MURDER ON THE NIGHT TRAIN TO PARIS

A POSIE PARKER MYSTERY #15

L. B. HATHAWAY

WHITEHAVEN

WHITEHAVEN MAN PRESS

First published in 2023 by Whitehaven Man Press

(http://www.lbhathaway.com, email: permissions@lbhathaway.com)

ISBN (e-book:) 978-1-913531-31-7
ISBN (paperback:) 978-1-913531-32-4

In memory of Harold File
(Trônes Wood, 13th July 1916)

Also by L.B. Hathaway

The Posie Parker Mystery Series

1. *Murder Offstage*

2. *The Tomb of the Honey Bee*

3. *Murder at Maypole Manor*

4. *The Vanishing of Dr Winter*

5. *Murder of a Movie Star*

(The stand-alone novella, *A Christmas Case*)

6. *Murder in Venice*

7. *The Saltwater Murder*

8. *Murder on the White Cliffs*

9. *Marriage is Murder?*

10. *Murder in the London Lights*

11. *Murder in Tuscany*

12. *Murder in a Chelsea Garden*

13. *Murder and the Mermaid*

14. *Murder through the Mirror*

15. *Murder on the Night Train to Paris*

Prologue
Belgrave Square, London (Late July, 1916)

'Ladies and Gentlemen, your attention please!'

The string quartet stopped playing immediately.

A small and very ugly man in his fifties, round-chested as a proud cock-robin, tapped his glass with a fork and smiled out at his hundred or so guests. He stood on a raised dais. Sweat was pouring down his face and he tugged at the tight collar of his white bow-tie.

'Has everyone got a glass? No? Waiters, make sure everyone is topped up with champagne, will you? Now where *are* the lovely couple? It's time for the toast.'

In truth, it was early for champagne.

Only three o'clock.

A time normally reserved for delicate China tea, and wafer-thin cucumber sandwiches. But today tradition had been forgone in favour of alcohol and platters of oysters brought up specially from Whitstable, packed on ice which was starting to melt in the intense heat.

A special occasion.

A party, with the crème de la crème of London society in attendance.

Lady Diana Manners, the most beautiful girl who had ever lived, was ensconced in a corner over by the dessert trolley, and Raymond Asquith, the ridiculously handsome son of the Prime Minister, was deep in conversation with her, their heads bent close together.

People had expected the dashingly gorgeous Prince of Wales to turn up; he *had* been invited, but he was yet to materialise.

A handsome cake built of five white-iced tiers, sparkling like a bewitched iceberg, was the centrepiece of all the rich food displayed on the sideboard, and the endless mirrors of this huge and sumptuous pale-blue Belgravia ballroom threw back the reflections of about thirty young society women who jostled together in an excited flurry of pale candy-coloured organdie dresses, rustling and quivering in the sudden silence.

Giggles were stifled, lips were licked and come-hither looks thrown across to the opposite side of the room at an equivalent-sized group of young men.

But today these men were not hunters; more like a group of cornered prey.

A bevy of older women in dark outfits thick with pearls frowned disapprovingly at the frenzy of pent-up excitement.

One of these older women bustled her way through the crowd in a proprietorial fashion, stately as a galleon, her enormous purple-satin bulk completely dominating a slender dark-haired figure walking in front of her.

As the tall and hugely fat woman propelled the smaller person forward, she could be heard hissing: 'Come *on*, Jane. Get a move on. Daddy's *waiting*.' The big woman's many chins quivered, and she smoothed away a lock of her strawberry-blonde hair which had come loose in the terrible heat.

Suddenly, the doorbell of the huge townhouse jangled into the silence.

Brrrrrrrrrrring.

Insistent.

Running feet could be heard on a staircase somewhere, and a man's shouted command. Everybody in the room froze, fascinated.

Several of the young men who were grouped together had visibly jumped at the noise, then they laughed it off casually. Most of these young men were sporting the officer's dress uniform of their regiments; their glimmery ribbons ominously prominent among so much frothy lightness.

There was shouting on the street outside, a shattering of the peace of genteel Belgrave Square itself.

The doorbell again.

A girl's shrill voice. 'I say! Let me in. It's my *right* to come in!'

Within the group of young men, a very tall blonde man in his early twenties stood out particularly.

His skin was golden with the heat of English summers long gone; tanned by a sun which had warmed countless cricket matches and umpteen tennis games at expensive private schools. But perhaps he had been exposed to a stronger sun, too; and more recently?

The freckles beneath the gold skin of his nose were endearingly childish, as were his long blonde eyelashes, and it was only his stature and his rather haughty air which made you think he might have anything serious to contribute to grown-up life.

He was an Adonis of a man, in an officer's uniform.

But if you looked closely, you would have seen that his body was shaking slightly, and, ever since hearing the girl outside shouting on the street, his right hand had gripped at his left wrist where a flash of something turquoise could be seen – a watch, maybe? – and it had fastened there, as if to quell his nerves. His champagne glass teetered precariously in his limp left hand.

The man next to him, slight and small, darkly handsome with a thin neat moustache, was obviously the leader of the group, and he muttered an instruction to those nearest him: 'Drink up, eh?'

The young men were putting on a good show. But in truth they were pretty much all in a bad way.

They were mere boys who, only months before, had danced with the rich young women opposite them in this very room. But fate had led them, by virtue of their age and prominent social standing, to play their parts as soldiers in a hideous war unfolding across the Channel on the fighting fields of France.

It was a terrible war which no-one else in this room could ever hope to understand; would never *want* to understand. Least of all these pouting, heaving beauties.

If these men survived, they knew their experiences would have to be hastily buried, zipped away; never spoken of again.

But right now, they were home on a short period of leave; an unexpected prize for having simply survived the appalling mess of the Battle of the Somme in northern France which had started three weeks before.

Sixty thousand British men had died on that first day of battle, and this group had seen it all. Names of locations which sounded innocent enough – Thiepval, Fricourt, Trônes Wood – would forever cause them anguish.

Anger and fear at facing the trenches again burnt in the hearts of all these lads today.

Some were good at covering it all up. Putting on a show.

The small, dark-moustached lad was one of those, and he elbowed his blonde neighbour conspiratorially, as if they were at the races and he'd just been given a good tip.

He indicated over to the dais with an exaggerated gesture, to where the huge woman and her much smaller charge were standing with the host of the party, looking out expectantly, anxiously.

'Good grief, Davey darling. There's your fiancée up there, and you're standing here with us like a wet weekend! It will never do. Go and stand at her side, won't you? This is *your* engagement party, for goodness' sake. Why we've all been dragged along! Don't hide among us rank and file!'

The blonde lad seemed to recover himself, and he grinned while snatching up his officer's cap and pulling it quickly onto his head.

He patted his companion softly on the arm. 'All right, Matilda. Keep your hair on. It will be all right; we will be all right. I know what's expected of me, okay?'

And so the blonde Adonis navigated the ballroom, conscious of the many hungry eyes on his uniformed back. He had always courted interest; had long ago realised his own peculiar brand of beauty, which had been both a blessing and a curse. As had his immense wealth.

He skirted the string quartet, and almost jogged up to join the hosts.

He stepped automatically closer to the petite young girl to whom he was engaged.

Jane.

Jane wore a stiff and expensive cream lace dress, sewn horizontally in thick sections, like a shroud, and her long face, below her sweaty dark fringe, was a faithful copy of her mother's. Only thinner.

The only interesting thing about Jane, and you'd have had to get up close to realise it, were the tiny specks of multi-coloured paint below her fingernails and a sort of heavy oily-nutty smell which seemed to emanate from her very pores like a strong perfume.

But, in truth, her fiancé had never noticed either of these things.

He had never usually got so near before.

Jane's father had started to speak to the room, sounding pleased and important, but Jane wasn't listening.

Instead, she turned her face, sunflower-like, up to David's

blonde sun-like beauty, and she hissed at him accusingly: 'David? I searched everywhere for you. In Belgrave Square Garden, and in the library upstairs. Where were you? And are you all right? You look like death, darling.'

David was vaguely dismissive. 'Oh, I've never been better, Jane. Don't fuss, please. I was probably having a ciggie out with Matilda down by your servants' quarters, in the backyard. Lost track of time.'

The enormous diamond on Jane's left-hand ring-finger, which he had had no part in choosing, gleamed brilliantly in the bright room, and the iceberg-white cake was being wheeled towards them on a silver trolley by a pair of immaculate serving-maids.

David stared at this spectacle and he grabbed again at the turquoise trinket he wore on his left wrist.

'By Gad, is all that cake just for us, *today*? It's not even the actual wedding. Talk about over-the-top!'

Jane gave a slight shrug. 'You know how it is here, David...'

'Mnnn. Yes. I do. Unfortunately.'

But now the cock-robin's moment had really arrived. Jane's father raised his glass and smiled indulgently at David, who automatically took Jane's arm, like an actor in a play.

'It is my pleasure to welcome home – on leave – my future son-in-law, Major David Greeze. He's been doing his bit over in France, eh? As have several of the lads here. We hope you will join in a toast to congratulate him and my daughter Janie on the news of their engagement. This is such delightful news for Ottoline and myself personally, and *professionally*, of course...'

David seemed to be searching the crowd, his smile fixed, his blue eyes restless, his focus locking on to the dark officer known as Matilda for a moment, before moving on again, as his future father-in-law continued on happily.

'As you all know, *our* family brewing business, Morrell

& Sons, has been in existence for centuries. It's how my dear father received his knighthood: for services rendered to the British beverage industry! The only other brewing firm of equal size and importance to our own in England today is that which belongs to the Greeze family, of whom David here is the sole rightful owner. So, we hope to come to some sort of *professional arrangement* between ourselves. And the future for both families, and both brewing dynasties, should indeed be rosy from this point onwards.'

But if this seemed an odd sort of congratulatory speech, or if anyone in the room had time to register the expressions on the soon-to-be bride and groom's faces, such thoughts were hastily abandoned and all eyes turned to the door to the ballroom, which was suddenly and forcibly wrenched open on its hinges and thrown back.

An anguished-looking Butler was trying to block the doorway.

'I say! Stop it, Miss! Please! First the noise outside, and now *this*. I will call the police, Miss. You're intruding... Oh, Master! Oh, Madam! I tried to stop her!'

But the Butler was shoved out of the way and a girl entered the room, all in a rush, as if she had been catapulted there forcibly by a great tsunami.

She was waving around a cream piece of card with a gilt scalloped edge. 'I have an invite! See? And yet I was kept out. What a scandal!'

Everyone gasped. Recognised the girl for who she was.

The intruder was famous. But not in a good way; not like Diana Manners.

This girl was a notorious society beauty whose gorgeous star fizzed brightly in a lonely firmament of drugs, drink and endless parties and whose exploits were often gossiped about all over town. Captured by photographers.

An example of what *not* to be.

Up close she was tall with a slightly crooked nose which, rather than dulling her beauty, lent her face an aristocratic, aquiline air. She wore a flimsy, romantic white puff of an organdie long gown, but it was her hair, looped up in a huge double bun and piled on her head like a splendid bird's nest, which caught the eye: flame-red, almost purple in its intensity.

And as the sunlight glancing through the room fell upon her, at that moment it seemed as if the girl's very head was on fire.

She was a pre-Raphaelite dream gone awry.

It was a bad-fairy-at-the-christening moment, and people stared at her, agog.

The red-haired girl seemed to be searching for someone, and for the briefest of seconds her gaze lingered on the Prime Ministers' son, then locked onto the dark lad with the moustache.

She swayed very slightly, holding on to her invitation as if it took all her energy to do so. Then she spat out her words in an oddly low, gruff voice: 'I'll tell all of London how Morrell & Sons run their parties, shall I? In my weekly column, *Girl About Town*...'

And then she dissolved in a fit of laughter and hiccoughs.

Jane's mother, Lady Ottoline Morrell, lurched forward quickly, capably, stepping off the dais. Immaculate in her fury.

She stormed up to the newcomer.

'There's obviously been a mistake! Let's step outside, shall we? I have no idea how you got hold of that invite, young lady. Did you pay someone for it? But you and your weekly column are not welcome here. *Not at all*. And I do believe you are blind drunk, Lady Duff-Shepherd! Shame on you!'

'Shame on *me*?'

The red-head threw back her head and laughed. 'Look at yourself, *Lady* Morrell. I certainly never paid for this invitation! So please don't insult me. Perhaps a famous young man gave it to me earlier? Perhaps he was bored by how very mediocre this party looked and he couldn't be bothered to polish up his golden crown and come on over here, so he thought *I* could have some fun with it instead, and write about it for my column, maybe? Anyhow, speaking of drink, isn't anyone going to offer me some of those nice cold bubbles? On such a hot, burning-up sort of day?'

The whole room stood, holding their breath, transfixed, shocked by the cavalier reference to the Prince of Wales, and unsure as to what would happen next in this stand-off.

But no-one could have predicted what was to actually unfold.

Because David Greeze, the multi-millionaire brewing heir, whose engagement party this was, whose eyes had been searching, searching, only moments before, suddenly became animated.

It was as if all of his life he had been waiting for this moment.

'Hey! Lady Duff-Shepherd!'

He pulled away from his bride-to-be, away from her odd smell and the certainty of her riches, and he stepped from the dais.

And as he moved nearer to the red-headed girl, he actively shoved his future mother-in-law out of the way.

A gasp of surprise ran around the huge blue room and Jane's mother stood frozen, horror-struck.

But David Greeze ignored Lady Morrell, and he was conscious only of standing right in front of the uninvited guest and handing her his own glass of champagne.

'Here you go, take mine. Let *me* welcome you here. It is supposed to be my party, after all. I think I may have met you before, but you and I were both children then? It was a long time ago: a birthday party in the woods with balloons and teddy bears, and, if I recall rightly, a tree house far, far higher than I'd ever been in before; all in the grounds of a lovely house... I thought I recognised your voice just now;

when you were shouting in the street. You really haven't changed, my Lady.'

'Gracious, I'm told I was a dreadful child, Major. I hope you don't remember me *too* clearly!'

'You were lovely. And by Gad, you still are.'

'How very kind of you.'

And then the girl threw back the drink in one go, full of bluster, watched by everyone, as if on a stage.

David Greeze was very aware of the red-headed girl's pride, her defiance. The shambles of all of this.

But most of all he was conscious of the wonderful way this girl made him feel in front of the stale, silent crowd.

Dangerously alive.

He felt as he had – three weeks earlier – at Thiepval, when he had led his division out over the top into no-man's land; when he had been about to walk a fine line between life and death, with a totally unknowable outcome.

David Greeze came closer, close as he dared.

'Everyone is watching us. Perhaps, my Lady, we could step out of the room together, and leave?'

Run. Run away.

Lady Duff-Shepherd licked her pale lips.

'Perhaps, Major. I suppose there's only one way to find out, isn't there?'

She grasped his left wrist, as if preparing for flight, her grey eyes meeting his blue gaze for the first time, and for David Greeze it was as if his life had really and truly started.

A strong scent of tuberoses came off of her, and something stronger. Whisky, perhaps? Something sweeter, with cherries as an undertone?

'Oh! But what's *that*?' the girl suddenly demanded, as if they might have all the time in the world to chat.

Around them the awful silence beat on. 'On your bracelet? Golly, I say! Is it a scarab? An *original* scarab?'

'Yes.' David Greeze grinned. 'I was lucky enough to be

on the archaeological dig at Abydos, in Egypt, last year, before I was called up.'

'How thrilling.'

'It was. I found two. Paid for them, of course. I wear one, and I'm happy to give you the other, if you'd like it? I can have it made fancier, if you wish? Set with jewels, maybe… Something to match the colour of your hair, my Lady? Rubies? Tanzanite? We'll go to Cartier; I'll get you whatever the blazes you want. God, I'll give you everything I own if you'll only be mine.'

The two were close now, closer than a bride and groom.

'That all sounds delightful, Major Greeze. But maybe a plain scarab, as it is, is better. More appropriate for *us*. Because if I'm not mistaken, Major, the Egyptians believed scarabs to be lucky because they symbolised new starts?'

David Greeze grinned wolfishly. Their faces were very close.

'I'm impressed, my Lady. But a scarab is also a good amulet for those of us who want to simply survive. I keep mine with me in the hell-holes of France.'

'Golly, well, my whole life has been about trying to survive. Perhaps we can do that together?'

'Absolutely.' He grabbed at her and tugged, pulling her towards the door, still watched by everybody.

'Let's go. *Now.* I'm staying at Claridge's. We'll head there. I have three weeks of leave. I'll marry you straightaway; no ceremony, no party, no fuss. By Gad, I tell you, we won't leave the hotel room for a minute.'

They were at the door. Pulling at it, pulling at each other.

His golden fingers were caressing the white lace of her back, fingering the skin of her wrists, the nape of her neck beneath the hair.

Someone sniggered. There were frantic whisperings in corners.

Then a sharp keening sound started up, like you'd hear at a wake.

'NO! Please. COME BACK!'

Jane Morrell, still up on the dais, was crying, and her mother, who was ashen-faced and standing frozen to the spot, watched open-mouthed as her future son-in-law disappeared from the room.

'Mama! Stop them! It can't be! No! Not *her*!'

But the door swung forlornly on its hinges and suddenly the candy-coloured women were up, all in a rush, surging towards the dais.

Because Jane Morrell had collapsed.

Her father looked as if he might do the same. He was puce-coloured, swigging directly from the neck of a bottle of his celebratory champagne, pacing up and down, shaking his head.

And over by the abandoned cake trolley, the officer whom David Greeze had called Matilda was getting busy with a cake knife, cutting the iceberg into careful thick squares of delicious royal icing, almond marzipan and top-quality fruit-cake.

He was neatly and calmly folding the pieces of cake into the pile of starched linen napkins, embroidered with a twisted emblem of a combined 'J' and 'D'.

Shouting at his friends, he ordered them about, as was his wont.

They started to collect about him, laughing off their unease.

'Come on, lads! Eat up. Get your teeth into a piece of this! It's Fortnum's finest, unless I'm much mistaken, and we won't see this amount of sugar again this side of Christmas. If ever, eh? And if we never make it home again to Blighty, at least we'll all die knowing we had a piece of Davey Greeze's engagement cake! Because we sure as blazes won't be having any of his wedding cake anytime soon: that particular horse has bolted, I fear…'

He picked up his empty glass, smeary with cake grease.

'Now, shall we all have a look for some more of that bally champagne?'

And he raised his glass in his own private toast.

* * * *

PART ONE
The Night Train

London

(Tuesday 19th January 1926)

Chapter One

'Can you believe it? She's gettin' married to this skinny painted *boy*! Imagine him as my new Master!' whispered a thin, ferrety-faced woman to her neighbour in the queue at the railway station.

Both wore the stiff white lacy collars above black uniforms which denoted they were ladies' maids.

'This scoundrel! As if things aren't bad enough!'

The first woman was jabbing at the cover of a magazine.

It showed a staged photograph of a couple, both in profile; the lady was sitting, elegant in a pale skull-cap, and the man, featured in purple, wore a rakish-looking hat at a foreign sort of angle.

The disgruntled maid went on: 'Of course, this *Picture Post* is old news to me: this mag is a week old. Magazines haven't printed anythin' new yet, what with all their workers stuck at home. All these strikes, Vera! Blimey, the rubbish-collectors must be on strike too. Look at the mess around here. Dead vermin, just lyin' around!'

'Aye, Maureen. It's disgustin', I quite agree wiv you on that.'

It was true that dead pigeons scattered the concourse of Victoria Station, fallen from their perches up on the iron girders above, frozen to death overnight.

Further up, at the ticket counter marked 'International Travel', a tall, thin woman all in black was waiting for tickets.

She bit at her thumbnail nervously and a flake of bright-red nail varnish came off in her mouth. She tried to spit it out discreetly without anyone noticing.

But Posie Parker, London's premier female Private Detective, was right behind her, and she noticed it.

Posie Parker noticed most things. She had to; it was her job, after all. And right now, she was bored.

She tried not to listen to the continuing stream of gossip from the two female servants behind her, all of it nasty tittle-tattle.

Posie hunkered down into the gauzy softness of her new cashmere stole.

It was a deep shadowy green colour that perfectly matched her grey-green overcoat and cloche hat. The colours were as muted as the month of January.

By Gad, January was an awful month.

You spent your whole life thinking next year when it came around it wouldn't be as bad. And every time, sure as bread was bread, you were disappointed.

It was even worse.

The dark, the cold, the freezing London pea-soupers which crept in through the brick-work froze right into your bones, and into your soul in a very depressing way.

Oh, roll on summer.

If Posie had smoked, now would have been a good time to light up.

She needed a distraction.

She concentrated instead on the tall woman in front again.

She noticed the black coat was made of real wool, but it

was obviously several years old, and cut in an unfashionable way.

It had gone sheeny at the elbows and at the rear, and there was no fur trimming or ribbons of any kind on it. The woman had instead draped a black scarf of some cheap, fake-silk material – rayon, maybe? – around her shoulders, to provide a bit of variety, and the effect was simply a mess.

A servant of some kind?

A governess? A housekeeper?

That would make sense. Posie was probably the only non-servant in the whole queue here today.

Most non-servants who would use this form of transport were still hunkered down at home, keeping warm.

A week of intense cold had thrown England, and London especially, into total chaos. Days of unprecedented sub-zero temperatures had culminated in a heavy, swift snowfall which had turned London into a difficult-to-navigate, sinister wonderland; more like a treacherous ice-rink than a city, and the wind had been Siberian.

During the last week, Londoners had been advised to stay at home.

Travel plans of every kind had been disrupted as all public transport had ground to a sudden halt.

Thankfully, a thaw had now set in.

Trains, trams, buses and boats were up and running again.

And now all those people whose journeys had been cancelled wanted to travel again.

Victoria Station, London's busiest train station, was in the grip of a frenzied chaos as every ticket counter was besieged by angry, impatient passengers, desperate for replacement tickets.

But right here, in the first-class 'International Travel' section, where trains had started running again only yesterday, those rich folk anxious to get to Paris, Brussels, Berne and Venice had sent their servants to queue for them instead.

But not Posie.

Posie *did* actually employ a Housekeeper, but she wouldn't have dreamt of asking the redoubtable Glaswegian Mrs Juniper to run any sort of errand for her; she would have been frightened of the response.

Besides, after five solid days of coping pretty much alone, cooped up inside the top-floor flat at Museum Chambers in Bloomsbury with three small children aged five and under, Posie didn't mind the outing.

In fact, she'd been desperate for a break and when Mrs Juniper had arrived on time at the flat that morning Posie had felt like kissing her.

Which she obviously didn't do.

The snow had been so bad during the last week that Mrs Juniper had been unable to get across town from Bermondsey to help out, and Masha, the ancient Russian live-in nanny, had taken to her bedroom in the flat, citing aching bones and chills.

And Richard Lovelace, Posie's important policeman husband, was inconveniently away.

He was up in Liverpool overseeing a big trial; the culmination of months of hard work for Scotland Yard which had succeeded in rounding up and putting in the dock one of England's biggest ever drug gangs. As Chief Commissioner of the country's most important police force, he had to see the thing out, even if it took weeks.

He'd been up there for most of January so far.

The advice from the government to stay inside during the last week had been difficult to bear for Posie.

Slowly, slowly, she had felt worn down.

She and the children were all fraught, nerves frayed; every game had been attempted, every toy played with to death, then angrily discarded.

Full-time childcare, without fresh air or the usual walks out to nearby Bloomsbury Square or Tavistock Square had proved a nightmare. The windowpanes had been frosted up with icy spidery fingers of snow, and wind whistled about their frames, making it seem as if Bury Place was somewhere in the Arctic. Cut off.

But yesterday evening had thrown Posie a life-line.

Of the very best sort.

A letter had been brought up to the top-floor flat by the ever-reliable, ever-stalwart Ted, the Porter for the whole block.

He'd proved a life-saver during the cold patch, bringing groceries in from the East End, all at vastly inflated prices. He'd also helped by taking out Posie's Yorkshire terrier, Patsy, for short walks at either end of his shift.

Ted had handed Posie a white envelope last night, edged in gold.

'Hand delivery, Miss. Just arrived. Looks like it's from your posh friend, the Earl. Oh, lawks! You've still got yer hands full there, by the looks of it, ain't you? Is that little Kit, walkin' already? I've not seen him properly lately. He's a big 'un, ain't he? What a strapping lad! How old is he, ten months?'

'Mnnn. Yes.'

'Looks more like two years old to me! And is that foreign nanny still not out of bed, Miss? Gracious! The cheek! If you need any more groceries, you jus' ring down, won't you? But they do say the snow will go tomorrow, thank the good Lord! I've been gettin' a lift in here with the rag-and-bone man, but today the Number 15 bus ran again, so I'll be ridin' that home tonight! But don't you worry, I'll be up again before me shift ends, and I'll collect the wee doggie for her walkies, eh?'

Posie had muttered a heartfelt thanks as she had closed the front door, impatiently ripping open the envelope, which was indeed of the sort used by Rufus, Eleventh Earl of Cardigeon, her 'posh' friend.

Actually, Rufus had been her elder brother's best friend at school, and following her brother's tragic death in the

Great War, Rufus Cardigeon and Posie had continued the friendship, which had become important to both of them.

On the back of the envelope was a small maroon crest, showing what looked like an impenetrable castle of the sort found in fairy tales. Or nightmares.

It was Rebburn Abbey, the Cardigeon ancestral pile.

With red-headed Kit holding on to her leg in a vice-like grip, and his older eighteen-month-old adopted sister Katie screaming blue murder on the parquet floor of the hallway, Posie had counted slowly to ten, then shaken out the letter in Rufus' familiar terrible spiky handwriting, blotting out all the noise.

The Chelsea address of the Cardigeons' London townhouse in Pavilion Road, SW3, was embossed in maroon on the top of the letter, and it had been marked with the day's date, which was a Monday.

The paper had stunk of whisky.

Posie had read very quickly:

Posie,

Trust you are keeping well? Haven't seen you since December in Rye, hope you and Richard had a good Christmas and New Year.

Sorry for my lack of correspondence, but with Dolly gone I haven't felt much like celebrating, to be honest. Hope you both understand.

I've been up to my neck employing one nanny after the other for the children, and not one of them will stick around. Trixie and Bunny are being devils, and Raymond is sick all the time.

I'm only just back into London, and sorting out everything I've been meaning to do since Christmas.

You kindly said you'd go to Paris for me. Search for Dolly?

I've finally got around to organising this. I saw the Golden Arrow service is shot to pieces in this cold weather, but the Night Ferry train seems to be running again with no problems, from today onwards. I've called them and booked you a single first-class berth for tomorrow night, Tuesday 19th January, departing at nine pm from Victoria Station. You can come back whenever you like – it's an open return. I didn't know how long you wanted to spend there. Or how long you want to be away from Richard and the children, and Grape Street, of course.

The only catch is that you or one of your staff will need to collect the tickets at Victoria tomorrow, Tuesday morning, early as possible. And show your passport. It's their standard procedure, apparently. What a dashed bore, eh?

I'd ask you to bring Dolly home with you, Posie, if I thought that was possible.

Of course, that would be best.

The very best outcome.

But as time passes, I'm not sure if that is even an outcome which is half-realistic. Just find out what's bally well going on, Posie, if you can. The Countess of Cardigeon needs to be located, at least.

Oh, and your car should be with you soon. In around a week, I reckon. Hopefully the roads will be less hazardous by then, eh? Less slippy.

Pip-pip and fondest regards to you both,

Rufus

P.S. I do hope you are eating well, Posie old thing. I know I've ribbed you in the past about being a bit on the tubby side of things but I was shocked by your appearance when I last saw you in Rye. Like a half-skinned cat, you were.

It doesn't suit you, that bag-of-bones look, you know. Bally well go and get yourself fed properly, eh?

Posie had folded the letter away, biting her lip, thinking.

The drunken wretch of a man Rufus Cardigeon had morphed into following the mysterious disappearance of his wife, Dolly – Posie's best friend – in the summer of last year, 1925, had shocked everyone.

He'd been in a dreadful state when Posie had seen him in December, in strange circumstances in Rye.

But this letter seemed cogent and well-written, and as if – despite the whiff of alcohol – Rufus was now on top of things and in the frenzied grip of a new-found purpose.

Well, that was a good thing.

Timely, too.

Posie had had Dolly on her mind for months.

She'd been meaning to go to Paris – where Dolly had been seen in summer the year before, and where Dolly was known to have links – for ages. But Posie had been thwarted on several occasions by life itself: the children; her own ill-health taking a tumble at the end of last year; and most recently, by Richard's absence.

It seemed that fate, or rather, Rufus and his fat wallet, and a newly-cleared head, had now intervened. Sending Posie on her way.

And by the Night Ferry, no less.

The Night Ferry was a one-stop service from London to Paris which ran at night and only took first-class customers, and whose navy-and-cream sleeper carriages were loaded onto a boat at Dover and then hooked up again to a locomotive in France to continue onwards to reach Paris in time for breakfast.

It was a hugely expensive and seamless service, which had only been running for one year so far.

Not like the Golden Arrow, which also provided a service from London through to Paris, and ran in the daytime, in a much more disjointed fashion, and catered for first-, second- and third-class passengers.

Last night Posie's thoughts had been broken into by Phyllis, her five-year-old stepdaughter.

'Mama, I'm hungry, I've tried to make dinner for us all but it's gone wrong.'

'Sorry? What? Oh, golly!'

Phyllis had, in her wisdom, opened a packet of Peek

Frean's Lemon Puffs and dipped them all in a bowl of water and stirred them up. The resulting grey mess on the carpet was eye-wateringly awful, and Phyllis had dissolved into floods of tears, immediately followed by Katie, then Kit.

Mrs Juniper would have had forty fits if she had seen any of it.

'Give me a second, darlings. We'll eat something properly in just a minute.'

Posie had cast a look of utter despair around her usually-tidy living-room and had hurried to the telephone, her little son still clutched to her black-stockinged leg.

She'd telephoned the Adelphi Hotel in Liverpool, hoping to reach Richard, who was staying there for the duration of the trial. She'd been lucky and he was intercepted crossing the hall.

'Darling? Richard?'

'Posie, you just caught me. I'm heading through for a briefing with our prosecution lawyers in a boardroom here. We've got to discuss evidence. One of our key witnesses wobbled on the stand today. Total bally disaster. Are you fine, my love? Are the water pipes at home holding up in this freeze? You're warm enough? The children? Is that Katie I can hear, crying? Or Phyllis? Or both?'

'Everything's fine. Look, Rufus has written and he's organised me a berth on the night train, to Paris. I leave tomorrow night. Is that all right with you?'

'*Paris?*'

'I'll get a Norland Nanny organised. Two, perhaps, simultaneously; that would be better. It's more than obvious that Masha can't cope anymore, but Mrs Juniper will be back tomorrow. She'll also hold the fort until I return. I'll make sure I travel home again on Thursday night; I'll only be gone Wednesday and Thursday daytime. I'm sure two days is long enough.'

There had been noise and footsteps in the background of the call.

Richard had sounded distracted, wrong-footed:

'Long enough? To find Dolly, you mean? Two days? And alone? But that's ridiculous! You know we've been liaising with the French police on this since last summer and they've made no headway, none at all, other than that first initial sighting at the Gare du Nord, and since then there's been nothing. The trail is cold. Freezing cold. There's been no news at all. And they are the *experts*.'

'*I'm* an expert,' Posie had almost growled, but her husband had hardly heard her, rushing on in a flurry of worry: 'And then there's the possible connection with all of this to…to, well, you know who…'

Her husband's voice had tailed off, grim.

Posie's mind had been clear despite the chaos about her. Kit had been biting at her leg, through the wool. He was teething, badly.

'Caspian della Rosa, you mean? My old *bête noir*.'

'Exactly.'

Caspian della Rosa was a Swiss aristocrat who also happened to be one of the world's richest and cleverest criminals. Not to mention being exceedingly dangerous.

Posie suspected that Caspian della Rosa was actually slightly unhinged; possibly quite mad.

He'd been obsessed with Posie since 1921, when she'd had the bad fortune to cross his path in an early case.

He'd been hell-bent on wanting her as his wife, and for several horrible years he had been the bane of Posie's life. Severely injured in a gun-fire incident in 1924, Caspian della Rosa had given Posie a welcome reprieve for the last couple of years.

But last year, in the summer of 1925, quite out of the blue, Posie had been contacted by a firm of lawyers in Paris, who had informed her that Caspian della Rosa had, at last, died.

This had obviously been on Richard's mind last night, too.

'Posie darling, do you remember that dashed odd letter the French lawyers sent you? Apparently, it was a letter from della Rosa himself, written on his deathbed. Informing you he was leaving you a hotel in his Will? As a parting gift!'

Richard had laughed coldly.

'What was the hotel called? The Palais Della Rosa? What rot! It turned out the hotel didn't exist, and neither did the firm of Parisian lawyers! It was all a big charade. Darling, do you recall, the building was there on the Champs-Élysées, that much was true, but there was no lawyers' office inside it? By Gad, I can't remember the exact name of those supposed lawyers off the top of my head…'

'Redon.'

'Ah, yes. And in his deathbed letter, della Rosa basically told you to go to that wretched fake lawyers' office on the Champs-Élysées and claim your gift. Thank the Lord you didn't go. It would have been a trap, darling. Because I think our lovely Caspian della Rosa is still very much alive.'

Richard had sighed down the line. As well he might.

The strange tale of the fake lawyers' letter and the fake deathbed gift had not ended there.

It had been further complicated when Richard had got Scotland Yard to investigate.

It had turned out that a telephone call had been made from the fictional lawyers' address on the Champs-Élysées, and it had been connected through to Dolly Cardigeon, in her home in Chelsea.

The call had been made on the morning of the very last day Dolly had spent in London before she'd gone missing, apparently having been summoned to Paris. Had she gone there, because of that call?

Whatever the case, there had been other coincidences in the tale, things which seemed neat when they shouldn't have been so.

Richard had sounded tired last night.

Worn out with remembering it all. 'Who was that French contact of Dolly's, named Violette – what was she?'

'She was Dolly's children's former nanny.'

Violette.

The odd, unexplained, unexplainable link.

'Oh, yes. Violette. Well, do you remember, darling? The French police – a jolly good chap called Inspector Jegouzo, who works nearby – worked out that the call had been placed from the fake office on the Champs-Élysées by a woman called Violette, luring Dolly to Paris for that devil Caspian della Rosa! That rotter must have got hold of Violette and turned her, somehow. Although *why* any of this happened, and *why* Caspian della Rosa wanted Dolly – there has never been a ransom note – is still beyond us all.'

Richard had paused, thinking hard. 'We all thought that Dolly was lured to Paris as bait, as the sole means of getting *you* to follow her. It seems to me that too much time has passed now for that theory to work.'

Posie had sensed him shrugging.

'We don't even know if Dolly ever ended up meeting with Violette, or with Caspian della Rosa, and besides, why did della Rosa then bother with the whole deathbed letter ruse being sent to you a mere month later?'

Posie had tried to sound reasonable. 'I don't think we can rule anything out, Richard. Where Caspian della Rosa is involved, anything is possible. Including the possibility that he *really* is dead.'

'Unlikely!'

Richard had harrumphed: 'Frankly, I can't believe old Rufus is expecting this of you, darling, although I do know he was jabbering away about it in Rye. Misses old Dolly awfully, I expect.'

He had sighed from faraway in the north. 'I know this is a personal crusade for you, Posie, as much as anything. You'll talk about this for the rest of our lives if you don't go. I know it.'

'If you're worried about the children…'

'Oh, hang them! I'm worried about *you*! But I suppose…I suppose I *can* send someone out with you. Fox is still in London, but he'd stick out like a sore thumb with his English hang-dog face and penchant for acting like an Inspector already.'

Posie had imagined Richard at the hotel's smart front desk, dragging his fingers through his red hair, thinking hard, trying to come up with a solution. He had sounded very stressed.

'Oh, dash it, I suppose I could even find one of our French counterparts; he'd have time to nip across and meet you tomorrow night on the Night Ferry train if I organise it now. I'll phone Inspector Jegouzo at the next break. But whatever happens, promise me you will telephone to me here, at the Adelphi, on your arrival in Paris on Wednesday morning and then again, every evening? Just so I know you're still in one piece. And do not, I repeat DO NOT, go inside that address of the fictional firm of lawyers, Redon, on the Champs-Élysées. Got it?'

'Fine. Calm down. You don't think I'll find Dolly, do you?'

'The possibility hadn't even crossed my mind, my love. It's a dead end.'

Tamping down a simmering anger at her husband's blunt words, but also brimming with the start of a tide of excitement, Posie had then telephoned through to Pavilion Road in Chelsea.

She'd expected the Cardigeons' Butler to answer the telephone, and had been surprised to hear Rufus himself on the end of the line.

She'd thanked him for the letter, and told him she'd be delighted to accept. Said how generous it was of him to allow her to travel like that.

'Wassat, Nosy old girl? Ah? Yes, yes, I'm delighted you're going to accept. Jolly exciting, eh?'

Rufus had been slurry, and blurry, and he was obviously very drunk despite the early hour and Posie had felt sad.

She'd resolved to breeze through the conversation, and deal only with the practicalities which needed addressing.

'It's very kind of you, Rufey, but where do you want me to stay, exactly?'

There had been a buzzing noise, and a sort of crash. Whatever Rufus had been up to, it hadn't sounded good. '*Stay?* Well, wherever you bally well choose of course. What's that to do with me? What am I now, your dashed Form Master in school, Nosy?'

'Very well.'

Knowing he wasn't one for details, she hadn't even bothered to ask Rufus about an expense account, and had decided she'd bill him later, much like one of her normal clients. It wasn't as if he couldn't afford it; Rufus was one of the wealthiest men in the kingdom.

'I'll say goodbye then. Wish me luck.'

'Good luck, Posie. Just bring the lady home in one piece, okay?'

'I'll try.'

'You'd better do a bally well darn sight better than just *trying*, Nosy. I didn't pay all that money for simply *trying*.'

'Fine.'

And then, amid all the children's hollering, Posie had telephoned down to Ted, at his desk seven floors below, and asked him to step out and order fish suppers from the nearest fish bar, off High Holborn, quick as he could. And to make sure he bought enough for a small, belligerent army.

She'd then phoned through to a pub near Mrs Juniper's digs in Bermondsey, The Dog and Bone, and asked them to get a message to her, pronto: asking if she would be turning up for work the next morning.

She'd also telephoned the London branch of the Norland Nannies and had, at great expense, booked the two most experienced women available at this short notice. Both women would start the next day, and remain at Museum Chambers until the end of the week.

Then Posie had cleared up the horrid biscuity floor. And fed the children.

That had all been last night.

But right now, at Victoria Station, with her mind wandering off with thoughts of Dolly somewhere, Posie found herself being ploughed into with the full force of a rugby tackle.

'OWWWW! Watch it!'

Papers went flying through the air.

It was the black-coated woman who had been in front of her.

Posie staggered to remain upright, her eyes smarting with tears at the pain in her shoulder and hip, where the woman had hit her.

'I say! Watch where you're going, won't you?'

But the woman was crouching down on her haunches, balancing on precariously high black heels, gathering up her scattered tickets and documents, cramming things into a big blue envelope.

Posie sighed and bent down too, helping to pick up flimsy bits of paper, handing them over wordlessly. She saw the word 'SCOTLAND' typed on several of the papers.

The woman was breathless, skittery. 'Oh, thank you! That's kind of you. Especially as I just nearly killed you.'

Posie saw that the woman had not been what she had imagined at all from behind. Her face was not pretty, it was too horse-like for beauty, but the look was captivating anyway, with heavy black eyebrows and bright full red lips, a testimony to a knack with lipstick. The woman's hair was worn longer than was fashionable right now, in shoulder-grazing ringlets.

She could have been Spanish, or Italian, or perhaps even Indian. Anything other than the boring English Housekeeper Posie had so wrongly labelled her.

They both stood up, awkward.

'I *am* sorry. I honestly didn't see you standing there!'

The English was spot-on, but there was a French accent beneath it, Posie would have bet on it.

Posie shrugged. 'Well, it's a queue. Chances are you would have run into someone.'

The woman flicked a long black ringlet out of one eye and Posie saw she was wearing a plain golden wedding ring on her left-hand ring-finger.

'The truth is, I'm selfishly rather on cloud nine – you English say that, yes? To mean being deliriously happy? I was a bit overwhelmed by my sudden good fortune. *Mais, oui. C'est incroyable!* I had no thoughts of anything or anyone else. I wasn't looking out for anyone at all. Can I make it up to you? Buy you coffee and a slice of cake? A macaroon? Chocolate éclair? A scone with cream and raspberry jam? There is a very good small French café around the corner from here. I haven't yet had breakfast.'

'Oh!' Posie was slightly wrong-footed by the invitation, and in truth, her stomach was rumbling at the thought of all of these treats.

But she shook her head resolutely: 'Normally, I'd have loved to have joined you, but I can't keep you from your breakfast: I might be standing here for yonks. They seem to be very slow after all these delays. But you enjoy your day.'

'Oh, I will. Have a good day, too.' The girl bit again at one of her red-painted flaking fingernails, and then left, smiling.

And then Posie found herself up at the ticket counter, passing across her passport and waiting several minutes for her ticket to be prepared and for the relevant customs forms to be filled in.

The railway clerk returned at last, clutching the standard-issue big blue railway envelope.

He gave all the paperwork one last check over.

'Enclosed is one first-class single ticket for tonight,

Madam. The other piece of paper here is an open return, also for the Night Ferry. Tonight you are allocated Berth Number Nine of Car Number One. Please be on Platform 2, here at Victoria for eight-thirty prompt and come already dressed for dinner. Cocktail dress or ballgown; your choice. A Pullman car will be serving a full dinner to you and the other Night Ferry passengers between here and Dover, before your sleeping carriages are loaded on the boat for France. The menu is enclosed within this blue envelope. Oh, wait a moment…'

The clerk paused briefly with a finger on a big teller on his desk, flicking between two entries there, before double-checking the number on Posie's blue envelope again.

He frowned.

'Is everything in order?' Posie asked, slightly harshly. She hadn't had breakfast yet, and it was almost nine o'clock.

'Oh, yes, Madam. All fine. It's just odd, that's all: it seems the passenger before you, the foreign lady in black, has actually been set up on the same…'

'Has been *what*?'

'Oh.'

The clerk blushed suddenly, caught out somehow. 'It's nothing, Madam. It's nothing. I shouldn't have let myself speak that way… Only, er, well, the passenger before you just now, she'll be in the very same sleeper car as you tonight, in the next berth, actually. Berth Number Eight. Bit of a coincidence, that's all. But perhaps it's not such a coincidence, eh? It looks like your Night Ferry train tonight is very select. It will only consist of two sleeper cars, the legal minimum for the ferry to run. Normally we run with four or six or eight cars. And there is a maximum of nine berths to each car, so not many passengers will be on board at all.'

Posie wasn't much interested in the warbling of the clerk about the usual number of train carriages, but she *was* intrigued to know that the strange woman she had just met would be a travel companion later tonight.

Very much *not* a servant then. To be travelling first-class on the Night Ferry.

Actually, the woman had looked good fun. And fun had been in very short supply recently.

A recent solitary trip around the quite wonderful exhibition by John Singer Sargent in Piccadilly had proved, despite the staggeringly beautiful paintings on display, a dry old stick of an experience, and Posie had found herself wishing she had had Dolly at her side, to hear her friend's unique take on the quite ridiculous fashions being sported by some of the other guests parading at the gallery.

And a trip last week, before the startling cold snap had begun, to see the new Irish play which had set London alight, *Juno and the Paycock*, had been almost unbearable to sit through alone, and Posie had left at the mid-way interval, and gone home, subdued, lost in her own thoughts.

Quite simply, London was not London without Dolly around.

How I miss you, old friend.

Armed with her blue travel docket, Posie crossed the concourse, avoiding the dead birds which still lay about, and she headed in the direction of Petty France, behind the station, where all the travel shops and travel companies had gathered together.

There were several cafés here: French, Italian, Portuguese, Chinese.

She looked about her in case she saw the dark girl from the station again but it was too cold to sit outside, and the pavement tables and chairs were understandably all empty.

So Posie charged towards the nearest Lyons Cornerhouse where you never needed to feel embarassed if you came in on your own, and where the cakes were pretty good anyhow.

She ordered black coffee and a choice of cakes on a platter.

A macaroon, a chocolate éclair and a scone with raspberry jam.

And she ate them all with great enjoyment.

* * * *

Chapter Two

It was a busy day. A day of preparations.

After her horribly sweet café breakfast, Posie set about her practical arrangements, which Rufus had quite understandably left her to manage.

She first popped into the Post Office and sent a telegram to Scotland Yard.

Then she organised a set of travellers' cheques and collected a docket of French francs from Thomas Cook & Son, before visiting Cox & Kings Travel Bureau in the same street; paying them to book her a room in a nice, friendly, central Parisian hostel.

Definitely *not* in an ostentatious city hotel where the smart set stayed, and played, and glittered, and where Posie's presence would be noted. Her only other instruction was that the accommodation should either be *on*, or else very near to, the Champs-Élysées.

The bureau was most obliging and promised to deliver the details of the hostel to Posie's berth on the Night Ferry train tonight, in time for her departure.

A haircut and 'set' followed, at Trumpers in Piccadilly; the usual shingled style, very short, with the bobbed length only just reaching past Posie's ears.

But today Posie had a fringe cut, a heavy square shape

in order to hide the deepening 'V' between her eyebrows, which these days seemed to be a constant feature of her face. The style felt good, and fresh, but Posie had quite forgotten the weather outside and almost gasped as she stepped out of the salon.

She pulled her scarf up further about her face to stop her neck feeling completely exposed in the chilly air, and dragged her hat down closer about her ears.

Sometimes fashion was utterly ridiculous, she thought with a half-smile.

But I keep up with it all the same, fool that I am.

And then Posie walked on through Piccadilly, rammed with what seemed like hundreds of buses and horse-drawn carts looped in a standstill around the Eros statue, and she walked briskly up into the ever-busy Leicester Square, the sky a clear blue arc overhead, with not a cloud to be seen.

Hot-chestnut sellers were doing a roaring trade with their coal braziers set up on street corners; the sweet, nutty scent of their wares rising temptingly in the air.

Posie was wearing long-unused black snow boots, clumpy in their practicality, and today they were proving virtually unnecessary. Posie had expected the streets to still be slippery and icy, but London had surpassed itself. Snow shovellers had obviously been out early, salting the pavements, and the whole city looked fresh and renewed, like it had been washed clean.

Posie purchased a small folding map of Paris at Stanfords Map Shop on Long Acre and then started to walk slowly in the direction of her office.

She dawdled along the glistening cobbles of Long Acre, which was busy with shoppers happy to be back out in the fresh air again, and the intersection was packed tight with the hordes of fruit and flower sellers who clustered around Covent Garden Underground Station, throatily yelling out their offers in cockney rhyming slang.

A group of ten or so girl ballet dancers, long-necked

and very young, perhaps only fourteen years old, their hair already lacquered into stiff buns, were buying apples at a fruit stand, obviously bound for the practice-rooms of the Royal Opera House, just around the corner.

Something about their youth and vulnerability touched Posie, and they reminded her suddenly of a flock of just-grown swans, all cast adrift on a terribly rough sea, whose choppiness knew no bounds and held no certainty of any approaching calm.

Who was to know which of these girls would fulfil their dream of becoming a new prima ballerina? A new star to rival Anna Pavlova, whose shows around the corner were always sold out, and whose life was already the stuff of legend.

And which of these girls would always remain destined to be part of the *corps de ballet*? Part of the ever-muted background.

Well, that was London for you, thought Posie. *It was a dream, where anything was possible. But it could be a hard-fought dream, too.*

And many fell by the wayside.

Not just dancers.

Posie walked on down Neal Street, up to the Seven Dials, all the while her mind remaining an unhelpful blank, free of any useful thoughts, although she knew she had stacks to prepare for this fast-approaching trip to Paris.

But *what*, exactly?

And anyway, what can you prepare for when you step into the complete unknown?

A shop she passed said 'FASHIONS FROM PARIS! JUST IN!' in the window, and some female shop workers were draping mannequins in the thinnest, most sparkly concoctions of evening dresses: black, sequined, beautiful, too sheer for anyone's own good unless you wore a bally good slip underneath it all. The dresses were ridiculously inappropriate, like fairy's wings.

A crowd had assembled and were gawping, drooling. And against her better judgement, Posie found herself also craning her neck and casting a lingering look back at the shop window as she passed.

As the nearby clock on the Swiss Church in Endell Street – where Posie had got married – struck ten-thirty, she was conscious of the office workers milling around the sharp grey windy corners of the Bloomsbury offices. This was the allotted 'coffee-time' for workers, a legal fifteen-minute break for all.

Posie crossed over to Grape Street, that shadowy little enclave which was special to no-one, but which had housed her Detective Agency for more than five years.

She jangled her keys in the lock of the outer door of the red-bricked building right on the corner, and headed inside, past four or five familiar faces, secretaries from other offices, clustered in the stairwell, gossiping.

They were a friendly bunch, cheaply lipsticked and over-rouged, and adorned with homemade versions of the scarves and knitwear they saw in the magazines.

One of the girls, with dyed black hair in a home-set bob, waved a cream card at Posie.

'All right, Miss Parker? What a start into the New Year, eh? Freezin', innit? 'Ere! This telegram just arrived for you. I was gonna bring it up in two shakes of a lamb's tail!'

'Ah, thank you.'

Posie took the telegram, read the telephone number and address on it quickly.

The black-haired girl carried on, cheerfully: 'We woz jus' sayin', we've all seen yer photo in the newspapers jus' before Christmas. Wow-wee! You looked like Louise Brooks; real gorgeous! And we was all dead proud to tell our folks that we shared an office buildin' with you: that we see you every day! That you're dead nice, as well as bein' famous!'

Posie flushed slightly, embarrassed at such effusive praise. 'Ah, yes. Well, I did happen to be standing in a good light for those photos, I suppose. But it's still very kind of you to say such nice things.'

Another girl chimed in. 'Oh, Miss? The dress you were wearin' in the photographs, that sparkly one? Was it designer-like, or was it shop-bought? We were all jus' wonderin'...'

'Shop-bought.' Posie smiled conspiratorially.

That much was true.

The dress in question had been plucked from the rails of a department store in Victoria; the Army & Navy Stores.

It had been a couple of years – busy years when marriage and children had transformed her life – since she had ordered anything extra special to be made up for herself from her preferred Fashion House, the House of Harlow.

Times change.

Posie started up the stairs. She'd not come into work for over a week, and the noise of typewriters and general chatter as she passed the many other offices on the lower floors of the building seemed extra jubilant today.

She clomped up to the top floor, where the Detective Agency was based. Posie needed to check all was well here before leaving for Paris, but she also hoped to actually get down to some work, too, in a way she simply couldn't ever do at home.

But on entering the office, she was met by a very depressing sight.

First up, it was perishingly cold inside the office.

No lights were on, no fire was lit, and the usually cosy clients' waiting room looked very miserable, and smelt musty, unused. Newspapers from at least a week ago, from before the big freeze, were still out on the coffee table, and old teacups, unwashed, sat accusingly all about the place. It was as if time had stood still here.

Len Irving, her erstwhile professional partner at the agency, had obviously had no clients in, and, like Posie, hadn't been in here himself.

The door to his inner office was closed. Work, even Len's ever-profitable work involving obtaining compromising photographic evidence for clients in divorce cases, seemed to have ground to a frozen halt.

Posie flicked on all the electric lights in the office, and they buzzed and dimmed in a wobbly way.

She cleared out the grate in the fireplace of the clients' waiting room and then managed to light a fire which soon roared into life.

Throwing her carpet bag down on the floor, but keeping her coat and hat on, Posie scanned the post heaped up on the secretary's desk.

It was all for her.

Bills, mainly, all for this place: electric, water, telephone. A couple of invitations for charity concerts later in the year, plus a fat navy envelope with the word 'Lagonda' emblazoned in gold on it, which she didn't yet open.

Not yet.

Rufus Cardigeon had, at the end of last year, madly generous as ever, promised Posie, who was hankering to drive again, that he would order her a new Lagonda. It was an unacknowledged but obviously thinly-veiled reward for undertaking to find Dolly, in Paris.

This navy pack must contain all the paperwork to fill in.

Well, it would have to wait until Posie was back from Paris. When she could feel excited about it, properly.

As yet this car was undeserved.

She needed to feel she had earned such an expensive reward.

Her heart sank slightly as she reached the end of the stack of post. There were still no new cases.

There had been no new cases for a month now, despite a fairly high-profile murder case that Posie had solved just before Christmas, involving a controversial magician and a good deal of glitzy photos splashed across the front-pages of several newspapers. One of which had obviously been seen by the girls downstairs.

But even Posie's photograph in the newspapers and some decent editorials hadn't led to any new work.

Perhaps she needed to give it time? For now she was left with the fag-ends of cold cases which every detective worth his or her salt is bound to take on from time to time.

And of which Posie had gathered up a fair few.

She sighed at the hopelessness of it all.

The most painful current cold case on her books was that of a woman, a widowed German House Matron, Mrs Brunhilde Walter, who lived at the prestigious boys' school, Eton College. Her talented son, Friedrich, had simply disappeared in the carnage of the autumn of 1917, when he had been fighting on the English side.

The woman insisted her son was still alive, and had tasked Posie to find him.

Normally Posie refused such cases out of hand, as they were always heart-breaking and ultimately frustrating for both sides, especially with eight years of distance now from the Great War. But this one had proved slightly different, as there was the added complication of a personal connection, although it was very slight.

Mrs Walter had actually been Posie's brother's old Matron while he was at Eton, and she mentioned Posie's brother often in her letters. Clingily so.

It seemed that the ghost of Posie's dead brother was as much a feature of this case as was the missing son, Friedrich. And perhaps Posie's brother, although dead and buried these last nine years, was the more substantial figure.

Who knew?

One letter in the pile today was from Mrs Walter.

'Rats.'

Posie sighed and opened it with a heavy heart and with a sharp pen-lid, pulling out a scrawled note in purple ink and a few pages of damp stuck-together newsprint and a school photograph.

There had been all sorts of mixed, mangled information

from this woman in the past, including cut-out articles from old newspapers about the Tomb of Tutankhamun, and cut-outs from old school magazines, featuring pairs of small boys, all looking identical in an array of fencing outfits, Roman costumes and sailor suits.

Nothing useful ever arrived.

Soon Posie would have to tell the old Matron that the case was a non-starter. And she half-suspected that poor Mrs Walter had lost the plot a little.

But suddenly Posie jumped out of her skin. The telephone was ringing over and over, but not at this, the secretary's desk; rather in Len's own inner office.

About to open Len's door and take the call, Posie got a shock as she heard the receiver abruptly handled, a jangling noise, a cough, and then Len's bleary, sleepy voice:

'Yes? Yes, that's right, Operator. That's me. The Blue Lion, you say? Oh, yes. Make the connection.'

Astounded, Posie stood stock-still.

So Len *was* in the office, after all! It had sounded from his voice as if he had been fast asleep.

Perhaps he'd been working on a case last night, very late, or worked an all-nighter, and had had to stay over in central London, unable to make it back home to Leytonstone with the uncertain transport?

But even so, it was a very late start.

Not wanting to listen in to what was probably a work call from a dodgy contact in a pub somewhere, Posie returned to the secretary's main desk.

But she couldn't help overhearing the sudden hoarse, angry roar from the inner office, through the very thin door.

'Keep your hair on, Agnes, we can *meet*, okay? I didn't say we couldn't, did I? I just don't want your parents there when we *do* meet, all right? Somewhere neutral, eh? You're callin' from The Blue Lion, well, we can meet there if you like. I know it's hard with all the kiddies. And yes, you've been on your own this last week in all this cold. What do you want? A medal for it? Couldn't your mam help you out? They live with us, don't they? *Someone's* got to earn the money, eh? Bring home the bacon. Well, that's *me.*'

Posie swallowed, trying not to eavesdrop on Len's very private conversation. But it was difficult.

'I didn't say anythin' about divorce, did I? I jus' can't sleep there in the house with all the ruddy noise. Not a wink. Kids cryin', and your parents arguin'. And the twins are the last straw. Colic, you say? It's been more than a year now…'

Posie tried to concentrate on the new enclosures from the House Matron at Eton, shaking out the newsprint which was revealed as being a page from a church newspaper with a feature about missionaries in Africa, with much frantic underlining in the usual purple ink and small, crabbed notes written around the margins. Posie looked up from the paper at the sound of her own name.

'POSIE? What the 'ell has she got to do with all this? Nah, you've got the wrong end of the stick, Agnes. There's nothin' goin' on there I can assure you. What? No, of course I haven't seen the *Woman's Penny Post*. What you goin' on about? It was a photo of Posie? Out at some play, alone? Lookin' like a vamp? Well, yes, she has lost a lot of weight, but what's that got to do with me? I wasn't there, was I? No, we're not in some secret tryst. Besides, she's happy: she's got Richard–'

There was a sudden crashing noise as the receiver was obviously forcibly replaced as one or other of Len or Agnes had hung up, or, perhaps, if she was in a pay-phone, Agnes had run out of change.

Posie sighed, aware her face was blazing with embarrassment, at both overhearing such a private conversation and also at the content of it.

Agnes and Posie had always had a difficult relationship, and now it seemed things were on a knife edge in Len's marriage. Once upon a time, years ago, before Richard Lovelace had become her husband, and before the children, Posie had desired Len madly, hankered for him. He was unmarried then.

But it had not worked out. Which was fortunate for everyone, of course. Work and play should always remain separate, and besides, Len was Len, he was more the sort for romance, but not for marriage.

Posie felt a stab of pity for Agnes, over in Leytonstone, weighed down with her parents and her four difficult children, and a husband whose presence was little more than a ghost's might be.

Sitting down in the secretary's chair, Posie breathed slowly to calm herself down.

She half expected Len to burst out of his room, and so she wanted to look composed, professional, but there was just endless silence.

It was nicely warm in the main room by now, and there seemed little point venturing into her own ice-cold box of an office.

She got down to work.

She pushed aside the bills, and threw the letter from Eton with its accompanying enclosures into her carpet bag. Perhaps she'd read it again in Paris in a down moment? Perhaps she could send Mrs Walter a postcard from there, and explain that she was sorry she couldn't take the case any further.

Clearing a space on the big desk, Posie made a little pile of French money, the blue envelope from the railway with her tickets and documents inside it, and her pocket map of Paris.

At home, late last night, she had also taken the opportunity to make up a small, neat file on Dolly for the purpose of taking to Paris. A red cardboard-covered file.

But it was slim pickings, really: a photograph of Dolly as she had looked last year; a photograph of Dolly with Rufus and their three children and a photograph of Caspian della Rosa which Posie had wheedled out of her friend Sam Stubbs, the editor of the *Associated Press* newspaper. But the photograph was at least five years old, and poor quality and probably worthless, as the man was known to be a chameleon when it came to looks and disguises.

Still. It was better than nothing.

Now she had to concentrate. She wanted to write a summary.

Posie took out a fresh silver notebook and opened the page.

A blank page.

She wrote the name 'COUNTESS DOLLY CARDIGEON' at the top, and underlined it several times.

She wrote dates and information, too. Dates she couldn't forget.

Would never forget, as if they were burned indelibly on her mind.

1. Monday 15th June, 1925

The last day I saw Dolly, here in London, in the evening. She came to my office in Grape Street, seemed flustered, nervous. Had been acting oddly all day, and had spoken of receiving a strange telephone call.

2. Tuesday 16th June, 1925

Dolly was seen at the Gare du Nord, Paris, in the early morning, stepping off the Golden Arrow train from England. The Golden Arrow Train Company confirmed her place on the train and her last-minute booking of the passage, paid in cash. The booking was made in her real name.

She was carrying a bald sphynx cat in a special travel basket. The cat was named Julius. It would have needed to be placed in quarantine on arrival in France, but no records have been found of this.

No further reliable sightings beyond this point have since been reported of Dolly or the cat.

3. December, 1925

In December, 1925, a telephone call was taken at the Mermaid Inn Hotel in Rye, in which Caspian della Rosa, or a man purporting to be him, called from Dieppe in France. In this call he apparently claimed that Dolly was with him in Dieppe, in the background.

The accuracy or not of this call cannot be proved and the source herself was unreliable.

4. Other thoughts?

Dolly's mother was from Paris originally, before Dolly was born. Dolly often spoke of visiting the city and was fascinated by her mother's past.

Also, Dolly employed a Parisian nanny, by the name of Violette. (NOTE – what was her full name? Investigate.) She worked for Dolly in 1922, when the twins were tiny, and became something of a confidante. She was sacked by Rufus who (I believe) was jealous of Violette's influence and also jealous of the dominant language in the household becoming French. Dolly spoke often of visiting Violette and catching up with her in Paris.

Was Violette the nanny really the same Violette who called Dolly (from Caspian della Rosa's fake law office on the Champs-Élysées) on the day Dolly left, enticing her to Paris?

Did this really happen? Is the name 'Violette' just a coincidence?

Why would Violette the nanny be working for Caspian della Rosa anyhow? Coerced? Money? (I must investigate.)

Posie flung down her pencil.

There was nothing more to write.

Posie tore out the summary and stuck it rather angrily into the slender red file.

She blew out her cheeks in exasperation, and reached for the receiver of the telephone nearest her.

She placed an international call with the Operator, asking for Inspector Jegouzo, head of the police station on the Rond-Point of the Champs-Élysées, in the 8th Arrondissement.

Posie had never spoken to him before; had only half-caught his name the night before from Richard in that snatched and unsatisfactory telephone call.

She'd asked Sergeant Fox by telegram earlier to look up Jegouzo's exact contact details and location in Paris, and he had obliged in the return telegram she had been handed by the girls in the stairwell downstairs.

After some minutes of trying to connect, and much bleeping, and murmurings, a deep mellow male voice came on the line.

'Mademoiselle Parker?'

'Inspector? *Parlez-vous anglais?* I think you do speak English?'

'*Mais, oui*. Of course I do. Can I help you?'

'It's kind of you to take my call. Has my husband, Richard, the Chief Commissioner of Scotland Yard, been in touch with you yet?'

There was a slightly awkward pause, and Posie could imagine a frown, a shake of the head. 'Pardon? The Chief Commissioner? Your husband? No, Mademoiselle, he has not. Perhaps he called and someone took a message? *Mais, non*, I cannot find any note. What is this about?' There was a slight sigh. 'Oh! Is this still the case of the missing Countess?'

Posie ignored the note of weariness in his voice, the resignation. She hurtled on: 'Dolly Cardigeon, you mean?

Yes. I'm coming out to Paris actually, tonight. On the Night Ferry. My husband said you might have organised someone to accompany me?'

But the ridiculousness of this request if Richard had not even had time to make contact with his French counterpart seemed to sink in as Posie spoke, and she swallowed, doubting the reason for her call, after all.

'I am afraid there has been no such request made, Mademoiselle. Perhaps your husband meant he was sending one of his own men? I cannot spare anyone to cross the Channel for an unspecified reason. But I can give you a man tomorrow morning, if you like? Here in Paris? To meet you off the train?'

Flustered, Posie found herself declining. 'Oh, no! No, I'm sure that's not necessary. I must have got my wires crossed, that's all. One of the London men must be joining me; that must be it.'

'Can I help you with anything else? You would like to come and see *me*, perhaps, at my police station, tomorrow morning? Eleven o'clock? I can tell you where we got to on this case last year. Although, I am afraid to say, we did not make much progress. But the file is still open.'

Posie agreed anyhow, expressed her thanks, wrote down the exact address, and rang off.

She marked the police station on her small map – Number 8 on the Rond-Point – which was a circle of interconnecting roads at one end of the boulevard of the Champs-Élysées. Probably like the Seven Dials in London, she surmised, only chicer, less grubby, and with better shops.

And then Posie marched over to her old carpet bag and she fished out a filled-up silver notebook from last year, which she'd brought from home.

Last summer, when Posie had received the strange letter from the Parisian lawyers informing her of Caspian della Rosa's supposed death, together with his handwritten note to her, apparently written on his deathbed, these papers had been taken away as 'evidence' – although evidence of *what* exactly, she wasn't quite sure – by Richard to the archives of Scotland Yard.

She'd never seen them again.

Fortunately, she'd had the presence of mind to write down in her notebook what she had read, and she'd remembered it, word for word.

She flicked through the old notebook until she came to the page.

Here it was: 'REDON – 77, Avenue des Champs-Élysées, 75008, Paris. Galerie FF.'

She leant over the desk and checked the map, and saw the location was halfway down the boulevard, about two blocks away from Inspector Jegouzo at the Rond-Point, in the direction of the Arc de Triomphe.

She marked the place and then folded the map back up.

Unsure what else to do, she started to place everything in her carpet bag carefully.

The red file, the map, her travel documents, the money, her old and new notebooks.

Suddenly Len burst out of his room.

'Oh! Hullo, Len!'

Well, what else could she say?

'Wotcha, Po. Thought I heard you on the telephone.'

'Mnnn.'

She couldn't exactly say the same thing, could she? She'd have to admit to overhearing everything, which was awful. 'I'm off to Paris later. Just grabbing a few bits and bobs.'

'Oh, yeah? Paris, eh? Fancy.'

Len looked awful. Truth be told, he was barely recognisable as the fresh-faced, cheeky cockney chappie Posie had first been entranced by, had set her heart on five years before when they had started up the Detective Agency.

He had lost his looks.

His curly hair was now grey, thinning. He'd put on weight, and his creased, greasy beige shirt seemed to strain around the belly area, but it was his lovely green eyes which seemed to have changed the most; they'd lost their fire. His face was grey and pallid.

He smelt dreadful, an overpowering scent of old clothes and sweat and alcohol emanated from him in waves.

Posie cast her eye over at the open door of his office, and saw a collection of whisky bottles on his desk, fish and chip wrappers on the floor, and a khaki-coloured sleeping bag in a kind of nest on the floor.

He's been living here.

Good job we haven't had any clients, Posie thought, worry seizing her. *But this can't go on.*

Len's eyes met her own and they held each other's gaze for a few seconds until Len ran a hand through his grizzled remnants of hair.

This pep talk was going to be difficult.

She was not his wife or mother, or even his lover. But as business partners they carried a shared responsibility, and owed each other a duty to be nothing if not scrupulously honest.

'Look, Agnes is not the only one who needs you to bring home the bacon, Len,' Posie said softly, but clearly.

'We rely on you here, it's often only your work keeping us going. I've hardly any cases on at the moment, although I sure am trying. Now, goodness me, smarten yourself up and if you *must* sleep here then do so neatly. Open the windows for a bit. Call up Sid and tell him to get on into work, and the two of you can start telephoning through to lawyers, seeking out new cases… We *must* get some new work, some money pumping in. For all our sakes. For our self-respect.'

Len nodded miserably. 'This wouldn't have happened if we still had Prudence working here, you know...'

Posie sighed heavily. It was a totally pathetic excuse but Len was probably right.

Prudence, their bossy but efficient secretary, had been with them from the very start, but she'd married Richard Lovelace's former colleague, Inspector Rainbird, last year, and she had recently announced the news of a pregnancy, while at the same time submitting her resignation, effective immediately. They hadn't yet tried to find a replacement.

It was high time to do so.

Posie got out her copy of *The Lady*, used by her last night to organise the Norland Nannies, who always ran an advert inside.

She flipped to the page marked 'APPOINTMENTS – SITUATIONS WANTED AND SITUATIONS VACANT. *SECRETARIES, NANNIES, HOUSEKEEPERS, SCHOOL MATRONS.*'

She ran her finger down the page, found two or three adverts for ladies who might be suitable and ringed them with her pencil.

'I'll call *The Lady* and ask them to contact these ladies, and I'll also ask them to place a nice big advertisement specially for us, too. To the effect we are seeking a first-class secretary. We can interview anyone who expresses a real interest next week.'

She picked up the telephone receiver, asked the Operator to put her through to the magazine offices.

As she waited, Len spoke on, desperate to make amends: 'That all sounds good. And I'm sorry, Po. When you get back here you'll find this place is shipshape, I promise.'

'Fine. I believe you. It will have to be shipshape, won't it? We've got a new secretary to impress, remember? Oh, hang about, I'm being connected at last…'

But as Posie placed the advert, speaking the lines out automatically, she felt as if she'd just encountered something which should have had a meaning for her; some odd connection which had been made, and which she'd missed.

Something which could help her.

But what was it?

She ran her fingers down through the current adverts on the page of *The Lady* again.

'Yes, that's right, bill it to me personally. Yes, of course...'

Yes, of course!

Last night she'd been looking for Nannies, hadn't she? Norland-trained ones. But Dolly had used *The Lady*, too. For almost everything.

'Oh!' Posie exclaimed to herself in some excitement.

Chances were high that the French Nanny, Violette, had been found through these very pages.

The Cardigeon twins had been born in May 1922, with Violette arriving soon afterwards, so Posie had a rough idea as to the date Violette might have advertised her services, or when she might have answered an advert Dolly had placed.

It was worth a try, especially as she was still on the telephone.

'I say, could you help me on another matter, Miss? I require a full name, please. You might need to call me back, and you might need to dig around in your archives. I'll make it worth your while. I'm actually looking for a French nanny you placed in employment four years ago...'

And as she got out her newest silver notebook from the old carpet bag, and turned a fresh page, she was hopeful of good news.

Or any news at all, come to that.

* * * *

Chapter Three

It was almost time to depart. Eight-thirty.

Tuesday night.

A few tables had been laid out next to Platform 2, for the Night Ferry passengers, and, despite the cold, it was quite warm under the huge glass-arched ceilings of Victoria Station, mainly due to the many coal braziers glowing cheerily all about the place, punctuating the darkness.

A plump serving-girl in the navy livery of the company was fretting about, topping up the urns for tea and coffee.

Posie presumed it was her first day on the job, as the girl kept spilling things and chewing at her large bucked front-teeth in spasms of nerves, or pulling at her straggly black plait. Her large, thick glasses seemed permanently fogged with the steam from the boiling water.

Posie thought it best to leave the girl well alone and not add to her worries by asking for a brandy, which was also on offer.

She would have dearly loved a drink though, as she had been sitting here alone, small duffle bag and trusty carpet bag at her feet, for about twenty minutes, although it felt like much longer.

She had read her file on Dolly twice, and congratulated

herself several times regarding the small breakthrough she had experienced earlier.

The girl from the magazine hadn't called Posie back.

Instead, mid-way through the afternoon Posie had received a telephone call from South Kensington, from a wary-sounding older woman with a northern accent who had been contacted by *The Lady* and given the option to ring Posie if she wanted to.

On hearing Posie's famous name, she had decided to call.

'You're after information on Violette Lagarde?'

'Er, yes: that's right, Mrs…er?'

'Mrs Bloom. I was Violette's landlady here while she lived in London, see? It's a French area of London here, but as you 'ear, I'm not French. It was my husband who was French, see? But he's been dead twenty years now: so I take in lodgers to pay our way. Violette was one of them. I acted as her reference for jobs, and for that magazine, too. Violette was a good girl, worked in the French Lycée before she got that posh job with those funny Cardigeon people over in Chelsea. She loved it an' all; she was right sorry when she was asked to leave, out of the blue. She was so shocked she decided to go back to Paris.'

'Mnnn. And when she left? Did Violette give you a forwarding address at all?'

'No. But she intimated she'd be going back to her old address and I've got that here. You got a pen, Miss Parker? Oh, and is she all right, Violette? I've not 'eard from her this last year. She normally sends me a card at Christmas.'

Now, at Victoria, Posie studied the Parisian address she had been given, and knew she'd been lucky.

Although whether or not the address would prove to be useful, only time would tell. And whether she'd be able to find anything out about Violette, as she had promised Mrs Bloom she would, remained also distinctly unclear.

Posie folded the paperwork away and looked about eagerly.

She seemed to be the only passenger to have arrived.

And no luggage had yet been loaded. Surely not everyone was like her, travelling light?

Posie was eagerly watching out for her fellow travellers, wondering if anyone famous might be making this expensive overnight journey. Politicians? The rising politician, Winston Churchill?

Or perhaps royalty, even? The glamorous and still unattached Prince of Wales, maybe? With his raffishly handsome brother George in tow?

Or some of the fashionable set from town: Emerald Cunard, or the Curzons, perhaps? Or the heiress Winnaretta Singer, who kept up residences in both London and Paris? All of them were known to travel across the Channel regularly.

So where were all the other passengers?

Were they all such seasoned travellers on this fairly new service that they took the instruction to 'arrive early' with a decided pinch of salt?

And even if all the berths were to be occupied as singles, there should still be eighteen first-class passengers – including herself – at least. Each of the two sleeper cars had nine berths, hadn't the man at the ticket counter said this morning?

Posie stared at the two sleeper cars much further down the platform, at their immaculate navy-and-cream paintwork glistening beneath the overhead lights. They were already attached to a smart black locomotive, whose body bore the distinctive yellow crescent moon symbol of the Night Ferry, and whose engine was noisily being stoked up.

There was much hissing and trying of brakes and the horn being sounded, as engineers in black-stained overalls clustered around the front of the locomotive itself, chattering.

Wreaths of pearly grey puff-like smoke from the engine

coiled and looped up the platform towards Posie, the stench of coal heavy in the air.

It was now twenty minutes to nine, and a dark-red Pullman dining-car nearest Posie was being attached to the back of the sleeper carriages, and men bearing metal canisters – presumably containing hot food – were handing up what seemed like enough provisions to feed a small army.

Posie sat upright at her table, taking it all in.

She was imagining how excited little Kit would be if he could see all of this; he had developed a recent and very enthusiastic love of trains, and he would have been in his element to be here.

For a moment Posie missed him badly; missed his sweet-biscuit smell and the rub of his red hair against her face, and the feel of his fat, cuddly little body held tight against hers, but then again, *no.*

She would be back with the children very soon. No use feeling guilty about leaving them, and by golly, it was good to be here.

In fact, it was wonderful.

To be on her own.

To shed all of them; all of that chaos. To step out alone. Alone for two whole days.

Posie realised her feelings were conflicted. On the one hand Paris represented the case at hand, pure and simple. She felt fear, and nerves, and anticipation at discovering what had happened to her best friend.

But it represented something else, something for herself, too: a personal adventure.

Paris for Posie had only ever been the Gare du Nord, a place for changing trains, for grabbing a quick, overly dry croissant before carrying on with a journey.

Nothing more.

But now the City of Light was waiting for her. Was it as entrancing and enticing as Dolly had always believed it to be? Had it been so good that Dolly had decided never to return? What on earth had happened to Dolly over there?

Posie felt as if she were on the very edge of something.

Heck, she'd even gone a little bit crazy and returned to the shop selling the diaphanous black French gowns in Covent Garden.

Right now, under her thick green woollen coat and muffler suitable for the winter weather, she wore one of the perilously-thin black lace evening gowns. This particular one was a giddy black swan of a dress, with tiny silver beading: it was an outfit destined for adventure.

But suddenly, all in a crush, people were now arriving in a frantic glut, splurging along the platform.

Posie was about to rise to get a better view, when a familiar scent crept up on her and took her breath quite away. Caught her off guard.

'Oh! I say!'

It was Blenheim Bouquet, by Penhaligon's.

A scent Richard wore every day, and had always worn.

Was he here? As a surprise, perhaps?

If so, where?

Posie's heart beat loudly, quickly. She didn't know whether to be happy or sad. But she turned her head, confused, and saw she had a companion sitting at her table.

Not Richard.

Another man, wearing the exact same scent.

Funny how one made such particular associations about a smell belonging to one special person, as if it was their right to own it.

The man sporting Richard's smell was probably in his forties, but it was difficult to say.

He had a spare-looking, handsome tanned face, but with grey hollows beneath his very blue eyes.

His dark homburg hat rendered most of his face in shadow, and Posie could see underneath his thick black cashmere coat he was wearing a turquoise velvet smoking jacket, and an immaculate, expensive white silk shirt. At his throat, where his black cravat was folded, he wore a turquoise scarab beetle tiepin. He made a show of checking a gleaming gold fob-watch.

Glancing up, he caught Posie's eye.

'Good evening, Ma'am.' He was American.

'Posie Parker, pleased to meet you.' She extended a gloved hand, which the man shook in a slightly puzzled fashion.

'The famous lady Private Detective? Say, is that so? You're on *this* train?'

'That's right.'

'Ah?'

Was it her imagination or did she see a slight raise of a surprised blonde eyebrow under the hat?

But the American smiled easily, lighting a cigar which had already been cut. 'I'm Lex Lennart. Well, I'm sure glad to find myself in such good company, Miss Parker. I've heard of you, of course. Gee, who hasn't? A kind of female Sherlock Holmes, they say, huh?'

A man-servant suddenly appeared, bearing a black leather box and a black leather valise, both monogrammed with a gold 'LL' and padlocked heavily.

The American nodded at the man. 'Thank you for these. And I'll see you in Paris, Jakes, tomorrow. Everythin' inside here like I asked for, eh? Good man.'

Lex Lennart stood, made a hat-doffing motion towards Posie, took his very compact luggage under his arm, turned on his heel and, without another word, walked away into the smoke rolling up the platform.

Taking her cue to get on board the train, Posie stood up hurriedly, but was tapped on the elbow.

Behind her was a thin, dark, bare-headed man in an inexpensive brown day-suit. He was quite good-looking, probably in his early thirties, tweedy and sensible, although with rather longer hair than was really quite fashionable just now.

He almost bowed in Posie's direction. 'I'd hurry on now, Miss. Everyone's on board, pretty much. And by the way, I'm Alphonse, Miss Parker. Alphonse Durrant. I'm travelling with you, but not in the same sleeper.'

He motioned with a flick of his head further down the platform, towards the sleeper car nearest the locomotive. 'I'm in Car Number Two.'

'Oh!' Posie said, feeling caught off-guard. 'Did my husband send you?'

She found herself bristling a little, if so. It felt like she was being chaperoned. And by this complicated man whose English was absolutely perfect but whose name was foreign and unplacable.

Was he really a policeman?

Alphonse Durrant had bright, almost-black eyes which creased merrily at the corners, but he had a rather pained expression overall, and his very pale skin made him appear almost sick.

'My husband is the Chief Commissioner of Scotland Yard, Richard Lovelace? *He* sent you here?'

Alphonse Durrant shook his head. 'No, not your husband. But I *am* following orders.'

He pulled out a navy leather fob from an inside jacket pocket, with a metal crest upon it. Flicking it open he revealed his own photograph, and tiny print, all in French.

He stuffed it away hurriedly, his eyes roving around quickly, to make sure no-one had seen.

'My senior, Inspector Jegouzo, telegrammed me at lunchtime today and ordered me to accompany you on the train and see you to his office tomorrow. *I* am French, but my father is English, and he teaches mathematics at a famous boys' school. He's very sick, and I've been visiting him. He might be nearing the end, and I wanted to say goodbye. I was due back in Paris anyway at the end of this week, so I was recalled a little bit earlier than was already planned. Inspector Jegouzo remembered after your call that I was already in England, and that my accompanying you on this train might be useful. He says he will send your husband the bill! I am a plainclothes policeman, Miss Parker. An Inspector in the French Police Judiciaire. And I am at your service.'

'Oh!'

He made the bow again, and ushered Posie towards the train.

She felt dreadful at having dragged this nice man away from an ailing relative, but she was impressed too at Jegouzo's organisational abilities.

'I do hope your father remains stable, Inspector, and this hasn't inconvenienced you too much?'

'Not at all, Miss Parker. There is a woman there who has taken good care of him, so it is all fine. He's in good hands.'

'Good.' Posie stepped up onto the first set of train steps to Car Number One, the nearest sleeper.

'I will see you at dinner shortly, Miss Parker.'

Guards in the livery of the company, cream and navy, were bustling along, and there was a general hurry going on.

From the top of the steps Posie caught sight of a small, elderly, hunched-up woman in a dark travelling cape, wearing a black lace mantilla on her head. The old woman was pursued along the platform by three maids and a porter with a trolley, all helping her to alight up the steps at the opposite end of Car Number One.

And then Posie saw the girl all in black from earlier, the one with the chipped red nails.

She was in a similar state of chaos as earlier: breathless, tottering on her high heels, lugging along a bulky, shabby canvas suitcase all by herself, tearing past the tables loaded with coffee, stopping there and almost upsetting the drinks. Then skittering along the main platform. She stopped for a moment to speak to a guard.

Panting, she stopped at Posie's steps, checked her

tickets for the car number and started to haul up the case.

Posie called out: 'Do you want a hand? Only, don't knock me over again, eh?'

The girl looked up in surprise, grinned widely. 'Oh, hullo! Fancy seeing you here!'

'You look like you might be going somewhere for a long time, with that big bag... Here, let me help you. I insist.'

The two women dragged the old bag up onto the polished floor of the carriage. It was very heavy.

'Goodness, thank you. *Merci*. It feels like I've got a body in here, doesn't it? But it's only shoes, really. A few books, too. Sentimental things.'

Posie was reading the name on the worn luggage tag. It said 'SCOTLAND'. She frowned, and something somewhere far-off seemed to be ringing a bell.

The woman followed Posie's gaze. 'Oh, that's me! "Scotland" is my *name*, not the country! *I'm* Suzannah Scotland.' The woman stuck out a hand with freshly-painted nails in the bright-red colour from earlier. 'I'm very pleased to meet you.'

'I'm Posie Parker.'

'*No!*' The woman squeaked in disbelief, then covered her mouth as if Posie might have told her she was actually Princess Mary in disguise.

'You're the detective?'

'Yep. That one. But your name – it confuses me – forgive my bluntness, but you're not from here, are you? You seem to deserve an altogether more romantic, artistic name.'

The woman laughed again, and it was quite a honk actually.

'You're correct! I *had* another name, *certainement*. I'm from Algeria, Miss Parker. My first husband, an Algerian like me, died at the start of the Great War, fighting for France, and then I got myself sent up to the Western Front, nursing, alongside some other Algerian ladies. I met my second husband, Christian Scotland, when he was a patient of mine in a Field Hospital. We married after the Great War finished. I took his surname and we lived a very nice life here in England, in Surbiton: nice little house; nice little garden. He worked as a shoe salesman at the local department store, Randalls in Uxbridge. It was a nice life, actually. *Oui*. Lots and lots of shoes, and new outfits. *Parfait*.'

The smile vanished suddenly.

'Well, *almost* perfect, Miss Parker. Unfortunately, we couldn't have children. And then Christian died last year. He was never strong, and they found he'd had lung cancer all along, *le pauvre*. He left me with a broken heart, and many bad debts. Turns out we'd been spending money we didn't have. Christian was never good with money… *pas du tout*. I sold everything we had, then all *my* own clothes, all *my* jewellery. I've paid some debts off by working like crazy, by taking anything I can get; mainly French translation work, which pays well, but it hasn't been easy. In fact, it's been rotten, not to mention very lonely. And I still owe money here, there and everywhere…'

Posie felt awkward, having basically forced this confidence out of the woman.

Suzannah Scotland was still a mystery, though.

Why was she here, now?

With her faultless English, but with its peppering of French words, and her bad debts?

Where was she going and why was she on this expensive train?

Posie flapped her ticket. 'Well, I'm in Berth Number Nine of this carriage. I bet you're in the one right next to me, aren't you? Number Eight.'

Suzannah Scotland looked amazed. '*Non!* You really are a good detective.'

Before Posie could explain how she knew this, there was a flurry of whistle-blowing, and Posie and Suzannah rushed to the window.

Outside, a jostle of photographers and journalists engulfed the platform, following a couple of stick-thin figures who appeared as little more than silhouettes set against the flash-lights and billowing smoke.

Posie cupped her face against the glass. 'Who are *they*? They'll almost miss the train at this rate!'

Suzannah Scotland squinted, then gave a gulp of excitement. '*Mais, non!* I know who it is! Under that big purple *hat*!'

The obviously-famous people were being pursued up the steps at the far end of the carriage and they were suddenly inside the wooden sleeping car, albeit still far away from Posie and her new acquaintance.

All she saw was a flash of bright purple, and a very big hat with an impossibly wide brim. The other figure seemed to be entirely dressed in black.

A Guard had accompanied these new guests and was fawningly opening the door to Berth Number One. And then they were gone, as suddenly as they had arrived.

Down on the platform the group of newspaper men were breaking up, some checking watches and running for the exits, some calling to each other conspiratorially over their shoulders as they left.

'Miss Parker, look at this!'

Suzannah had pulled out a folded-up magazine from her inside coat pocket and she shook it out eagerly.

Posie recognised it as the exact same one the gossiping maid had been regaling her pal with in the queue earlier that morning.

It was the *Picture Post*, with the profile shots of a man and a woman on the cover.

Posie felt the train shudder slightly beneath her, groan, and a whistle went as it heaved off.

But then she saw a streak of shimmering darkness tearing itself along past the train carriage outside, fast as a whippet, silks and glittering scarves streaming.

Posie saw a hat go flying up into the night, and a desperate face beneath a short black crop.

It was a girl running alongside the train, a bolt like lightning, lithe as an athlete, insubstantial as a ghost.

She was keeping pace with the moving train, trying to reach Car Number Two.

'Oh, look, Suzannah! A real latecomer! Golly, you reckon she can make it?'

'*Le pauvre*. She cannot outrun a train, *non*?'

Posie pulled the corridor window down a little, heard amid all the puffing of the train a desperate shout.

'DON'T GO! DON'T GO! I *must* make this train! I just paid a *fortune*...'

She heard a slightly-familiar voice calling out: 'Here! Give me your hand! Step up. Onto this step. I won't let you fall, I promise.'

A good Samaritan, a brave one, had intervened further down the train.

Posie presumed the girl had got aboard, as she didn't see her fall back. She felt unaccountably pleased for the girl, and slightly guilty at not having done anything to help her herself.

She turned her attention to the *Picture Post* again, which Suzannah was obviously gripped by. Posie read the caption:

'THE ENGAGEMENT IS ANNOUNCED BETWEEN LADY CAROLINE GREENLOW AND THE SOCIETY PHOTOGRAPHER, DADIE SPENCE.'

Posie raised her eyebrows in surprise. 'You mean these two are travelling with us to Paris? On this train?'

'Yes, I think so.' Suzannah nodded. 'I thought I saw another man down on the platform who looked famous, too: he's always in the newspapers, but not glamorous at all. Old and boring. With a funny old red suitcase clutched in his hand. But these two, well, they look so fresh and exciting, don't they, Miss Parker?'

Posie refrained from commenting.

Lady Caroline Greenlow was a highly controversial figure at the best of times, and always had been, and Dadie Spence was such a newcomer to London society that he was a completely unknown quantity.

All Posie knew of him was that he was part of the crowd known as the 'Bright Young Things', and that his lifestyle was probably, as a result, wildly decadent, and possibly, sometimes, illegal.

'Perhaps they will simply stay in their berth for the whole journey?' Posie suggested, hopefully.

The thought of dinner with two love-birds as part of a group was not a particularly attractive one, famous love-birds or not.

'Perhaps they are simply wrapped up in each other, and want for nothing else?'

'How thrilling!' replied Suzannah Scotland dreamily. 'Oh, the romance of being a couple only-just-arrived in love! Those first few honeymoon-ish weeks! And to be together on the way to Paris, too! I envy them.'

'Mnnn.' Posie felt distinctly non-committal about such things. Perhaps she was getting too old?

'Dinner will be served in twenty minutes in the dining-car!' shouted a navy-and-cream liveried Guard as the train rumbled its way out of Victoria Station, and Posie and Suzannah hastened to their own berths to settle in and freshen up.

As Posie turned her key in the door of Berth Number Nine, she knew she should have been feeling excited, but for some reason a growing feeling of unease was stealing over her, little by little, and she could not for the life of her work out why.

****

Chapter Four

Outside it was pitch-black and it had started snowing again as the train puffed through the sprawl of the London suburbs.

Bromley, St Mary Cray, Swanley.

Posie checked her reflection in the small round mirror above the tiny basin, and nodded, satisfied.

The sheer black dress with its silver glitter was really lovely. It worked like a sparkly pick-me-up. It needed no jewellery to accompany it, no further embellishment.

She took a deep breath, dabbed for the last time at her cupid's bow of scarlet lipstick.

Not bad.

She'd found all the information from Cox & Kings about her Paris accommodation – the Hotel Maigret, situated off the Champs-Élysées, at Number 8 on the Rue de Berri – here in her immaculate berth, on the small bedside table. Just as she'd been promised.

And everything else seemed to be in perfect order.

Berth Number Nine was clean and mahogany-panelled, and carried the strong scent of furniture polish. It was all very well-appointed and stylish, obviously prepared for a female guest, with a pink glass ashtray, pink glass carafe of water, and a pink glass bowl of apples on the bedside table.

Snack wafers and a small leather-covered Bible were on the desk, next to a pad of Night Ferry embossed writing paper, with a matching pencil.

She was on the verge of stepping outside when there was a brisk knock at the door. It was the Guard.

'Oh, hullo. Am I late? I'm coming along now.'

'Not to worry, Madam. Actually, I'm here to deliver this to *you.*'

He proffered a plain silver platter stamped with the Night Ferry insignia. On the platter was a very small white envelope with 'P. PARKER – STRICTLY PRIVATE' typed in black.

The train jolted particularly badly, and Posie frowned as she clutched the doorframe with one hand and took the envelope with the other.

'This is from someone on the train? Just now? A fellow passenger?'

The Guard, a harassed fellow with very red, spotty skin, in his early thirties, looked immediately sheepish. He shrugged.

'Nah, Madam. The note was actually passed to me on the platform at Victoria but I can't for the life of me remember who by. I agreed to get it to you immediately, but, well, we're very understaffed tonight. It's only me, plus the one Pullman Waiter who will leave when we get to Dover, when the dining-car is unhooked. And what with the unexpected extra lady passenger arriving like that, all in a whirl, and having to prepare a berth for her, and all the excitement around our *famous* guests, I'm afraid I've only just remembered this 'ere note.'

'No harm done.' Posie smiled. 'I'll read it now, in case it's important, then I'll be along in a minute.'

'Right you are, Madam.' And he was gone.

She ripped the paper open, expecting maybe some kind of sudden last-minute instruction from Rufus, or even from darling Richard, perhaps, who might have had to get one of his underlings at Scotland Yard to type something up and dash it around the corner.

But no.

The paper inside when unfolded was revealed as being small, lined, with one jagged, ripped edge, like it had been torn from a pocketbook.

It looked dirty, and had a piece of thick parcel-tape stuck to its rear.

The thing was decidedly odd. And not in a nice way.

Posie quickly read the typed message:

LISTEN

What do you make with this?

Find the answer.

This is what your fancy friend remains.

'What on earth?'

Posie read it again.

It could have been the ravings of a mad person. She sat down hurriedly on the single bed with its crisp white sheets and navy woollen blanket, the train swaying slightly.

'"*Listen?*" But "listen" to what, exactly? And to whom? How, exactly? And what kind of mad person doesn't sign their letters?'

She was unconsciously pulling her fingers through her new thick, blunt fringe.

Was this some kind of threat?

Was Dolly Cardigeon the 'fancy friend' mentioned in the note? Well, who else could it be? Posie didn't have many other fancy friends.

Even friends plain and simple were few and far between these days.

Posie felt sick to the pit of her stomach.

If only the Guard could remember who had passed him the note.

Suddenly she felt a presence next to her, a movement. Posie looked up quickly, and then relaxed.

It was Suzannah Scotland.

'I hope you don't mind, Miss Parker, but your cabin door was open? Just banging back and forwards with the motion of the train. I tried knocking but you didn't hear me. And my heels are too high to stand about in for ages. But, oh, look at you! How beautiful you are! Like a movie star. That dress! It's stunning!'

Suzannah sighed. 'I've only brought two dresses with me, and this is much the best. But I'm nervous, going to eat with all those important people. So, I called here first.'

Posie smiled wanly, putting the weird note down on the bed.

She saw that Suzannah was wearing a woollen black, plain serviceable work dress with a wide boatneck, but it was shiny in places with age. Suzannah had tied her black sateen stole about the waist as a sort of unsatisfactory belt, and Posie's heart lurched with pity.

The woman had made an effort with her face though and reapplied her make-up carefully, pink powder over her beautiful dusky skin, and the red, red lipstick again, plus she'd twisted her hair up into an elegant chignon with a small tortoiseshell comb.

Posie reached down to her as-yet unpacked duffle bag, which she'd stowed hurriedly under the bed, where she'd packed one slimline dark-pink woollen outfit for Paris.

Underneath the outfit was her small jewellery roll, into which she'd packed her single string of creamy pearls, and a pair of sapphire pear-drop earrings, with tiny diamonds webbing out below set in droplets of gold, like stars trailing in their wake. Rufus and Dolly had given these earrings to Posie years ago; they were made by Cartier, and they were her favourites.

'Here.'

She handed the precious jewels to the woman at her side.

'I think you'd probably suit emeralds better, or rubies, given your lovely colouring, but we'll have to make do with what we have. Wear these, please, if you fancy; they'll add some glitter and sparkle in the lights at the table.'

'Oh! Oh, how kind, are you sure, Miss Parker? *Mais non!* They're real.'

But Suzannah was already eagerly clipping the earrings into place, and twisting her neck to-and-fro, feeling the weight of the stones, checking her reflection in the small mirror.

Posie smiled. The earrings suited this girl, and she looked like some lovely flamenco dancer, gearing up for the high-point of the evening.

'Shall we go?' Posie reached for her clutch bag, and then saw that the horrible note was on the floor, fallen from the bed.

At the very same time Suzannah Scotland saw it, and trying to be helpful, also reached down for it.

'Here. A note! Oh, but what's this?'

The parcel-tape at the rear had come off the note, and remained on the floor. Posie picked it up, suddenly seeing a small piece of newsprint stuck to the parcel-tape, folded down to about the same size as a postage stamp.

Posie levered at it carefully with her unpainted fingernail, prised it from the tape and unfolded it.

'Oh! Golly! How *horrible*!'

A clipping from a newspaper showed a photograph of a beautiful face, a girl, asleep. Or more like, on closer inspection, she was dead.

Yes: definitely dead.

There was a paragraph of French text beneath the picture. Below, a title read: '"*L'Inconnue de la Seine*", 1880s.'

'What does that say, please, Suzannah? My French is terrible.'

The woman looked pale, swallowed, then nodded and translated quickly:

'The title means "*The Unknown of the Seine*". And the clipping is a review for a new book, just out, by Ernst Benkard. It's a weird book all about death masks. This is the most famous one featured in the book: a girl who drowned more than forty years ago, and who was washed in at the Quai du Louvre, in Paris. That's all it says. Does this make any sense to you, Miss Parker?'

'Oh, do call me Posie, please. This formal guff is getting boring. You're wearing my diamonds: we must trust one another. And no, it makes no sense at all. I suppose it must be some crazy person who I've got on the wrong side of, or someone trying to scare me, perhaps. It does happen. I must confess I'm not wildly happy about this missive. But I'm relieved, too. Sad though I feel for whoever this "Unknown of the Seine" was, I'm relieved it seems to be a forty-year-old cold case, and that it's no-one I know. For a horrible moment there, I thought it might be a pal of mine.'

Posie placed the newsprint on the night-table and made to rise.

Then she saw Suzannah Scotland was holding the original note with its typed heading of 'LISTEN'.

Suzannah shook it in Posie's direction:

'This note came with *that* clipping, Posie? About "*L'Inconnue de la Seine*"? *Mais, tout alors!* This sender is charming, are they not?'

Posie shrugged dismissively. 'Oh, yes, you've read it? Well, that's something else which is bizarre. I have no idea what that note is going on about. *What* am I supposed to listen to, exactly?'

'*Non*, Posie, you are wrong!' Suzannah Scotland was pointing at the paper excitedly.

'You're not supposed to "listen" to anything. This is like a crossword clue. You are simply meant to take the letters of the word "LISTEN", and you are asked to *make* something with them.'

Posie looked at her new acquaintance blankly.

'What am I supposed to make with it?' she whispered.

'This is an anagram, that's all,' said Suzannah quickly, clearly. 'You need to make a new word. From the word "LISTEN" you make the word "SILENT". And that's it. There's the answer. So, the writer says you have a fancy friend, and the fancy friend remains silent. And that is all.'

Silent?

Posie stared in horror at the note which had been passed back to her, and then at the screwed-up picture of the death mask, and she shivered in her thin, cobwebby dress.

Dolly, silent?

Silent like this poor girl who had died so long ago? A girl who had died in a watery grave in a city known as the City of Light, but for some it was obviously a city of dark, fathomless shadows instead.

What was Posie being warned of here, exactly?

To stay away? To not investigate? To clear off? To keep her nose out of things?

Yes, perhaps that was 'all'.

Or worse, was Dolly already dead and this was all a waste of time? A 'mare's nest', as Richard would have called it.

Posie tried to remain calm, avoiding the dark, searching eyes of her fellow passenger, who was obviously intrigued, as well she might be. Suzannah was obviously clever, and on the ball, and Posie chided herself for being so sluggish today.

Grabbing at all the horrible bits of paper, Posie quickly stuffed them in her carpet bag.

'Let's go,' Posie said brightly, throwing down her clutch and picking up her carpet bag instead. 'I'm famished. And I'm not going to let a few odd-ball notes put me off my dinner.'

But as they started to walk in single file along the swaying mahogany corridor towards the Pullman dining-car, something else happened to make Posie, already nervy and tightly wound, want to scream out loud.

* * * *

Chapter Five

The most frightening-looking man Posie had ever seen had stepped out into the corridor.

It was like seeing the dead, newly resurrected.

But very, very badly.

He was locking the door to Berth Number Six, and he stood in a blaze of bright light, key held aloft, staring at them, immaculate in black-tie.

Behind her she heard Suzannah stifle a gasp. Willed the woman to keep quiet.

Don't scream, Suzannah. You were a nurse, weren't you?

Don't scream.

He doesn't deserve that.

Smile instead.

Posie had seen most things, actually.

In the Great War she'd worked as an Ambulance Driver on the Western Front up until the winter of 1917, and she'd witnessed the horrors which senseless war could inflict on mortal man, on both the body and soul.

She'd become used to dreadful, gruesome injuries on a daily basis.

Posie had become an expert at masking her own feelings – fear, guilt, disgust – as she helped scoop up the injured men onto stretchers and into her ambulance, making soothing noises to distract them as harried doctors at the camp hospitals yelled out hateful yet necessary labels as each man was assessed for medical care.

They were labels etched forever on Posie's mind: an 'A' for 'actionable'; 'M' for 'maybe later, but only if time allowed'; and the dreaded 'U', which meant the case was 'unrecoverable'.

This man, turning to them now with the full glare of the overhead corridor light shining in his face, must have been a 'U'. Impossible not to have been.

Poor fella.

Caught unawares perhaps, with a crisp, new, unseasonal Panama hat clamped under a withered right arm, the man's entire right-hand side had obviously been caught in a wartime bomb blast, with most of the lower part of his face on that side missing.

What was left was an ugly criss-crossing of scar tissue and bad skin grafts, a gaping nostril-hole and a green-coloured glass eye staring out horribly from behind a jaunty *pince-nez*, which had obviously been added for no other purpose than as a diversionary tactic. His lips had been ripped away on that same side and his mouth and teeth were exposed as a terrible half-snarl, which made him look unearthly and dreadful.

Putting the hat on quickly, and turning himself round so only his left side was to the fore, the man bowed quickly.

'Good evening, lovely ladies. I am sorry if I shocked you there; your calm faces do you much credit: I am aware I resemble Frankenstein's monster, but I hope to assure you I am anything *but*...'

The voice was mellow, laughingly upbeat.

Posie strode right up to the man and held out her hand. 'Posie Parker. And you need assure us of nothing, Mr...?'

'Doctor Dance. Derick Dance. At your service.' But now the voice held a streak of uncertainty in it, too; a biting worry.

'*You're* Posie Parker?'

He looked at Posie full on, the remains of one badly burned eyebrow raised improbably, his one real green eye watering horribly. 'The *detective*? Well, by Gad, that's quite the surprise. I've heard we've got a bobby from the French Police Judiciaire on board, as well. I suppose you aren't in cahoots with him, eh? A group of crime experts, all travelling together, perhaps?'

'No, Doctor Dance. The man you speak of and I, we are not in cahoots.'

'Well, well. We must all be on our best behaviour though, mustn't we?'

The man grinned, and there, beneath the tatters of the face, was an echo suddenly of a man who had been used to being important.

He introduced himself briefly to Suzannah, who was loitering uncomfortably behind, and then stuck out his good left arm to Posie.

'Would you do me the honour of accompanying me to the table? I assume you are travelling alone?'

'That's right. My husband remains in England.'

'Well, that's his loss. And what a treat for me. I cannot remember the last time I had such a beautiful woman by my side.'

Posie smiled at the ridiculous flattery, but took the man's arm anyway, glad to see the French policeman, Alphonse Durrant, suddenly appear behind them in the corridor, smart in an old-ish black velvet blazer, introducing himself to Suzannah in French, making up a loose pair with her.

They walked as a group of four down the corridor and opened the door into the dining-car.

The Pullman car was beautifully and dimly lit, with amber-coloured sconces flickering along each wall, and a thick emerald-green carpet throughout.

The walls were gleamingly wood-panelled, and the still-undrawn curtains were a matching emerald green. The effect was ostentatious and opulent, like walking into the very best sort of gentlemen's club.

A bar at the entrance to the car was picked out with tiny fairy lights, and its counter of bottle-green glass was covered in an array of jewel-coloured flacons of drinks and liquors.

Tiny cocktails on a silver tray had been prepared and set out already, and a Waiter was busily at work preparing canapes.

A rather tight space in front of the bar included a couple of hastily-arranged seats and a low glass coffee-table, and this was obviously where pre-dinner drinks were to be taken.

Posie felt the man on her arm suddenly relax on entering the dining-car. Felt him exhale.

Out of the bright light, into familiar territory.

Close up the man smelt of cinnamon, and musk, and something stronger underneath: disinfectant, perhaps? Iodine?

The Pullman was obviously used to catering for big numbers of guests. Groups of tables ran the length of the car, set in blocks of four places at each side. So a group of eight could sit together, albeit divided by the narrow aisle.

There was capacity here for five groups of eight people to sit and eat. For forty people in total.

Posie scanned the car. *Not today.*

Most of the blocks of tables were not laid for dinner and the chairs were still folded up. She saw that only the furthest end of the Pullman was being used today.

Two blocks of four places, alongside each other but divided by the aisle, had been set with cutlery for dining, plus two cosy settings placed immediately behind.

Ten people! Posie frowned. *Were there really only ten people eating?* It hardly seemed worth the effort.

Whatever the case, they were certainly the very first to arrive.

The Waiter brought around the cocktails on the tray: tiny glasses of a bright-green liquid, each replete with a shining candied maraschino cherry and a curl of thin chocolate.

'Mint Julep cocktails,' he murmured and everyone took one politely, as if they might be taking communion.

He then offered around tiny blinis piled high with gleaming black caviar, which Posie saw were only taken by the French policeman and Suzannah, who wolfed them down hungrily.

The train wobbled and Posie could quite see that standing about for pre-dinner drinks on a train was almost impossible.

By the bar, the lone Waiter was opening bottles of Vichy water, and lining up bottles of red wine, and stirring up a punch bowl filled with orange liquid, all the while emptying tins of fruit into the mix.

She heard Suzannah speaking in quick, excitable French with the young Inspector, and saw her unfolding a blush-pink card from inside a pocket of her dress, showing it to Durrant, pointing animatedly, the long sapphire and diamond earrings sparkling.

How good they look on her, Posie thought, pleased.

She watched as Suzannah's fancy card glittered with a burnish of rose-gold at the top.

Posie's natural curiosity got the better of her. *What was it?* Was it the reason why Suzannah was on this train? The reason she had been on 'cloud nine' earlier? Perhaps still was?

She realised to her embarrassment that Doctor Dance had said something at her side, and he was now coughing pointedly, trying to get her attention.

'I'm so sorry, Doctor. You were saying?'

He laughed heartily. 'I was just being as curious as you obviously are about others and their interesting situations. I wondered why *you* are on your way to Paris, Miss Parker? Is it a last-minute trip?'

'Er, well, sort of. Funny you should say so.' Posie frowned. 'Do I look like I'm in a mad last-minute rush, then?'

'Not at all. The picture of composure, but the last few days have been a hell of a mess for everyone, travel-wise.'

'Mnnn. Well, I'm on a case, actually. Someone has employed me as from tomorrow. I'm staying on the Champs-Élysées.'

'The Champs-Élysées, eh? How lovely.'

She saw Doctor Dance look past her for a split-second, to where the couple beyond them were still chattering in French, saw a flash of something – was it anger? Envy? Jealousy? – cloud his one still-good eye.

But then he turned back and gave her his full attention, the dreadful smile. 'I'm staying just along from there, two minutes' walk, on the Avenue Kléber. You know that street? It's lined with these big, upmarket hotels. The Majestic, the Raphael, you know. Mine isn't quite as grand, nor as beautiful, but still jolly nice.'

Posie didn't admit she didn't know Paris at all, that those names meant nothing to her. 'Are you in Paris for diversion, Doctor?'

'By Gad, I wish. No, I'm lecturing on my speciality at the Sorbonne tomorrow. Part of a big medical conference for all the students. I do it every year. Unfortunately, this time round I've got the dreaded dead slot to lecture in, just after lunch. But the pay is usually very good. It's been in my diary for ever: the secretary at the Sorbonne organises it all. I came back from Africa specially for this. Oh, rats! My bally eye…'

The Sorbonne.

Posie had once met a medical student who was studying at the Sorbonne. Despite being far too young, he'd pursued her and carried on writing to her after they'd parted. He'd been a charmer, though.

Like this man, Dance, obviously once had been.

Posie tried not to look too closely as Dance fumbled

with the bright-green drink, sloshing it down his front, and digging in the pocket of his black smoking jacket for a handkerchief with which to wipe his ever-watering real eye.

The scent of iodine was very strong again, and it seemed the handkerchief was doused in it.

But Posie couldn't help noticing, this close up, how two of his fingers on his right hand were completely missing, and how the rest of his hand was scarred in a cross-hatch of white and livid pink scar tissue, despite the many years which had passed.

He caught her looking, and grinned with that awful skeleton's smile. 'They do say a person's personality can be read by their hands, don't they? Oh, and that the eyes are the mirrors to the soul: isn't that another old saying? Well, turns out I'm screwed both ways, aren't I? That bomb I intercepted at Passchendaele, 29th October, 1917, it really scored a hat-trick, didn't it? Took me years to recover and even get to this current handsome state, would you believe?'

He dabbed at his eye again. 'I still dream of all the noise.'

'Golly, I'm so very sorry, Doctor Dance. Were you with a bomb-disposal unit? It must have been dreadful work. Terrifying.'

'Don't be sorry. Plenty more I knew died that day near Hooge, and never made it out of Château Wood alive. I'm lucky. Here I am, nearly ten years on, speaking to a beautiful woman and on my way to the best city in the world. I'm proud that I did my bit, and call me Derick, for goodness' sake. And no, I wasn't in the bomb squad: I was already a doctor then, very junior of course, just out of Oxford really. Picking up the scraps where they fell; trying to pull the pieces of just-about-alive lads out of the mud. Then later on of course the boot was on the other foot and my medical colleagues had to pull *me* out.'

'I see.' Posie started to talk of her experiences as an Ambulance Driver, trying to find a little common ground, but then stopped, as the Pullman doors were opened by the Guard who ushered in some more guests.

First came the American man Posie had shared a table with briefly on the platform, Mr Lennart. Now, without the protection of his hat, it was clear that he was older than she'd first assumed, at least in his fifties.

He was smoking yet another cigar, and Posie saw how his eyes almost exactly matched the turquoise scarab he still wore at his throat.

An eccentric, Posie concluded, *albeit a very wealthy one.*

And behind him lurched a much bigger, taller man, also in his fifties, who had crammed himself tightly into a dinner suit which had obviously been bought in trimmer times.

This big man, with his bald, pointed, egg-shaped head had a self-important look on his face. As well he might, as he was very famous.

But not at all loved. Far from it, in fact.

'I say!' Posie exclaimed under her breath. '*Now* there may be fireworks!'

This was Sir Charles Loxley, the famous government minister. He was a hugely controversial figure. Loxley was attached to Stanley Baldwin's Conservative government, and he was currently Chancellor of the Exchequer, and he had very controversial views.

He was, it was rumoured, in the process of bringing in legislation which would drastically reduce manual workers' pay allowances, especially for shipbuilders and mineworkers.

The daily newspapers liked to stoke the flames of ordinary people's fear by printing dire headlines: 'GRIM REAPER LOXLEY TO STEAL YOUR KIDDIE'S MILK MONEY!'; 'LOXLEY LIVES THE HIGH LIFE WHILE PLANNING TO STEAL YOUR WAGES!'

And the like.

But Loxley was hated by many women, too, and with a

passion. And this was nothing to do with money, but about basic human rights.

While women over the age of thirty and with money or land had been granted the right to vote eight years before, there were constant calls for women to be treated as equal to men, and for *all* women over the age of twenty-one to be able to vote, regardless of their wealth.

Loxley was very vocal in opposing this, frequently thundering in Parliament that women already had 'enough' when it came to voting rights.

He was an object of hate for women's groups throughout the land; and he didn't seem to mind it at all.

Posie, who had voted before and believed it a fundamental right, was all in favour of lowering the age-limit and making things equal. She had always viewed Loxley with a mixture of curiosity and hostility, the latter of which she was doing her best to hide.

Loxley was looking round beadily, holding one of the green, minty drinks suspiciously; the low lights reflecting off his sweaty forehead and bald pate, and Posie saw that in his other hand he was holding on tightly to a red boxy-looking case of paperwork stamped with the golden portcullis design of Parliament.

Important paperwork, probably. Which he doesn't want to leave lying around, not even here.

Loxley had obviously been the famous man Suzannah had seen on the platform, that she had recognised but thought was old and boring and not glamorous.

Well, she'd been right about that.

Loxley struck up a polite, superficial conversation, aiming his words towards the men of the group, which Posie found rude, but rather convenient, as it meant she didn't have to talk to him at all.

Hands were shaken awkwardly, glasses balanced.

'Lennart? Ah, yes, yes. Of course. Financier? You used to own Lennart Morgan Investment Bank, yes, of course.

And you've been really very decent over those gifts to the British Museum, dashed decent of you. I dare say you'll be doing something similar for the French, eh? Nice that so many can enjoy it all. Especially after all the bad publicity, eh? Lot of bally suspicious nonsense, of course.'

The American looked angry and clamped his lips down tight on his cigar. 'Of course, it's a load of darn nonsense, Sir Charles. And no, I'm not meeting the French government. I have a dinner tomorrow night, at the Blue Garret. It's become a tradition for me, I go every year. I usually take the normal boat and connect to the Golden Arrow in Calais, but my man booked this, thinking it would be more convenient as a "through" service. He's had me booked on this train for months; ever since the Night Ferry started running. Although it's my first time travelling on it.'

'The Blue Garret, eh? Sounds lovely, wish I had time for a spot of dinner in Paris,' brayed the Chancellor, 'but I've been summoned over on urgent business by the French government. Only knew I was travelling late last night.'

He took a swig of the crème de menthe and looked momentarily surprised, but then took another sip.

'I've travelled on the Night Ferry a few times for governmental business, and it's all pretty smooth, except for the terrible clanging of the chains as they lash all the sleeper carriages on to the boat securely at Dover Marine Station. It's a ghastly noise! And the sea crossing to Dunkirk is rather long; three hours. But my solution is to take a good dose of Veronal after dinner. Then I sleep through all the noise. If you need a sleeping powder, Lennart, you let me know, eh?'

He then turned to Doctor Dance, and didn't flinch once. Which Posie gave Loxley a glimmer of credit for.

'And you, my fine fellow, must be in the berth next to me? I'm in Berth Five. Thought I saw you earlier, darting about with a medical bag, eh? You're a doctor?'

'Yes, that's right, Chancellor. Of course, I trained generally, but infectious diseases are my thing now.'

'Ah, perhaps I can bend your ear on the subject of inoculations, eh? Costly business, eh? Jolly expensive. There are proposals to bring in compulsory inoculation for…'

Parts of the previous conversation had passed Posie completely by, especially the bits about 'bad publicity' and 'suspicious nonsense', and she had no desire to continue listening to the self-important government minister wittering on, so she tore her gaze away and saw Suzannah Scotland and the French policeman, Durrant, had very sensibly sat down on the chairs.

They were talking and joking together as if they had known each other for years, not minutes. Posie looked away, not wanting to intrude.

And here were more passengers arriving, with the blotchy-faced Guard fawning attendance upon them as he opened the door. These were his famous guests.

First came the 'Bright Young Thing', Dadie Spence, who was perhaps only twenty-one or twenty-two years old, but was greyer and more exhausted-looking than his pictures in magazines and newspapers let on, and not as tall.

He's nervous, thought Posie, watching carefully. *But why?*

Everyone turned and stared, most with distaste.

Dadie Spence was quite a spectacle.

He was wearing a feminine and bright-purple day-suit, in a colour which almost perfectly matched his wide-spaced, large-pupiled violet eyes. He was obviously wearing orange pancake and thickly, immaculately-applied powder all over his face, and he wore dark-purple lipstick.

In his long fingers he held a violet Sobranie cocktail cigarette, already lit, in a long amber cigarette holder, and upon joining the group he pouted self-consciously and took one of the green drinks, raising it half-heartedly:

'Wotcha, folks! Cheers!'

The voice was nasal, quite common. Like a shop-boy.

But his demeanour was confident, like a King. Posie assumed the boy was on a cocktail of drugs; it seemed almost certain.

But she felt a pang of sympathy at the silence he was greeted by.

Fortunately, he was quickly joined by a much taller woman in her early thirties. She smelt strongly of a perfume Posie had spritzed on just once, and adored, but which was difficult and expensive to buy: Chanel No 5.

The woman also picked up a bright green drink and downed it quickly, hurriedly taking another one and throwing it back in the same manner.

So, this is Lady Caroline Greenlow, thought Posie, and tried not to stare quite as much as everyone else was doing.

England had only ever boasted one *real* beauty. And that was the ethereal-looking Lady Diana Cooper.

But Lady Caroline Greenlow, slightly younger, had always run a very close second, and was recognised as being the most famous beauty of her generation. Hers was a face which sold magazines whenever it was on a cover.

Up close, Posie saw that Lady Caroline looked as if she had been through a good deal, and her legendary beauty was dimmed now, but it still burned away underneath.

It was a beauty made up of embers, not flames.

Lady Caroline was obviously dressed by a very modern designer.

Perhaps Chanel herself?

Her black jersey outfit had an exaggerated dropped-waist skirt, and a very high collar, which completely concealed her neck. She wore no jewellery at all, but her hair, cut boy-short, much shorter than Posie's actually, was dyed purest white with peroxide.

Below this luminous cap of hair her beautiful eyes were ringed in creamiest, blackest kohl, and a generous helping of freckles had been powdered into submission by white and chalky make-up which also covered up big dark circles beneath her eyes.

In her hand she held a bright gold hip-flask. No handbag.

Lady Caroline said nothing, but stared around with contempt, eyes blazing.

She glanced at the American, and Posie saw her eyes narrow for a couple of seconds as she took in the blue scarab tiepin, and Posie watched Lady Caroline swallow, as if with distaste, then pause to gaze at Loxley and give the Chancellor an utterly withering look.

'Lady Greenlow,' Loxley murmured, bowing his head slightly in her direction. 'What an unexpected pleasure this is.'

Yes, now for the fireworks.

Because Lady Caroline Greenlow was Loxley's sworn enemy.

Lady Caroline was a stranger to Posie, but she'd been much admired and raved about by Dolly, and she was perhaps the most vocal of all the supporters of a new bill of rights for women – all women – to be able to vote.

Caroline Greenlow had hounded Parliament mercilessly for a couple of years, day after day, for a new bill to be put through both Houses. She wrote hateful and clever letters to newspapers about the subject and was often found standing on the box at Speakers' Corner, shouting about injustice.

Part of her newspaper campaign was to write open and vicious 'letters' to Sir Charles Loxley, basically tearing the man and his policies apart, and then to wait for his self-important replies, which were always printed the following week, full of reliable bombast. Then she'd reply to Sir Charles again, and the circle carried on.

People said Caroline Greenlow had been too young to be a Suffragette, but if she had been, she would have given the Pankhursts a run for their money.

A heartbeat of a moment passed, and then Lady Caroline bit at her lip savagely. 'I assure you, Sir Charles, there is absolutely no pleasure on my side in meeting like this. And had I known *you* would be here, on this train, I would have stayed away.'

She threw the words out snappily, fiercely.

She turned to Dadie Spence, her unlikely-looking fiancé, and pointed at one of the tables laid for four at the very end of the carriage.

'By Gad, Dadie, let's go and sit down, shall we? We're on a *train*! I can't think why people are milling about. And I'm just dying for a proper drink. You go and sit nearest the window and pull the blinds down for goodness' sake, will you? I know it's nice and warm in here but I still don't want to be reminded that it's icy cold outside.'

The boy, because he was not much more than a boy, obediently scurried down the carriage and into the seat and did as he was bid, fussing with the blinds.

Lady Caroline then stalked down the carriage and dropped into the seat next to Dadie, nearest the aisle.

The Guard called out: 'Perhaps you could all go and sit down, please? Dinner is served.'

Loxley and Lennart shuffled awkwardly along the aisle, approaching the tables. Posie and Doctor Dance followed, slowly.

'No! No way!' almost shouted Caroline Greenlow, turning, looking over her shoulder.

'Don't sit here, with us. Not you, Loxley. Over my dead body. Never in a million years. Take your wee pal and sit away on the opposite side of the aisle, perhaps with that happy Frenchie couple, eh? And you two…' she pointed at Posie and Doctor Dance, then at the seats opposite hers, 'whoever you are, *you* can both sit here. With us.'

'How jolly for us all,' said Posie, speaking in an undertone, but smiling sweetly, shuffling along into the window-seat opposite Dadie Spence.

Across the aisle, Charles Loxley and Lex Lennart were seated with Suzannah and Alphonse Durrant, and at the small table set for two, behind them all, but in view, Posie could see the back of an old, old woman, a black lace mantilla on her head, a black velvet cloak wrapped around her fragile shoulders, being helped by the Guard to sit down.

She would obviously be sharing a table with the girl who had run alongside the train, *if* she deigned to join them.

Suddenly the girl in question appeared.

She sashayed through the Pullman, a short, petite, dark-skinned, all-glittering person wearing top-to-toe gold, with a gold lamé turban on her head. Up close she was a dead ringer for Josephine Baker, perhaps in her late twenties, with black short, greased hair, and almond-shaped eyes and a beautiful, mischievous grin.

Robbed of the chance to introduce herself properly, and now placed away from everyone, the girl came forward for a moment, through to the main tables.

She winked over at Alphonse Durrant and then grinned at Posie: '*Bon appetit*, all. I was late for the train, and it seems I'm late for dinner. I'm Daphne, in case any of you are wonderin'. Daphne de Bengy. I'm sure after tonight we'll never meet again, but I sure am glad to be here tonight wiv you all!'

The girl, who looked all-out American, was as cockney as Dolly had been.

But no-one paid the girl any attention at all. Loxley and Lennart were chattering together in a soft undertone, and Caroline Greenlow and Dadie Spence had not even bothered to turn around.

Posie smiled over at the girl, trying to look welcoming: 'I saw you running earlier. You should have won a medal for that sprint!'

Daphne laughed good humouredly as the Waiter arrived with the wine.

'I know, luvvie! I had a Good Samaritan tonight, and

that fella over there…' she indicated to Alphonse Durrant, '…he pulled me on the train and he saved my bacon. What a day! I'd already had trouble gettin' a ticket! I only got me contract of work today and I simply *have* to make it to Paris for tomorrow. My employer is puttin' on somethin' special for Paris Fashion Week. And the silly beggars at Victoria made a bad mistake and said I couldn't ride this train tonight as it was full up! But look at it, it's like a ghost train. Almost empty, innit? So they were either wrong, or they were lyin'!'

Daphne motioned backwards with her head.

'In my carriage back there, Car Number Two, it's just two of us: my Good Samaritan and me, and the Guard in his little compartment!'

'How did you manage to get a ticket then?' asked Posie, curious.

Daphne laughed with glee. 'I got around the stubborn ticket clerk eventually. Well, toodle-pip!'

She winked at Posie and slipped back into her seat.

The Waiter was pouring the old woman's wine, and the Guard was lifting out steaming silver tins of food from a heated kitchen-cupboard behind the green bar. He was hurriedly opening the food canisters and organising ladles.

Posie forced her gaze away from the girl, Daphne, and roused herself, pulling herself sharply back to the here-and-now. Willed herself to be good company.

She was politeness itself, and introduced both herself and Doctor Dance very succinctly to Lady Caroline and to Dadie Spence, who both nodded and looked bored and stared out of the window, ceaselessly smoking.

But in truth, Posie's thoughts were elsewhere: reeling, clutching desperately at facts she had heard tonight but not quite understood or put together properly.

A jigsaw with missing pieces.

Why had the ticket clerk told Daphne de Bengy the Night Ferry train to Paris tonight was full, when it so clearly wasn't?

Things here were jolly odd.

There were only ten people for dinner. And there were heaps and heaps of empty bunks, and empty tables.

But her thoughts were broken into.

Because suddenly, beside her, on her left side, Doctor Dance, still in his Panama hat, had began to spasm, and to shake uncontrollably.

* * * *

Chapter Six

Posie said nothing at all, but placed a hand on Dance's ruined, scrawny right arm.

Below her steady hand she felt bones as slight as a bird's, with no flesh upon them at all, and she sensed a fragility which was at once pitiful and shocking.

After a few seconds he stopped shaking, and nodded almost imperceptibly.

'I'm fine,' he muttered, obviously disgusted at himself.

'Always happens, damn it; at least once an hour.'

Out came the handkerchief, the iodine stink. Lady Caroline screwed up her nose in disgust but said nothing about the incident.

Fortunately, the Waiter was pouring red wine for everyone, and it served as a distraction, but Lady Caroline was shaking her head, displeased.

'Haven't you anything stronger, man?' she asked, belligerently.

'I need something with a little extra vim. Perk me up a bit, you know? And not that horrid green stuff which tasted like mouthwash. Well, actually, talking of *green*, if you have green chartreuse, that wouldn't be so bad. Or, absinthe; now, that would be something. Whatever you have which is *strong*.'

'Let me check, Madam.'

'Oh, here, man,' Caroline Greenlow passed the Waiter her hip-flask. 'This is empty. Wash it out, will you? And then fill it with something as a nightcap for me later. Port, or whisky, or brandy? Ideally cherry brandy. Not sherry: I hate sherry.'

'Of course, Madam.'

Posie's eyes took in Dadie Spence, opposite her, constantly smoking. His strange violet eyes were fixed on Posie in a languid, slightly inappropriate fashion. Lecherous, almost.

Although, were it but for his engagement, Posie would have said he was probably not a man who loved women.

Whatever the case, he and his celebrity fiancée made a jolly peculiar pair.

There was a distance, an emptiness between them. It was almost a loathing. They seemed completely mismatched.

Perhaps it was only drugs or alcohol that had thrown these two together? Or perhaps it had been a brief blast of unbridled passion which was now spent?

Dadie Spence now blew a perfect smoke ring, then another, and then another, in quick succession, and for a second Posie was reminded of Dolly, whose trick this was, too.

A holy trinity, Dolly used to call it, and then she would laugh.

'*That's the only holy thing you'll ever catch me doin', lovey*,' she'd always said with a wink, taking another deep draw of the smoke, relishing it all.

When Posie had first met her, Dolly had smoked Sobranies, too. Cocktail packets, which included the candy-colours. And later, when she'd come into all those riches from Rufus, Dolly had had special blue and silver cigarettes made for her, with a tiny Cardigeon monogram on the side.

What was Dolly smoking now?

If she was smoking at all…

The Waiter was back, looking worried. The Guard was serving soup at the other tables, but the Waiter was holding the big punch bowl Posie had seen him preparing earlier.

As the train lurched over some unsmooth points the orange liquid sloshed onto the white cloth he had placed around it as a wise precaution.

'This is our classic fruit punch, Madam. It's very, very strong: four parts alcohol to one part Vichy water. It's really for after dinner. Lots of sugar, a jot of lime, rum, angostura bitter, a touch of nutmeg. It's very sweet, and very potent. The fruit is simply for decoration.'

'By Gad, Caroline darling, that sounds just your thing!' drawled Dadie, grinding out his smoke on the chrome ashtray right in front of Doctor Dance, making him cough. 'Very sweet? Sickly, he means. No-one else can ever bear sweetness like that, eh? If we had it at our wedding next week, you'd be the only one drinking it.'

'Oh, do shut up, Dadie,' snapped Lady Caroline. 'It sounds perfect. Fill my glass up, man.'

As the Waiter swayed with a punch ladle, Doctor Dance coughed again and turned in his seat slightly to fix Caroline Greenlow, opposite him, with his one good eye.

Posie saw how he flicked the brim of his hat up very slightly on the left-hand side of his face, so she could see him out of shadow, and he spoke properly for the first time since everyone had sat down.

'I say, Lady Caroline, do you really think that is wise?'

The aristocrat stared at Posie's 'date', caught off guard.

'*What*?'

Lady Caroline looked suddenly very shaken, like she had seen a ghost.

'What did you say? What the blazes? Did I hear you correctly, man? Who the hell *are* you, anyhow?'

'A medical doctor, my Lady. Someone who can see your condition in plain sight.'

There was a sharp intake of breath. 'Oh, yes. A medical doctor, I should have known. Well, how dare you. *What* condition?'

Her eyes very wide, her mouth an open, aghast 'o' of outrage, Lady Caroline picked up the punch glass and threw the orange drink back in one easy go.

She licked her lips, nodded for more to the Waiter, who lingered nervily, filling up her glass a second time.

A horrible silence hung over their table, and when everyone else shook their heads at the proffered punch bowl, the Waiter disappeared, obviously relieved.

Lady Caroline and Doctor Dance continued to stare at each other, as if suddenly locked in a newly-found force-field of energy, which pulsated with hatred, at least from her side.

Dance didn't say anything more, and Posie couldn't see his expression under the hat which shielded the utter ghastliness of his right-hand side.

He's touched a nerve.

She hates him as he had the nerve to name her as an alcoholic, thought Posie, over-cheerily thanking the Waiter when the split-pea soup was served, and taking a roll from the bread basket which was offered.

Posie ate hungrily, as if she hadn't seen food in weeks, although the food wasn't that good, and not hot enough, either.

She took small, careful sips of her red wine, a good burgundy, conscious of Dance, at her side, eating his soup in painfully slow movements which she didn't dare watch.

How difficult his life was; every single little thing.

Eating. Using cutlery.

Swallowing.

Things everyone else took for granted.

She didn't dare look at Caroline Greenlow, who wasn't eating anything at all, just staring fixedly at Dance, so Posie watched instead as Dadie Spence picked apart his roll, threw it all into his soup dish, stirred it childishly, and then pushed it aside, completely untouched.

It reminded Posie of Phyllis, with the lemon Peak Frean biscuits.

But Phyllis was only five years old.

The man saw Posie watching him, grinned. She felt awkward, greedy.

Don't they eat?

'You didn't like the soup, Mr Spence?'

'Oh, I rarely eat. I might try the main course. I would have stayed in the cabin, but Caroline wanted to come into the Pullman, mainly for the drink, of course. But I'm glad I came now.'

'Oh? Why?'

'To watch *you*, of course. You really do have the most delightful face, Miss Parker. Splendid bones underneath, shame about the fringe, of course, and that ridiculous dress, which just looks tawdry, but then one cannot have everything...much as one wants it. I could really make something of you, though. *If* you let me.'

Posie didn't know whether to be insulted by this strange boy, or whether to laugh at his idiotic comments.

What was he going on about? Was he a hairdresser?

A dress designer?

A lunatic?

She crossed her arms defensively. 'And what is it you "want" to do, Mr Spence?'

But it was Lady Caroline who replied, and crossly, her face peculiarly flushed.

'Oh, ignore him, Miss Parker. Dadie is rather a good photographer, that's all. Very talented, quite astonishingly so. He will be the next big thing. He has a fancy to photograph as many beautiful women in London society as possible. He's had several of these portraits published, and is getting quite a name for himself. But he only wants to photograph *famous* women. As I said, in *society*.'

This snub was so blatantly rude, and intentional, that Posie wanted to laugh.

Besides, Lady Caroline was correct. Posie wasn't an aristocrat, and wasn't in 'society': had never been a debutante.

She didn't give two hoots about any of that stuff anyway, never had. It had been interesting to peer in on the whole charade every now and then, in later years, when Dolly had joined that particular circus.

There was a sudden forceful cough at her side. A frantic dabbing of the eye beneath the *pince-nez*.

The Doctor's voice was strong, and almost angry: 'I am not sure if you are aware, Lady Caroline, as to who the lady next to me *actually* is. She may not be in "society" but she *is* famous. Very famous.'

Posie flushed. 'Oh, come, Doctor Dance. It's not necessary, really…'

'No. It *is* necessary. I may not have known you very long, but you do not deserve to be spoken to like that, Miss Parker. My Lady, you should know that Posie Parker is the most famous female Private Detective in England, and quite possibly the world. Often in the newspapers. In fact, I spotted her only a couple of weeks back, looking very glamorous. She will not tell you what she is up to right now, of course, but I can assure you, that unlike *you* on your frippery of a trip, she is on a top-secret mission. Is that not correct, Miss Parker?'

'Well…'

That was overstating it, surely? But how nice to have a defender, of sorts.

Lady Caroline stared. 'A Private Detective?'

'That's right.'

'I see.'

Lady Caroline swallowed, took another more restrained sip of the fruit punch. 'Well, I suppose Dadie *could* photograph you, then. I've not heard of you, but if you are famous, it's a different story.'

Yes, Posie thought to herself. *That did seem to be true.* Fame cast different shadows, and altered many things, and not always for the good.

Dadie Spence pushed a purple card in Posie's direction. 'Call me when you are back in town, eh, Miss Parker? You can come to my studio.'

She played with the card and smiled. 'Oh, I think you and I would stay better friends if there are no photographs, but thank you. Thank you for your "interest".'

Plates were cleared and dishes of fish and white rice were put down in front of them, and Caroline Greenlow's hip-flask was delivered back to her, placed inconspicuously next to her on the snowy-white cloth.

A dead silence hung over their table, and Posie gabbled, desperate to break the tension and the heavy claustrophobia engulfing them all: 'And you are both travelling to Paris for something enjoyable, I hope?'

Posie was remembering Doctor Dance's strange throwaway comment about Lady Caroline attending a 'frippery', and she wondered what he had meant.

In fact, she was intrigued.

Did he know why Lady Caroline was travelling? Was it common knowledge? Or had he simply made an assumption, which might prove to be wrong?

Dadie Spence took the bait.

'Oh, yes.' Dadie Spence smirked in his strange lecherous, teasing way. 'We're going to attend something *very* enjoyable. Can I tell them, Caroline, my love?'

His fiancée was spearing her food angrily, eating nothing.

She stared at Doctor Dance again, and anger glittered in her eyes. 'Perhaps it is not the secret we think it is. Other people seem to be well-informed. So yes, you can go ahead. Besides, by tomorrow night it will be all over Paris. As well as London.'

Dadie Spence ferreted about in an inside pocket of his

purple jacket, and drew out a thick piece of blush-pink paper. Rose-gold embossing in fancy swirls covered the top, and upside down Posie could just make out 'POIRET'.

It seemed familiar.

Spence shook the paper out somewhat dramatically, licked his purple-painted lips in a satisfied way: 'Caroline has been invited to Paris, by none other than *Paul Poiret*! She got the invite a week ago. But she needs to be there tomorrow.'

A distinct hush fell upon the entire group, even at the next table, and it seemed for the very first time that everybody in the Pullman car was united. Forks and knives were put down quietly, and every eye was staring at the pink paper.

But suddenly the silence was broken, and a small, excited squeal broke through the carriage.

'Oh, *c'est incroyable*! *Mais, moi aussi!* Oh, sorry! I mean, how wonderful, and bizarre! Me too! Me, too! I am invited to Paris, too, for tomorrow, by the famous, wonderful, genius of a man that is Paul Poiret!'

It was Suzannah Scotland.

She had pulled out of her pocket for the second time that evening a piece of pink paper, an exact match for that being held aloft by Dadie Spence.

Posie was very conscious of everyone staring across at it, and there was complete silence in the carriage.

It felt as if everyone had sucked in their breaths; in horror, perhaps, or perhaps in complete disbelief.

The paper Suzannah was holding aloft had a big scrawly signature covering the lower bottom half. Looking from one piece of paper to the other, Posie could see they were a match.

Both were typed, both had the same signature, albeit signed in a different coloured ink.

Caroline Greenlow was now looking at Suzannah Scotland as if for the first time. She was taking her in, assessing her minutely, obviously wondering what on earth connected them.

Well, what on earth *did* connect them?

What did these two women, apart from being on the same train, and being in possession of the same letter-headed paper, have in common?

Posie was suddenly and ridiculously glad that Suzannah was wearing such lovely jewels right now, for they were being assessed too.

And they sparkled nicely, more than Suzannah herself.

'Golly, well, how wonderful,' Posie said, into the odd silence, faking cheer. 'Is it a party you are both invited to by Mr Poiret?'

'Hardly,' spat Caroline Greenlow.

'Oh no!' Suzannah Scotland smiled confidently. 'I've been invited by Mr Poiret to come and work as his secretary; his last one has just left him. It's terrible timing, as Paris Fashion Week is about to begin. And it's oh, simply *parfait* for me! I'd put an advert in *The Lady* during the last week to advertise my services as a secretary, and then I got this letter! Last night! It's a dream come true. He's paid for me on this train, and he's even putting me up at one of those lovely hotels on the Avenue Kléber, just until I find my feet, of course.'

Posie stared at her new acquaintance in the borrowed earrings. She now understood Suzannah being on 'cloud nine', and why she was travelling first-class. Well, she deserved it, surely, after going through such horrible, hard times.

Posie now also remembered something which had struck her as incongruous earlier, when Suzannah had lugged her big case aboard. It had been the name 'SCOTLAND' on the luggage-label. It had seemed familiar to Posie at the time, or, at least, slightly so.

And it hit her now why that was.

With Len, earlier, looking through *The Lady*, Posie had

come across the name 'Scotland' in the section advertising secretarial help. In fact, it had been one of the box numbers Posie had told the magazine might be suitable for their own agency on Grape Street.

Well, Suzannah had obviously had even better good fortune than being employed by a dusty little Detective Agency in Bloomsbury.

Posie was genuinely glad for her.

Suzannah smiled warmly at Caroline Greenlow, craning her neck as she edged out a little in her seat to see the woman fully. 'Will *you* be working for Monsieur Poiret, too, Lady Caroline?'

The aristocrat almost coughed in disgust. '*Hardly!* How dare you? If you must know, and the whole world will know tomorrow, Poiret has asked me to be his muse for Paris Fashion Week, and how could I refuse?'

Finding her glass of punch empty, Lady Caroline unscrewed her gold hip-flask and took a swig. The smell of artificial cherries and strong alcohol hit the air in a noxious wave of kirsch.

She grabbed at the dusky-pink paper in Dadie Spence's hands, and shook it in the air, as if it was the ticket to explain her very existence.

'He's making me a pure silk wedding dress, too, for my forthcoming nuptials, which will take place on Saturday the 30th at Westminster on our return to London. Our engagement was announced only last week, by the *Picture Post*, in an exclusive scoop. Not even our closest friends knew! Mr Poiret saw the magazine and decided I was perfect for him to showcase his talents as a wedding-dress designer. He's made the dress already, and I'm told it is *divine*, but tomorrow I will try it on for real and have final alterations made. I will wear the dress on the cat-walk, obviously, and Man Ray will be taking my photograph for the cover of all the editions of *Vogue*. Obviously, Dadie here is excited about that, and has come along with me purely to watch and learn from the best photographer in the world.'

Lady Caroline Greenlow took another glug of kirsch, narrowed her eyes in irritation at Suzannah Scotland. 'So, no, I will not be "working" for Monsieur Poiret, my dear. *Mine* is about as far from that sort of situation as you can get, in fact.'

A muttered, muted round of 'congratulations' emanated from around the tables, but without much enthusiasm.

At her side Posie heard a slight chuckle from Doctor Dance.

And a slip of a remark, loud enough to be heard by all at the immediate table: 'But here you both are, travelling on the same train, anyhow! Both of you are in the same position really, aren't you? At least right now.'

And Posie thought she heard an edge of amusement in his voice.

And then she felt him shake in those violent and uncontrollable spasms yet again.

****

Chapter Seven

The train juddered to a stop suddenly.

Brakes squeaked; steam hissed.

The low-lit amber lamps running along the length of the Pullman car flickered and died.

For a few seconds all was in darkness.

Then there was a sudden cold breeze, and a collective shiver rippled through the passengers at the table. Were people standing up?

It wasn't really long enough to be frightened, but Posie's heart skipped a beat anyhow, as if in anticipation of fear.

Breathe.

A woman's gasp cut through the air, but just as suddenly as the lights had gone out, they came on again.

Charles Loxley, his red boxy bag in his hands, was standing. 'What the devil is going on here?' he said, testily, to no-one in particular. 'This doesn't normally happen on this train. There are no stops!'

Doctor Dance had pulled open the curtains by the table. 'It's fine. I think we've pulled in at a station. Canterbury, is it? It's probably all this wretched snow. Look at the size of the flakes coming down! It's possibly drifting across the tracks? But we're fine.'

The red-faced Guard appeared. He seemed calm enough.

'Don't fear, folks. We're being put onto a different track; got to wait for the points to be switched. We'll be off again in a minute. It's another half an hour to Dover where this dining-car will be detached. I've spoken to the Waiter and, bearing in mind the small numbers of passengers tonight, and for your own comfort, we think it would be easier for all concerned if we finish the table service now.'

He motioned behind him, to where the Waiter was putting more chairs out by the bar. He'd also folded away some of the unused tables to make more of a space. 'You can mix a bit more over there in that parlour area, and we will serve you coffee and after-dinner chocolates and any alcoholic beverages you may like there, shall we? For the last half-hour.'

General murmurs of assent were made, and people stood up, happy to move.

Posie got up, attentive of her dinner companion at her side. They moved out into the newly-constructed 'parlour', where the Waiter was setting up a tray with coffee cups and flasks of coffee on it and the Guard was busy stacking dirty plates in a big pile.

The curtains at the windows here were not drawn and Posie saw how the flakes of snow really were huge, and coming down heavily, settling on the station sign: 'CANTERBURY'.

The small, brightly-lit station was completely deserted, apart from one lad, little more than twelve years old perhaps, who was kicking the metal front of a chocolate bar machine on the station platform, either for fun, or perhaps because he had genuinely lost money in it.

I know how that feels, thought Posie, suddenly with a hankering for a bar of milk chocolate herself. Or several, actually. She wasn't full at all.

She found herself eyeing the plate of green-foil-covered Bendicks mints on the table, and wondered if she would be thought greedy if she took one without waiting for the coffee to be poured.

But before Posie could venture to do so, the small older lady with the black mantilla on her head – who Posie had not yet seen or spoken to properly – suddenly swooped down on the plate of mints and took all of the sweets on the plate, laughing a little as she did so.

The lady sat down quickly on a chair and looked up, and Posie saw bright, hazel-brown, nut-like eyes.

Gosh. She's not so stuck-up, or old, after all, thought Posie. *But she has seen hardship.*

She noticed how folds of skin hung off this woman's plain work-worn face, and how her cheeks were deep hollows which spoke of past anguish. But why was she dressed so severely?

Perhaps she's in mourning? Perhaps someone has just died and she's on her way to a funeral?

One should never assume anything about another human being.

The older woman beckoned.

Posie went over and sat down in the empty chair next to the woman, noting with some relief that Doctor Dance had moved off to the bar.

He was standing next to Inspector Durrant now, who held a bottle of water. The two men were very close together at the tiny bar and Posie couldn't help noticing that Durrant seemed tense; his free hand gripped at the green-glass counter and made a chopping motion, as if to illustrate a point.

What was he saying? Posie strained to hear Durrant's usually clear voice, but there were just snatches:

'I tell you…she deserves better. Better than you…'

Was that what Durrant had said? Had Posie heard correctly?

What on earth were they taking about, if so?

About Suzannah? Had the Doctor made an unlikely-seeming play for her? If not, what was it about?

About herself, Posie? Did Durrant think Dance was making a play for *her*?

Whatever else the two men were discussing, it was not audible from where Posie was sat. And where was Suzannah, anyhow?

Posie gave up and turned her attention to the old woman, whose outstretched hand was full of mints.

'I must apologise! I beat you to it, I'm afraid, my dear! Take one, or several,' said the woman. 'I saw you ogling, same as me. I'm very greedy. I do love these sweets. But I really mustn't eat all of these.'

The woman's voice was soft and hushed, as if she was speaking in church, but also as if she perhaps really had a big, loud voice, which she was afraid of using.

Posie grinned. 'Thank you. These are rather a weakness of mine, too, as it happens.'

Posie took a chocolate and introduced herself.

The tiny woman under her black headscarf looked curious.

'Oh! The famous detective? My, how exciting. I'm Mrs Shepherd. No mystery about me, sadly. Just off on a yearly trip to visit a lonely relative in Paris. I go every January for a few days. It's been in my diary for ages, and I hoped against hope I would still be able to travel. That this wretched snow wouldn't spoil things.'

'It seems we're lucky so far.' Posie took a cup of weak coffee which was passed to her, and sipped at it politely.

All of a sudden Lady Caroline was at Posie's other side, sinking down into an empty chair there, sitting well back, with her arms crossed over the expensive ruching of her black jersey dress, her unpainted lips curled in a sort of twist of impatience.

Lady Caroline closed her eyes, and the shadows beneath her eyes looked positively cavernous now.

Posie thought that after the amount of alcohol Lady Caroline had drunk, she would be pretty well sozzled by now. Sleepy, perhaps.

Or feeling sick.

Dadie Spence was at the bar, making polite, bored chat with the American and Doctor Dance, another violet cigarette on the go.

Inspector Durrant had disappeared.

Mrs Shepherd edged forwards in her seat eagerly, looking past Posie and addressing herself to Lady Caroline.

'I say, Lady Caroline, I was sitting at the table behind your own, but I couldn't help overhearing: congratulations on your upcoming wedding. And also, congratulations on the Paul Poiret appointment. A "muse", eh? *That* must really be something.'

Posie made a pretence of wanting more coffee, stood up and fetched some, then lingered, so the two women could communicate over the distance of her empty chair.

But Caroline Greenlow didn't look as if she was up to communicating, she kept her eyes closed deliberately, as if to blot out everything, including the old woman's talk.

Undaunted, Mrs Shepherd had quite come alive. The mints were uneaten, forgotten, lying in her lap. '*I* remember Paul Poiret, from his heyday. You know, the days before the Great War, and even in the Great War. They say he's lost the magic now though, don't they?'

Finding Lady Caroline unresponsive, she addressed Posie: 'Do you know Monsieur Poiret's work, Miss Parker?'

Posie shook her head. 'Afraid not. Not first-hand.'

Mrs Shepherd nodded, then sighed. 'It used to be wonderful. Everything embroidered, silk with everything. He had a magnificent Grand Salon on Rue d'Antin, you know, with a theatre inside it. Now, I gather, he's moved to much smaller quarters on Rond-Point, Champs-Élysées. He's been in trouble, that's for sure. Overspending, I'm told, doing everything in an over-the-top way. He's sold off his perfume line, what a shame...and he's weighed down with debt. This wedding-dress line must be a last chance for him, I suppose. A last hurrah. Still, I'm surprised he can afford to pay anyone to be his muse anymore.'

The woman dug in a soft black pouch she wore around her neck on a string, and brought out a packet of small, black cigarillos, and a packet of matches.

She stuck one in her mouth and lit up quickly, expertly, without offering the packet around.

She took a deep inhalation of the heavy, tarry smoke, released it, enjoying every second, before carrying on: 'And did either of you attend the Art Deco Exhibition in Paris last year?'

Posie shook her head and Lady Caroline remained shut-eyed and silent.

'No? Oh, a shame. Poiret bought three barges for it specially, and he moored them on the Seine. He went crazy to showcase his designs: twenty-four-hour catwalks of his fashion; a piano that wafted out different scents from his perfume house on a revolving basis; home decorations and even furniture. As I said, it was vastly over the top. People want something different now, I think. Don't *you* both think? All this talk in the fashion magazines of Chanel, and Jean Patou. Simpler things.'

'Did you attend the Exhibition yourself?' asked Posie, interested. 'It sounds wonderful.'

Mrs Shepherd shook her head mournfully, blowing out smoke. 'No, I only read about it, took cuttings from all the newspapers. I don't travel to Paris in the summer, dear. It would be too hot, and unpleasant. Think of all those tourists!' She shuddered a little, but then seemed to lose herself in a distant memory, and she smiled faintly.

'I did write to the House of Poiret for the brochures, and got sent a few free items. Mainly because I used to spend a good deal of money there. I used to buy Poiret dresses, whole wardrobes of them, but that was in a different time.'

Mrs Shepherd turned to Lady Caroline, spoke despite the woman's non-participation. 'You're too young to remember, my Lady, but I suppose your mother and your aunts wore Poiret. *My* sisters certainly did, although all their beauty and all their many dresses were to no avail as they met utterly tragic ends at the hands of a dreadful little arsonist…'

Posie watched as a tear trickled down Mrs Shepherd's face.

Horrified, Posie wondered whether to intervene, but then the old woman was chattering on again: 'Yes, it was *that* generation who glittered in all the opulence of his dresses. Good times. A long time before the Great War. A very different time.'

Posie noticed that Lady Caroline wasn't actually asleep, and hadn't been.

A muscle by her mouth seemed to contract with a spasm every now and then, but of what? Rage? Frustration? Boredom? Fright?

But Caroline Greenlow was now rousing herself, checking for her hip-flask, which she patted, as if for reassurance, before hauling herself out of her chair.

'Anyhow, my Lady…' called Mrs Shepherd aloud, trying to get the younger woman's attention.

'Yes? WHAT?' Lady Caroline looked back over her shoulder, and almost spat the words out.

It was daringly rude.

'I just wanted to say that I am sure you will make a huge success of it all, dear. Turn Mr Poiret's fortunes around for him. You'll be like a lucky charm, like you always are. I do look forward to seeing the pictures in *Vogue* in due course.'

'How kind of you. How supportive.' But Caroline Greenlow didn't smile.

Then she turned her back on them and muttered aloud, 'Oh, here's Dadie. Good grief, he's actually bringing me a *coffee*. I hope it's at least got some bally whisky in it.'

Posie watched Caroline join her fiancé and start sipping at her hot drink.

She heard Mrs Shepherd mutter something about 'girls these days', and watched the old lady start to demolish the pile of chocolates, when all of a sudden the train groaned and jerked, and started to move again.

Feeling suddenly and wretchedly tired, Posie checked her watch and saw it was half-past ten.

She thought she would turn in, although it wasn't late, and try and get some sleep, so she would be fresh in the morning.

She had started to say goodnight to the other passengers, when the dark, beautiful girl who resembled Josephine Baker came up to her. She glittered in her gold column dress, and she had a powder-blue card between her perfectly-manicured gold fingernails, with which she tapped lightly on Posie's arm.

'We ain't spoken, lovey, have we? Not properly. But 'ere's my card anyhow.' She passed it across.

'Oh, er...thank you.' Posie introduced herself properly.

'Nice to meet you, Miss Parker. I've given my card to everyone 'ere. Even that odious government minister. Well, I reckon he's just the right sort for it, really, isn't he? I can probably get you free tickets for the show, if you like? Perk of the job, innit?'

Posie read the name and address on the card quickly, the text glittering gold on blue.

DAPHNE DE BENGY

SENIOR WARDROBE MISTRESS

Moulin Rouge

82, Boulevard de Clichy, 75018 Paris

'Goodness,' Posie exclaimed, grinning at Daphne, and trying not to look too shocked.

The girl stood with her beautiful head to one side, like an inquisitive robin, and laughed.

'Fancy cards, aren't they? Do you like 'em? Soon as I 'eard I'd got the job today, I got 'em printed up: cost me a fortune but what do I care? I'm feelin' proud of myself. I had to do about five interviews for this job, and two of 'em were in Paris, but I got through to the end, thank the good Lord. It's a decent employer, too: payin' for me to travel first-class so I can make it there on time. I'll miss Blighty, but a new life awaits me. London is done for me. I needed to get away.'

'Oh?'

'A bad romance gone wrong, if you want to know. So, all in all, this timing is perfect. Nifty, eh?'

Posie looked at the card again. It was unique. Around the writing on the card were printed figures of tiny dancing girls, but it was all in very good taste.

'Can-can dancers! I say! And yes, I do like the card, Miss de Bengy. Congratulations on the job. I had a friend who would have been thrilled to talk to you about this…'

She tailed off, thinking of Dolly, who had also worked as a Wardrobe Mistress in London's West End, before meeting Rufus.

But Daphne suddenly clutched at Posie's arm, and spoke in a soft, lower voice, almost a whisper, almost a warning:

'If you need anythin', lovey, you can come to me. I know Paris pretty well. I know all the good shops, all the tailors, all the best couturiers. Although,' and she grinned, 'you look pretty dazzlin' already, if you ask me. But you watch yourself in Paris, Miss Parker, won't you? You're a beautiful woman, alone; you're a target for creeps, and pick-pockets, and worse. Keep your eyes peeled, and your purse close, eh? Paris is wonderful, but it's a treasure-box of darkness. Filled to the brim.'

Posie looked into the girl's eyes.

Yes, she thought. *You seem a good sort.*

Very close up, Daphne was older than Posie had first thought, nearer forty than thirty, and there were creases at the sides of the girl's eyes, well camouflaged with thick greasepaint in a metallic hue.

'How come *you* know Paris well, Miss de Bengy?'

'Oh, call me Daphne, love. I trained in a designer's atelier there, actually, to learn couture: three years, and then I decided I'd go into the theatre as a Wardrobe Mistress in London. I speak French, fortunately, as my dad was from Paris, by way of the Seychelles, and then he ended up in glamorous Shadwell! Workin' the docks. Poor fella!'

Posie suddenly remembered something from earlier, when Daphne had first come into the dining-car, and it had piqued her curiosity.

She *had* to ask.

'You said you nearly didn't get on the train, Daphne, that the clerk at the ticket counter told you this train was full? And you also said you "got around" him eventually. I suppose you promised the clerk free tickets to the Moulin Rouge, did you?'

Daphne nodded, looking coy.

Posie thought it would have been hard for the clerk to turn down.

She pocketed the blue card. 'Well, I'm not sure I'll have time to visit you, or the Moulin Rouge. My trip to Paris is a flying one, I'm afraid, but I'll bear it in mind, Daphne.'

'You do that, lovey.'

'Well, goodnight, then. See you at breakfast in France, if we *do* actually get put on the ferry tonight, what with all this snow.'

'Oh, it'll be fine, lovey.' Daphne winked. 'I've been on the Night Ferry in December, and again right after Christmas, both times for these Moulin Rouge interviews. It was packed solid wiv passengers both those times though, not like tonight. Back then you had to queue for dinner! Anyhow, it ran fine on both occasions, apart from the choppy sea. Let's be optimistic. The City of Light is all ablaze, just waitin' for us. All those stories waiting to happen!'

'Yes, perhaps.'

But as Posie made to leave, a horrible sound erupted behind her.

Turning, she saw something awful, but not that surprising, somehow.

It was Caroline Greenlow, coughing, choking.

She was standing in the centre of the space with everyone staring, useless, and she had her hands around her slim, black-encased neck. Her face was blue, swollen, her eyes bloodshot, panicked. Silent tears were coursing down her cheeks.

She's choking to death.

Posie's heart hammered in her chest. She willed the scene to stop.

Where on earth is Doctor Dance?

I can't remember what to do.

I used to know this, back in those awful days of the Great War, when I took all those training courses. I'm going to have to try, anyway…

'Help! Help!' shouted Dadie Spence, at his fiancée's side, but useless, wary, almost in tears himself. Like a small child at a playground, raising the alarm.

The Waiter looked on, gobsmacked, white-faced, retreating to the very back of the bar.

Posie ran forward, suddenly calm and practical. 'Let me see. I used to know what to do.'

But here came Doctor Dance, rushing along, bending the much taller woman over in one fluid motion as you might with a heavy silk dress, carrying its weight over your arm.

He was suddenly slapping her hard on the back with a surprising amount of force for such a slight, injured man, and Lady Caroline was coughing and gasping for air, almost screaming out the fact that she was still alive.

'I'm fine. It's fine. It's all gone. I coughed it up. It's out.'

Her rescuer stood back, hands on his knees, panting, himself breathless with the exertion of the manoeuvre he'd just performed. He took out his handkerchief and dabbed at his eye frantically.

'You must have got something stuck in your throat, my Lady. Fruit, was it? From that punch, again?'

Everyone looked to the bar for the punch, but the glass bowl was now empty. The Waiter started to clear it away, as if he might be implicated in any blame which might be allocated.

Lady Caroline was rubbing at her throat, down on her knees. There were thick lines of smudged kohl make-up running down her face, like a clown who had painted on hideous tears as part of his act, and the make-up was rubbed right along the ridge of her nose, which now seemed to look crooked. Her famous, beautiful face seemed grotesque and almost as disfigured as that of Doctor Dance.

'I was simply drinking a coffee,' she said, defensively, hoarsely, getting to her feet. 'There was something in my drink! Something unexpected. I swallowed it, choked…'

Dadie Spence was down on the floor, his hands gently patting at the thick green carpet.

'Aha!' he said, triumphantly. He was holding something small, and turquoise, and about the size of a woman's thumbnail.

He held it up, towards his fiancée. 'Was *this* what you choked on, Caroline darling? But what the blazes is it?'

Everyone was gathering around in a silence which was broken only by the noise of the train and its now-familiar beat.

Posie watched Caroline Greenlow and her sweating, grey face, trying to recover her composure after her awful and frightening experience. The woman looked down into her fiancé's hand, and was it Posie's imagination or did her pale face grow paler still? But Lady Caroline was shaking her head.

'What is it? I simply haven't a clue, Dadie darling. Not a clue.'

Charles Loxley leant in to see what Dadie Spence was holding. Then he turned his head sharply and spoke to the American.

'Here, isn't this the same as what you're wearing, Mr Lennart, one of these turquoise critters? It's not the very same one you had on, is it? Did you lose it, somehow? An accident?'

Lex Lennart came closer, but not before touching the cravat at his throat with a slight caress and smiling when he found his own little carving was still there and intact.

'No, Mr Loxley. Mine is not lost. It is still here, of course.'

He peered at the object in Dadie Spence's hand, his bright-turquoise eyes sparkling with a sudden and unfeigned interest.

'And *what* is that thing? Well, gee, I'll tell you all: it's a turquoise scarab beetle. Plain and simple. The ancient Egyptians used to wear them for good luck. A kind of lucky charm. This one is your bog-standard edition, worn by everyday folk, but it's real all right: old, I mean; not a modern copy. Looks like Thutmosid Dynasty to me, Eighteenth Dynasty. So it's four thousand years old. Nice little thing, huh? But probably not so nice halfway down your throat.'

Posie looked at all her fellow passengers standing around in that green space, in the beat of unsure, sticky silence following this pronouncement.

Everyone was present, except for Alphonse Durrant and Suzannah Scotland, and the Guard – who had gone off a few minutes before – to speak to the Driver about their progress.

What on earth was going on here?

Why had Caroline Greenlow ended up swallowing a scarab beetle which was four thousand years old?

A lucky charm?

Not so lucky, after all.

Had it been by accident? Or design?

But who would do such a thing?

And why?

The awkward uncomfortable moment seemed to pass, and then people started drinking hurriedly again, especially Lady Caroline, as if to forget, perhaps.

To pretend things were normal.

Even old Mrs Shepherd was downing brandies and calling for several refills, which the Waiter seemed more than happy to oblige with, happy for something to do.

But Posie touched her own throat, frowning, trying to imagine the panic Lady Caroline must have felt a few moments ago: the dreadful experience of not being able to breathe; the awful dawning realisation you were being killed by something the size of a small button, or a small jewel.

It now seemed utterly ridiculous, but the scarab could have been utterly deadly.

The train twisted and groaned and lurched and swung, and the Guard suddenly returned, very cheerful, oblivious to what had just happened, telling everybody that the train was, despite heavy snowfall, staying on course, in time to meet the ferry at Dover, which would leave on time.

Posie looked around herself one last time, tamping down the terror which seemed to be growing in her whole being.

She left the Pullman and walked to her berth, but while she undressed and brushed her teeth, she couldn't get rid of the image of Caroline Greenlow's face when she had choked.

She tried to shake it off.

But it wasn't just the choking Posie couldn't forget.

She couldn't erase the memory of Caroline's Greenlow's face as she had looked at the scarab. At the slow, dawning horror on the woman's face, and Posie was certain, sure as bread was bread, that Lady Caroline had been lying, and that she had known very well what the scarab beetle was.

But what did it mean to her? Because it had meant something.

I hope we do all stay on course, Posie thought. *That we stay alive on this train.*

Just until we reach Paris tomorrow morning, at least.

Then I'm off and away.

Away from this strange claustrophobic train with its horrid anonymous notes, and horrible passengers, and not enough staff, and terrible near-death occurrences.

Posie turned off the light. Next door she heard what sounded like muffled laughter, a flirty giggle.

She buried her head in her pillow.

It had been an odd night.

And now it was time to close the door on all of this, and sleep.

****

Chapter Eight

She was dreaming of London.

Of Lincoln's Inn Fields. With the summer scent of blown roses in full bloom, mingled with the grit and tar of the busy roads around the law courts.

Posie dreamt she was walking past the huge square with its tennis court at the centre, past the big, formal gardens, and the London plane trees framing it all, whose pollen was the scourge of every Londoner who worked nearby. But in the dream Posie was anxious; unprepared for some task or another.

Richard was at her side.

But Richard Lovelace as he had been *before* he had become her husband, years back.

Slimmer, maybe. Not so grey, but his face was more subdued.

He was in summer plainclothes flannels, with no hint yet of the uniform he would be required to wear in years to come, with all the glittering gold buttons and braids of the Chief Commissioner's rank on show for all to see.

His words were clear and ringing: 'I don't like the sound of any of what you're telling me, Miss Parker.'

'No, I don't either.'

'What smells "off" *is* usually "off", you know that?'

'I'll bear that in mind, Inspector. I wish...'

He turned in the dream to face her, his green eyes sparkling with mischief, with kindness, with a sensual energy, but filled too with an acknowledgement of futility: of dreams long crushed and packed away, although with something underneath it all that whispered of hope. 'What do you wish...?'

'I wish you were coming with me, sir. It feels wrong to go on my own.'

'You've made a name for doing things on your own, my girl.'

'Even so...'

'You'll be fine. I know it.'

Posie must have been deeply asleep; far, far under the rolling waves of consciousness. Comfortable, too, in the crisp sheets of that single bed in Berth Number Nine on the Night Ferry.

In the warmth of the toasty space.

She was completely unaware of any chains lashing the carriage onto the ferry to secure it down, and completely unaware of waves rocking the boat, or the choppiness of the cold, fathomless sea beneath the bleak, relentless snow.

Unaware of foghorns, or sirens, or the flashing beams of lighthouses. Unaware of everything, in fact.

She was sleeping the sleep of the drugged, the dead.

Until a sudden and violent banging woke her up.

It was frantic in its intensity.

Almost breaking down the thick, glossy, mahogany door to her berth.

BANG.

BANG.

'Miss Parker? Are you in there?'

She got up blearily, uncertain for a moment where she really was, uncertain if whoever was calling her was male or female, and then she felt the train lurching, grinding, swaying slightly below her.

Oh, yes.

The Night Ferry, to Paris.

She checked her watch, and it read half-past five. She pulled up the blind, but all she saw was endless darkness outside, punctured by a few beams of light far off, red, then green, and white.

For a horrible moment she thought the train had been in an accident, but she grabbed at her thin silk oriental-style dressing gown and shrugged it on over her pyjamas, then pulled off the lace nightcap she had worn to keep her hairstyle in place.

'Come quickly, Miss Parker. Help me.'

'Yes, yes, I'm here,' she called, stuffing her feet into her velvet slippers.

She coughed, wondering at how feeble her own voice sounded. 'I'm coming.'

Posie hadn't recognised the voice summoning her at all, but unlocking the door and pulling it open gingerly, she saw that the person was Dadie Spence. However, this Dadie Spence was quite different from before.

Now, he was wild and make-up-less, his slightly grey hair grizzled and standing on end, dressed in gone-awry lavender silk striped pyjamas.

In addition, he was covered in some awful-looking dark, slimy substance, and a terrible smell emanated off him.

He beckoned Posie out into the corridor, which was empty and lower lit than it had been earlier. All the blinds were drawn.

She pulled her flimsy gown tighter around her. It felt much colder out here.

'What is it?' Posie demanded.

'It's Caroline,' the young man panted. 'She's really bad. Something's wrong. I can't seem to rouse her awake properly. She was very sick earlier on the sea crossing; threw up everywhere, awful mess. But I just thought it was sea-sickness.'

'Or the alcohol,' Posie muttered, looping back on herself, snatching up a couple of small, fresh towels from the side of the basin in the tiny bathroom of her berth, and grabbing the pink glass carafe from her bedside table, still filled with water. They charged along. The corridor was eerily quiet.

'What about Doctor Dance?' asked Posie, as they walked past Berth Number Six. 'He'd be better than me by miles. Have you tried him, knocked on his door?'

'Of course! Again and again. I thought the knocking on his door would have woken you all up, but he didn't answer. The Guard isn't around either because they are connecting the carriages to the French locomotive outside: I think we are in Dunkirk. *You* looked like you might know what to do earlier, when Caroline was choking, so you seemed my next best bet.'

'Mnnn. I suppose Doctor Dance took a sleeping draught. Most people did, I expect. And the walls and doors on this train do seem very well constructed: solid, well sound-proofed.'

They were outside Berth Number One now, and the door stood ajar, with all the lights on inside, blaring away.

Posie elbowed her way in and almost retched at the smell.

'Golly.'

Although identical in design to her own cabin, this place was a grotesque mess. The top bunk, where Dadie had obviously been sleeping, was pulled out above one which was the same as her own bed, and in this lower bunk lay Lady Caroline.

The woman was sprawled out, having kicked off the white sheets and the navy woollen blanket with its moon emblem.

Her feet were tangled in the sheets, and she was wearing a white cotton nightdress more suited to the summer.

Her head lolled off the bed onto the nearby night-table

at a horrible angle. A glass of water had overturned there and Lady Caroline's bleached hair was lying in the pool of water, soaked through.

Pills were everywhere, as were small green prescription glass bottles, lying about open, and some were even broken, the glass smashed.

Also on the floor were several small tiles made of mirror with lines of white powder laid along them.

Cocaine, probably.

The place was wrecked.

The smell was pure alcohol, the sweetness of cherry kirsch, but underneath it all was something very strong, and worse. There was vomit on the bed, and on the carpet and all over Lady Caroline.

'Pull up the blind,' ordered Posie sharply, still holding her breath, bossy in her practicality.

'Draw down the window and get some blasted fresh air in here, will you, Mr Spence? Then try Doctor Dance again, and if not, the woman at Number Eight. She used to be a nurse.'

Posie rolled up her sleeves, edged to the lower bunk, and picked her way gingerly through the mess on the floor, thankful for her sturdy slippers.

She kicked aside the gold hip-flask.

As she got closer, she realised the woman on the bed was shivering horribly, uncontrollably. But the room, with its small radiator, just like hers, was unbearably hot.

'Lady Caroline? It's Miss Parker here.' She tried to get Lady Caroline back into the bed, putting a dry towel under her wet hair. Posie did her best to pull away the dreadful sheets, and as she did so she tugged off her own dressing gown, placing it over the woman.

She wetted the other clean towel with water from her carafe, and tried to clean up the woman's face. Posie cleared a small space on the floor by the bunk, and knelt there.

She smoothed the woman's brow, not knowing what

else to do. 'You'll be fine, Lady Caroline. You just drank too much; we'll get you better. You'll be off this train soon and into a nice smart hotel where you can relax.'

Lady Caroline seemed to be speaking between the rolling bouts of shivering.

'I can't hear you, my Lady. Sorry?'

Posie came even closer, close as she dared, to try and pick up what was being muttered, and then she saw it. She grabbed at the small sconce wall-light by the bunk and she angled it quickly, full beam, cruelly, on the woman's face.

Oh, no.

No, no, no.

Without the powder, or any make-up, Lady Caroline's face was sweaty, greasy, and a horrible, distinctive pale blue colour which turned Posie's stomach and made her panic.

Posie had, unfortunately, seen this before, but only in the recently dead.

Poison.

She must be pretty near the end.

Posie grabbed at the woman's hands, and they too were blue, with darkening indigo patches around the fingernails.

Not shivering, then, but spasms.

Posie moved the beam of light away, carried on automatically smoothing the woman's hair, thinking nineteen to the dozen. What could Lady Caroline have taken which was poisoned?

The answer was surely anything, and everything.

The floor was strewn with the detritus of the drug-taking lifestyle of these people, and maybe she had taken one pill too many? A bad one.

Although, based on what she could see, this looked to Posie horribly like poisoning with arsenic, which, when given in high, concentrated doses, killed in exactly this manner.

And its calling-card was this awful blue patina.

Dadie Spence was hovering at the doorway, gripping

the frame. Posie turned to him from the bed, spoke calmly but clearly, tamping down the panic bubbling inside her.

'We need proper help here.'

Dadie whimpered: 'I can't rouse the lady you said was a nurse, but Doctor Dance is up: he shouted that he's just pulling on some clothes.'

'Good. Try and get the Guard again. Tell him to make sure we stay here. Keep the train as it is. We must not move off.'

'Okay.'

In the moments of quiet which followed, Posie realised the woman in the bed was speaking again. Posie leant in even closer, but careful not to touch anything at all.

'Lady Caroline? We'll get you comfortable, I promise…'

The stupidity of her assurances hit her. *How could she promise anything?*

This woman must be in agony.

Up this close, the grey eyes were very wide, glittering, but the whites were also turning a milky-blue, and the effect was unearthly.

'I only have moments left…' the woman breathed, 'I know it, Miss Parker. Don't pretend. I need to tell you something.'

'Tell me.'

'I didn't kill him. *Never*. I loved him with all my heart. I would have loved him forever. And you must make that known, Miss Parker. Make it known, okay? As for all the other stuff, I took my pleasures where I could, and I have no regrets… Here, take this.'

Caroline Greenlow was pulling at her neck now, working herself up into an awful state, trying to sit up, and Posie saw there was a tiny silver cord there, at her throat, fine as gossamer thread.

She was about to help the woman, when Posie saw the thread had broken, and she was being passed the necklace.

Posie stuffed it automatically in the pocket of her pyjamas without looking at it.

'You *do* understand me?'

'Well… *who* didn't you kill, Lady Caroline? I think it's all fine, you're imagining things. Try and relax. Help is coming.'

'Tell me you understand.' The breathing was growing fainter, ragged, juddering.

Posie held onto the woman's hands. 'Yes, I understand. I will do that for you, my Lady. I promise.'

'Thank you.'

And then Lady Caroline collapsed back into the pillow and turned to the wall of the berth.

Posie knew she was gone.

She went to the window, yanking the pane even further down, forcing down the bilious panic which was making her shake.

A sudden gust of wind blew through the tiny compartment, cleansing everything and taking with it the soul of a complicated, clever, famous, beautiful person who was too young to die; who had had everything to live for.

Posie had been with men when they'd died before, but always out on the battlefield, or else with stretcher-bearers in the waiting rooms of chaotic field hospitals, as they sat waiting to take their charges in.

She'd never been on her own with anyone at their point of passing before, never in such a small space.

She'd never before felt that emptiness which comes to a room; never experienced those moments of knowing completely that the person has really gone.

She closed her eyes and said a quick prayer for Caroline Greenlow.

But anger flooded her veins quite suddenly, and a terrible resolve settled over her. A resolve to find out what had happened here to Lady Greenlow, who, to Posie's mind, had been undoubtedly murdered in deliberate cold blood.

In the most brutal, awful way.

And somehow, Posie had found herself agreeing in those last few moments to undertake a task she hadn't understood; couldn't possibly understand.

Who was it that people thought Caroline had killed?

And who exactly were these people labouring under that bizarre misapprehension?

Were the odd words nothing more than the murmurings of a dying woman?

Or had Lady Caroline really known what she was talking about in those last moments?

But a promise was a promise, and Posie would have to investigate. To set her own mind at rest.

And at the very least, to right this terrible wrong.

* * * *

Chapter Nine

Doctor Dance suddenly arrived, hat-less and dreadful-looking; bleary and heavy with sleep, still under the effect of a strong mix of sleeping draught and painkiller, desperate to be of some help, but useless.

And too late.

As was the medical bag at his side.

He rushed in.

'What's all this? By Gad, I didn't hear a thing. I was out like a light all night. I'm so sorry. What a bally mess of a thing, eh? Oh! Oh, no. Oh, my Good Lord...'

He paused at the dead woman's bedside, seemed to shudder for a moment, his shoulders pumping up and down; a wheezy, gassy noise emanating from him.

'Doctor?'

'I'm fine. You never get used to it, even though you think you will...'

He stepped away, took a deep breath and pronounced Caroline Greenlow dead. He confirmed Posie's suspicions that poison, probably arsenic, was at the root of the death.

'See the blue tinge, eh?'

'Yes. I saw it.'

The Doctor hadn't had time to put his glass eye in yet, and he was wearing a black canvas pirate-like eyepatch instead, while his real eye watered ceaselessly. Thick greasy creams covered the bad skin grafts on his face and hands, and in his striped cotton pyjamas he seemed very small, much slighter than in his evening clothes.

Posie and he both stood as far away from the body as the small space had allowed.

'By Jove, *poison.* How awful. But please don't touch anything, Miss Parker: who knows what receptacle the poison was placed in? Those stains… It could be all around us. You don't want to ingest some accidentally, do you?'

'I'll wash in a minute.'

'Make sure you do. Yes.' Doctor Dance was jittery, shaking his head constantly. 'Good grief. What a shame. What a real shame, and in her condition.'

Posie frowned, confused. 'What "condition", Doctor? You mentioned that last night, at the table. You mean as an alcoholic?'

Doctor Dance shook his head. 'Mr Spence will have to confirm for us of course, but in my professional opinion it looked to me like Lady Caroline was at least six weeks or so pregnant. It was certainly starting to show…'

'A *baby*?'

'Yes. It accounts for their bally rush to get married, don't you think? Both of them completely unmatched, unsuited. And he, Spence, is far too young. But these things happen in life.'

A terrible sadness crept up on Posie, but she stood up straight and steeled herself for more awfulness to come.

Because someone still needed to tell Dadie…

And it fell to her.

Breaking the dreadful news to this louche, languid, famous want-to-be-photographer was heart-breaking, as was witnessing him, white-faced and silent, crawl into the tiny bathroom cubicle, where, behind the closed door, he became an inconsolable bundle of fury.

He hurled himself at the walls, breaking the mirror, from the sounds of things.

'Dadie?' Posie stood outside the bathroom door, her forehead resting on the polished wood, wondering what to do.

'I'll wait for him here, Miss Parker. I have sedatives,' Doctor Dance said, seeming to pull himself together more with each passing second. He started to rummage in his black bag, fishing around for a syringe and vials of liquid.

They were suddenly aware of a slight, unwelcome noise behind them, out in the corridor, and they turned to see that a few sleepy passengers had gathered in the corridor outside in a curious gaggle.

The American, Lennart, looked surprisingly alert, wrapped in a luxuriously thick satin-quilted turquoise dressing gown, and Mrs Shepherd was also there, tired eyes curious, trying to peer inside.

The Night Ferry Guard, who had already been put on alert that something was wrong by Dadie Spence and had been unsure what *exactly* was the matter, had arrived and was sweating profusely, his blotchy red face riven with worry, with no clue as to what to do next, his navy cap gripped in his hands for something to occupy himself with.

Posie found herself taking control. There was no sign of Inspector Durrant.

She stepped into the corridor, leaving the Doctor to minister to Dadie Spence, and she spoke succinctly:

'I regret to inform you that Lady Caroline has passed away. And in possibly suspicious circumstances. Guard, you or the Driver of the locomotive should inform the local police to come on board. Her berth needs to be sealed up; it's a crime scene, or could be. Oh, and Guard, please could you call through to London immediately and ask Scotland Yard to get on the case? I know it's very early, but you can leave a message. Tell them what has happened. You can ask for Sergeant Fox, or Inspector Oats, I suppose. And the Pullman car we were travelling in earlier, the one that was unhitched at Dover? Well, that should be searched thoroughly, immediately. By a proper Forensics team. Have you got that?'

The Guard swallowed, very pale and scared. 'Yes, yes, I think so, Miss.'

'One more thing, the Waiter who was attending on us at dinner will need to be questioned, too.'

'Right. I understand.' The Guard nodded and fled out into the darkness of the very early morning.

And then things moved along quickly.

Inspector Durrant, sleepy-eyed and tousle-haired, but a figure of authority, nonetheless, suddenly appeared.

'Let me get this sorted out, Miss Parker. I'll close up Lady Caroline's cabin as soon as we can get Mr Spence out of there, once the sedative is working. Meanwhile, I'll get what we need from outside, including men. The Guard already left? I'll follow him now.'

Thank goodness, Posie breathed to herself, with almost desperate relief.

Durrant jumped off the train, hurriedly pulling out his leather police fob as he went.

Posie and the group in the corridor watched him heading across the snow-covered tracks and hurrying over to the main 'Douane' office of Dunkirk, where presumably there was some sort of police presence, and where one amber light burned in the supposed calm of early morning.

They stood together in an awkward silence, but thankfully Inspector Durrant returned quickly, looking purposeful.

The Night Ferry Guard followed Durrant back into the carriage, looking happier than before, and he gave Posie a thumbs-up sign to indicate he had placed her requested call.

'I've called that Inspector Oats, Miss. Scotland Yard said they will sort out everything at Dover.'

'Thank goodness.'

Durrant nodded. 'I have alerted the French police,

and I await local support. Now, the next priority is to get everyone out of their berths. *Safe*. I'll address everyone when we are all together.'

Within ten minutes, four smartly-uniformed local *gendarmes* joined the train, all obediently carrying out the orders of Inspector Durrant, whose authority and senior rank they seemed to automatically accept.

Quick decisions followed.

The berth of Caroline Greenlow was locked up, with the body still inside, and one policeman placed outside it, sentry-like.

Then each passenger, if not already awake, was woken and told to dress hurriedly, and ordered to assemble in the newly-attached French Pullman dining-car, only bringing bare essentials. All of the berths were then sealed, and all keys were handed in to Inspector Durrant.

Posie dressed quickly, washing thoroughly in cold, cold water and spritzing herself liberally with her usual Parma Violet scent before donning her dark-pink plain woollen jersey dress.

She pulled on thick navy woollen stockings, and her new dark-pink suede shoes, and then made up her face as fast as she could.

She added a shimmery rouge to both lips and cheeks, and layered up grey eyeshadow on her eyelids. She spat quickly in the Maybelline eye-black, and drew on big wings of eyeliner; an effect she'd normally reserve for night, but she had the feeling her make-up might need to be capable of withstanding long hours without touch-ups.

Posie grabbed her old faithful carpet bag and stuffed the strange cryptic note she had received the night before inside it, too, and then hurried off, leaving her virtually-empty duffel bag behind on the floor.

'Sit where you like, please,' Inspector Durrant commanded everyone. The Guard fluttered behind him, and two of the *gendarmes* hung about, too.

The French Pullman dining-car had been set up with many, many tables, and all of them were laid, as if the French had got the wrong message and expected to be serving breakfast to a hundred.

People sat down at different tables, everybody still half-asleep and flummoxed. It was warm in the carriage, and small flickering low-lights were turned on along all the walls. It would all have been very cosy, if the whole thing hadn't been so unutterably horrid.

Hot flasks of coffee, and fresh croissants, still warm from a bakery in Dunkirk, were laid out on a buffet table, all set up before the alarm was raised, when it had seemed the train would be running on as usual.

But none of the passengers had any desire to eat anything, and the only people who helped themselves generously were two of the French policemen.

Inspector Durrant explained what was going on: 'Ladies and Gentlemen, I am afraid we are, right now, in the middle of an emergency situation.'

He spoke briefly of the death of Caroline Greenlow, and of potential foul play. The word 'murder' was not mentioned, but it was understood plainly, and the silence in the dining-car was awful.

'With a dead body aboard, and her being such a high-profile person, we must ensure things are done properly,' Durrant explained calmly, as if humouring his audience.

'We will need a proper Forensics team to go through everything, but being so early in the morning, the local Dunkirk force were not up to dealing with this tragedy at all.'

Durrant shrugged resignedly. 'The local Commandant thinks it better if the train continues on to Paris. We are therefore a moving "crime scene", with me in notional charge, with these good *gendarme* boys assisting me. I will hand over control on arrival. Paris has been forewarned and is expecting us, and I believe the case will be run at the most senior level, by the legendary Inspector Lucille, the Director of the Central Paris Police Judiciaire, the equivalent of Scotland Yard. So, please, I entreat you, it is important we stay *here*, and no-one tries to return to their berth. It would be futile anyway, as I have all the keys, and also the Guard's fob of master keys. There is one bathroom allocated to use, and you will seek permission from one of us if you need to use it. We will alight in Paris at almost exactly the expected time of arrival, and you should not be inconvenienced very much at all by this.'

'I bally well hope not!' Charles Loxley roared unpleasantly.

He'd been surprisingly quiet since being forced to wake up and leave his berth, but Posie put this down to the effects of the Veronal, and the fact that its effects had probably not yet worn off. Loxley was wearing a lopsided pinstripe jacket over a white silk shirt with the buttons done up all wrong. On his lap, as ever, he was nursing his red governmental briefcase.

Durrant waved a pad of baby-blue paper above his head. It looked like it carried the moon logo of the Night Ferry company at the top of the pages.

'I will ask you now to write down your name and place of intended accommodation in Paris on one of these sheets, and I will collect them and pass them to the Inspector who will take charge in Paris. Unfortunately, I do not have any proper forms with me, as I am not really travelling in an "official" capacity, but we will have to make do. You will be interviewed briefly on arrival in Paris, and then you will probably be free to go. Your belongings will be searched, and then sent on to you at your given hotels.'

The train then moved off at six-thirty, prompt.

And after the blue forms were completed, and collected up, they all sat in the Pullman dining-car, on a surreal journey all the way to Paris.

It took a little over three hours; the locomotive rumbling on through the frozen January countryside.

The light outside the windows changed during the journey from darkest obsidian-black to the milkiest of pinkish-silver dawns, revealing the snow-covered fields of northern France and the frosty-roofed villages with their glistening ochre roof tiles, glittering like a strange stardust.

It was actually a beautiful dawn.

A dawn Caroline Greenlow would never get to see, Posie thought to herself, sadly. *And Paris was now a destination she would never get to arrive at.*

Not properly, anyhow.

Nor her baby…

Chugging along with their dreadful cargo on board, the passengers stared at each other, half-fearful, and half-gruesomely intrigued by the story unfolding all around them: the like of which they'd never live through again.

Posie observed them all.

Charles Loxley looked very nervous, and despite holding on for dear life to the red bag with the portcullis emblazoned upon it, he seemed unwilling to do any work, or take out correspondence. He dozed off a couple of times, using the red bag as a pillow for his overly-large head.

Dadie Spence had been given something to make him sleep, and he lay outstretched on the green carpet near the coffee, sleeping fitfully, covered in a black, luxurious sheepskin coat, which was presumably his own. His powdered face was tear-stained and puffy, and in his hand he still clutched the dusky-pink letter of invitation from Paul Poiret, now much crunched and crumpled.

Next to him, on the floor, cross-legged, dressed properly and with his customary hat and glass eye in place, Doctor Dance sat doggedly working, reading through a big wodge of typed lecture notes, and occasionally making comments in a shaky hand, in green ink.

Daphne de Bengy, obviously not an early riser at all, slept the whole journey with her head in her hands on an empty table, a big velvet coat with a hood pulled up over her face.

Lex Lennart, the American, was dressed in yesterday's clothes, but immaculately so. The scent of Blenheim Bouquet was strong today. He sat at a table all alone, with a set of business accounts, together with a ruler, a pencil and an eraser, and he worked his way through the lot, occasionally darting inquisitive looks about the place, at his fellow passengers. His two black leather boxes were at his feet.

Mrs Shepherd sat at a table alone, too.

She had a detective novel to read. The new one from Dorothy L. Sayers, *Clouds of Witness.* But she spent most of her time staring out of the window, or tugging at her black lace mantilla and shaking her head, looking downcast.

Posie sat cloistered with Suzannah Scotland, who was still dressed in last night's clothing, and still wearing Posie's earrings, which were quite the freshest thing about her. She looked mussed-up, in need of a wash and brush, and like she could have done with some new make-up and a spot of freshening scent.

'Where *were* you, this morning?' Posie hissed at the woman, as they finished completing the pieces of blue paper with their personal details. 'I could have done with a hand with Lady Caroline, to be honest. Some proper medical help.'

To Posie's surprise, Suzannah flushed a deep red under the duskiness of her lovely tanned skin. 'Yes, I'm sorry. This whole thing is dreadful, even if Lady Caroline wasn't the nicest person I'd ever met…'

Suzannah then flicked the tiniest glance over in the direction of the Inspector, who was collecting in the blue papers which he had distributed to every passenger, the Guard helping. She fluttered her black eyelashes and then looked bashful, but pleased, too.

The Inspector made a concerted effort *not* to catch Suzannah's eye, and pulled at his collar, as if he felt suddenly hot, before sweeping his long fingers through his thick fringe of black hair.

Posie suddenly understood. 'Oh, *ah*.'

She stifled a small smile. 'I see. Well, that makes sense.'

Posie then whispered: 'So that's why it was near-nigh impossible to get hold of either you, or the Inspector. You were *together*...'

Suzannah inclined her head slightly in assent. 'First in my berth, then in his. All night. And *what* a night! It was as if he didn't care; had no inhibitions. Like it was his last night on earth.'

Posie raised an eyebrow but said nothing.

Suzannah hissed an urgent whisper: 'Are you shocked, Miss Parker?'

'I *told* you to call me Posie. And of course not. Why would I be? I'm glad for you. If you're not hurt by it, that is. Will you meet him again, outside of all of this mess, I mean?'

'I don't know. He didn't say anything to encourage me.'

'Ah, well...' Posie yawned. 'I'm glad you had a good night, anyway.'

It was true.

Posie didn't care how people lived their lives, and so far she had been impressed with the Inspector's sleek handling of the situation and his general demeanour. He seemed a good man, and life was short, and you had to take what happiness was afforded you, in the ways you decided worked best for you.

Besides, it seemed Suzannah and the Inspector's secret was probably of a very harmless sort; compared to some secrets which endangered life, and caused real harm.

And it seemed certain there were secrets like that, dangerous ones, contained within this very train, entombed within these carriages, hurtling towards some sort of resolution.

Towards Paris.

Posie remembered suddenly how the dead woman had entrusted her with something, with a request, not yet understood.

How in her dying moments Caroline Greenlow had pulled at something from her neck, had given it to Posie, who had automatically stuck it in the pocket of her pyjamas, meaning to study it later.

A necklace of some sort?It might be important, Posie thought to herself, chiding herself for leaving the item behind.

I must dig it out. When I am allowed my things.

If the police don't confiscate it.

She saw Inspector Durrant now standing, his back turned to everyone in the carriage, staring out of the window, his arms crossed, his expression mirrored in the glass was one of consternation, as if he was weighing up some great conundrum.

Posie watched him say something to one of the junior French policemen and then stride from the carriage, his tweed-blazered back very straight. At her side Posie was aware of Suzannah asking for permission to use the lavatory, and there were others standing up, too. Everybody was restless. Understandably.

But then tiredness overcame Posie, and she put her arms down on the table, folded her head down, like a swan wanting to hide, and, only meaning to shut her eyes for a minute, she fell into a deep, tremulous sleep which lasted all the way to Paris, but it gave her almost no rest.

And barely any comfort.

****

PART TWO
Murder and Mayhem

Paris
(Wednesday 20th January 1926)
Chapter Ten

On entering the Gare du Nord at nine-thirty sharp, the train came to a stop – heaving and panting, as if in relief – amid wreaths of curling white smoke. Posie was shaken awake at her table by one of the *gendarmes* who had boarded at Dunkirk, and she watched, bleary-eyed, as about fifty smart, uniformed Parisian police officers lined the platform, forming a barricade against potential escape.

A crush of navy-blue-and-gold uniforms were suddenly everywhere, swarming onto the train, and each passenger found themselves being allocated a policeman, as if they were under arrest.

'What the devil? Do you even know who *I* am?' Loxley was shouting, as red in the face as the bag he carried. 'I'm very important! My government is relying on me!'

'We don't care. We are following our orders. *Dépêchez-vous! Move!*'

The passengers were to be marched off the train, and French instructions were being shouted in loud voices.

'*Dépêchez-vous maintenant! Let's get a move on, quickly now!*'

Posie had no idea where Suzannah had got to, and she'd also lost sight of Inspector Durrant in all the fiasco, but she saw the blotchy-faced Night Ferry Guard ahead of her in the queue. She pulled on her dark-green coat and tugged her matching hat into place.

'Posie watched as the French Forensics team, and a small team of undertakers with their big black briefcases, trooped onto the train and took over the Pullman. They were busy setting up, all their grisly paraphernalia laid out on the floor: two canvas stretchers; a multitude of metal knives and boxes; metal trolleys with small bottles of chemicals and testing apparatus at the ready. The Guard was looking about warily: 'Looks like something else is afoot now, Miss, eh? What could it be?'

'Sorry, what else has happened? Oh…'

But they were being moved off; a police escort at every passenger's side. And as Posie stepped down onto the platform below, and the cold of the frozen morning air hit her, and the familiar smell of tar and croissants and melting chocolate wafted up to meet her nostrils, she gripped her carpet bag tightly beneath her arm.

Take it all in.

This is where Dolly was last seen.

Focus on why you are here.

But it was hard. There was so much going on around her.

Ahead of her, Posie saw the four *gendarmes* who had boarded at Dunkirk, together with the French train Driver, and the nervous Night Ferry Guard, all being taken aside into a huddle. They were to be quizzed by a huge man in his thirties who was brandishing a notebook aloft and looked very un-French, more like a Norse God. As wide as he was tall, with thick, blonde hair styled in crimped waves, he seemed to sparkle with the amount of gold buttons and medals attached to his front, and he was resplendent in high polished black boots and a voluminous navy cape.

'So *that* must be the legendary Inspector Lucille,' Posie whispered to herself in some awe. Behind her, Mrs Shepherd smoked one of her black cigarillos silently in the queue, and in the harsh light of day she looked even more withered and crabbed in her black clothes than she had seemed last night at dinner. Like a puff of the frozen wind might blow her right away.

Behind Mrs Shepherd, Doctor Dance was bundled up in a huge black overcoat, studying his script for his talk. Lex Lennart was holding his black bags warily, looking all about, and Charles Loxley had already been marched away, presumably on account of his important governmental status.

No-one spoke or even tried to make eye contact with their travelling companions. Each passenger in the queue had withdrawn into themselves; become separate islands all of their very own. Probably because of the policemen standing threateningly at each and every side.

Posie tried not to look at her own guard too much, other than to note he was very young and plump, and full of a sense of self-importance, which didn't need stoking.

And then there was a sudden slight movement beside her. A tap on her shoulder. 'Miss Parker?'

'Oh, hullo?'

A small man in his mid-forties was right up next to her, delicate-looking but immaculate. He was wearing a shiny black leather trench-coat, and sported a black, greased moustache under a small, pointed nose, which had turned blue with cold. He was holding a big black ugly briefcase and his hands were encased in white kid gloves.

At first, Posie confused him for one of the undertakers, and frowned. *What did he want with her?*

But it was immediately noticeable that her young, plump police 'guard' had come over all subservient. He almost bowed low to this man in the black leather coat.

'Miss Parker?' repeated the man in black, doffing his black bowler hat to her and putting it back on again.

‘Shall we step out of this line? Can we speak? I am Inspector Lucille, Police Director at 36, Quai des Orfèvres. I am in charge here. I was looking out specially for you.’

Posie swallowed, nodded. Her young police guard fell back.

How could she have been so stupid?

She should have learnt by now that one should keep an open mind about almost everything.

Throwing one last backward glance at the train, Posie crossed the vast marble-tiled concourse of the station, following the wily, wiry little black-clad man as he snaked through the crowds, her police guard trailing in their wake. She wondered briefly where Inspector Durrant had got to – he was supposed to be here with her, wasn’t he? – and also where Suzannah had got to. Both had been noticeably absent on the platform. And Daphne hadn’t been there either, which was odd.

But right now Posie had to make an effort to keep up, her pink suede shoes with their small heels tap-tapping aloud in a rather frivolous fashion on the shiny floor.

Hundreds of men in black bowler hats, wearing thick fur coats and with newspapers tucked securely under their arms, swarmed up the two vast ornate sweeping staircases at the front of the station, all on their way to trams and buses and the Metro, and on to work.

And above everyone, at the top of the two grand staircases, was a huge cathedral-sized window made up of seven gigantic panes of leaded glass, with an ornate art-deco clock placed like an all-seeing eye at the very centre of the design.

Posie saw Inspector Lucille glance up and check the time, and she followed him hastily up one of the staircases, holding onto its gleaming golden banister.

The Inspector marched across the floor which was at the very top, and he opened a small wooden door in the wall there, almost hidden behind a coffee-seller’s stand. He turned and beckoned for Posie to follow him with those strange white gloves which made him look like a director of traffic, or perhaps a magician.

Very odd.

They were suddenly cloistered inside a tiny office, which turned out to belong to the Station Master. It had been requisitioned specially for Lucille, for this emergency.

Inspector Lucille motioned for Posie to sit down on one side of a desk while he sat on the other. He had a notebook in front of him, filled with scribbles.

Behind him was a huge window that looked out over the entire concourse, which was very distracting.

Posie had to keep pulling her gaze back to this insignificant little man, and try to not look at the beautifully sleek black locomotives pulling in at the many platforms spread out below. Everything was laid out like a toy station beneath her, with crowds of ant-like people far far below.

Suddenly the Norse God appeared through the tiny door, with a tray of coffees from the stall outside, and he murmured to Inspector Lucille in hushed, urgent tones.

He handed across a couple of telegrams and pieces of yellow scribbled-on notepaper and then he swept out again, his cape rustling like the hero in an opera.

The Inspector read the messages and frowned slightly before putting them down on the desk.

'Apologies, Miss Parker. That was my Sergeant, Jean-Luc de Caunes, reporting that everyone has now been accounted for and is in the process of being questioned. The body of Lady Caroline has been removed for an immediate post-mortem at the City Morgue. On the initial evidence it does seem that the deceased was poisoned and we are therefore treating this case as murder. The cabins are all being searched and we have already found some unusual things.'

Posie remained silent, waiting.

Inspector Lucille pushed a cup of coffee across the desk

to her, and peeled his gloves off his hands. Posie saw with a sudden awful start that his hands were a raw mass of wounds.

Old scars.

Not quite as bad as Doctor Dance's hands, but almost.

The Inspector followed her gaze, shrugged. 'Those trenches, Miss Parker, they have a lot to answer for, *n'est-ce pas*? But I was lucky, Miss Parker, and I remind myself of that every day.'

He sipped at his own coffee, carrying on briskly: 'I have already spoken to your husband, the good Chief Commissioner, but very briefly. He cannot come over here immediately, unfortunately, but his Sergeant…' he consulted one of the pieces of paper, '…Fox, is it? Like the animal?'

'Yes, sir.'

'He will fly out immediately to Le Bourget. He will be here in Paris by about three-thirty this afternoon.'

Posie nodded, not particularly caring either way, the highly-anticipated idea of her jaunt here alone obviously in tatters anyhow.

'I see. Well, that may be helpful.'

She tried her coffee which was good and strong and very, very sweet. It would have been even better with a biscuit.

Inspector Lucille watched Posie carefully. 'I need you to help us, Miss Parker. If you would be able to write for us an account of Lady Caroline's last moments – we understand you were with her as she died? – that would be wonderful. But did anything else on the train journey strike you as unusual last night, or this morning?'

Posie felt like laughing aloud, almost hysterically.

'What *didn't* strike me as unusual, you mean, sir,' she answered. 'The terrible weather; the reduced staff; the very few passengers; not to mention the oddness of all of the passengers…' She tailed off before shrugging, chewing at her lip. 'But perhaps the passengers were not so odd after all, sir.'

Lucille smoothed his moustache and frowned: '*Que voulez-vous dire?* What do you mean?'

Posie sighed. 'We were on a first-class train, sir. The rich and entitled are *always* a little odd, aren't they? They are often self-absorbed, and that can make them horrible. I'm afraid that was the case with regards the murder victim and her fiancé: they were quite obnoxious.'

She shrugged. 'The only pleasant, helpful passenger was Doctor Dance. And I suppose the younger women, Mrs Scotland and Miss de Bengy, were good sorts, too, but they weren't your typical passenger for that train.'

The Inspector shook his head. 'No, they certainly weren't typical, *non*.'

He shuffled a yellow page of his Sergeant's notes, reading it again quickly. 'I understand that Lady Caroline almost died even earlier, with something down her throat? Any idea who was behind it?'

Posie shook her head, but explained succinctly about the scarab which Lady Caroline had coughed up, and about the similar one worn by Lex Lennart.

'Where did the object end up, Miss Parker?'

'I am afraid I do not know, sir. Her fiancé, Mr Spence, had it in his hands the last time I saw it.'

The Inspector changed tack: 'And I understand that in your country there was a long-running sort of public hatred between the murder victim herself and your very esteemed Chancellor of the Exchequer?'

Posie nodded. 'About women's rights, yes. They had heated exchanges on the topic, but always through the medium of *words*; very punchy articles or letters. They didn't have a history of physically attacking each other.'

Lucille cocked his head to one side. 'Would it surprise you, Miss Parker, if I told you that so far Sir Charles Loxley is suspect number one in this case? We have him already in the little cell…'

Posie was astounded. 'Loxley? *No!* He's a blithering fool; a well-connected one, of course, and full of stupid self-importance. But…'

She remembered his lugging around the prized red briefcase, the importance he had accorded it at all times. 'I don't like him, but I *do* think he's proud to serve in our country's government, and that alone should stand for something, shouldn't it? He wasn't on the train for pleasure. Sir Charles was coming over for some sort of urgent meeting which was only organised late on Monday.'

The Inspector shook his head. '*Non*. That is not true, Miss Parker. We have ascertained there was no invitation from our government; no work reason for Sir Charles to travel here. It seems to have been a bluff of some kind…*un truc*. A trick. He was probably on board that train specifically to kill his great enemy, Lady Caroline Greenlow. That, most likely, will be what we will conclude.'

Posie stared at the Inspector in complete disbelief.

Charles Loxley was a buffoon of the highest order, and in Posie's experience, buffoons were not good liars or dissemblers.

'But why is he your top suspect, sir? Apart from the feud?'

Inspector Lucille checked his note. 'We have evidence. On an initial search of Sir Charles' belongings, a bathroom sponge-bag was found to contain two similar packages of white powder which purported to be tooth powder. One looks like genuine tooth powder, but the other has the clear characteristics of arsenic. It is being tested as we speak. Sir Charles will be retained in custody, but we will be discreet, of course. As I would like *you* to be, please. No word of any of this to anyone. And certainly not to the press.'

Posie nodded, then sat, silent, her thoughts racing ahead of her.

The search teams had only had a few minutes, surely, to look through things, when that blonde Sergeant had come crashing up here with updates?

This meant that all searches so far had been ridiculously superficial, and the packets of white powder supposedly belonging to Charles Loxley must have been so obvious as to be utterly ridiculous.

Any serious poisoner would have got rid of such compromising evidence, surely?

So, they must have been placed.

Or else, Loxley was carrying them for a different reason.

The Inspector was checking the time on a big wall clock above Posie's head. It was ten minutes past ten.

He handed Posie a piece of very official-looking paper and instructed her to fill in what she could remember of Lady Caroline's last moments.

Inspector Lucille was clamping his big black bag together, pulling on his gloves.

'Why are *you* in Paris, Miss Parker? Your husband mentioned one of my good colleagues at the Rond-Point Station, Inspector Jegouzo? Your husband said it was a personal matter which you could not let rest? I have to say, he did not sound particularly happy that you were here, to be honest. Still less when I told him about the murders on the train.'

Posie tried not to scowl.

It might be a cold case to Richard, but Dolly's disappearance was very much an ongoing matter of the most pressing importance to her.

'You have one minute, sir?'

'*Oui*.'

Silently, she opened her carpet bag, pulled out her small red folder and opened it on the desk. She pulled out Dolly's photograph and pushed it towards the Inspector.

She explained as briefly as she could.

He took the photograph in his white-gloved hands, and his mouth turned down beneath the moustache.

'Ah, I remember this case. There was the possibility of Caspian della Rosa, that old fiend, being involved, wasn't there? Yes, last year? And Jegouzo was given control of it purely because of the location of this fake lawyers' "office" on the Champs-Élysées; the need to monitor it for a while.'

He handed the image of Dolly back to Posie, and gave a smile which held sympathy, but not encouragement.

'Good luck, Miss Parker. I hope poor old Jegouzo did not give you any encouragement? I would not have thought there is much hope for you to discover anything new here.'

His dark, clever eyes suddenly alighted on something else in Posie's red folder. It was the crumpled, newspaper-sourced picture of the drowned girl's death mask.

He flicked it around and winced.

'Ah, "*L'Inconnue de la Seine*". Our famous dead lady. She is like a mermaid, and has led many good men astray. Good job you are not searching for *her*! I suppose you had the thought to question the City Morgue about your friend, and whether she ended up there, too, eh? Clever of you, yes. That's why you brought her photograph. *Oui*...'

Without pausing for Posie to confirm or not, he took a piece of paper from the Railway Manager's own desk-jotter and he took up a pen which also did not belong to him, and he struck a big line through the emblem of the French Railways, and scribbled a few sentences on it with a slow, crabbed, gloved hand.

Then signed it all with a big flourish.

'Here,' Inspector Lucille said pleasantly.

'This will admit you to the City Morgue, and to any official city organisation you need. It should open most closed doors to you. I *do* understand you need to know what happened to your friend, otherwise these things haunt you. And if you need anything else, drop by to our Headquarters. We are on one of the two natural islands on the Seine, by the Palais de Justice. The Île de la Cité. Sergeant de Caunes will make himself of use to you, if needed. Now, do you need a lift anywhere when you have completed that statement, Miss Parker?'

Posie thanked him, grateful for the sudden courtesy, and explained that she was going to the Rond-Point for eleven o'clock, to speak to Jegouzo personally, and that she would not need Sergeant de Caunes at all, as Inspector Durrant had promised he would escort her there.

Posie explained that Durrant had been on the Night Ferry train entirely because of her.

'I suppose he's helping you with enquiries now, is he? I haven't seen him for hours, not even when we all got off the train. If Inspector Durrant is finished here, perhaps *he* can accompany me to the Rond-Point Station?'

Lucille was at the door by now, and he turned suddenly, his white, peaky face even whiter than before.

'This is most awkward, Miss Parker. It seems I have more bad news for you…'

'Oh?' Posie stared hard. *What on earth was he talking about?*

'*Oui.* The police station on the Rond-Point has suffered some very bad luck in the last couple of days.'

The Inspector leant against the door, heavily for such a light man. 'The first bad news concerns Inspector Jegouzo. He was reported as missing yesterday afternoon. I do not know if he has yet returned to the office. I'm not even sure the office is open, actually. It's a very small one. And as for young Inspector Durrant, well…' There was a moment's strained silence.

'Sir?'

Posie stood quickly, her heart beating much quicker than before.

She strode to the huge window, and looked right out across the concourse, across the hectic scrambled busyness of the Gare du Nord. Thoughts crowding her head, spilling over.

What does he not want me to know?

This legendary policeman?

She turned to the left, to where the shiny black locomotive which had pulled the Night Ferry carriages was still to be seen, right at the buffer, with its French Pullman carriage still attached. Behind this, the two sleeper carriages were also still there.

Crowds of professional-looking men with heavy apparatus and wearing white coats were still buzzing around the sleeper carriages, with uniformed policemen forming a cordon around the whole train to keep away interested-looking onlookers.

But as she stared, she realised that the men were focused, swarming even, around Car Number Two. Which was weird, as most of the passengers had been allocated berths in Car Number One, and Lady Caroline Greenlow had actually died in Car Number One.

As Posie watched, a group of policemen swarmed on the platform near one of the doors of Car Number Two.

Into their midst came a small procession, and Posie saw that it was two stretcher-bearers stepping down, having negotiated the steps with a stretcher between them.

On the stretcher was a body, covered in black cloth.

But hadn't Inspector Lucille said Lady Caroline's body had already been taken to the City Morgue?

So, who on earth…?

Posie saw all of the policemen around the stretcher and all of the policemen in the cordon line suddenly whip off their caps, holding them to their chests; making a salute.

'Oh! I say!' She covered her mouth in horror.

She suddenly remembered seeing two stretchers being brought onto the train earlier, but in her tired, addled state she had thought nothing of it.

And then she remembered something else. A slip, she had thought, just a few minutes ago. When Inspector Lucille had referred to '*murders*' which had taken place on the Night Ferry.

Murders, not a murder.

She turned in a flash and caught Lucille's dark gaze. He seemed to be challenging her.

'Inspector Alphonse Durrant is dead? Murdered, as well? But he was fine this morning, at Dunkirk.'

Lucille exhaled wearily. 'I am not allowed for the time being to either confirm or deny what you have just asked me, Miss Parker. We need to inform family members, and so on. It is complicated, a police death.'

'So, he *is* dead?'

'You must wait for the official line, Miss Parker. But I think it is safe to say Inspector Durrant will not, unfortunately, be accompanying you anywhere this morning.'

Posie felt sick to the bottom of her stomach.

He was on that train because of me, she felt like wailing. *It's my fault Durrant is dead. Pure and simple.*

She thought suddenly of the young Inspector's visit to England, to see his ailing father. A man who was dying, who had now been predeceased by his only son. How would he take such news? It didn't bear thinking about.

Posie was remembering Durrant striding from the Pullman as she rested her head sleepily on a table; that slight crush of people moving behind him.

'But *why* was he killed?' Posie's words sounded angry. 'Was it something to do with Lady Caroline's murder? Perhaps he knew who had done it, and he confronted them?'

Inspector Lucille shrugged. 'I don't know. But I can tell you, Miss Parker, that our second murder victim was stabbed. Viciously. I do not think Charles Loxley, our main suspect for Lady Caroline's death, would have done such a thing. The stabbing looks to be a crime of passion, or, perhaps, an opportunistic crime by a low-life.'

'A low-life?'

'You said yourself that there were two people travelling on the train last night who were not typical passengers.'

Posie frowned. Remembered. 'Oh! You mean Suzannah Scotland and Daphne de Bengy? But they're not low-lifes!'

She could hear her voice pitching higher. 'They are both decent sorts, not rich, but certainly not murderers. Absolutely not.'

Lucille smiled sadly. 'Not rich, no. But both are suspicious. One is little more than a call girl at the Moulin Rouge, and the other is a registered bankrupt. We have detained both of them. They have both been found in compromising positions this morning. And evidence has been found for both women in Durrant's berth itself: a blue calling-card from Ms de Bengy, and a cheap black scarf which we believe is Mrs Scotland's. We will see how this ends up.'

Posie sat speechless, anger consuming her.

How could one blue business card, of a sort doled out to nearly everyone on the train, incriminate someone for murder?

And a scarf! Well, it was obvious how the scarf had found its way into Durrant's sleeping space. But she wouldn't mention that particular tryst; not now. It might fuel the idea of a crime of passion having been committed.

That wouldn't help Suzannah one bit.

Inspector Lucille made a mock-salute at her: 'If you *do* need us, you know where to come.'

After the Inspector had left, Posie sat for a few minutes, shocked to the core. Angry, too.

And then she saw the time, which was half-past ten, and decided to try and get to the Rond-Point anyway.

She had to do something. This was her only appointment in Paris and she'd be blowed if she missed it.

She scribbled a statement and handed it to the young policeman outside the Railway Manager's office. Then, companionless and unaccompanied, Posie stepped out into the huge cacophony of noise outside the main station, where hundreds of taxi horns were blaring together on the great grey concourse. Adverts for 'CINZANO' and 'MACEDONIA CIGARETTES' flashed above in bright lights.

Having hailed one of the noisy motor-taxis, she headed off for her scheduled meeting, passing buses and policemen, and women with tiny dogs, who were smoking impossibly long white cigarettes, and on and on and on past frozen avenues of winter-bare trees. Posie watched a woman with a smart bob and a navy-blue pram navigate a pile of old snow on a kerb, two little girls clutching at her coat.

She's like me, thought Posie. *Trying to do it all.*

Keeping on.

Other women with fashionable shorn bleached hair were coming out of a florist, laughing, holding huge blooms of expensive hot-house flowers.

And perhaps they are like Dolly.

Loving all of this.

Every minute of silvery, enchanting, beautiful, but very dangerous Paris.

* * * *

Chapter Eleven

The police station on the Rond-Point was located to the side of a beautiful toyshop with a striped yellow-and-pink awning, set back on the very outer ring of the vast roundabout.

It was right on the corner of the Rue Jean Mermoz, where all the uniformly tall and elegant Parisian yellow-grey houses, with their giddying height, and rows of elegant glittering silver balconies, looked cold and frozen today.

Posie arrived on time, with her little red folder about Dolly already in her hands, feeling business-like and as if she had a point to prove.

What that was, she didn't yet know.

What would she do if Jegouzo, a man she had spoken to only yesterday, wasn't here, as Lucille had intimated?

And what would she do if he *was*? Would she tell him about his colleague, Durrant, and his yet-to-be-made-official fate, or simply act dumb?

A gleaming brass sign on the wall announced the location of the police station, and doors stood open to the street, revealing a courtyard inside.

Posie went in.

A small and pretty garden with snow-covered shrubs in terracotta pots was revealed. Several large floor-length windows faced onto the courtyard, and Posie saw, looking about, that all of the rooms were police offices.

Behind the glass of the windows, she could see many uniformed policemen going about their daily business: on telephones; writing up reports; shouting across to each other in a friendly fashion, waving paperwork. A big, heavy door had a bronze sign marked 'ENTRÉE – VISITEURS' and Posie rung the bell outside it.

The Duty Sergeant was small, very thin and polite, with buck-teeth and yellow-grizzled skin and sad eyes. He spoke no English, but he seemed to be expecting Posie, and he quickly shepherded her out of the small, empty waiting area which smelt of disinfectant, and where a small green budgerigar was perched in a cage which hung from the high-beamed ceiling.

They proceeded along to a small office at the back of the station, having walked through the busy hubbub of the warm, comfortable offices first.

The level of noise was unexpected, as were the sheer number of uniformed policemen around. Posie had been led to believe by Inspector Lucille that this was a small office, and she wondered with some cynicism quite how big the main Police Headquarters were, over by the Palais de Justice, if *this* was small.

Lucille must have hundreds, if not thousands of men working for him over there.

Inspector Jegouzo opened his own door before the Duty Sergeant had knocked, and the two men smiled at each other.

'Ah, come in, Miss Parker, and welcome to Paris,' the big Inspector said, and in a torrent of quickfire French he ordered the Duty Sergeant to organise refreshments. A telephone on Jegouzo's desk was ringing, and went unanswered.

A wide, messy desk stacked high with paperwork almost filled up the dark, window-less room, and behind the desk an enormous map of the 8th Arrondissement was pinned to the wall. There was no fire in the grate, but heat pumped out from a good-sized radiator and Posie took off her coat.

The scent of cigar-smoke was all-pervading here. A couple of ashtrays overflowed, and a dark, ashy old residue covered the surface of the desk, even the visitor's chair, which Posie dusted off before sitting down, as inconspicuously as possible.

A couple of cheap prints featuring the Arc de Triomphe were on the wall in plain frames, and a silver-framed photograph of a middle-aged woman in an Edwardian hat was prominent on the top of a single bookshelf, sitting among a good many sets of red-leather-covered textbooks.

Black folders were lined up below these red textbooks, at least a hundred of the things.

A typical policeman's office, thought Posie. It felt familiar. Cosy. Inspector Oats at Scotland Yard kept his office like this: old-school.

'Wait a moment, Miss Parker, I will see what I can find on this case, eh?'

Inspector Jegouzo was older than Richard, at least fifty, older than Inspector Lucille. He wore plain clothes rather than a uniform, including a silk cravat and a woollen waistcoat, everything in tones of forest green.

The Inspector resembled a friendly old walrus, with the moustache to match. He had twinkling blue eyes and a big, pock-marked fleshy nose and he looked like the sort of man who would normally be inundated every year with requests to play Father Christmas. He did indeed seem to be the 'jolly good chap', whom Richard had described.

He started to pull a slim black folder out from the bookcase and opened it, scanning the pages.

A slender young woman in white overalls and wearing a white paper cap over her peroxide-blonde bobbed hair suddenly appeared, pushing a tea-trolley. Two coffees and a plate of finger-sized sponge cakes filled with cream were placed upon the ashy desk, and the woman left again.

'*S'il vous plait*, help yourself,' said the Inspector kindly, sitting down and passing a cup of the coffee over.

'Thank you.' Posie took a cake, ate it in one bite. It was utterly delicious, vanilla and coffee and cinnamon flavoured, all at the same time.

'And thank you for seeing me, Inspector. I'm especially glad, as Inspector Lucille told me when I got to the Gare du Nord this morning that your office here had had some bad luck recently? He seemed to think *you* wouldn't be here to meet me, at all. That perhaps the office would be closed?'

'*Comment…?*'

Jegouzo raised his eyebrows in genuine surprise. He sipped his coffee which was thick with foamy milk and it caught on his splendid moustache. He dabbed at it with a sage-green handkerchief.

'You spoke to the great Inspector Lucille?' He sounded incredulous. 'This morning?'

'Yes, that's right,' said Posie. 'There was an, er…an *incident* on the Night Ferry which I was travelling on. And he seems to be supervising the case.'

'It must be high-profile. Big.'

'Perhaps, sir.'

'Where is Inspector Durrant? You know I arranged for him to accompany you, Madame?'

'Yes, thank you. You had better ask Inspector Lucille about Durrant.'

Jegouzo shrugged in a very French way and blew out his cheeks.

'Well, I am not sure what bad luck the great Inspector Lucille is referring to. Perhaps the fact my mother died a few days ago, and although it was very sad, she was almost one hundred years old! Of course, I took a day or two off but I was here yesterday again, was I not, Madame, when you telephoned? We spoke in the morning, did we not? I also left early yesterday afternoon, as I needed to arrange the funeral service. But why would this office be closed? All my men have jobs to do! *Oui*, I had better call the good Inspector Lucille at the Île de la Cité. Right away. Especially about retrieving Inspector Durrant: there is work for him here. I must see what all this is about.'

Jegouzo reached for the receiver of his telephone, but then seemed to change his mind and dropped it back in its cradle.

'Lucille is probably tied up, with this "big" case. I'll call after you leave. Now, before we look at the file on the missing Countess, do *you* have anything new to show me, Miss Parker?'

Posie shook her head. For some reason, which she couldn't quite understand, she wanted to keep that strange note with the word 'LISTEN' and the horrible little clipping about the death mask to herself.

It added nothing, did it?

Nothing to this.

Instead she got out her timeline of the dates when she had last seen Dolly, and when it had been reported that Dolly had been seen.

Together, they worked through the dates, which matched exactly with what the Inspector had in his file.

He sighed. 'When we got the information linking your missing friend to this "fake" lawyers' office on the Champs-Élysées, we kept a policeman watching the place for months.' He snapped his thin file closed.

'I had to withdraw my man before Christmas, Madame. I had run over budget. And no-one was ever seen inside that office. Not once. *Jamais!* It was always completely empty. A waste of time. My superiors, in fact, I think it was Inspector Lucille, he ordered the money to be cut. The case is still open, theoretically, but, well...'

Posie nodded grimly, biting her lip. She understood that funding had been taken away. Richard would have ordered the same in the circumstances.

From her red folder Posie pulled out the one image she had of Caspian della Rosa. Medium-height, quite stocky and with short hair and plain small eyes in a strong face with a square jaw. She pushed it across the table, trying to avoid the ash and cakes and mess.

'Would you be able to show this to the man who was watching the "fake" office? See if he recognises him?'

Jegouzo munched on his cake. 'I will get it checked out, of course. It's Caspian della Rosa, is it not? But I can assure you we have our own library of photos. We have consulted them at all times. Although, as you are no doubt aware, he is a master of disguise…'

Posie saw the Inspector glance at his wall clock. Twenty-past eleven. He had nothing more to say.

Just at that moment she thought she heard footsteps at the office door, a pause.

She hurried on before he was interrupted:

'Oh! One other thing, sir. I think I have found out the full, proper name of Violette, the girl who worked as a nanny for my friend, Dolly. The girl we think may have been the link; the girl who called Dolly from the fake lawyers' office, and then disappeared.'

'*Non*!' The Inspector looked genuinely shocked, taken aback.

'*Mon dieu!* You have done awfully well, Miss Parker.' The big policeman picked up a fountainpen which was oozing black ink and sat waiting, ready.

Posie read aloud from her current silver notebook. 'The name I picked up in my research is "Violette Lagarde". Her former landlady gave me an address in Montparnasse.'

'*Montparnasse?*' The Inspector groaned. He pulled at his moustache. 'That will be like searching through a *meule de foin*, a "haystack", you say?'

Posie nodded, then read aloud the exact address. 'I'll go there maybe later today, sir. On the Metro, to the Vavin, that is correct, is it not? On the Nord-Sud line? I do appreciate you don't have anyone to lend me, but Inspector Lucille has kindly given me a Search Warrant, so I can have a look around.'

'Search Warrant' was stretching it a bit, really, thought Posie, slightly ashamed of her exaggeration, *but it made it sound like she had more standing than she really did.*

Which was always good.

A flash of alarm had crossed the Inspector's face. He quickly cast his blue eyes down and pulled out a drawer in his desk, then rattled around in it. He pulled something out, and checked a label on it. As he did this, Posie heard the footsteps at the door suddenly retreating, running almost.

'Here, Miss Parker.'

The Inspector passed across a key. 'This key is for the "fake" lawyers' office, on the Champs-Élysées. It's for Number 77, Galerie FF. I still have it, even though I pulled my man out of there. And while I do not have anyone to lend you, if you are in possession of a Search Warrant, then I am sure you can go and have a look: put your mind at rest that this is all a dead end. Then I should probably return the key to the administrators of the building. It is an empty space up there, but perhaps it will soon be sold or rented? There is the Porter who sits in an office by the lift. You could ask him to accompany you up, if you liked?'

'The Porter? Well, perhaps…'

Posie found herself gingerly accepting the key, tucking it away in the capacious depths of her bag.

She was slightly surprised the Inspector was willing for her to go looking about on her own, but he had seemed pretty awe-struck by her association that morning with the great Lucille, and perhaps Jegouzo didn't want to stand in the way of that highly-esteemed man.

Or maybe he thought he was helping Posie out, one final thing – *the only thing?* – he could really offer her which was in his gift.

But in Posie's mind she could hear Richard's voice, and his tart, strained warning:

'*...do not, I repeat DO NOT, go inside that address of the fictional firm of lawyers, Redon, on the Champs-Élysées. Got it?*'

Posie had actually agreed with Richard wholeheartedly, and hadn't even thought it a possibility she would get inside the building, mainly as she wouldn't have got the opportunity, but here she was, being handed opportunities on a plate.

'Thank you, Inspector. I'll bear this in mind.'

They both stood up, and Jegouzo walked her out of the building, through all the interconnected warren of offices with the never-ending telephones ringing and jangling, and the policemen scurrying around being busy.

And at the door, as she said goodbye, Posie heard him giving orders to the Duty Sergeant to telephone through to Lucille and then she heard him angrily muttering the word 'Durrant' over and over, several times. She saw him opening the door on the cage of the little green bird, and taking it upon his finger with what looked like a good deal of affection. She heard him speaking to it: '*Salut, Charlie! Comment ça va, Charlie?*'

What a funny, kind, odd type of man he was.

A bit of a loner, perhaps, among the Paris police. A maverick; a man who liked to do things his own way. Probably a thorn in the side of someone like Lucille. No wonder that misunderstandings occurred.

Outside, heading through the small courtyard garden, Posie tried to free her mind.

What on earth should she do next? There seemed so much, and yet so little to do, somehow.

And through all of it, Posie couldn't stop thinking about Caroline Greenlow in the early hours of that very morning; the blue face, the dreadful sickness, the desperate plea to Posie which had seemed to mean so much to the dying woman, and which had meant so little to Posie.

She recalled Lady Caroline's dying, dreadful words, spoken in pain and fear: '*I didn't kill him. Never. I loved him with all my heart. I would have loved him forever. And you must make that known, Miss Parker.*'

What on earth had the woman meant?

Had she been speaking of the child in her belly, an innocent borne away forever on a sea of reckless alcohol and poison? Killed before it was even given a chance to live?

Or was she speaking of a previous child?

Or a previous lover?

It had sounded as if Lady Caroline had been protesting her innocence in the face of some kind of opposite, established opinion.

But *what* opposite opinion?

Had it got anything to do with Caroline Greenlow's horrific death by arsenic?

Because, much as Posie disliked Charles Loxley, she didn't for one second believe he had killed his old foe in cold blood. He had been wronged, too, and deliberately, it seemed.

Yes, I must investigate all of this. And quickly, Posie resolved.

I don't have much time. And this was all before any consideration was even given to poor old Inspector Durrant and how he had ended up dead. And the way Suzannah Scotland and Daphne de Bengy were being held in custody on account of a crime they almost surely couldn't have committed.

It was all too much at once.

She wandered out onto the empty pavement of the street, the Rue Jean Mermoz, and found herself standing mesmerised in front of the toyshop window.

'Oh, I say! How sweet!'

For a minute all thoughts of Dolly, and Lady Caroline, and Alphonse Durrant, were displaced and she thought instead only of her three children, and the looks of joy on their faces when she presented them with the treasures on display here.

A simple but beautifully-made wooden black locomotive, very much like the one which had pulled the carriages of the Night Ferry train, curled enticingly on wooden tracks, with fake snow dusted all about. It was lit up cleverly with fairy lights, and Posie knew that little Kit would love it.

Adore it, in fact.

And in the very centre of the window were two beautiful dolls: one a girl doll, dark and sensible-looking, like Phyllis, in a little French school uniform; the other a baby-doll, ice-blonde, like Katie. They were positioned so as to be sitting with teddy bear friends, with a tea set arranged on a miniature picnic rug. Tiny paintings of the Eiffel Tower decorated the miniature cups and saucers.

It was all perfect.

Posie walked briskly into the beautifully-arranged but minute toyshop, where fairy lights twinkled and tiny model carousels spun around. She was the only customer, and she spoke to the very neat, bobbed-haired girl at the counter there, asking to buy the train, the dolls, and the tea set.

'Oh, and the teddies too, please.'

The immaculate girl smiled. '*Bien sûr, je vais emballer les choses*. I will package them all up nicely.'

Posie pulled out her purse which held the folds of French francs collected the day before in London. She moved to open it, and then dropped everything on the floor. Notes and travellers' cheques and old receipts were all over the place, coins rolling.

She stooped down, gathered it all up into her purse again, tried to regain her composure.

'How much is it?'

The girl named a fairly exorbitant price, which Posie had expected, and Posie started to pull out the correct money.

As she did so, she noticed her hands were dusty with a gritty grey ash which had a strong smell. She tentatively sniffed at her fingers.

It was cigar ash. Probably from the chair or the desk of Inspector Jegouzo's quite filthy office, which Posie had either tramped in here, then got on her hands as she touched the floor, or else it had been so prevalent in the air in the office that it had settled all over Posie's bag, and got into the purse and money itself.

Posie also noticed a tiny, tiny green feather on the floor, bright in its intensity.

How on earth had that got there?

She frowned, slightly puzzled.

I must have somehow got a feather on me from Jegouzo's office. Perhaps Charlie, the office bird, is really his pet? Perhaps it normally lives in his actual office?

The girl Posie had paid was drawing up a complicated receipt.

Posie checked her watch, a touch impatiently.

Half-past eleven.

She sighed. *I have so much to do. What, I don't know yet. But stacks… And my time here is short.*

'I can send these items to your hotel, Madame?' said the shop girl, politely, seeing Posie's harried expression. 'At no extra cost. I will make sure they arrive in the next couple of hours. Perhaps it is more convenient for you, too? You can then walk without heavy baggage, *non*?'

And agreeing wholeheartedly with this good idea, Posie left.

****

Chapter Twelve

Posie walked up from the toyshop, stalling and lingering outside 'Number 77' on the Champs-Élysées ten minutes later.

This was the address Caspian della Rosa had provided Posie with as housing his law firm. This was the address a 'Violette' had telephoned to Dolly from. The very same day Dolly had run away.

But if she'd been expecting anything very unusual, or illuminating, Posie was disappointed.

Number 77 was a building like all of the others on the Champs-Élysées; smart and perhaps ten storeys high, festooned with immaculate gleaming balconies and replete with fluttering French flags. A jewellery store took up all of the lower floor of Number 77, and its turquoise awning, rich with gold lettering, lent the place an easy, old-fashioned opulence.

Posie peered to the immediate side of the jewellery shop, where an archway in the yellow-grey stone housed a sparkling glass door under a big carved '77', and she saw that inside was a very smart reception, with creamy marble floors and a gleaming golden birdcage lift.

There were dark-wooden pigeon-holes for mail running the whole side of one wall, and a mosaic of the skyline of

Paris in the current art-deco style taking up the whole of the opposite wall.

Posie stepped closer, her hand almost on the polished door handle.

The Porter was sitting at a desk, dressed in a smart burgundy livery, writing letters, engrossed, his capped head turned away from Posie.

Posie grinned. This chap was nothing like good old salt-of-the-earth Ted, at Museum Chambers. The comparison was laughable, and yet Posie knew which Porter she preferred.

Posie then stepped back slightly, terrified for some reason that the Porter would look up and see her, and also very aware of the key to the place, almost burning a hole in her carpet bag, and of the possibilities it might, or might not, unlock for her.

Later.

Perhaps later.

Besides, Posie felt uncomfortable. Ill at ease outside Number 77.

In fact, the unease had started when she left the toyshop.

All the way down the Champs-Élysées she had had a pin-prickly feeling down her neck which normally meant someone was following her, or looking at her.

She'd turned several times, but no-one had ever been there. No-one in *particular*, that was.

Of course there were crowds of people, it went without saying: a mass of bundled-up tourists in thick coats and scarves, and office workers, out for errands or an early lunch.

But once, *just once*, Posie had had the sense of a man turning away from her hurriedly, a blur of brown which had flickered away into nothingness.

And it was the same outside of Number 77. She had the clear and horrid sensation that someone was directly behind her, a little way off, on the pavement, watching what she was doing, biding their time.

I'll catch you out.

Again, she turned, whip-fast, and again a flicker of movement near the empty bench under the nearest tree made her worry.

This is the reason I will not go inside this building, she promised herself.

Out in the open I think I am fine. But inside, I am done for.

But perhaps I am simply becoming paranoid after all that has happened?

She scurried on to her hotel, the Maigret, which was only a few comforting minutes away.

The Rue de Berri, just off the sleek, immaculate Champs-Élysées, was a sliver of a narrow connecting street, made dark by the high, rising houses on either side.

Here the pavements were not the golden, polished marble of the main thoroughfare, but rather a greasy grey stone covered in lumps of dirty snow.

Carts and horses obviously used this street for delivering to the modest hotels lining the street, and motor-taxis were also parked up here, their horns mercifully quiet, as the drivers used this slip of a road for a quiet snooze between fares.

Patrons entered Number 8, Rue de Berri at street level, through a huge double wooden door, but that was the only grand thing about the place.

The entrance inside was all brown, with shiny brown tiles on the walls, and it was dimly-lit with one antique chandelier which had had most of its electric bulbs removed. Those which remained flickered unreliably.

There was no Porter.

The hotel took up only the top floor of Number 8, and you had to take a ramshackle birdcage lift up to it.

Posie was intensely cold and more conscious of her very damp feet with every passing second. They felt like they might freeze up.

I must warm up. Change.

The lift wheezed up to the tenth floor, and Posie stepped out.

Here, the place was flooded with light, and it was very bright and clean, but not for the very tall, as it was made up of attics. It also felt wretchedly draughty.

'*Bonjour, Madame. C'est Miss Parker?* From London?' A smart young man with unruly red hair sat behind a tiny reception desk, eager and welcoming.

'Yes, that's me. I say, can I use your telephone?'

'Of course. It's half a franc per minute. You pay immediately at the end of the call. Exact coins only, Madame. You start now, and I will time you. *Oui?*'

He took off his watch and studied it intently.

And so Posie turned her back on the receptionist, picked up the receiver and placed an international call with the French Operator, trying to reach Richard at the Adelphi in Liverpool.

She was acutely conscious she hadn't yet spoken to him, although Inspector Lucille had obviously done so. And she'd promised to make regular contact. Her experience standing outside Number 77 on the Champs-Élysées had made her feel vulnerable, and she wanted Richard to know she was okay.

In fact, she'd almost sent a telegram at the busy little Post Office on the corner of the Rue de Berri, but she'd charged on, anxious to change and get warm, telling herself she was being over-cautious about everything.

The call was quickly connected by the English Operator, and the line was good and not a bit crackly when a receptionist with a Liverpudlian accent eventually answered the call.

'I need Richard Lovelace, the Chief Commissioner. He's not there? Can you take this quick message for him? I need him to have my address here in Paris. I don't think he has it yet. Yes, I'm his *wife*.'

Feeling she had at least discharged her duty in

reassuring Richard as to her whereabouts, although not to a particularly bright receptionist, Posie paid her one-franc-fifty, and then got a tour of the Hotel Maigret which she hadn't asked for from the red-head.

He proudly showed her a cramped breakfast room tucked under the beams of the attic, with a view out across the dark street.

'Mnnn, lovely.'

Neat white sofas were placed at the back of the breakfast room, and a couple of American women tourists were looking at a map of churches and pointing excitedly, with coffee on the table in front of them, alongside newspapers in French and English and German.

An elderly English vicar was sitting in a rattan chair, reading a copy of *The Church Times*.

Posie wondered briefly if she should say hullo, be polite. But her damp feet niggled at her, and she felt a shiver building up through her entire body.

So, so cold.

'Monsieur, is there any hot water? Do I need to pay more for it as it's not the early morning? I would love to draw a bath.'

'*Mais, oui*. Of course. I will go and run it for you. Normally baths are only allowed up until eight o'clock in the morning. But we can make an allowance for you: the hotel is not full *maintenant*. We have only a few guests, with all this snow.'

The hotel receptionist then showed Posie a white corridor with a line of doors running along it, ten rooms in all, with two bathrooms located at either end.

'If you need bath towels, it's twenty centimes per item of fresh linen. If you need soap, it's the same again. A sachet of perfumed bath salts, the same price. A bottle of essence, same. The scent we use is very luxurious: "4711". There is no change given, I'm afraid. Exact coins only.'

'Fine. Bring me all of those things, with a towel.'

Posie pulled off her gloves, dug around in her purse and counted out four silver coins of twenty centimes apiece, and passed them across to the lad.

A small green feather suddenly floated down to the floor, and Posie ignored it, thinking it was probably the same one from earlier, but the receptionist watched it, blue eyes wide and disbelieving, horrified somehow, as if she had just performed some magician's trick which had gone badly wrong.

He picked the feather up pointedly, almost theatrically, gave it back to Posie, who smiled tightly.

Some strange expression crossed the lad's face – he seemed genuinely spooked, actually very frightened – but Posie had no time to wonder at it and she hurried on: 'The *bath*, Monsieur?'

'*Certainment*, Madame.' The receptionist stopped abruptly outside door seven, and brought out a key.

'Your luggage arrived here about half an hour ago, Madame,' he said, still wide-eyed. 'From…' and here he dropped his voice to a complete whisper, frightened eyes darting about lest anyone hear, '…the *police*!'

'Ah yes,' said Posie, matter-of-factly.

Some lies here wouldn't go amiss, evidently. Playing things down.

'The police have been very helpful, actually. The train company had lost all the luggage of the passengers from the Night Ferry service. The police have retrieved it. It's nothing serious.'

'Ah.' The red-haired lad looked relieved, almost disappointed. He was obviously the sort to thrive on bad news.

'I'll run the bath now, Madame. I need to check the boiler in the cupboard at the end there: give me five minutes. I'll leave a key for the bathroom and the things you paid for outside the door here.'

'Fine. Oh, and get me a newspaper, would you, from

your breakfast room? One which won't be missed? An old one is fine. In English, of course. I like to read in the bath. And yes, I will pay you twenty centimes for it.'

'*Certainment.*'

Posie's room was simple, clean, small, with one neat single bed and one white desk, and a tiny basin with a cheap mirror screwed on the wall above it in a corner.

But what Posie mainly noticed was that it was cold in here, and there was no fire or radiator. It felt as if the room hadn't been heated for months, years, and couldn't get warm.

One window in the attic roof looked out over the sloping, jagged vista of the shiny silver Paris rooftops, and from here she could just make out the top of the Eiffel Tower, scratchily black against the scudding grey of the clouds above.

Posie opened the window and threw out the green feather into the icy wind, snapping it shut again quickly.

She watched the green feather whirl away.

She removed her coat, scarf and hat, then kicked off the wet pink shoes and peeled her damp stockings from her chilly legs.

Delving into her carpet bag, she got out her red folder about Dolly, and placed it on the white desk, on the far left.

Scrunched at the bottom of her bag, Posie found the horrid note she had received last night, on the Night Ferry. She snatched it out and pressed it open carefully, and laid it, with its accompanying grisly newspaper cutting, on the desk on the left-hand side.

The desk looked pretty impressive now, actually. Like the workplace of a detective worth their salt; a detective about to crack a case with ease.

'Here I am, Dolly,' she whispered in a falsely-cheerful way. 'I'm nowhere nearer to finding you, but I'm not further away, at least. What all this means, I have no clue. But bear with me, eh?'

She took out the photograph she had brought with her of Dolly, and placed it on the left-hand side of the desk, too.

And then she went over to her small attaché case, which she had last seen in her berth on the train early this morning, and now delivered so promptly by the police.

Posie unzipped it and started to throw things out on the bed, willy-nilly: her black sheer dress from last night; her leather jewellery-roll, minus the sapphire and diamond earrings which, like an idiot, she hadn't thought to ask for back; her change of underwear and a pair of stockings; her slippers and her pyjamas, sealed in a brown paper police evidence bag; her make-up bag, which had obviously been searched through by men, the make-up compacts and perfume containers all open, lids askew.

The pyjamas.

They were what she was after.

To be honest, Posie was surprised the pyjamas had been returned to her, covered as they had been in streaks of Lady Caroline's vomit and perhaps even poison.

It was possible that the French police had not made the connection with Lady Caroline's death, and had assumed it was Posie who had been ill in these clothes.

She had simply left them on the floor of her berth, after all.

Or perhaps they had made the connection, and had tested the clothes, and found them safe?

Whatever the case, the pyjamas and the slippers would need to be thrown away immediately.

But Posie needed to check something first.

She took a large pair of tweezers from her make-up bag, grabbed up the hand towel from the sink and tore open the paper bag, careful that her skin didn't come into contact with any of it.

Posie nearly gagged.

The smell was truly dreadful, and brought immediately

to mind the terrible last minutes of Caroline Greenlow, wretched in agony on that small, cramped bunk, up against the wall.

Posie willed herself on.

Is it still here? Or did the police find it and take it?

She was searching with the tweezers inside the pockets of the pyjama jacket for the jewel Lady Caroline had ripped from her own throat in a blind panic only moments before she died.

And oh, here it was!

A tiny hard object on a fine, fine chain.

The police had obviously been in a hurry. Missed this. Or thought it was Posie's? And left it well alone.

Posie felt a mounting excitement growing within her.

Would this help at all?

Help sort out whatever it was which Posie had promised to do for the dying woman?

She pulled the item out properly, clamped in the tweezers, her hands wrapped like a mummy in the towel. Automatically she sealed up the paper bag as best she could and left it on the floor.

There was a sudden knock at the door.

'Madame, the bath is ready. It's the bathroom on your right as you come out.'

'Thank you.'

And here it was.

Posie's heart sank.

This was not what she had been expecting.

She took the object to the sink and let the hot tap run over it, washing away any left-over poison.

Then she sat on the edge of the bed, and stared at the object in her palm.

On a golden chain, fine as lacework, was a single intricately carved bead.

A scarab.

Another scarab.

This one was different, though from the one Caroline Greenlow had choked on. Whereas the thing Posie had seen the night before had been plain, this little bead was outstanding. It was the same size; about the size of the French centime. But this one had diamonds for its eyes, and tiny rubies for its antennae, and sapphires picked out the detail on its folded wings.

It was obviously vastly expensive, and it had meant a good deal to Lady Caroline.

Posie flipped it over. Saw that the back was encased in solid gold.

Within the gold were tiny words: '*Spread yourself over me, so that I may be placed among the imperishable stars and may never die.*'

Posie rose, shaking her head, confused.

But it was more than that: she was deeply worried.

She placed the charm on its chain on the very far right of the white desk. She looked from Lady Caroline's precious necklace to the horrid note she had received.

She drew the note right into the middle of the desk.

'Two lost women,' she whispered to herself. 'Nothing linking them at all. And who knows how many imperishable stars there are in this dratted case?'

Something made Posie throw her coat over the small desk, hiding what was there from view.

There had been something about the red-headed lad she hadn't quite trusted – a ghoulish curiosity, perhaps? – and she wouldn't have put it past him to break into the room with a copy of the room key, to search about.

She locked the door and then left her room and walked to the small, immaculate bathroom with its clean scent of soap and fresh paint amid the rising steam from the bath. She was carrying the items the lad had left out for her, including yesterday's edition of *The Daily Observer*.

She planned to read it in the bath, which, for all the small annoyances so far, was actually very hot and deep.

Posie threw all the scented stuff in the water, undressed, and settled down for a good soak, letting the water work its magic, heating her freezing body and easing her addled mind. Washing away the stink of the dying woman, of the train, of a pretty awful journey.

But she didn't have the luxury of staying in the bath very long.

She'd only just started reading a story in the newspaper which had immediately caught her eye, when an urgent knocking sound interrupted her.

'Hullo?'

'Madame, sorry to disturb.' It was the receptionist's voice, tentative, apologetic, the other side of the door. 'But you'd better come quickly.'

Posie sat up, sloshing water all over the floor. 'What is it?' she called.

'A friend of yours, Miss Parker. She says so, anyhow.'

No-one, except the police, knew she was here.

A rush, a thrill of excitement flooded her veins suddenly. *Could it be Dolly?*

That would be wonderful, easy. The case done, finished already.

Or, if not, perhaps it was the mysterious Violette, somehow alerted to the fact Posie was looking for her?

This would also be good, if she had come of her own volition and not as a spy or employee of Caspian della Rosa.

Even if it was just to protest she had not been involved in any of it.

Perhaps, thought Posie suddenly and hopefully, *it had it been Dolly or Violette who had been tailing her today, accounting for the pin-prickly feelings?*

And if so, it was nothing at all to do with the dark unfathomable reaches of Caspian della Rosa's vast network of paid employees and spies.

'A friend? A woman, you said?'

'Yes, Madame. A woman. I have put her in your room. *L'étrangère, elle pleure…*'

'Do I understand you correctly, Monsieur?' Posie got out of the bath, took the scratchy, small, inadequate hotel towel, hurriedly dabbing at herself. Good job she hadn't yet decided to wash her hair.

'Did you say someone is *crying*?'

'*Oui*. You had just better come out, Madame.'

Posie was pulling on her pink dress again. She had no stockings with her here, and no slippers anymore, either, but no matter.

It seemed she was destined to be cold again in a matter of moments in this hotel.

Posie grabbed at the damp *Observer*.

'On my way.'

****

Chapter Thirteen

Posie rushed to her room, where the door was ajar.

A tray with a cafetière of strong coffee, two cups and a plate of plain biscuits had been placed on the floor outside, and Posie felt immediately grateful to the red-haired lad, and guilty she hadn't warmed to him before. Nor trusted him. She'd read too much into his worry over that stupid green feather.

She picked up the tray and shouldered her way into the room eagerly, anticipation building.

Who would it be?

Could it be…

But no.

Posie's heart fell, just a little, the excitement in her releasing like air from a filled balloon.

'Miss Parker?'

It was Suzannah Scotland, black tresses wild about her shoulders; her make-up gone, washed away by tears which hadn't yet dried.

She looked simply dreadful and sat perched on the single bed in the very small room. It seemed even smaller now that there were two of them in here.

Posie tried to hide her disappointment and smiled what she hoped was a convincing welcome. 'Oh, er…hullo!'

How had Suzannah found her?

But then Posie felt a snap of relief.

The police had obviously finished with Suzannah, at least.

They obviously hadn't been able to find enough evidence or grounds for her to be charged with Durrant's murder, no matter what assumptions they had made.

Posie hoped Daphne de Bengy had been released, too.

'I hope you don't mind me coming here like this, but I had nowhere else to go.'

The woman rubbed at her eyes. 'And I had no-one else to turn to.'

Posie glanced about the room and saw that Suzannah's large battered black case was stashed in the corner, near the white desk, taking up a lot of room. Her scruffy old black coat was thrown on top of it.

Posie took a deep breath and headed towards the desk, putting down the tray on the floor.

She noted that Suzannah had returned the earrings, and had left them sitting on top of Posie's green coat, where they caught the only bit of sunlight filtering through the white room, and they twinkled beautifully.

Posie put the jewels quickly into her leather jewellery roll, and then moved her own coat and set up the coffee tray properly in a gap between all her paperwork. She pressed the handle down firmly on the cafetière and then poured.

'Here you go.' She passed Suzannah a cup.

'So, what's happened?' she asked gently, sipping at her own coffee, which was lukewarm at best, and sitting down on the flimsy desk chair.

'And how, if you don't mind me asking, did you know where to find me? Not that I'm not happy you did find me; don't get me wrong. I'm very happy. I'm just curious.'

Suzannah blushed slightly beneath the tears, shrugged.

'I've always had a photographic memory,' she said, somewhat apologetically. 'I saw what you'd written on that blue paper on the train, early this morning, when

Inspector Durrant asked for our addresses, and I suppose I memorised it. I would have tracked you down anyhow, whether in Paris, or London, to return those lovely jewels you lent me, for which I thank you. I felt beautiful.'

Posie nodded.

She had to approach it.

The topic of Durrant. But how best? Had Inspector Lucille even told Suzannah why she had been held? Or what had *actually* happened to Durrant? It all seemed so hush-hush.

Posie swallowed uneasily. 'You were held by the police this morning, is that right? In a cell? What happened, Suzannah?'

Suzannah froze, covered her face in her hands, spoke between her long fingers. 'They say he's dead. Stabbed, in a frenzy. *Le pauvre*. I can't quite take it all in.'

The woman didn't cry, but took a long shuddering breath. 'They accused me of attacking Alphonse. This great big blonde policeman in a cape kept shouting at me, telling me I had killed Alphonse as we had had a night of passion, and that I was angry when Alphonse refused to leave his wife for me. But that is *not* true. We never even got on to discussing a wife!'

Suzannah shook her head, placed her hands carefully together in her lap.

'We *did* have a night of passion, that is correct. But I would never have hurt him. *Never*. Alphonse was a wonderful man. It's true I *did* try and follow him, early this morning, after he'd collected up those blue forms. He seemed to be heading back to his berth. You may not have seen? You looked like you were falling asleep at that table... I didn't even tell those *gendarmes* where I was going, and they didn't try and follow me; they had a good deal to do. I only wanted to get my silky scarf back; I'd realised it was missing and thought it must be in his berth. I use it for everything...'

Posie nodded, encouraging the woman: 'So you followed Inspector Durrant? What happened next?'

'Nothing.' Suzannah bit at her pale lips. 'When I got to his berth he was already in it, and the door was locked. I knocked but there was no answer. I could hear him talking though, to someone in there, and he was angry. Angry like you wouldn't believe.'

'Did you hear the voice of the person he was talking to?'

'No. It was only Alphonse who raised his voice. But they were speaking in English, I'm certain. I heard the word "school" mentioned by Alphonse, I'm sure. And the word "love", again and again.'

School?

Love?

These terms were too abstract for Posie to do anything with, so she hurried on.

'What did you do? Stand there for ages? Your berth was locked, like everyone's, but I don't think you came back to the Pullman car, did you? I didn't see you again.'

Suzannah explained that something odd had happened.

She *had* hung around the corridor, sitting there on the floor, waiting for Alphonse's visitor to leave, but after a bit she must have dropped off, fast asleep.

And when she'd come around, it was nine-thirty in the morning, and the train was drawing into the Gare du Nord.

Suzannah had awoken to find herself locked in a bathroom of one of the empty, unused berths in Car Number Two.

There had been a bloody knife in the sink of the bathroom where she had been locked, and when the police found her there, they had naturally thought the worst.

But the knife had since been tested for fingerprints and none had been found. It was clean as a whistle.

The police had had to let Suzannah go, albeit unhappily, and with plenty of threats of further action.

'*Oui*, but the strange thing is that the dark beautiful

girl, Daphne de Bengy, the Wardrobe Mistress, she had almost the same story to tell. *C'est incroyable.*'

Posie tried to look surprised by this. But in truth, not much would surprise her anymore.

Suzannah explained. 'Daphne says she had sought permission to use the allocated toilet, and then the next thing she remembers is being whacked around the head by something heavy. She woke up this morning in a locked toilet too, in another unused berth. It was in Car Number Two, but it wasn't Daphne's own berth. And there was Alphonse's bloody tie in the sink of the bathroom she was locked inside, and so the police had it in for her, too.'

'Is Daphne still in police custody?'

'I think so, yes. She was calling her employer frantically on the telephone, all the time in handcuffs, trying to explain, but it did not sound good.'

Posie blew out her cheeks in exasperation.

'We will have to help her then, won't we? Fix things up with her employer. We *must* get the French police to back down and find the real culprit. I must admit this murderer is chillingly cool and effective: they must have killed Durrant and then, when the opportunity arose to frame you and Daphne, minutes later, they must have looped back, returned to the body and stolen Durrant's fob of master keys for all the berths. They must then have locked Durrant's berth, and locked both you and Daphne in those empty bathrooms. It's a confident hand, isn't it?'

Suzannah nodded, dark eyes big and scared.

Posie tried to sound upbeat: 'My husband's Sergeant is coming over later: he'll help Daphne, I'm sure. He's called Fox. What I really hate here is that this whole thing smacks of fixed evidence, and the French police have taken it all at face value. It's dreadful.'

Suzannah nodded again, stifling tears. 'But at least Daphne had a job, and an employer. It was *real.* And if she walks free, she can try and get them to understand, can't she? Plead her case?'

Real?

An employer?

What the blazes was Suzannah talking about?

Posie waited, saying nothing.

Something had obviously happened to Suzannah this morning which had nothing at all to do with Inspector Durrant and his dreadful death, and nothing to do with the despicable way she had been treated by Sergeant de Caunes.

Because every little speck of joy in this woman had gone.

Suzannah sniffed, and at last she spoke. 'Something awful has happened to me, Posie. As soon as the police were finished with me earlier, I decided I needed to freshen up and I went to the hotel, the Raspail, which was booked for me on the Avenue Kléber. I was longing for a bath.'

Posie nodded, encouraging the girl. 'Nice.'

'It wasn't. The people at the Raspail said there was no booking for anyone with my name, or in Mr Poiret's name. They were actually quite rude.'

Posie frowned, unsure where the story was going. 'Go on.'

'So, I thought there must be an administrative mistake, and I'd better go and see Mr Poiret, the designer, himself, as he had seemed to want me to start work right away, for Paris Fashion Week. It wasn't ideal, as I had wanted to look fresh and smart when I first met him, but I couldn't help that. So, I spent the only francs I had getting from the Avenue Kléber to the Rond-Point in a cab with my big bag. It's where his salon is.'

'And?'

But Posie knew that this story couldn't end well.

Had Paul Poiret, the famous designer sacked Suzannah on the spot because of her dishevelled appearance? Before she had even had a chance to prove herself?

But no: it was worse.

Suzannah took a deep breath. 'I'm used to difficult circumstances, Posie, *mais oui*. But this situation was awful. The man is a genius, obviously, and quite a pleasant man, under all the proud bluster and his silly yellow silk coat which is his trademark, but…'

'*But?*' Posie prodded.

'He nearly had me thrown out!' exclaimed Suzannah, her thick eyebrows raised in twin arches of disbelief.

'He was busy, of course, preparing for Paris Fashion Week to start. He said he'd never heard of me, and had never written to me. He had never answered an advert placed in an English magazine: why would he? He already has a perfectly good Parisian secretary right here! He said he didn't need anyone else, least of all me! Mr Poiret obviously thought I was crazy, and maybe I looked it: standing there with my suitcase, looking desperate, saying I had no money.'

Posie could imagine. Her heart sunk. 'Oh dear.'

Something suddenly struck Posie as strange.

'But what about the Night Ferry train? You got a first-class berth from London, apparently because Mr Poiret needed you with him urgently. Well, that was paid for by him, wasn't it?'

'I told Mr Poiret all of this. He said he'd never heard of me, and definitely wouldn't have paid for me to travel first-class anywhere. It wasn't him. It must all be a funny trick. A cruel trick.'

It certainly seemed so.

But why?

Who else would have wanted this odd, beautiful, clever, scruffy girl on the train last night?

For what reason?

As a distraction?

As a potential and conveniently-placed suspect in a murder case?

Posie bit at her lip.

The more she thought about it, everything about last night's train journey had been off kilter. Like the article she'd been reading in the bath, before she was interrupted.

'Suzannah, tell me what you think of this…'

Posie got up and picked up the *Observer* newspaper again. She read aloud:

'It's from yesterday's newspaper. "*The Night Ferry Service, previously a popular choice of travel to the Continent for many of our well-heeled readers, has come under fire in recent days. In the chaos following the recent inclement weather, most transport is now running as normal. Not so the Night Ferry! The service has been inundated with angry passengers trying and failing to re-book seats, and since Monday night the service has been forced to operate at its fullest capacity, running eight sleeper cars per journey, all with shared berths. There is still not enough capacity and the Director of the company, Mr Daniel Brookman, has said it may take several weeks for passengers to get a single booking and for the service to get back to normal. But passengers should certainly keep on trying.*"'

Posie threw down the paper on the floor, stalked to the window and looked out at the sliver of sky.

She rubbed at her arms to keep herself warm.

'This newspaper article accords perfectly with what Daphne de Bengy was told when she tried to get on the train last night at the eleventh hour: it was the "official line". Or maybe it *was* the truth, generally. Daphne was told at first that all the Night Ferry trains were full, booked out. But that wasn't at all true last night, was it? Our train last night was fabulously empty, and we only had two sleeper cars, not eight. And we were all sleeping in single berths! There were even spare berths, plenty of them! So, I think there was something fishy about our train. Something different.'

'*Mais quoi?* What was different?'

'I don't yet know.' Posie spun around from the window. '*When* did you get your letter from Mr Poiret, Suzannah? Was it on Monday, two days ago?'

Suzannah nodded, ashen faced.

Posie frowned. 'Same here. I heard on Monday evening that I could travel by yesterday's Night Ferry train. And Inspector Durrant was only ordered back to Paris yesterday, last-minute, by his boss, Inspector Jegouzo, and a berth was found for him immediately on the train. So, some of us were found places on the train at short notice, it seems, despite the apparent massive demand. It's all jolly odd.'

Posie picked up her coat, put it on. She was freezing, especially with her bare legs, and her feet on the icy floorboards.

She moved the coffee things off the desk and looked at the separate areas she had made for Dolly, and for Caroline Greenlow. Posie dragged her gaze away from Dolly's face in the snap and stared hard at the scarab beetle on its chain. At its luminous jewelled richness, its bizarre inscription.

Suzannah Scotland interrupted. 'What are you thinking, Miss Parker?'

'Please, I told you to call me Posie. And I'm wondering *why* you were on that train, if there was no work here for you. I'm also wondering *when* Caroline Greenlow got her invitation from Paul Poiret.'

Suzannah Scotland narrowed her dark eyes. 'Didn't her fiancé, that odd boy, Dadie, say she received it one week ago? He told us all at dinner, very proud.'

'Interesting,' muttered Posie, thinking very hard. 'Yes, I think you are right. And I wonder too if…'

Suzannah Scotland stood up suddenly, facing Posie. The tears had dried on her face and there was a tiny spark of excitement in her black eyes. 'Are you wondering if the invitation for Lady Caroline, for Paris Fashion Week and all the other stuff which went along with it, like meeting that famous photographer, Man Ray, was all a trick, too?'

Posie nodded, slowly.

Suzannah Scotland spoke fast. 'It could be! *Oui*, it could be. Because I saw that boy, Dadie, arriving at Paul Poiret's salon on the Rond-Point, right after me, clutching at the pink letter Lady Caroline had been sent. I presumed he was there to tell Mr Poiret about the tragedy, or perhaps to meet Man Ray? But perhaps Dadie Spence knew something was up: perhaps he'd turned up at *their* hotel and realised it wasn't paid for, either, and then thought he'd straighten it out with Mr Poiret, like I did. Realised they were caught in a trap.'

'A trap which has led to death,' Posie replied.

Suzannah clapped a hand to her mouth. 'Oh, and I've been so stupid! I forgot to tell you something important! Mr Poiret laughed at me when I showed him the fake letter, supposedly from him. He said anyone could have created it! He explained that last year, at the Art Deco Exhibition, the pink-and-gold notepaper with his name on the top was available to buy, in great big boxes. It was available on all of his barges, alongside his perfumes. So, the trickster could have paid for a box, and fooled lots of people, just for fun!'

'No,' Posie said slowly. 'Not for "fun", and not to fool "lots of people". Perhaps just to fool you, but mainly Lady Caroline.'

Whatever was going on here was sinister, not fun.

But what was going on, exactly?

And what was it which linked these two women who had both received letters on the same paper, purportedly from the same designer, bringing them here to Paris on the same day, on the very same train?

'Come over here, Suzannah.'

Posie beckoned and she picked up the beautiful scarab in her hands, holding the weight of its cold, fatal beauty.

'Do you recognise this, Suzannah? And I need to ask you: did you know Lady Caroline at all? From before? From some other time in your life? Or do you know something about her, anything at all, in fact, which might help us work out what is going on?'

Because the past throws long shadows, Posie thought to herself.

And not all of them are kind. Some are grasping, destructive.

She knew she was clutching at straws, but Posie was still disappointed by the quick shake of the dark girl's head, and she watched as Suzannah studied the scarab charm intently, turning it around in her palm, eyes transfixed.

'Does the charm mean anything to you, Suzannah?'

Suzannah sighed. 'Nothing at all. I've never seen it before, but it's lovely, *n'est-ce pas*? It's quite new, too, isn't it? It's not antique. You see under the mouth of the beetle, where the chain runs through it, there's a hallmark, and a large "C" for…'

'For *Cartier*?'

'Yes.'

'You're jolly good. I missed that.'

Posie picked up the beetle and she put it into her red-leather money-purse, and then she started to pick up her 'Dolly' items, too, placing them back in the red folder, packing up her carpet bag.

She didn't have much time, and she would have to make the best of it and go out, with or without Suzannah.

She pulled on her one fresh pair of stockings, smoothed down her coat, adjusted a brooch.

'Who was the blonde girl in your photograph, Posie?' asked Suzannah softly.

Posie sighed. 'She's the reason I'm here. Her husband has asked me to find her; she means a great deal to him. She means a great deal to me, too.'

'*You* didn't receive an invite from Paul Poiret on pink paper?'

'No. Nothing like as glamorous.'

Posie went to apply fresh lipstick in the mirror over the sink, and powdered her cheeks carefully.

She watched Suzannah in the reflection, digging out her own cheap red lipstick from a small scuffed leather handbag, and apply it in the mirror of a compact. Posie took advantage of this moment of shared frippery.

'Are you okay, Suzannah? About Inspector Durrant, I mean? You've had a dreadful time of it, what with his murder and now this shock over Mr Poiret.'

Suzannah nodded stoically. 'I'll be fine. As I said, I've been in worse situations.' She dabbed at the bright-red greasepaint, splodging a little onto her cheeks as well, a good old trick.

'You're going out now, Posie?'

'Yes, I must.'

'Of course. I'll leave with you.'

Suzannah was now over by her huge bag, opening it, tugging at its broken zip, and lots and lots of once-good, black, high-heeled shoes tumbled out. Suzannah thrust her feet into one of the pairs, patent leather with vertiginous heels.

But Suzannah was delving inside again. She grabbed a clothes-brush and tried to make herself neat, and then ran the same brush through her own hair, all to very little effect. Posie shuddered at the chaos of it all.

The woman had suddenly decided to talk, and she talked and brushed at the same time.

'I think the worst part, after Alphonse being killed, I mean, was the way this awful Sergeant de Caunes spoke to me this morning, when he was interviewing me. Like dirt! Like a cheap girl. We were waiting for the results of the fingerprints on the knife, and he was trying to get me to incriminate myself. He said that Durrant was a ladies' man, and a collector of waifs and strays, and a hopeless helper of those in need. And that anything was possible with Durrant!'

Suzannah shrugged, pulling on her own coat. 'I got the feeling he had been jealous of Alphonse, maybe? Even though he was now dead! Or that the Sergeant was angry at how things had turned out; that a plan had gone wrong?'

Posie nodded. *Yes, it was all a bit weird.*

Her thoughts were scrambling.

Perhaps it ran deeper than any of this?

What if Inspector Durrant had actually been much more senior than he had let on, maybe from the French Secret Service?

And rather than simply accompanying Posie to Paris, might he have been tasked with protecting someone?

Perhaps the police had had a tip-off to alert them that someone faced mortal danger?

And if so, had the police had something to do with the curiously empty train last night?

Perhaps by cancelling the places of other passengers who had booked, and limiting the number of carriages to only two – the bare minimum required to run – the police had hoped to make any protection operation they were running much, much easier.

That would make sense.

But it hadn't worked, had it?

And if Alphonse Durrant had actually been a policeman from the Secret Service, tasked with protection, he had failed spectacularly.

He hadn't even been able to protect himself.

Perhaps Lady Caroline's killer had realised what Inspector Durrant was tasked with, and had killed him because of it?

Or, as Suzannah had heard from behind the locked door, perhaps Durrant had confronted the killer with their crime and things had got nasty?

Poor man, thought Posie.

But there was no way of proving any of this, and for now she kept her thoughts very much to herself.

There was so much to think about here; and for the moment the picture was too confused.

Focus on Dolly now.

Posie looked at her snow-sodden pink suede shoes, pretty well ruined. She bent to pick them up.

But Suzannah Scotland was there first, with a black, worn, but fairly decent pair of shoes. Not too high. Obviously once nice.

'Take these, Posie. I think we're the same size.'

'Thank you,' said Posie, grateful for the unexpected stop-gap. She'd buy some more things at the Galeries Lafayette, later, and truth be told, she'd been dreading putting on those cold, wet shoes again.

There was a sudden knock at the door. Posie answered it, holding it slightly ajar, and found the red-headed receptionist outside, holding a stacked tower of immaculately-wrapped black-and-gold parcels.

'Madame? A delivery came for you. Toys, they said. It's very heavy, certainly.'

'Ah, yes.' Posie reached out for the parcels, anxious not to let the man see inside the room, with its chaos of clothes and Suzannah's old shoes everywhere. Posie put the boxes down on the floor and found a franc in her purse and pressed it into the lad's hands before snapping the door shut again, anxious to be away from those prying blue eyes.

Posie checked the room one last time.

Oh, she'd almost forgotten.

She strode to her duffle bag and pulled out a packet of pale-yellow papers, tied together with a hair-band. She shoved them into her carpet bag and grabbed at her jewellery roll and placed it into her carpet bag, too, without quite knowing why.

'What are your plans today, Suzannah?'

The woman, all ready in her outdoor clothes, shook her head. 'I don't have plans. Not anymore. I'll just walk outside for a bit, think about what to do. I don't even know how I can afford to get back to England at the moment. Perhaps I could volunteer here and do some laundry, or dishes, or something?'

'I don't think this is that kind of helpful place, Suzannah. It's a bit weird.'

'Another hotel, then.'

Posie opened her purse hurriedly, and split what money she had in two.

'Here. That's for you. Take it.'

She put one half of the money into Suzannah's hands and the woman looked at it, half-desperate, half-thankful.

It was a mixture of coins, notes and travellers' cheques. A jolly generous amount.

'Oh, I can't take that! It's too much. More than I'd use in several months at home! No...'

'Please. That should be enough to get you home to England, today, and then some over to get yourself going again, until the next job. But you are welcome to stay on here, if that suits you better; although I am meant to be leaving again tomorrow. Mine is a short trip. As I told you, I'm supposed to be working on a case, so I need to spend most of today out. The evening too, probably.'

Posie thought of Suzannah's excellent French, and her scruffy feminine charm, which could, perhaps, work to Posie's advantage when out and about, investigating.

If ever she had needed help, it was probably now.

Besides, she had had that strange sensation of someone following her around, hadn't she? And there was safety to be had in numbers.

'Or, Suzannah, how about you take that money as payment for helping me today: translating; investigating and so on? You would be most welcome to accompany me.'

'Oh, yes, if you're sure. Thank you.'

Suzannah looked relieved, and purposeful, too. She stuffed her half-share of the money into a small square purse at her belt, as if ready to earn it properly.

'Where are we off to first?'

'Montparnasse,' Posie said. 'And quickly.'

She was about to snap her own purse shut quickly, when she suddenly noticed something curled up, squashed, right at the bottom of it, almost in the lining. It was bright green.

She picked it out, dusty and bedraggled. It was the original feather from the floor of the toyshop.

So where on earth had the green feather she had thrown out of the window come from?

It was a mystery. As was so much else here.

* * * *

Chapter Fourteen

The two women walked quickly away from the busy Vavin Metro Station, south of the Latin Quarter, their high heels clicking on the salt-encrusted pavement.

Posie held onto her pocket map of Paris from Stanfords Map Shop, checking their progress as they walked.

They were on the bohemian-feeling Carrefour Vavin, which consisted of a jumbled clutter of packed-out cafés with bright awnings, most with smart rattan chairs and teeny-tiny round tables outside.

Braziers burned brightly, and large groups of people were at the tables; talking, smoking, arguing, pouting, kissing, drinking coffee.

Shouting. The noise level was high.

There were beautiful women in smart black furs, and others with wild theatrical headdresses and daring green and yellow lipstick, and there were young men in painting-overalls, and bare-headed men with big beards in tatty blazers.

A mixture of American voices and quick French chatter rose in the cold air like frenzied birdsong.

The most prized seats seemed to be at the very front of the pavement; an unobstructed view out onto the world and everything amusing in it.

One café was called the Dôme, and – with its red awning and fairy lights picking out its name – it looked very inviting. Waiters buzzed around with pots of coffee and the famous caramelised apple-cake of Paris, *tarte-tatin*.

Waiters at all the cafés were beginning to bring out tempting lunch blackboards with '*PRIX DU MENU FIXE, DÉJEUNER*' chalked on them in scrappy white writing.

Posie's stomach grumbled rowdily. It was midday, but lunch, or even a solitary piece of apple-cake, would have to wait.

'Here it is,' she announced calmly, taking a sharp corner. 'The Rue Delambre.'

'What number are we looking for, Posie?'

'Twelve. Apartment E.'

The street here was narrow, dirty, with many overflowing rubbish bins. But it had a distinctive feel to it, and then Posie saw that rather than grocers and bakers and fishmongers, which you would normally expect to line such a street, this was a street for artists.

Small second-rate galleries and stores selling paint and supplies, and a few rough-looking bars lined the road.

They walked past an all-night bar, with 'DINGO AMERICAN BAR AND RESTAURANT' emblazoned in gold above huge, dark, smoked-glass windows.

The smell of old beer and wine snaked out onto the street from the open door, and peering inside, they saw the place was rammed full with both women and men. A saxophonist was playing, and women were dancing in glittering cocktail dresses like exhausted shadows, as if it was already midnight.

'Goodness,' said Posie, coming to a stop at the very next door, which was a long, narrow townhouse of typical Parisian grey stone. 'I think Violette, my pal Dolly's French nanny, must have found London very boring if *this* is where she lived before. What a place!'

'I do not think we have seen the half of it, Posie.'

'Mnnn, probably not. The mind boggles. Here is Number 12.'

Posie ran her finger down a list of names written in ink beside various bells at the door. 'ISADORA DUNCAN, JULES PASCIN… Oh, there's a blank at "Apartment E". Top floor. It's the *only* blank, and there's no Violette mentioned here, so I think this *must* be it, or must have been it.'

She was about to ring when she saw the front door itself was ajar. She pushed at it.

'You think it's safe for us to go in, Posie?' asked Suzannah calmly, rubbing her gloved hands together for warmth. 'Are you expecting danger?'

So far, they had not spoken of Posie's case in terms of safety, and the name or existence of Caspian della Rosa had not yet come up.

'I think it's safe.' Posie nodded. 'It's just a girl's address. If anyone asks, we can say we are looking for Violette; that we are friends of hers from London.'

'*Certainement.*'

The place was not salubrious, and old, withered autumn leaves and industrial salt from the roads lay about the small entrance vestibule. There was a strong smell of alcohol and the stink of paints, all mixed together in a scent which suddenly caught your breath and burned at the back of your throat.

They climbed up six flights of tiled stairs, and didn't see a single soul.

On the sixth floor there were three once-white doors, all in need of a good clean and a new coat of paint. The middle one was obviously a filthy shared bathroom.

The door on the left, marked 'D' was closed, but the one on the right, marked 'E', swung open on its hinges, and it moved in a gust of icy wind. Posie hunkered down into her cashmere scarf.

'Hullo?' She rapped on the door. There was no answer. She pushed the door and stepped inside, followed tby Suzannah.

The place was empty, empty of anything except the cold.

The apartment consisted of two modest green-painted rooms with sloping attic ceilings. There was a small kitchenette, and a fireplace in both rooms. A wrought-iron Juliet balcony faced out from the bigger room over the dark, narrow, fascinating street, and the view was intriguing, with a bit of the Eiffel Tower again showing on the skyline, and otherwise just the higgledy-piggledy silver roofs. Both women stood at the window, as if waiting.

But for what? thought Posie, irritably. *Violette Lagarde, if this had ever been her home, was obviously long gone.*

It was a dead end.

Sighing, Posie turned, and then almost jumped out of her skin to see a stocky figure standing in the open doorway.

'Oh! I say, we didn't mean to intrude.'

It was a woman, silhouetted against the light of the landing. Large, boxy, wearing what looked like a summery kimono or a beach drape, with a short sharp bob. With completely bare legs and feet.

Posie stepped forwards, aware that she and Suzannah were fenced in, blocked in this flat, with no escape other than the useless, decorative balcony.

The woman stepped right into the room, came closer, and Posie saw she was holding a bottle of champagne. She was in her fifties, and was still very beautiful.

'I *thought* I heard English voices,' the woman said, in a soft, friendly American accent. She walked forward extending her hand. 'How divine. I'm Isadora. I take it you're looking for Violette?'

'That's right. I used to know her, in London.'

Posie stretched the truth here, but the woman in front of her – Isadora – barely seemed to be taking in what Posie was saying, anyhow.

Posie hurried on: 'This is the address I was given by Violette's landlady in London, as being her permanent Paris address. I thought I'd visit Violette while I was over here.'

'Gee, you're too late, darling. But only just.'

The woman took a swig of drink from the bottle. Up close her tired grey eyes seemed to hold all the sadness of the world, and her doleful mouth turned downwards, as if always on the verge of being about to cry.

'It's the oddest thing; I've known Violette for the last couple of years and it seemed like she'd always live here; she'd got a long lease on this place, you see, years back. But this morning, after coffee-time I suppose, perhaps eleven-thirty, if you stick to such conventions, there was a helluva noise and I saw she was moving out! I couldn't believe my eyes! There were men running up and down the stairs with her furniture and clothes; I thought I must be dreaming. Violette loved that apartment. I wondered privately if she'd got herself into trouble financially? They seemed to be bailiffs escorting her away. I saw her go down the stairs with them in tears, holding her cat.'

'Her *cat*?' Posie asked quickly, bluntly. 'It wasn't a bald cat, by any chance, was it?'

'Oh, how clever you are! Yes. You must have stayed in regular contact with Violette to know that; although I've never seen you here before. Yes, you're right. She got it last summer. July, I think it was. She had no name for it. Just "*Chat*"...'

These cats were ever so rare.

Dolly had obviously come here last summer, with her cat, and then she'd disappeared.

But why? And where to?

Posie described Dolly's distinctive appearance to Isadora, and asked if she had seen her here, on the Rue Delambre. She pulled out her photograph of Dolly and passed it across.

'Was this girl here last summer, Isadora?'

The woman took another swig of drink as she stared at the snap. 'No. I don't think so, sorry.'

Isadora shrugged. 'I'm out most nights, though, dearie, down at the Dingo Bar, with other Americans. So if your pretty little blonde friend came here at night, chances are high I wouldn't have seen her.'

Isadora shook her head in a stately way.

'But I don't recall Violette having any English visitors at all. And even the French ones were few and far between. There was a dark, tubby girl here last summer, very unfortunate-looking, with bad teeth and glasses as thick as the bottom of a bottle. But she was from Belgium. A cousin, I believe. Here on a library course, and poor as a church mouse, from the way she dressed. And occasionally Violette had men here, too, but then, don't we all? She had one who used to come over a fair bit, small, sickly-looking. Sometimes wore a beret. A funny little man!'

Isadora moved further into the biggest green room and stood in front of one of the fireplaces and stretched out a bare foot, into the fireplace itself, as if toasting it on an imaginary fire.

Her feet were blue and purple with the cold and Posie shivered at the sight of them.

'Gee, what's this?'

Isadora pulled in her foot quickly, as if she'd been stung; she held it underneath her, like a dancer, examining it.

'Oh, it's just some sticky resin, or floor polish, I suppose. Anyway, I'm sorry for you; for your wasted journey. I'm sorry for me, too. Violette was a good neighbour, and discreet too. Good friends are hard to find these days, huh? Violette was a nice girl; she was even willing to share her money around. She'd often help me out with my own rent, when I was short.'

Suzannah piped up. 'What was Violette working as? To have such money?'

An unfortunate and tawdry implication seemed to hang in the air and Isadora shook her head quickly.

'Nothing like *that*, my dear. She was a good girl. Last year she was working as a gallery assistant, or a secretary, or something, I do believe. On the Champs-Élysées. I don't have the exact address, but I think the job finished. And since then, I think she was looking for other jobs, but she always seemed to have enough money to live on, somehow. Perhaps this little man with the beret… Now, I must get on, or get back to bed, maybe. It's so hot in here, don't you find? Gee, I'm positively burning up.'

'Poor woman,' whispered Suzannah as they watched the woman teetering off.

'Gracious. If that's the same Isadora Duncan I believe her to be, then she was once very famous, and very talented,' said Posie softly, in awe.

'She was a dancer. But more than that: a marvel of the stage. *I've* never seen her dance; I was too young. But when I was a little girl, I remember my mother gushing about having seen her, once, on the stage at the Coliseum in London. Isadora Duncan was Titania in a ballet of *A Midsummer Night's Dream*. And she wore a dress made of real ivy. She received three standing ovations, and my mother said she deserved four. They say she's the most tragic American in the world: she had everything, and now she's lost everything. Even herself.'

And as they watched Isadora Duncan navigate the landing, stately and beautiful, although fallen on hard, hard times, they saw that she had something stuck to her foot. Where she had said it felt sticky.

It was something bright green.

****

They obviously weren't fashionable enough to get a seat right out on the pavement, but the food at the Dôme, and the general atmosphere made up for it.

Posie polished off a plate of omelette, and then ate a medium-rare steak, with crusty French bread and mustard, and then ate two pieces of *tarte-tatin*, which was utterly delicious.

Suzannah ate nothing, simply drank coffee and lit up several long, thin cigarettes, one after another, from a packet of Gitanes she had bought, along with a slip of matches, from a vending-machine by the Metro station.

She smoked them with obvious enjoyment, without a holder, with her battered copy of the *Picture Post* from the train on the table before her.

Here were Lady Caroline and Dadie Spence captured for eternity, the vivid colours giving the sense that these people could go on living for ever.

As if…

Posie suspected Suzannah normally smoked, or would have done so, but hard times had forced her out of the habit, and it was only now, having the luxury of change in her pocket, that she had resumed.

Dabbing at her mouth, finished, Posie was pondering what was nagging her about the magazine, when she looked up and caught sight of someone she recognised.

The person was two rows away, with her back to them, having been placed in the very front row of seats on the pavement.

'Look, Suzannah!' she hissed. 'Look who it is! Our friend from the train!'

'Oh? Who? Where?'

'Look! But what is *she* doing here, of all places?'

Because Posie had spied the black-clad, bent, small, hunched figure of the elderly Mrs Shepherd.

Her black lace mantilla was visible beneath a big black velvet snood which she wore half-off, as if she were going to a Catholic mass, or to a funeral. Mrs Shepherd was drinking coffee, and there was a carafe of red wine at her side, too, with two empty, clean glasses set up. A plate of cream cakes sat untouched.

'Is she expecting someone?' whispered Suzannah.

'Maybe.'

But as they watched, Mrs Shepherd poured out two glasses of red wine, and then took them in each hand, and lightly touched the glasses together, as if she were saying 'cheers'. She drank a sip of wine from one glass, and then from the other, then put both glasses down. As if she was taking part in a blessing, or a ritual, which was now finished.

'That's the loneliest toast I ever saw in the world,' muttered Posie, seeing Mrs Shepherd calling for the bill and pulling out money.

'Quick,' instructed Posie, also finding money and placing it on their table as fast as she could. 'We need to follow her. See what she's up to.'

'*Vraiment?*' Suzannah was stubbing out her cigarette, shaking off the ash from her lap. It had gone everywhere, all over her black coat and all over the white tablecloth.

Mrs Shepherd was already on her feet.

'Yes. Leave that mess. We need to move.'

In a mad rush, while trying to appear calm, Posie and Suzannah rose, pulled down their hats, linked arms, and walked a good distance behind Mrs Shepherd.

For an older woman, and one who looked so frail, she moved along quickly.

She slipped in and out of the groups of artists and tourists who thronged the streets, and past dog-walkers, and past cigarette-vendors and match-sellers.

They followed Mrs Shepherd with enthusiasm and deftness, sometimes hanging back in the shadows of shop awnings, sometimes in the doorway of a church, so as to be unnoticed if the older woman turned about.

They found themselves on a brisk walk down the busy Boulevard Raspail, then taking a sharp right, down the freezing, blowy thoroughfare that was Rue Huyghens, a road filled with schools and gymnasiums.

'She said she always visited a relative in January…' muttered Posie as they went along. 'Perhaps a teacher?'

But they walked on, south, crossing the big Boulevard Edgar Quinet, which seemed a place for night, rather than day, lined as it was with closed nightclubs and shut-up dancing bars.

'Where do you think she's going?' asked Suzannah, puffing slightly. Ahead of them were massive rows of tall, leafless trees, running along a neat grey wall.

'A park?' Posie didn't dare get her map out for fear of losing sight of Mrs Shepherd.

She'd also felt, once or twice on this fast, jittery walk, that someone was following them, really quite closely behind, and she'd wanted to turn around sharply on at least two occasions but hadn't done so for fear of losing their quarry.

Besides, she could just have been being fanciful and she didn't want to look paranoid in front of Suzannah.

They hurried on, keeping Mrs Shepherd in view. The old woman turned a corner, and so did they. She went through some gates. And so did they.

'Oh!'

They stopped, surprised.

It was a cemetery.

Montparnasse Cemetery.

And it was huge. Impossible to imagine in scale. Green Park, doubled, tripled.

It was an enormous space of frozen grass with trees and shrubs planted all about, with tombs and vaults built everywhere, as far as the eye could see, seemingly with no uniform plan.

Grey slabs and angels and crosses seemed to have been placed here in their thousands.

They watched as Mrs Shepherd stopped at a flower-seller's small stall, and bought a bunch of white hot-house roses, quite the biggest bunch on offer.

Other black-clad people milled about, and, for the first time, not wearing black, Posie felt conspicuous.

She stepped back a little, towards the gate.

'Suzannah. We don't need two of us here: you're all in black, and you blend in better. I need *you* to follow Mrs Shepherd. See where she goes. Is it a grave she's visiting, or is it an actual meeting? Keep your eyes and ears open. If you feel up to it, follow Mrs Shepherd some more. You've got coins, haven't you? Take a cab, if you need one. Try and keep your senses alert. If you're in trouble, or you feel like you are being watched, return immediately.'

'Return *where*?'

Posie frowned. 'Inspector Lucille is at the Police Judiciaire. We'll use that as a meeting point.'

She checked her little red wristwatch. It was just after one o'clock.

'My husband's man, Sergeant Fox, will be with Inspector Lucille in two and a half hours. Fox is a good man, very approachable. He will help us, if we need it. So please, go to that address and ask for Sergeant Fox. I'll be there too, at three-thirty. Wait for me.'

'Fine. Although I was already at the Police Judiciaire this morning, don't forget. In one of their horrible little cells! It's not exactly my favourite place.'

Suzannah was lighting up another Gitane, one eye still on Mrs Shepherd, who was starting to walk off again. Suzannah blew out her first hit of smoke quickly.

'Couldn't we meet back at the hotel, Posie?'

Posie shook her head. 'No. Not the hotel. Oh, and can I have your *Picture Post* for the next couple of hours? I've got to do some research.'

'Sure. I feel like I never want to see those faces ever again.'

And then Posie walked out of the cemetery, away from the trees and bushes and graves, and on to start her process of investigation properly.

She needed information, but it wasn't here in Paris that she would find it.

It was back in London.

Of course.

* * * *

Chapter Fifteen

Posie needed a telephone.

And the more public it was, the better.

She needed to be surrounded by noise, and by people, and not listened in on, not timed, not charged stupid hotel rates.

For these reasons she chose to go back to the Dôme, where she'd seen three public telephone booths inside the main hub of the café, over near the bathrooms.

She paced along, clip-clopping on Suzannah's unfamiliar heels. Once or twice she turned, that pin-prickly feeling very strong again, but there was no-one there.

Once, she even dived into a small empty Post Office, in order to get off the street and see if anyone was really behind her, to catch them out as they walked past on the pavement outside.

Inside, she'd found herself killing time by sending an unnecessary and pointless telegram to Richard, over in Liverpool, reiterating the address of her hotel on the Rue de Berri, and telling him she was fine.

She'd craned her neck the whole time to see if anyone stopped outside the Post Office, looking for her, but no-one came past, or darkened the doorway. Not once.

It was probably just the wind in the trees, or the rubbish blowing against the dirty snowy kerbs.

She set off again.

And as she retraced her steps to the Vavin, Posie's thoughts were twirling like an out-of-control spinning-top with too much information, and the result was a hideous, nauseous blur.

So, in all likelihood, it seemed that Dolly's unusual cat had made it to Paris. *But where was Dolly?* And where, for that matter, was Violette? Why had she had to up-and-leave that very morning? Having had an attachment to the same flat for years?

But now it seemed more and more certain, at least, that the Violette at the Champs-Élysées 'office' and Violette the nanny who had worked for Dolly in London were one and the same woman. Isadora Duncan had helped on that point; confirming Violette's last location of employment, even if the facts were, understandably, slightly skewed.

So what had Violette's role been in all of this?

And then Posie's kaleidoscope of thoughts twisted again. Another image spun in front of her.

This one was of the *Picture Post*. With its week-old news of a high-profile engagement.

'Oh! Blast!' Posie stopped suddenly in the street, mind clearing. 'Perhaps it's been staring me in the face from the very start!'

Had *this* magazine cover, or the news it had reported, become Caroline Greenlow's death sentence? Had it been her undoing?

Perhaps, yes.

Perhaps.

Because the timing fitted.

Just over a week ago that magazine had been published, and then Caroline Greenlow had almost immediately been invited on to the Night Ferry, departing one week later, as part of a staged deception designed to kill her.

But why?

Who wouldn't have been able to bear the news of her engagement to a strange but promising young man?

Was it someone else who was in love with Caroline?

Or was it someone out for revenge?

Lady Caroline had said the engagement was top-secret before the magazine 'reveal'. She'd hinted that nobody had known a thing. And so, whoever had been galvanised into action by this dramatic news had had to act very, very quickly.

'If this theory is correct, then the killer had lots to prepare,' Posie whispered to herself. 'It must have taken a superhuman effort of organisation. And a spectacular amount of money. Masses of money. The murderer would have had to do the work of several people in arranging everything.'

They would have had to have rigged up the whole of Lady Caroline's Paul Poiret deception, and got her booked onto the Night Ferry train, and then booked their own ticket on board, in what was quite a last-minute manner.

But this reasoning, and timing, ruled several passengers out immediately.

Posie knew that Lex Lennart, the rich American, had had his train ticket booked for a good long time beforehand, perhaps for months. As had Mrs Shepherd, who came out to Paris at the same time each year.

And Doctor Dance had come specially back from Africa for his annual talk at the Sorbonne, so he must have had his ticket booked a while back, too.

All these tickets had been booked before the *Picture Post* was even published. Before news of Lady Caroline's engagement broke a week ago.

So that ruled them all out.

And what of Dadie Spence himself? He was young, clever, seemingly opportunistic, and obviously 'on the make'. But what on earth would *he* have to gain from his fiancée's death? In fact, he had had everything to lose.

Although it would have been easy.

Dadie had been the one person nearest Lady Caroline at all times.

The scarab beetle in the coffee, the poison in the…

In what, exactly?

Well, poison could have been placed anywhere, and in anything, really. The punch? The golden hip-flask Lady Caroline had carried with her? And where was that flask, anyhow? No-one seemed to have mentioned it since the murder. Surely it would have been retrieved and tested?

Posie sighed. It would be best to keep an open mind, but Posie found she had already mentally struck Dadie Spence off the list of suspects.

And this only really left herself, Charles Loxley, Suzannah Scotland, Daphne de Bengy, and Alphonse Durrant. And none of these others seemed likely to have colossal wealth at the ready, with which to plan a murder in less than a week, for reasons as yet unknown.

Unless Charles Loxley had wealth?

And Charles Loxley was the only one currently suspected of the murder, and actually detained for it, because the police had discovered a stash of arsenic in his belongings, and a personal out-and-out grudge with Lady Caroline, which was bitter and public.

But a grudge wasn't enough to kill a person for, was it? And Loxley's grudge was long-running, not a recent thing.

So, what wasn't Posie seeing here?

Posie started walking again, the cold air and adrenalin pumping through her veins. Perhaps her theory about the engagement news one week ago galvanising a murderer into action was pure rot. A dead end.

It had been a good idea but it didn't work in reality.

She sighed.

What Posie hated most was that the murderer had cast a net of blame about for other so-called 'suspects' to fall into. Convenient people like Loxley, with his supposed stash of arsenic and his history of a grudge with Lady Caroline, or Suzannah Scotland with her identical pink 'Paul Poiret' invitation.

But why had Alphonse Durrant had to die, too?

Because, to Posie, these two murders were interlinked.

It had to have been the same killer, surely? Because again, with Durrant, the same technique of laying blame at the door of easy suspects had been used.

And that was unforgivable. It wrecked lives.

Posie was back at the café.

She stood in an empty telephone booth and rested her head against the beige baize of the backing cloth, which smelt of churches and old cognac.

Now get what you need, she told herself sharply.

She needed to make three calls.

Posie grabbed her silver notebook and her pencil from her old carpet bag, scribbled a list with three points on it, and fed the slot on the machine at the side of the telephone.

She picked up the receiver assuredly, asked for the International Operator, and waited, then gave the number for an office on Fleet Street. She asked for the editor.

'Connecting you…'

She fed the machine with another half-franc, and then another one, and then heard a man come on the line.

'Posie? Hullo, what's all this about? Rita here says the call is from Paris… News, is it? Real news? A scoop of some kind?'

Sam Stubbs was the editor of the *Associated Press*, a newspaper which had grown to have the second-widest readership in the country.

Sam was hard-working and a true news-hound, but he owed Posie virtually everything, as she had given him a 'leg up' in the business in the uncertain days when both of them were starting out, about five years ago.

As a result, he had never failed to make himself useful to Posie, offering her the vast resources of the *Associated Press* archive room on Fleet Street whenever she needed them, or even helping out by 'placing' stories, or locating the sources of stories, which was sometimes invaluable. In return, she sometimes fed him scoops.

But Posie didn't have a scoop for Sam this time.

She was painfully and acutely aware that Caroline Greenlow's death had not yet been announced publicly, and when the news broke in England it would be best if it were dealt with by Scotland Yard, especially with the Chancellor of the Exchequer being muddled up in the murderous mix, and being held in Paris as a potential suspect.

'Er…I need your help, Sam.'

'Oh?' Sam sounded wary, as well he had reason to.

'I'm a little pushed, actually. The front page needs to be "set" in under half an hour for the evenin' edition. We're only just back up and runnin' properly after the printers stayed home over the cold snatch, so I need to get our readership back and engaged. So, what is it? Is this about your Richard? I can't change the news, I'm afraid. Not even for you.'

'*Richard?* My Richard?'

Her heart contracted and hammered at her ribcage.

She almost had to stop herself from screaming aloud, but she heard the panic, clear as day in her voice: 'What's happened to Richard? Is he okay?'

'He's fine, Posie. Calm down. I didn't mean to scare you. He's fine personally, but probably not professionally. You haven't heard?'

'Heard? Heard *what*?'

'The big trial Scotland Yard were runnin' up in Liverpool. It's all fallen flat. Backfired like billy-o. The sentence was read out about an hour ago: the gang has been acquitted on all counts and they are all free to go. Scotland Yard, and the Commissioner, look right fools. The evidence wasn't strong enough. There are calls already for Richard to leave. To resign.'

Posie leant her head against the partition, closed her eyes, barely heard Sam Stubbs going on.

'Scotland Yard's failure will be front-page news today. I was just finalisin' which snap of Richard to place on *our* front page when you rang. There's a good one of him lookin' distraught; holdin' his Commissioner's cap in his hands apologetically.'

Poor Richard.

And she was over here, too far away to help. But she would help. *After this was done.*

Posie cleared her throat, spoke brusquely.

'I'm not calling about that.' She made it seem inconsequential. Which it obviously wasn't.

'I need three things, Sam. You know how I value you for information-gathering?'

'Mnnn.'

'I'm going to dinner tonight in Paris, with a big group. At the Blue Garret.' The name popped into Posie's head easily, smoothly, almost without thinking. 'There's a man I'm sitting with who I've never met before. Know nothing about. Lex Lennart? A rich American? You know of him?'

Sam Stubbs whistled incredulously, and Posie could imagine him grabbing for a pencil.

'Cor! That's like saying Nestlé is a milkman! You keep some company, don't you? Well, Lennart is American, that's true. But he's never over there. He's either in Europe, or Egypt. He could run the British Museum, from what I hear. He's an expert on ancient Egypt. You know the big quest to find Tutankhamun, in 1922?'

'Of course.'

'They say it was Lord Carnarvon who financed Howard Carter's expedition, but it's widely believed Lennart put his hand in his pocket fairly deeply for it, too. Gave a fortune. Some have said he lost his fortune over the whole affair, and others are starting to hint that his financial affairs in America are crumbling. Whatever the case, he was certainly out there. And so far, four years on, he's one of the only survivors. At least five of the main players on the dig have died so far. Tragic, innit? I reckon it's only Lennart and Carter left, now. Not that Carter likes to talk about it; he's gone notoriously quiet, reclusive even. You know, there's talk of a curse attachin' to all those who were there, when the tomb of Tutankhamun was opened? By Jove, nothing's happened to Lennart, has it? Is that why you're REALLY callin' Has the curse caught up with him?'

Sam sounded excited at this thought, but Posie quickly disabused him. But now she understood parts of the conversation on the train last night between Charles Loxley and Lex Lennart, when they had spoken of 'bad publicity' and 'suspicious nonsense'. It must have referred to gossip about the curse of the already-legendary Tutankhamun.

Well, this was interesting.

It certainly explained Lennart's knowledge of, and love of scrab beetles. But it got her no further.

Posie scratched off the first point, and moved hastily on to her second point.

'I saw the *Picture Post* has announced Lady Caroline Greenlow's engagement,' she said blandly. 'What do you make of it, Sam?'

'Mnnn. The wonderful Mr Spence, eh? He with the jolly lipstick. Yes, that *was* a surprise. But it's not "new" news, Posie. I think that was a week ago; the *Picture Post* has been delayed, like we all have, in bringing out new editions. I *am* fairly annoyed with Lady Caroline, though. She duped us royally.'

'Oh?'

'She agreed to an interview with us, a big magazine-style article with photographs and all the latest fashions, you know, for our lady readers. I wrote the copy personally. We paid her very well for it, and we had it finished before the big freeze. It was to celebrate her thirtieth birthday. She made a really big deal of it, reaching thirty, which is a bit odd, isn't it?'

'Oh? When was her birthday?'

Sam sounded cross.

'It hasn't been yet. It's next Friday, the twenty-ninth of

January. I only know as I've got my big newspaper diary right here with me, with all the articles we've already prepared, allocated to the correct day. Lady Caroline was adamant it had to go out on the *actual* day of her birthday.'

'I see. Did the interview contain any scoops? Off the record stuff?'

Posie stood with her pencil poised, but she was disappointed.

'Nah, it was a complete washout.'

Sam Stubbs sounded weary. 'Lady Caroline is known as a political animal, quite popular with women for all her campaigning, and popular with our male readers as she's so easy on the eye. I was hoping for something spicy, because she's known for being colourful: been an alcoholic most of her adult life, apparently due to some childhood tragedy.'

He laughed bitterly. 'But in our interview, she gave nothing away. It was all quite boastful, mainly about reaching thirty years old, but it was very flat, boring. As drunks often are. She drank steadily through the interview, from a gold hip-flask. And our talk certainly included nothing about an upcoming marriage to Dadie Spence! That's what I mean about being duped! She could have given us some *hint*. Romances are much in demand. And she's never been married before. So, this engagement news is big. We blimmin' well paid her enough.'

'Perhaps the *Picture Post* paid more?'

Sam made an exasperated noise. 'That sounds about right. I got the feeling money might be an issue.'

The pips started to go, and Posie fed the machine again.

'And has there been any reaction in any of the newspapers to the news of Lady Caroline's engagement, Sam? Perhaps something negative which came out immediately after the *Picture Post* scoop was published? Letters? Articles?'

'Negative? Well, Dadie Spence isn't popular. But most people have simply been concerned about the snow.'

'Sam, if you suddenly think of anything malicious you

might have seen about the engagement, or really anything at all, can you let me know? Or if you think of anything downright *odd*.'

She gave him Inspector Lucille's details and heard Sam noting it all down.

'Mnnn. Why the sudden interest in all this, Posie? You sitting next to Lady Caroline at dinner tonight, too?'

Posie shivered at the thought. 'Something like that,' she replied.

'That will be a mixed bag. She's quite abrasive. Well, don't turn her into one of your cases, will you?' Sam grumbled. 'Lady Caroline can quite help herself.'

She can't. She's beyond help, now.

And she wasn't able to help herself, even when she was alive.

'And why are you in Paris, anyhow, Posie? Is it for this wretched Fashion Week we're all being forced to cover? Such silly photos! At least the big fashion houses pay us to advertise, I suppose. That's something, at least. So, are you over there buying dresses?'

'No, I'm here looking for Dolly, actually.' But she said it without any excitement.

'Oh, Posie.' There was a slight sigh down the line. 'That old chestnut, eh?'

'That one. Yes.'

'You said you had three things I could help you with, Posie? What's the last?'

'You're not the best editor in town for nothing, are you?'

'Funny, aren't you?'

'Can I send Len and Sid around to your archive room today?'

'Is that all?' Sam had sounded relieved. 'Of course. And if there is a scoop out there, in Paris…'

'You'll be the first to know. I promise. Now you get back to destroying my husband's career with those lovely pictures of yours. Go on!'

Posie then placed another call, this time to her very

own office on Grape Street. She'd left the place, and Len in particular, in such a state yesterday that she hardly expected anyone to pick up the telephone.

But the telephone was answered in a friendly, cheery manner.

'Grape Street Bureau! 'Ow can I 'elp you?'

It was Sidney, their office boy. They'd had to reduce his hours lately as there simply hadn't been sufficient work for him.

There seemed to be a lot of noise in the office background, banging and thumping.

'What's happening there, Sid?' she asked suspiciously.

'It's Len, Miss,' said Sidney, matter-of-factly. 'He's havin' a good old tidy up. He's fair possessed wiv it! He got me in to help with the work; we're tryin' to contact all the lawyers we know, see if there's any work needin' done. Just to get them to take us on when the weather gets a bit better again. Oh, and he's got his parents-in-law in here too.'

Posie almost choked. 'What? Why?'

'He said he's tired of them eatin' him out of house and home, and they can jolly well earn their keep. They're clearin' the place, and cleanin' it too. Aggie has also been around, helpin' out.'

Pigs might fly.

But if this was part of some big reconciliation, who was Posie to object?

'Good. Well, that all sounds wonderful. But now I need your help, Sidney. It's urgent, and I'll pay you extra if you do a good job for me, okay? Get some cash out of the office tin, and get yourself over to Somerset House. Take a cab if you have to. Go now.'

'Right you are, Miss. What am I looking for at Somerset House?'

'A history, Sid. Births, deaths, marriages, and anything in between. We know a girl was born on 29th January

1896. But we need certainty here as to other things. Get all the official certificates you can.'

She gave him all the details.

'And then get along to the *Associated Press* archive room. Sam Stubbs knows to expect you. I want you to search for stories which feature Lady Caroline Greenlow. Go back as far as you can. See if there are any recurrent patterns you find, eh? If Len is free get him along too.'

She gave him her contact details in Paris. 'I'll be there from three-thirty my time. Can you try and call me as soon as possible?'

Posie imagined Sidney, who was getting on for seventeen now, scrawny and eager, jotting everything down in his notebook.

'Got it, Miss. Oh, and somethin' else, really exciting,' he could be heard turning pages nearby, as if checking a point, 'is that your Lagonda is ready! Brilliant, isn't it? The garage called yesterday evenin', at five past six, and again today, at half-past nine, askin' why you hadn't been to collect it yet! I said you'd contact them on your return.'

'Good.'

Normally this news would have been as exciting for Posie as it obviously was for Sidney, but today the Lagonda seemed far removed from her own bubble of experience, and certainly from the weirdness of Paris, and everything which had happened there lately.

For the third, very last call to the International Operator, Posie had to steel herself. Gather as much energy as she had. Because she was about to call an old adversary.

A man who had always, in the past, doubted her and put her down, right up until the point at which she had married Richard.

This old-style policeman was a hateful old moaner, but for the job she had in mind, he would be absolutely perfect. He wouldn't let up in harrying the truth out into the light of day.

'Can you connect me to New Scotland Yard, please, in London. Inspector Oats, please.'

Something had been troubling Posie about that Night Ferry train they had taken last night, even while they were on board. And certainly, ever since reading the article in the bath, her concerns had grown.

Because it seemed pretty certain to Posie that the train last night had been made to run artificially empty.

But why? And by whom?

She'd thought it might be the police themselves, as part of some protection job, gone wrong.

But increasingly it seemed unlikely. More complex, and darker.

Perhaps it was easier to start with *how* had the train been able to run empty? And that was going to be very easy.

Because at the root of all impropriety there usually lay a great heap of money. Bad, blackened, filthy money.

Whose money exactly, Posie still didn't know – not at all – nor *why* the money had been paid over, but perhaps if the existence of the money could be found, located, the donor of the money could be uncovered and rooted out.

'Miss Parker?' came a gruff, tying-to-be-conciliatory voice.

'Inspector Oats, golly, what a pleasure.'

'You're calling from *Paris*?' He made it sound like Sodom and Gomorrah rolled into one.

'That's right. I need your expert help here, sir.'

A lot of throat-clearing followed. 'Are you looking for your 'usband, Miss? I cannot help you there: I cannot vouchsafe as to his exact location. There have been some setbacks at Liverpool, unfortunately.'

More throat-clearing.

Posie made herself sound cheerful, gung-ho. 'No. It's not Richard I'm after, Inspector Oats. It's *you*, very specifically. As I said, your expertise. I have something which may be of interest. To the public interest, actually. A case of massive financial impropriety, Inspector.'

'Oh?' She could tell she had whetted the Inspector's appetite, and she'd crucially flattered him.

She could have chosen a younger man, someone cleverer. But Sergeant Smallbone, whom Richard favoured, was too inexperienced and had no gravitas. And Inspector Rainbird was too passive, and too slow.

Oats, older, was like a terrier, refusing to give in until he had the truth.

'Go on then, Miss. I've got me pen at the ready.'

'I need you to go and interview a Mr Daniel Brookman, at the Night Ferry train service at Victoria. He's the Director. Tell him you suspect fraudulent dealings with regards to his transport service: tell him you are investigating a report of financial impropriety connected to *last night*, sir. Regarding the Night Ferry train service which left last night for Paris. Tell him that withholding evidence is a crime.'

'Right. And will he talk?'

'I'm not sure, Inspector. You should put a notice out at all ports and airports that if Daniel Brookman tries to leave the country, he should be arrested and his bags thoroughly searched.'

'I see.' Oats sounded very pleased with all of this. 'And where is the evidence for this, Miss? What "report" am I meant to be dealing with here?'

Nothing yet. No report at all.

Just a lot of suspicion and a healthy dose of gut feeling.

'I don't have any names or details to share quite yet, Inspector, but by tonight I'll be able to give you the lot.'

'Fine. And is there anything else, Miss Parker? Apart from Mr Brookman?'

Posie had been wondering at the logistics of how it had all been achieved.

She was groping in the dark here, but the smallest of

cogs which had helped effect this murder could only have been oiled and forced to move with that same heap of money.

And where there was dirty money, there was guilt. And fairly often, guilty people ran away.

She nodded, certain: 'Yes, there is one more thing, Inspector. Sergeant Fox is working with the Paris Police Department, for Inspector Lucille, on a case which only blew up today. I believe he is on his way out here, now. But could you go through his file, and find two names for me? Names he will have asked for background checks on, only this morning.'

She fed another coin into the meter. 'One Waiter and one Driver. They are people who need to be questioned. If you can, bring them in. But I think for safety's sake you should also inform the ports and airports about these two people. In case they bolt.'

'Very good, Miss. Paris, eh? Very nice. Nice work if you can get it. Which Sergeant Fox obviously can. The lucky beggar.'

Then, with that bitter end note, Oats rang off.

And Posie was now out on the intersection of the Vavin again.

It was almost two o'clock, and the air was icy and petrol-scented, with a lingering note of linseed oil atop it all. A scent of oil paints maybe, and old, old cheap wine.

She looked about Montparnasse one last time: this was a place for dreams and dreamers. And dreams gone bad.

Not for her.

Posie got out her map, studied where she needed to get along to next.

The Sorbonne.

It was close. At the top of the Left Bank; a twenty-minute walk from here. And actually, the timing was perfect. Because now it was certainly after lunch; that 'dead slot', spoken of by Doctor Dance. Perhaps she would see him talking, in full flow?

But he was not the main reason for her journey.

She started to walk, patting the packet of yellow letters in her bag which she had brought with her specially, and she was rewarded by hearing the familiar rustle of the crisp letters through the scratchy carpet material of her bag.

It was a bag she loved, adored, even; which, despite Richard's pleading, she'd not yet had the heart to replace.

By contrast, the letters inside were unwanted, uncherished, needing to be returned. For Posie's peace of mind.

It was timely.

And now she headed for the Medical School at the Sorbonne, the best university in France. Where a few mutual interests coincided.

* * * *

Chapter Sixteen

He spoke well, Posie had to admit.

His talk was jokey, wide-ranging, light, but hinting at darkness.

She'd slipped in at the back of the full lecture hall, being nosy, and had gone in unnoticed, nearing the end of the talk.

The lecture hall was grand, built for more than a thousand students. Overheated, today. And the heat cooked the place: it smelt of hair oil, and musk, patchouli, but underneath there was a stink which couldn't be covered, and Posie realised with a start that it was the scent of formaldehyde; that preservation-agent for death in all its many guises.

Posie took off her outside clothes and looked about.

Golden velvet seats, and marble carvings above, and a red-canopied lecture stand lent the place the feel of a real theatre, and the slight figure of Doctor Dance, jaunty in a white Panama hat, and a carefully-pressed cream suit, was centre stage.

The way the lights illuminated him it was almost impossible to see the extent of his terrible injuries. And Posie felt very glad for him.

A panel of other doctors sat on red-velvet armchairs

behind him, like a set of chessboard pieces, waiting to play. Doctor Dance spoke in English, with a translator at his side, and he'd obviously been talking for a while.

After ten minutes, Posie rose, most of the talk on 'inoculation plans' having gone almost completely over her head.

She cast a last look at the small, far-off, illuminated figure down on the stage.

Heard him start to wrap up; a sort of endorsement to the students not to forget their general training.

'You never know what you may end up dealing with, as a doctor...'

Doctor Dance flipped over his lecture notes, apparently finished, but he spoke out into the darkness in a conspiratorial way, gripping the lecturn.

'Only last night, I was on the night train to Paris, when I was required to aid in the successful dislodging of a foreign object which had been ingested probably in a cup of coffee, and then rather predictably got stuck in a woman's throat.'

He spoke confidentially: 'And I have recently returned from a very remote part of Africa, where all sorts of black magic is still practised. There, as a medical doctor, you have to hold a difficult line: you must be courteous to local beliefs and customs, but try and help out where necessary, too. There the concept of "doctor" is different to our own, and poisons are much used, unfortunately. It's a particularly cruel way of dying. I've seen it. Hated it. Hardened my heart to it. Several times...'

He tailed off, as if alone, not in front of a thousand strangers.

Posie thought she saw his arms at the lectern begin to shake. He didn't mention last night again, on the train, but it must have been foremost in his mind. But then he carried on brightly:

'So, knowing the antidote to a poison, and keeping on top of your basic initial training in this area, may save lives one day. Because life is rich, and you never know where you will end up, or where you will be forced to run to. Or where the world will tilt on its axis and throw you, headlong. So, good afternoon, and I wish you all good luck!'

Posie slipped from the room, hoping to avoid the crush, as the hundreds of students in their identical flapping black academic robes stood to leave.

Behind her a mad, frenzied chatter was breaking out.

She pulled on her coat as she went down a magnificent set of stairs, drew the cashmere scarf up over her head, pulled out the packet of letters from her bag, and entered a cavernous entrance hall.

Black wooden boards were the only decoration here; gold-inscribed with the hundreds and hundreds of names of male students who had died in the Great War.

It was a sombre place. A focus of nothingness, except for the record of death everywhere.

But Posie was looking specifically for student pigeon-holes.

She was holding on to the yellow letters, and she had in mind to return them to their owner, by depositing them in his pigeon- hole.

Casting about, she saw a small ante-room over on the right, and she headed there with some relief.

This whole situation with the letters was awkward. Jolly wrong, too.

It had all started at the same time as Dolly had disappeared, last summer, 1925. Back then Posie had met a French boy on one of her cases.

His name was Count Anatole de Poilac. He had been almost eighteen. And he had been part of a group who had witnessed a murder.

Posie had given him no encouragement of any kind to think there could ever possibly be anything romantic between them, and yet Anatole de Poilac, a medical student at the Sorbonne, had started up a completely one-sided correspondence with Posie.

And these letters had arrived ever since, sent regularly to Museum Chambers, at the rate of about one a week; missives written on primrose-coloured paper with an emblem of a golden peacock atop them all.

They were teasing, chatty, humorous letters, in a charmingly almost-perfect English, full of details about life as a medical student, with various mentions of friends acquired along the way, and girls, too; who had mostly been lost along the way.

But at the bottom of it all, what marked the letters from Anatole out as odd was that there was always a subtle undercurrent of lust, of desire, and of a sense of holding out a hope for some long-term resolution within the carefully-written pages.

And despite never having written a single reply, and having burnt a good many of the letters before Christmas, the letters from Anatole had continued to come.

This needed to stop, now.

Posie stood in the small ante-room, scanning the hundreds of narrow pigeon-holes for names. Here it was.

'*POILAC.*'

She stuffed the bundle inside, heard a corner rip, the paper tear, but she turned quickly.

Job done. Message conveyed.

Hopefully Anatole would write no more.

A young man in shirtsleeves and flannels with floppy hair and his dusty black robe thrown carelessly over one arm, was pinning fresh notices to a board which took up part of one wall. Posie lingered out of interest, seeing that most of the notices were about lectures, and rooms for rent, and for some sports clubs. Swimming, fencing, indoor tennis.

But then something caught her eye.

Mainly because it was written in English.

THE BLUE GARRET CLUB welcomes you to an EVENING WITH TUTANKHAMUN!

Meet those who were there at the opening of the ***LEGENDARY*** *tomb.*

Handle some of the **TREASURES** *yourselves.*

Ask questions about the ***FAMOUS CURSE.***

(Location: Wednesday 20th January, 8pm. Rue Lepic.)

(Cost: Seventy francs per person.)

SPECIAL GUEST: LEAD ARCHAEOLOGIST HOWARD CARTER!

'Golly!'

Posie now realised what it was that Lex Lennart had been travelling over for. A talk, not a simple dinner.

But Mr Lennart didn't seem to be the sort who would relish public speaking, nor a gathering of this sort.

Perhaps the famous Mr Carter would come up trumps? Because Lennart hadn't seemed very sociable at all, really, and this talk at the Blue Garret – which was planned for tonight – seemed by the very nature of the invitation to promise a cosy sharing of secrets.

But what shocked Posie most of all was the price.

Seventy francs was an exorbitant amount to charge! Even for well-heeled students at the Sorbonne.

The student in shirtsleeves turned, smiled, with a stash of old notices in his hands which he'd just ripped down.

Posie pointed at the one about the Blue Garret, and asked in her haltering French:

'*C'est une vieille publicité?*'

The boy laughed.

Spoke in a clipped, upper-class English accent. 'Don't worry, I speak English; I was at prep school there! And no, it's not an old advert. I only put it up early this morning. Even so, there's been a lot of interest. In all of my five years here so far, I never saw interest like it! I would imagine that talk will be packed out tonight… Ancient Egypt is all the rage everywhere; a craze. But the *location* of the talk is quite a draw, I'd say.'

'And have you seen this talk advertised before? It's a yearly event?'

Posie remembered Lex Lennart saying he came across every year to this Blue Garret event, that it was a tradition for him.

'No. I've never seen it advertised before. This is completely new. New is always good, is it not?'

Humming, he left. And as soon as he'd gone, Posie pulled the advert down and stuck it in her bag.

She hurried out across the hall, which was full of students and professors, and she saw Doctor Dance, his white hat the only thing visible of him, almost being crushed by a big group of students, all wanting to ask him questions, all edging closer and closer, like a group of black crows, pecking at their quarry.

Posie rushed on, out.

Out past students who were milling out into the courtyard, smoking, or chattering, desperate for air after the stuffy lecture hall.

She hurried past fountains, was about to cross the busy road, filled with charabancs and motor-taxis, when she heard her name being shouted behind her.

'MISS PARKER! Wait! Please. WAIT!'

She turned, and then she felt her heart melting.

Pity, dread, something unbidden, all hit her at once.

'Anatole?'

She stood stock still, saw her breath clouding the cold air.

He was suddenly right upon her, and behind him she saw a small crowd of worshippers – friends who obviously adored him and basked in the reflected light of his glory – step back, melt away. Unsure.

Anatole de Poilac was taller than she remembered. She only came up to his shoulder, even in Suzannah's high heels. He was broad in his black academic gown with the gathered shoulders, and he appeared older than last year.

He'd obviously been lighting a cigarette when he'd seen her, and one smouldered in his big thick-fingered hand, unsmoked. He threw it away hurriedly. Impatient.

'What are you doing here, Miss Parker? You are looking for me, *non*?'

'Yes, and no.'

Posie looked up at the young Count, at those grey-green ocean-coloured eyes which never stayed still, never fixed at one colour, which were as consistent as the shifting sea, and she smiled.

'I'm a friend of Doctor Dance, actually. I was attending his lecture. But I left you a note, too. Notes, in fact.'

'Oh?'

His eyes were round with surprise, inquisitive.

He put out a hand, with the peacock signet ring of his family's old lineage carved upon it, and he touched Posie's cheek softly. For a second there was a jolt of something like a fizz of electricity between them, but Posie stepped back slightly, to break it.

Behind him one of his pals wolf-whistled cheerily, and there was much laughing.

Posie shook her head.

'*Come with me*,' Anatole whispered, pleadingly. This close the boy smelt of lemon and vetiver, and pure lust. 'Come with me to my flat. It's just around the corner, or, if not, come with me into the Jardin du Luxembourg. It's very private in there.'

'I bet it is.'

Posie waved her left hand in the air, where the diamonds of her engagement ring and the gold of her wedding ring didn't sparkle at all. 'I'm a married woman,' she hissed.

'So? *Mon Dieu*, I adore you. Have done since I saw you for the first time. I'd do anything for you. Anything.'

Posie threw back her head and laughed: 'Oh, Count Anatole, you are amusing. And lovely, and utterly gorgeous. If we were in another time, another place, another configuration of ourselves, then *perhaps*. But now forget all about me, and go and find someone your own age to pester, and stop all this nonsense. And stop the letters too.'

The boy glowered, his face red. 'You mock me, Miss Parker. But I will not forget you. No, not at all.'

'Fine.'

He dug around and pulled out a fresh Gauloise from inside the black gown, lit it from an expensive silver Zippo lighter, breathed in a lungful of smoke.

'You say you are friends with that crazy Doctor Dance? Pah!'

Anatole looked scornful. 'He's pathetic. In the past they only invited him along because they felt sorry for him. He never says anything new. I know the university secretary rather well – a pretty little girl called Josette – and she said they gave up inviting him two years back; that he'd offered himself virtually for free this time around. As I said, pathetic! He once told Josette he'd lost the love of his life as a young man, and he threw himself into the war to forget about it all, and ended up like that…imagine. He looks like a monster. It's pitiful!'

He exhaled smoke out of the corner of his mouth, his eyes never leaving Posie's face.

Posie shrugged. 'I don't think you can judge someone on gossip. And Doctor Dance is a good man. Don't pity him. Perhaps you could go and hunt down this charming Josette? She sounds really delightful. Go and listen to some more evil lies. But please, don't contact me again. Goodbye.'

There were titters from the group of students behind them, a sort of slight jeering.

'You have made me look a fool, Miss Parker. That is not very sensible.'

'What's that supposed to be, Anatole? A sort of empty threat? What do you propose doing?'

Posie turned on her heel, fast, and as she stalked off she was aware of several pairs of eyes following her, and sniggering. And she really didn't care.

She emerged onto the Rue des Écoles. Cross. Fuming, in fact. Trying to decide what to do next.

From here she could see the twin towers of Notre Dame, silver and gold and turrety, over on its island, the Île de la Cité, which it shared along with another legend, Inspector Lucille. It seemed unlikely that he, tonight, would be on the front of newspapers, fighting for his professional survival. Like, it seemed, Richard would be now be doing.

Posie sighed and checked her watch. It was only a ten-minute walk from here, she guessed, checking her map, to reach Inspector Lucille.

But Sergeant Fox wasn't due for another forty-five minutes, and she reckoned she could make it somewhere else first.

Just about.

Because something else was nagging at Posie.

It was the necklace Lady Caroline had tugged from her neck before dying, and which was now inside Posie's own little red purse.

Lady Caroline's strange last words as she tore off the necklace played again in Posie's head:

'*I didn't kill him. Never. I loved him with all my heart. I would have loved him forever. And you must make that known, Miss Parker.*'

Could Posie make that strange message known?

How? If she didn't understand it?

She flagged down a motor-taxi, but suddenly realised

she was unsure as to where the exact location she required was.

'Cartier? The jewellery house?' she said to the taxi driver, hopefully, her hand on the rear door handle.

The taxi driver looked at her blankly.

But just then she heard a male voice behind her which she recognised. But she recognised it from very far-off, as if in a dream.

She turned on her heels, completely confused. And then she thought she would scream aloud, and never stop screaming.

'Oh! Oh, my days!'

Her heart was in her mouth and she felt icy cold. Because she was looking at a dead man.

'*Rue de la Paix, s'il vous plait. Mais s'arrête à la police judiciaire.*'

It was Inspector Durrant, and he jumped into the back of the taxi quickly, and Posie followed him in.

'*Cartier, Rue de la Paix, Madame?*' asked the driver, over his shoulder.

'*Oui*. Yes, thank you.'

Durrant turned to Posie and grimaced, bouncing a little on the hard leather back seat as the taxi set off, slowly rocking over the cobbled streets.

'Sorry for creeping up on you like that, Miss Parker; I need a ride myself, to Inspector Lucille's office. And I'm not doing a very good job today of protecting you, am I?'

'Not particularly. Oh, my gracious! I thought you were *dead*. We all thought you were dead! Poor Suzannah! Goodness, this is madness: I even saw a body on a stretcher...a guard of honour! What the blazes happened? What's going on, Inspector?'

'Sorry, they are circumstances beyond my control.'

He flicked his long greasy dark hair out of his eyes. He was still wearing his brown tweed blazer and it looked even more crushed now. There was a big bruise beneath his eye, too, and Posie stared at it for a second before wrenching her eyes away and forcing herself to look out of the window.

Silver-gold-silver-gold-silver-gold houses flashed by, and the huge avenues rushed past.

'How did you find me, Inspector?'

'I followed you around for a bit.'

'Ah.'

Well, that explained those pin-prickly feelings.

'As have others, Miss Parker. Followed you, I mean. You need to be very careful: don't open the door to your enemies, and, if you are handed a key, don't use it.'

Posie turned and stared at the young Inspector. 'You sound like a riddle in a Christmas cracker,' she said icily.

'I wish I could be as cheerful.'

She thought of the key to the office on the Champs-Élysées, which was somewhere in her carpet bag even now.

'I *was* given a key, by your boss, Jegouzo,' she replied carefully. 'But I have not used it. I wasn't planning to, either.'

'Good.' Durrant nodded. 'You must not use *any* key, Miss Parker. I need to speak to Inspector Lucille, about Jegouzo. My boss may not be thinking straight just now. In fact, I don't think he's thinking at all.'

Posie shrugged. 'Well, I don't know if you should trust Inspector Lucille. *I* don't trust him. He's making some very rash judgements about people in the Lady Caroline Greenlow case. He has Charles Loxley imprisoned, and also that nice Wardrobe Mistress, Daphne, and that's for *your* murder, when here you are, alive and well!'

Inspector Durrant laughed bitterly. 'Yes, that will have to be put right, Miss Parker, if it hasn't been already.'

They were driving fast over a bridge connecting to the island in the Seine, and big grey buildings lined the sides nearest the huge, pulsating, grey river's edge.

'I always hoped I'd end up working here, at the top office.' The young Inspector grinned, resting his head on the glass, as if for relief.

'Maybe you will be moved here?'

'I think not. My ambition in that regard is all gone.'

'Will I tell Suzannah that I saw you? Could you meet her later? I think that would be nice for her. She liked you, I know.'

'Tell her to find someone else,' Durrant whispered, looking quickly away. 'There will be someone around the next corner for her. I know it.'

'And for *you*?' Posie said, snappily. She thought his behaviour shoddy, cad-like. 'Sergeant de Caunes apparently said you were a ladies' man, and it seems he was right.'

'Oh, come. You, Miss Parker, more than most, must realise that everything connects, don't you? Everything here must come full circle.'

Posie stared at the man, wondering if he had been drinking, or in an accident, or if indeed he had been tortured.

They were speeding along very fast, and Durrant suddenly put his hand on Posie's. His skin was burning up, she could feel it even through her gloves.

'Tell the driver to stop here, will you? Yes, here we are.'

Confused, Posie rapped on the glass divide, and the motor-taxi pulled up at the kerb.

The building which housed the most important police force in Paris was squatter than the usual Parisian buildings; greyer, too. It was like an imposing Medici palace, hunching over the banks of the Seine, with hundreds of watchful glittery windows.

She suppressed a shiver.

Ahead of them, parked up, was a van, its sides made of black canvas. A team from the Morgue? A police ambulance? A team of uniformed policemen were surrounding it, and there was much noise as they shouted out commands.

'Looks like there's been an accident,' said Posie, getting out with Durrant. He stood next to her, hair blowing in the wind.

‘There’s always an accident in Paris.’ Durrant smiled. ‘Always a dead body. Ten a penny here. Don’t get upset.’

The Inspector pulled a small bundle wrapped in brown paper from his pocket, about the size of a chocolate bar, but slightly bulkier, and he made an elaborate bow, holding the bundle carefully, as if afraid he might drop it, and it was precious.

‘I hope I can redeem my reputation later to you, Miss Parker. But for now, good luck. And wish me the same. And oh, by the way. Please keep the fact you have seen me a secret please. Don’t mention this to anyone, not anyone. Okay?’

She nodded, and got back in the motor-cab, and they drove on.

* * * *

Chapter Seventeen

Posie sat perched atop a high chrome stool, not at all designed for comfort. It gleamed in the light of the beautiful crystal chandelier overhead.

One assistant had already shown the scarab beetle to the jewellery workroom above the shop, and the Master Jeweller in charge, a bald, immaculate man in his fifties, had immediately come down, slightly breathless.

Very concerned.

'*Who* did you say you are, Madame? And how have you got this jewel in your possession?'

She'd waved her handwritten pass from Inspector Lucille, and mentioned his name, and said she was his agent. And the questions had immediately stopped.

'Excuse me, just a minute, Miss Parker. I need to telephone to London. I need to speak with Mr Cartier himself. He is in our London office, and *this* is his exquisite work.'

Posie sat with her silver notebook out, ready to write. As she looked about her, she was aware of the Manager, a whey-faced man in a black frock-coat, and the sales assistant, both staring at her curiously.

The jewellery shop was calm, soothing, with an intoxicating scent of beeswax, musk and jasmine, wafting into the air.

It was a deceptive foil to the extremely busy street outside, where all the smart clothes shops were festooned with flags and balloons, all celebrating Paris Fashion Week.

Traffic had been stopped, but the honking of car horns could still be heard, as irate motorists blasted out their annoyances from either end of the street. A catwalk had been assembled in the middle of the street outside, and braziers burned along its length, providing warmth to the people sitting in rows on rattan chairs. Cold-looking models were bunching up, smoking, chattering, not yet walking down it. The show was about to start.

The staff of the shop bunched at the window to watch.

Posie twisted her own rings as she waited for the call to end. These were not from Cartier.

But she *had* owned a ring from here once before. A beautiful sparkling daisy of an engagement ring, given to her by a man no longer alive; a love long gone, dead and mourned and buried.

The ring from that dead love had sparkled on, though.

Talked out of throwing it to the bottom of the sea in a fit of anguish and despair, by Richard Lovelace of all people, long before they had become lovers, the ring had been sold, and the sizable sale proceeds had been placed into a secure bank account for Phyllis, who at the time had simply been Posie's godchild.

Posie and Richard, and Richard's first wife Molly, had all sat down over a good strong drink and decided the funds would be for Phyllis to use as an adult. To provide her with a start in life; money for university, or a house.

But, in the event, Molly had died in a tragic accident and strangely enough, Posie had ended up marrying Richard, and now Phyllis was her stepdaughter. But the thought of the money helping Phyllis one day – dear, good, practical, uncomplicated little Phyllis – still made Posie feel light inside, and she knew the money would be put to wonderfully good use.

Everything connects, everything comes full circle.

Posie smiled.

But for now, the presents being handed out to Phyllis were much, much smaller.

Dolls and tea sets, not priceless jewels, or the sale proceeds of them…

Posie frowned, as something she had just thought about had not quite rung true.

But before she could reassess, and track back again, the Master Jeweller was back, looking flushed with excitement.

'Miss Parker?' He was cradling the small jewel in his hands, as if it might have been a new-born child. And a perfect one at that.

Laying the jewel in Posie's outstretched hand, he inspected a small notepad on the glass counter, patted at his bald pate, and lowered his voice, so the staff couldn't hear.

'I have spoken to Mr Cartier, and he consulted his file on this piece for me, so I have detailed notes. This was ordered from us in 1916, and it took a few months to make. It was ordered in London, and made in our workshop there, too. There was no expense spared. The price paid eventually was one thousand pounds. *Une pièce rare*. Special.'

Posie stopped herself from gasping aloud.

The Master Jeweller continued. 'The scarab itself was one of a pair brought in to us, both original, almost identical in size. *This* one was chosen as being of higher quality than the other, which was returned to the customer. I do not know what became of it.'

Posie bit at her lip in excitement. She had no idea what had become of it in the intervening years, but she would almost have bet her last penny that the second scarab had ended up down Caroline Greenlow's throat last night.

Sure as bread was bread.

The Master Jeweller read the last of his notes, pointing at a final paragraph. 'The inscription apparently came from a coffin lid, honouring Queen Nut, or the Goddess of "Night" in the ancient Egyptian world.'

'How utterly delightful.'

'*Oui.*'

'And the customer?'

It must be Lex Lennart, surely?

The man coughed. 'A youngish man, based in London. Very rich. A regular client, with a unique customer number which was engraved on all his items.'

'You have a name?'

'*Mais, oui.* But he is dead now, Miss Parker. His name was Major David Greeze.'

****

In the motor-taxi on the way back to the main police station on the Île de la Cité, Posie replayed the conversation again in her mind, staring at the words she had written down.

DAVID GREEZE.

It was a name which meant nothing to her, and yet, hadn't she heard it, or seen it, somewhere before?

But where?

And the man was dead apparently.

Which accorded with what Lady Caroline had said.

I didn't kill him.

Well, even if she hadn't, Lady Caroline had clearly believed someone blamed her for this man's death.

The question was, who was David Greeze?

And what was his connection with the scarab beetle he had had so beautifully adorned, at such extravagant cost?

Had he bought the ancient Egyptian scarab beetle, or the pair of scarab beetles from someone? From Lex Lennart, perhaps?

And more pressingly, what had been David Greeze's connection to Caroline Greenlow? Had they been married? Lovers? Sister and brother? Posie would have to find out.

And there was only one reliable way.

It was a little after three-thirty when Posie arrived back at Inspector Lucille's station, and there were no black vans anywhere outside, thankfully. Nobody outside at all, in fact.

There was one handy telephone booth out on the street, right up against the grey river wall, and Posie headed to it briskly.

The Seine was high here, and, although not as busy as the Thames, barges and tug-boats ploughed hardily through the choppy waters, with a few low-down tourist boats charging along purposefully, flags fluttering in the wind on the river.

She felt horribly exposed out here, and looked about tensely as she asked for the International Operator.

Posie placed two hurried calls, searching for Sidney, her office boy.

She crossed her fingers for luck, hoping to make contact, and speedily. She was down to her last few coins. She stared out through the glass at the huge, pulsating river. The grey infinite nature of it all.

The first call, to Somerset House, was unsuccessful, as Sidney couldn't be traced there. He'd been and gone.

But the female receptionist at the *Associated Press* office relayed better news.

'Scrawny lad, keen as a ferret? Yes, he's here all right, in our archive room, miles off though, and no telephone. A message, you say? You want what? How do you spell it? G-R-E-E-Z-E? Right. Everything and anything on him, you say? Lovely. Yep. I'll pass it on now.'

Breathing a sigh of relief, Posie looped back and entered the police station.

Inside the grey, sparse building which smelt of disinfectant and which had long, echoing grey marble passages snaking off everywhere, Posie immediately caught sight of the tall, lean, blonde figure of Sergeant Fox, filling in forms at the front desk, and looking jolly smart for once in a navy greatcoat with a red tartan scarf.

Posie clattered to a stop.

'Sergeant?'

She saw his familiar wolfhound's jowly face turn and look at her full on, and saw his expression change from one of pursed-up worry to one of absolute relief, and delight. 'Miss! Oh, my! Thank the good Lord!'

Sergeant Fox threw down his pen and bounded towards her, and for a strange second, she thought he might actually be about to scoop her up in his arms and hug her for sheer joy, but at the last minute he pulled back.

'Oh! Let me telephone your husband immediately… he's been going spare, Miss. He's beside himself with worry.'

'What?' Posie was confused. '*Why?*'

'He hasn't heard from you at all. No messages. And what with all these deaths and murders, he told me he would never forgive himself if something had happened to you. He started to believe something *had* happened to you when you didn't call.'

'But I *did* call him, Sergeant. Earlier. I called the Adelphi, in Liverpool. Left a message before lunch.'

Fox shook his head. 'He didn't get it, Miss. And there's been a problem from the start. He was told that Inspector Lucille had your hotel details, and they were duly passed on, but when the Chief Commissioner tried to contact you, he found the hotel didn't exist.'

Fox pulled his hands through his short bright-blonde hair, mussing it up. He'd pulled out his police notebook, quickly turning pages.

'I think he was going half-wild, Miss. He contacted Cox & Kings, who he thought you would have used, and they gave him an address for a hotel they had organised for you, which *did* exist, but when the Commissioner called, you weren't there. They said you hadn't turned up.' He jabbed at a page. 'It was The Hotel Aurora, off the Champs-Élysées?'

Posie shook her head stubbornly. 'No, the hotel I was allocated was the Maigret, Number 8 on the Rue de Berri. It's a slip of a place, easily missed. Right on the top floor.'

Fox jabbed at his page again. 'That's the information you'd given the police here, yes. And your husband had that information, too. But it doesn't exist. Not at all. Number 8 is all apartments, and the whole top floor has been sat vacant for years. Since coffee-time this morning both your husband and Inspector Lucille have been working on finding you. On top of all the other problems.'

Posie stared at Fox in utter amazement. '*What?*'

What Fox had described sounded crazy, stupid.

In fact, it sounded like the ridiculous sort of cover-up which Len often ended up working on.

Len would recount the tales to Posie over tea – when they laughed together hilariously – whereby a husband or wife who was carrying on an affair created an elaborate fiction around their exact, usually illicit, location, so they couldn't be found by their anguished spouses. These were usually complex stories involving hotels which didn't exist, or which had changed names, or which had miraculously lost that person's details.

Oh, Posie thought with a sudden pang, *is that what Richard has believed of me?*

That I am here for something like that? A love affair?

A complicated twist of a story which I am hiding from him?

Richard had known about Anatole's adoring letters last year. Had he imagined there might be more to it than that?

She looked at Fox straight in the eyes and he looked at her, then stared away again, flushing red.

So, yes.

That possibility was in Fox's mind; probably Richard's, too. That was the sum of it.

Sergeant Fox turned to the desk and placed a call to Scotland Yard, leaving a message for Richard, who was not there.

This was all utterly ridiculous.

'There must be some stupid mistake,' insisted Posie. 'Cox & Kings must have mixed me up with another passenger. Besides, I've got a woman friend who came to the hotel with me this morning; we met on that wretched train. *She'll* vouch the hotel exists. Awful cold place that it is!'

Fox shrugged, but his red face looked more normal now. 'Inspector Lucille has organised an incident room as a base for me here; it's not much, but it will do and it's warm, at least. He'll join us when he can. It seems there's all sorts of internal problems going on today. I'd love a bite to eat, though…' he tailed off wistfully.

'Yes, the food here is jolly good.'

'Haven't had a chance to taste it, yet, Miss,' Fox said miserably, and pointed ahead to a green door opposite the reception desk. It had a paper sign pinned to the door scribbled with the words 'SGT. JAUMES FEX – POSIE PARKEUR'.

He took it down, sighing, and re-wrote the names properly. Opened the door.

'What a case, eh, Miss? And old Loxley here too, banged up in a cell downstairs. It doesn't look good for him, not at all. But they're also holding that young lad, Dadie Spence, now, too. As a likely suspect.'

'Oh?'

'They reckon he could also have murdered Lady Caroline.'

'But *why*?' Posie shook her head resolutely. 'I've considered this for a split-second, and it makes no sense. He was on the cusp of marrying Lady Caroline. If they were married, he would automatically get her fortune on her death, surely? And if not, he would get nothing. So, he gets nothing. If he was going to kill her, why not wait another week or so? It doesn't make any sense.'

'Dunno, Miss. I've got Sergeant Smallbone back home checking on Lady Caroline's Will, and her financial situation.'

'Good. But what led the French police to think Dadie Spence was a suspect in the first place?'

'Some fancy designer called the police at lunchtime, asking them to come and arrest Dadie Spence; he was acting crazy. Spence wouldn't leave, apparently. Said he'd been invited to the designer's salon. But he hadn't: the designer had never heard of him before.'

'Mnnn. If the designer was Paul Poiret, then Dadie Spence was speaking the truth: he truly believed he and Lady Caroline had been genuinely invited there.'

'Really? Well, he made himself sick anyway, and vomited up all over the floor. Sick as a dog. This fancy designer was horrified and got him taken away.'

'He was *sick*?'

'Apparently, Dadie Spence ingested a small amount of arsenic, which made him sick. The police think it was the same stuff he gave to Lady Caroline, and that this is evidence enough to make him a suspect. But *he* says he must have got a tiny amount on his fingers by touching a scarab beetle which was in his jacket pocket, when he was fishing around for one of his pretty little cigarettes earlier today. The police here have analysed this beetle and they say it must have been saturated in arsenic recently, but it only has traces on it now. Mr Spence says he put it in his pocket after his fiancée choked on it, and then forgot all about it. It's hard to believe.'

'Is it? I think Mr Spence is right again,' stated Posie, insistently. 'I *can* imagine him pocketing the beetle in the panic after the choking incident, then forgetting about it with everything getting much, much worse, later on. I wondered what had happened to it.'

'Wonder no more. Anyhow, there's even more compelling evidence against our friend Dadie Spence, which I will tell you about in a minute. Shall we go in?'

Fox flicked on the electric lights of the small meeting-room, which remained dim, regardless.

'I'll have to try and get both Loxley and Spence back to England, without alerting the international press as to what's happening. Almost impossible, I'd say, Miss Parker. I've never managed that before. They always get wind of it. What a messy old tale this is turning out to be, eh? I feel like a grisly chaperone.'

'And do we know *exactly* what Lady Caroline died of? It was arsenic, was it?'

Fox shook his head. 'We don't know yet, Miss. Post-mortem results will be in shortly. But look at this, the London Forensics team have excelled themselves already!'

They sat at a plain table in the small, dark room, which had one window looking out over an internal courtyard, at some rubbish bins. There were no refreshments. But paperwork and slim files covered the table, and a fire blazed merrily in the small hearth.

For a second Posie thought of that small flat in Montparnasse which she and Suzannah had visited earlier, uselessly, with its empty, cleared-out, still-warm hearth, where Violette's neighbour, Isadora, had placed her bare feet, to warm them.

Feet which had got sticky, picking up something bright green from Violette's floor.

Green.

A green feather.

Fox was showing Posie some Forensics reports, and she had to force her mind back to the job at hand.

There was a heading on a slim manila file saying 'FORENSIC REPORT FOR PULLMAN DINING-CAR' and several typewritten pages followed, with much underscoring in red, and complicated chemical configurations. Posie ran her finger to the bottom, to the summary.

'Nothing? *NOTHING?*'

She felt confused. Sat back, arms crossed.

'This says that on a search of the English Pullman dining-car, which was detached at Dover, there was no poison found in any of the food, or on any of the plates. And all of the bottles of alcohol behind the bar were tested and all were fine. The pots of coffee were fine, as were the mint chocolate wrappers which were tested. There was no poison anywhere. Well, that's all quite a relief, isn't it? It means no-one else has ingested it.'

'Where did *you* think the poison was, Miss?'

Posie bit at her lip. 'The fruit punch, I suppose. It was the only thing Lady Caroline had which nobody else partook off. She drank a lot. It was apparently right up her street; very sweet, very alcoholic. It was never offered again to anyone later. So I suppose I found that suspicious.'

'The Waiter was just in a hurry, I suppose, Miss. Serving punch is a messy old job. Our poisoner needed things to be neat.'

Posie read through the text again. 'Mnnn. This says that the remaining punch and the bowl itself and the tins of fruit used as decoration were all fine. Clear. And you're right, I think what we are looking at here is a neat job. It's impeccable, in fact. A masterclass in organisation.'

'Yep. I agree. Here, look at this.'

He slipped another buff-coloured file across to Posie. It only had one page inside, and it was marked boringly as 'ANCILLARY FINDINGS'.

She read what was on the page. And then gasped.

'You found Lady Greenlow's gold hip-flask?' Posie exclaimed excitedly. 'I wondered what had happened to that. No-one has mentioned it to me at all today.'

'Yep, it was handed in very late last night. Tested early this morning.'

'Handed in? Sorry? Where was it handed in?'

Then she read on.

A Canterbury boy, who'd been in trouble at home, had been killing time at the railway station to avoid going back there. Even though it was cold, snowing heavily.

Ah, yes, the boy at the chocolate machine.

He'd heard a strange clunking noise while the train was sitting stationary at Canterbury Station, and had had the distinct impression something had been thrown from the train, and, upon its leaving, he decided to investigate.

He'd searched the tracks, the platform, in the bushes. All while thick snow was coming down, covering everything and obliterating any clues. And then he'd chanced upon it, right on the ground in undergrowth.

A gold hip-flask, smelling of alcohol but otherwise empty.

'Attaboy!' exclaimed Posie, but frowning, as the story didn't make complete sense to her.

Posie read on. Read how the father of the boy had come looking for him, discovered the lad standing, uncertain, in thick snow on the platform with the flask in his hands.

The father had been worried that the boy had stolen what was obviously an expensive possession. He'd walked the lad around to the Station Master's house, and explained it all. Handed it in.

It had made its way to the police at Canterbury pretty soon afterwards. And Scotland Yard had been informed as a matter of course, due to the value of the object.

'Good lad, wasn't he?' said Fox. 'If he or the father had realised the value of that flask – you know it's solid gold? – I wonder if they would have handed it in. It would have kept his family going for a year or so, comfortably. It's from Cartier, you know. Bears their hallmark, but no inscription.'

Cartier.

'Mnnn.' Posie frowned. 'The boy deserves a reward, Sergeant. Something more than chocolate.'

She read to the end of the report. Closed the cover. 'But his good deed was all for nothing. It says here that Forensics found nothing suspicious in the flask at all. No poison. Just a mixture of traces of alcohol. Mainly whisky, and some cherry brandy. Golly gosh, but actually, this makes no sense.'

Posie was desperately trying to recall a series of events and timings from the night before.

She spoke aloud, remembering how Caroline Greenlow had ordered the Waiter to re-fill the hip-flask, and how it was replaced on her table during the dinner. She described how Lady Caroline had been drinking from the flask just before the train had stopped unexpectedly at Canterbury.

Posie paused. 'There *was* something odd at Canterbury. We were still at the dinner table, all of us, when for a minute the lights went out and we all felt a breeze, and several people were standing up, panicking. It's possible, I'd say, that a window was opened. And that's when the hip-flask could have been thrown out…'

Posie frowned. 'But no, this all makes no sense. No sense at all. I definitely saw Caroline Greenlow with her hip-flask after dinner, sitting in a chair. So that was *after* the flask was thrown from the train window, according to this report. And then later, when Dadie Spence begged me to come to Caroline's help, I distinctly remember kicking a hip-flask out of my way,' Posie explained, flummoxed.

She watched Fox nod.

What wasn't she seeing here? This was like a magician's trick.

She looked at another report.

This one with a gold, French crest upon it, jemmied firmly under Fox's hand. Posie watched him light a cigarette, a Player's, and shake out the match.

'Ah,' she said, the truth dawning suddenly. 'Could it be that there were *two* gold flasks. Both exactly alike?'

Fox inhaled his smoke with obvious relish. 'Yes. Exactly.'

'There was a switch, wasn't there?' Posie whispered. 'It was at Canterbury. The original flask which Caroline had had topped up was thrown out of the window. It was clean. The flask which was the replacement however, was filled with something similar, but mixed with poison, pre-prepared. The first flask was thrown away so it would look like there had always been just the one flask, so the fact it was arranged on the train wouldn't be "clocked".'

'I agree with all of that, yes.' Fox nodded and tapped off some ash from his smoke, and he pushed forward the blue French police report.

'This is all in French, which is not my strong point, but I can understand enough. This is a preliminary report, but the gist is that the gold flask recovered from the train contained cherry-flavoured alcohol, and it was shot through with a drug which looks a lot like arsenic.'

'*Like* arsenic?'

'They couldn't be sure on the first findings. They are testing again, but from what I can make out here it's the same family of drug.'

'Where was the hip-flask found? In the cabin, on the floor? Where I saw it last?'

Fox shook his head slowly, smoked some more.

'You know I said there was compelling evidence against Dadie Spence? Well, the flask *is* that evidence. It was deep inside the violet-suede duffle bag belonging to Dadie Spence. Along with a lot of other drug paraphernalia. Well, he's a known user, isn't he? As are most of his "set". The famous "Bright Young Things", eh? Not that that helps Mr Spence now. The police discovered the flask in their search through everyone's possessions this morning. He protests that he never had it in his bag, and that it was Lady Caroline's, to do with as she liked.'

'And are the two gold hip-flasks exactly alike, Sergeant?'

'Apparently so. Although one is here, and one is in London now. But they bear the same hallmark, and the size and gold composition is identical. They must have been made together. Both were not new. Cartier's serial number indicates they were ten years old.'

'How utterly odd. So, Lady Caroline wouldn't have known the difference at all. But how, after ten years, would our murderer have managed to obtain exactly the same hip-flask as their murder victim? It was obviously special to her.'

Fox shrugged.

'Dunno. And that's it really, Miss. So what with Loxley with his packets of arsenic, and Spence with the flask filled with poison, we have an abundance of suspects. And I have heard there was a girl being detained here, too. But about some other case, slightly related. She's been let go now, though. New evidence, or lack of evidence, or something…'

'Good.'

Posie let out a sigh of relief. Daphne de Bengy could hopefully get herself back on track now after a horrible morning. She'd seemed like a survivor, and hopefully she would survive this, and have the life and career she so obviously deserved.

'But I don't like what we've uncovered here one bit,' snapped Posie. 'Surely the only person who could have made this swap was the Waiter? Or the Guard? Perhaps one of them was known to Lady Caroline, wished her dead and masqueraded as a worker on the Night Ferry, in order to effect this murder?'

'Perhaps. But more likely is that one or both of them were acting as an agent, being paid to do this. Or being paid to ensure things ran in a certain way. Perhaps along with the English Driver? What *does* seem suspicious at present is that the Guard, whose name and details were left with the police this morning, has disappeared off into Paris, and, when checked, his details in England don't add up. His lodgings in Bromley have been vacated, and his landlady there told me on the telephone that he had said he was "going away" for a while. I've put a call out to the ports in France and England, with an order to stop and seize him, of course, and I was about to do the same for the Waiter and the Driver. I should have done that before I left London, but I was posted off here pronto.'

'I rather think Inspector Oats may be helping us on that front already, with his own rather awful brand of efficiency.'

'OATS? What the...?'

But Fox's squeal of disgust was interrupted by the door opening, and three figures stood there: little black-moustached Inspector Lucille; the caped and magnificent Sergeant de Caunes; and behind them, bearing a big box of cream cakes, a beautifully chic woman who Posie didn't recognise.

Not at first.

****

Chapter Eighteen

It was Suzannah Scotland, but not as Posie knew her.

The black messy tresses were gone, and Suzannah's hair was now short and cleverly bobbed, revealing an elegant, long, dancer-like neck, and the untidy make-up was gone, too, replaced with a simple flush of apricot blush on her tanned face.

The worn black coat had been changed for a neat, dropped-waisted woollen coat, also in that peculiarly-suitable apricot-coral shade. The scruffy high-heeled shoes were gone, too, and smart, warm, heeled grey leather boots had taken their place. The black bag had been changed for a soft grey matching leather clutch.

The effect was one of tidy elegance.

The woman was beautiful, and she had a new smell, too: patchouli and vanilla, with a little spice on top.

Posie smiled, and thought that Suzannah must have blued all the money she had given her at the hotel, in one easy go, and she'd only had enough left for the cakes, as a final fling.

She watched as Suzannah placed the cakes in the centre of the table, and distributed café serviettes quietly, efficiently.

Suzannah winked at Posie and gave her an excitable

thumbs-up. *Success, thank goodness, with Mrs Shepherd at the cemetery.*

Or news of some sort, at any rate.

'I'll be waiting outside.' She motioned towards the door, towards the waiting room.

'Fine.'

Suzannah closed the door behind her softly.

Inspector Lucille was very out of sorts. That much had been obvious from his initial stance at the doorway, and Sergeant de Caunes looked nervy, kept checking his watch. But the bad mood didn't stop either of them from sitting down and reaching for a cake, munching hurriedly, without any obvious enjoyment.

Sergeant Jean-Luc de Caunes passed a telegram across to Sergeant Fox, without speaking, and Fox frowned, reading it over twice.

Lucille flipped open his notepad.

'Let's quickly bring ourselves up to date on the status of the Lady Caroline Greenlow murder, shall we? I will allow Miss Parker to stay in here on account of her unique position as Richard Lovelace's wife, and on account of her, er, her *professional qualifications*.'

Posie helped herself to an éclair, and saw how Sergeant Fox had taken a croissant filled with strawberry jam and whipped cream, and that he was munching hurriedly, with a view to taking a second.

Fox had a slightly faraway, intrigued look on his face and Posie had noticed his gaze had lingered a second or two longer than was quite necessary on the door as Suzannah had closed it behind her.

The way to a man's heart... Posie thought to herself with wry amusement.

How simple they are, and how simple the traps are we lay for them.

Even unwittingly.

Inspector Lucille was flipping through reports which

Sergeant de Caunes was placing in front of him, like cards in a pack, one after another. He smoothed his thin moustache in annoyance, or exasperation, Posie couldn't quite tell which.

'The post-mortem is here,' he said softly. 'Dreadful case, this one, made worse by the fact Lady Caroline was pregnant. The baby was six weeks along. *Mon Dieu…*'

He crossed himself and everyone waited.

So, Doctor Dance had been right about that, thought Posie. *Perhaps too about the motives for the sudden wedding.*

What a shame.

Inspector Lucille was continuing, reading aloud, translating. 'The murder victim was not healthy. She was a confirmed alcoholic and there was marked damage to the liver as a result of this addiction. *Years* of damage. But death was caused by internal haemorrhage and a massive cardiac reaction: the classic response to poison. The poison used was antimony trioxide, and in a hugely concentrated dose.'

'Antimony?' whispered Posie, confused.

'Yes,' sailed on Inspector Lucille. 'It behaves in the same way as arsenic, of which there was also some evidence of ingestion, but far, far less. Probably that came from the beetle she accidentally choked on earlier, which was found to be soaked in the stuff. But the alcohol found in the gold flask in the bag of Monsieur Spence contains antimony, in a pure, concentrated form. And thus, we have located the type of poison, and how it was administered.'

Lucille flicked a blue-covered file with that now-familiar golden crest on it shut with a bang, as if everything was complete, finished. Solved.

'Antimony?' repeated Sergeant Fox incredulously, putting down his half-eaten second croissant. 'I've never heard of that as being fatal, not enough to kill a person, anyway.'

Jean-Luc de Caunes read from his notebook in a

faltering English. 'It *is* enough in this variety. I've checked. This drug is rare, though. It is used abroad and also by addicts here and in London, to mix with other compounds, usually heroin or cocaine, to raise the heart-rate. For *une frisson.*'

'A thrill? It doesn't sound very safe, though, does it? Where can it be bought?' asked Posie, curious.

Jean-Luc de Caunes gave a great shrug and his cape swished. 'At every street corner, I suppose, Madame. Paris is a city of darkness as well as light. It is in all the universities, and places where the young experiment. It is apparently extracted in its original form from mines in Russia, China and South Africa.'

'Yes, yes,' cut in Inspector Lucille, snappishly. 'Do you have anything else to add at this stage, Sergeant Fox, apart from that odd little story you gave me earlier about twin gold drinking-flasks? Which I think does not go very far in helping us with this case. Any news on our missing Guard?'

'No, Inspector. But I *do* have some news, yes.' Sergeant Fox picked up his new telegram, placed it on the table and explained that he had now heard about Lady Caroline's Will, and her finances.

'My colleague, Smallbone, in London, has ascertained that Lady Caroline's Will leaves everything she owned to an institute for delinquent girls, in London. This Will would, however, under English law, have been automatically revoked on her marriage to Mr Spence, which I am told by Miss Parker here was going to happen next Saturday, the 30th January. Mr Spence then, at that stage, would have received *everything.*'

Inspector Lucille nodded. 'Perhaps he thought he would *already* receive everything, this Dadie Spence? Couldn't face marrying such a difficult, alcoholic woman?'

Fox shrugged. 'I don't know, sir. But I think your hypothesis is unlikely. If Mr Spence was going to kill

Caroline Greenlow, why not wait a week and be certain of the cash? But this brings me on to my second point. And this is important. Caroline Greenlow's finances. It's really shocking.'

Fox explained there was nothing.

'Really, I mean it: she had nothing at all.'

He explained that Lady Greenlow had been an orphan and an only child, and her ancestral home, Greenlow House in Surrey, had been destroyed in a fire years before, and the land sold off to provide an inheritance for the girl.

Fox shrugged. 'Lady Caroline whipped through that inheritance years ago. She had no earned salary at all, and relied on payments from an unidentified business, which arrived by cheque every month. Smallbone has checked and says that these payments stopped in summer last year. Since then, Lady Caroline has been flat broke: she's since sold almost everything she ever had, and she's lived in rented accommodation in Paddington. She kept one maid-servant, and had no luxuries. In fact, I don't know *how* she was eking out a living. No wonder she jumped on that train over here when she was invited, all expenses paid! She was giving interviews left, right and centre with magazines, just to make a bit of cash. And heaven knows how she would have paid for that fancy wedding next week! Oh, I nearly forgot: there *are* two precious items which belonged to Lady Caroline, listed by her solicitor, but these are in a separate codicil to her Will.'

Fox fidgeted with his packet of matches. 'There is a gold drinking-flask, and a precious scarab beetle. The solicitor told Smallbone that Lady Caroline had insisted the flask should be thrown away, into the sea, if possible. But the scarab beetle needs to be returned to Egypt, apparently. To a museum in Abydos, where it apparently belongs.'

Lucille stood up, angry. And de Caunes followed suit, scooping up all their paperwork into piles and loading it into his arms.

Inspector Lucille made an explosive noise: 'Wretched scarab beetles! Why is that thing precious? *Ma foi!* Who on earth would trek to Egypt with that arsenic-infested rubbish? Who has *time*? Our experts say the beetle is old, but not valuable. And that drinking-flask? Well, I'm sure someone can make use of it at the end of all of this, once it's been cleaned of poison. We'll try and wrap this up as quickly as possible, send the body back with you, Sergeant Fox, as well as the suspects, to stand trial on British soil. It's probably best.'

'Mnnn,' muttered Fox, resignedly.

But Posie was not thinking of bodies, or trials. She was thinking of scarab beetles, and Egypt.

Posie knew that the scarab beetle Lady Caroline was referring to in her Will as being precious was the one currently in her red money-purse, and it *was* priceless, set as it was by Cartier.

But so far it was still unknown to the French police, who only thought there was one scarab, the one Lady Caroline had choked on, and which she had insisted she had no knowledge of.

Posie reached into her carpet bag surreptitiously, anxious the jewel didn't fall out.

'Before you leave, Inspector Lucille, and talking of Egypt, sir...' She passed over the advert she had stolen from the Sorbonne, for the talk tonight.

'It is regarding one of the passengers on the train last night. I think Mr Lennart, the American, may be speaking at this, Inspector. Or perhaps he's just attending. I wonder, either way, could Sergeant de Caunes call the club up and see if this talk happens every year? I thought Mr Lennart said it was a regular fixture, but maybe I am wrong?'

Sergeant de Caunes made a face. 'You know where this is, Miss Parker? It is a *gentlemen's club* – no women allowed – right next to the Moulin Rouge!'

Posie had been unprepared for this. 'Oh, right. Do you

mean an upmarket club, or a downmarket club?' she asked, matter-of-factly.

Sergeant de Caunes went red. 'This Blue Garrett is upmarket. Select: dinner; a full library; academic talks. That kind of thing. But it is a kind of grey area. You know? I am sure the location is also a nice draw, for men who want to go on, you know, on to the Moulin Rouge. Or to the other places around Montmartre. They are filled with dancing girls, and harlots.'

Posie laughed. 'Oh, well, I don't give two hoots about any of that, why should I? Can you find out anyhow about the talk, Sergeant?'

The big blonde man shrugged. 'Of course. As you like. I will attend to this straightaway. I will find out what has happened in the past, of course. *Tout de suite*.'

At the door Inspector Lucille turned and bowed slightly apologetically. 'I must apologise to you both. We are a little at "*sixes and sevens*" today, you say? Out of sorts. Miss Parker, you may recall talking to me earlier about Inspector Jegouzo, down on the Rond-Point, who had kindly offered to help you out yesterday?'

'Yes,' Posie said brightly. 'He *did* help me out. As much as he could, anyhow.'

'*What?*'

The Inspector almost leapt over the table to her. 'When was this?' he demanded.

'I told you, sir. I had to be there this morning, at eleven o'clock. Inspector Durrant had said he would come with me, but there was obviously all this, er…confusion. So I made my own way there. The Inspector was very polite. He gave me coffee. Nice cakes. He was upset you hadn't yet released Durrant. He said he would call you.'

The slight rebuke as to the lack of his own hospitality here obviously fell on deaf ears, and Lucille was licking at his lips. 'What did this man look like?'

'Inspector Jegouzo?'

'Yes.'

'He was big, kind. Wore green. Messy, with a big walrus moustache, nothing like yours, sir. He smoked, too. There was ash everywhere.'

'*Mon Dieu*, it sounds exactly like Jegouzo. Well, perhaps they have the times wrong, eh, Sergeant de Caunes? It has happened before.'

Posie stared at both men, standing in a sort of frozen way. '*What* time is wrong? *Who* has the time wrong?'

De Caunes ran his hands through his lacquered, crisp blonde hair. He looked nervous.

'We were informed this afternoon that Inspector Jegouzo is dead,' he said, simply. 'He was reported missing yesterday, already. His body has just gone to the Morgue.'

Inspector Lucille stood up very straight, formally.

'There *must* be an explanation. But the attending medics say he has been dead since yesterday; a gunshot wound to the forehead. Shot point-blank, in cold blood. A terrible thing. We know he took a call from *you*, Miss Parker, yesterday morning. We also know he sent a telegram to Inspector Durrant, who was visiting his father, near Windsor. We have a copy of that telegram. And after that, the trail goes cold. We thought he had disappeared yesterday, but maybe the times are wrong...'

Inspector Lucille shook his head stiffly: 'What a terrible case. Who would do such a thing? Poor Jegouzo was stuffed inside a cupboard in that little office on the Rond-Point, and no-one would have noticed for days, or weeks. Not with Durrant absent. We would not have looked for Jegouzo without the tip-off we got. But you are right, Miss Parker. Perhaps he did not go missing yesterday but was, in fact, killed after meeting you today?'

Posie felt confusion, sadness, complete incomprehension flooding through her.

For some reason she thought she might cry.

'Wouldn't all the other men working in the office

have noticed the exact time when Jegouzo went missing?' she asked, but she received completely blank looks from Lucille and De Caunes.

She suddenly remembered Inspector Durrant in the taxi with her, telling her he needed to speak to Lucille.

Durrant knew that his boss, Jegouzo, was dead, realised Posie.

He had been going to tip them off. She remembered his odd words: '*My boss may not be thinking straight just now. In fact, I don't think he's thinking at all…*'

'Was it Inspector Durrant who came and told you about the death of Jegouzo?' she asked.

Inspector Lucille drew a deep, grim breath. Shook his head. 'No. Somebody came here and left the body of a green bird at reception. A budgerigar. No explanation.'

Posie was remembering Durrant with the small package which he had handled so gently, wrapped in brown paper.

She remembered too the green budgerigar at the office earlier. 'It was called Charlie, wasn't it? The bird?'

Lucille nodded, firm. 'That's right, Miss Parker. Well, you must have been there right before it happened. Our medics must be wrong with the time of death. The bird was distinctive, and old Jegouzo was famous for his love of this little bird. When we got the body of the bird here, we knew it was a sign. Dead bird, dead Jegouzo. *But why?* He'd never done anyone a wrong during his whole life, I swear it. *Mon Dieu*, what a dreadful day!'

Posie found she was clenching her hands tightly as the men left the room. A tear trickled down her cheek and she flicked it away quickly, angrily.

She looked over at Fox, whose face was a concerned frown. 'Listen…' he started to say in a low, concerned voice, 'you know one of the reasons I was sent here so promptly was–'

But he was cut off by a knock, and Suzannah Scotland entered the room again. She was like a triumphant schoolgirl, tasked with a project which had come off very well.

Suzannah glanced at Sergeant Fox, seemingly oblivious to the effect she was having on him. She took out a picture postcard in black and white, and slapped it down in front of Posie.

And then another, and another and then another.

Fox goggled.

As well he might.

Because in all of the postcards the woman shown was completely and utterly nude.

* * * *

Chapter Nineteen

Posie made the briefest of formal introductions.

'This is Suzannah Scotland, Sergeant Fox. Suzannah is the lady I met on the train, and she's been to my hotel, this morning, which *is* real.'

His eyes widened again.

The postcards were all, probably, of the same young woman, with shoulder-length hair and large, blank sad eyes, wearing nothing at all, reclining on a couch in different positions. They were photographs of paintings; paintings in a very modern, abstract style, so much so that the girl was rendered almost featureless, doll-like.

The postcards were all slightly curling at the edges.

Posie half-laughed. 'Well, Suzannah, you certainly have a good line in shocking people, but what is this all about? I thought you had news about Mrs Shepherd? Who we left at the Montparnasse Cemetery? We wondered if she might be meeting someone? Visiting someone? She told me on the train she comes to visit a lonely relative, every year.'

Suzannah pointed at one of the postcards. 'This is the person she was visiting. I'm sure of it, Posie, *oui*.'

'*How?*'

Suzannah sat down and explained how she'd tailed Mrs

Shepherd through the cemetery, and the older woman hadn't stopped to speak to a soul.

After ten minutes of walking, Mrs Shepherd had come to a tree-filled area which had bigger, more exotic monuments than the other, more conservative areas.

This area was filled with modern sculptures which had been erected in place of gravestones, and painted in shocking colours and inlaid with mosaics and mirrors.

Mrs Shepherd had come to a stop at a small headstone, rather conservative for this very modern section of the graveyard, and she had stood in front of it for a good, long time.

'I don't think she cried,' reported Suzannah. 'But after about five minutes she placed that big white bouquet of roses on the grave. Then she bent down and she seemed to be organising things.'

'Flowers?' Posie asked.

'That's what I thought. But then she straightened up and headed to a nearby bin. I stayed back under the shadows of a big tree, so she wouldn't catch sight of me.'

Suzannah explained how she had rushed over to the grave as soon as Mrs Shepherd had walked away, and she'd written down the details of the name there.

'It was very simple,' said Suzannah, sadly. 'It said "*JEANNETTE DE MONTPARNASSE 1898–1920*". But the grave was obviously visited by others, too. It seemed like a kind of shrine. There were ribbons there, and a few silk flowers. And when I was certain Mrs Shepherd had really gone, I went over to the bin and I dug around. And *these* are what I pulled out. I think they had been placed there by other, earlier visitors, and the snow has made the postcards curl.'

Posie and Sergeant Fox turned the images over.

Each one said the same thing: '*Amedeo Modigliani, Jeannette de Montparnasse, 1917. Galerie B. Weill.*'

'Oh!' exclaimed Posie. 'Suzannah, what good work!'

Suzannah smiled, pleased. She took a cigarette from the packet of players which Fox offered to her, and let him light it for her. 'There's more, Posie.'

She took a deep, greedy breath of smoke. 'I managed to see Mrs Shepherd again, as I was leaving the cemetery. She got into a motor-taxi, and so I did too, following her.' Suzannah grinned, obviously having enjoyed it all.

'Mrs Shepherd was going to the Rue Laffitte, which is miles off. Her motor-taxi stopped and I watched her get out there, and I wondered why, and then I realised we were actually sitting outside this very same gallery which is mentioned in all these postcards, the *Galerie B. Weill*.'

'I say, you did well, Miss!' Sergeant Fox looked impressed as he smoked, still turning all the postcards over, back and forth.

Suzannah smiled in response to the praise. 'The gallery is a tiny place, like a front room, but very beautifully arranged. I couldn't go in, Mrs Shepherd would have seen me straightaway, but I peered through the glass. She was their only customer, and for about twenty minutes she sat in front of one painting, a red painting, staring, with that black shawl of hers over her face. She didn't even look at any other artwork! *Incroyable!* Fortunately for me the Rue Laffitte is lovely, and interesting: full of art galleries, and restaurants, and with the Sacré-Coeur rising above it all like the dream it is. I remained posted outside the gallery. Well, just as I was wondering what to do next, all of a sudden, Mrs Shepherd stood up to leave. I hurried off down the street so she didn't see me. I stood in a doorway and watched Mrs Shepherd come out and get another taxi-cab. Perhaps on to her hotel?'

Posie didn't dare ask if Suzannah had gone further, dug deeper. As *she* would have. But perhaps there was enough to go on here?

But Suzannah *had* gone further.

She'd gone into the gallery itself and spoken to the

owner, a Madame Berthe Weill. Suzannah explained she had seen the red painting from the street, and had wanted to see it closer.

'What did she say?' Fox said, intrigued.

'She was happy I wanted to see the picture: said that was what it was displayed there for! She also told me, oddly, that I was just in time.'

'Just in time for what?' asked Posie, puzzled.

'*Je sais pas*, Posie. No idea. But the gallery owner was happy to tell me all about the painting: that it had been painted by Amedeo Modigliani, and he had had his first – and only – show with her. His exhibition, in 1917, had been a riot. It caused a scandal, as most of the paintings were of nudes. The police came and shut it down! Modigliani became a legend in his own right, overnight, and he sold all the nudes immediately to private collections.'

'That was a good bit of publicity, then!' said Fox, impressed.

'I don't know, Sergeant,' replied Suzannah Scotland. 'Three years later Amedeo Modigliani was dead; a mixture of bad living and ill-health. Berthe's gallery has always traded off her "fame" from that one exhibition, and she keeps postcards of the nudes from that old exhibition which customers can still buy. They are very popular. She has also kept one painting from the original exhibition up on the wall. She is allowed to, as it is not a nude. It is the head of a girl with flame-red hair. Set against a bright-red background.'

'Is the red painting of Jeannette?' whispered Posie.

Suzannah nodded. 'I asked *who* she was, this Jeannette, and Madame Weill said Modigliani used "Jeannette" a good deal; she was one of his favourite models. Madame Weill said while she particularly loved this painting, and wanted to buy it from Modigliani, back in 1917, she had been beaten to it, by another collector. But this collector had generously let Berthe keep it in the gallery ever since, for all to enjoy.'

'Jolly decent of them,' said Fox.

'Yes,' agreed Suzannah. She ground out her smoke. 'What was interesting is that Berthe Weill told me that Mrs Shepherd comes every year, every January, and has done for many years. She always sits in front of the painting, taking it all in. Always for about half an hour, then she leaves.'

And then Suzannah had confessed, rather shamefaced, that she had found herself tantalisingly close to the Galeries Lafayette, on Boulevard Haussmann, and that she had blown the rest of the money Posie had given her on a new look.

'Money bally well spent, I say,' remarked Fox, appreciatively.

But suddenly Suzannah was bending over, picking something up from the floor and handing it to Posie.

It was a slip of paper, and at first Posie thought it was the telegram from Smallbone to Fox, about Caroline Greenlow's Will and finances, but then she saw it was written in French.

It was actually a copy of a telegram, on thin facsimile paper, and it was addressed to Eton College, Windsor, to Alphonse Durrant.

It had yesterday's date on it.

'Suzannah, can you translate?' she asked hastily.

'Of course. It says "I WOULDN'T NORMALLY BOTHER YOU IN THESE CIRCUMSTANCES BUT PLEASE CUT SHORT YOUR TRIP NO MATTER WHAT AND GET TO VICTORIA STATION FOR THE 'NIGHT FERRY' TRAIN TO PARIS AT 9PM – STICK LIKE GLUE TO POSIE PARKER – CERTAINLY AS IF YOUR LIFE DEPENDS ON IT – I BELIEVE SHE AND INDEED OTHERS ON THE TRAIN NEED YOUR HELP. SOMETHING IS AFOOT. I AM FRIGHTENED FOR THEIR SAFETY. YOURS, INSPECTOR JEGOUZO."'

Posie swallowed, took the telegram copy and folded it away quietly.

Jegouzo's telegram had been convincing: no wonder Durrant had left his father so hurriedly.

What had Jegouzo been afraid of, though?

Posie had only asked him for someone to accompany her; had not said she was in danger. Had Jegouzo been tipped off about the Night Ferry and the murderer who planned to kill on it? It certainly seemed so.

Posie tried to be constructive.

She scribbled in her notebook, a name.

Jeannette de Montparnasse.

Who was she? Was she important? She would have to find out.

But just then Sergeant de Caunes stuck his head around the door. He looked slightly more jovial than before, and obviously had news.

'The Blue Garret, Madame?'

'Yes?'

'The talk tonight, at eight pm? It is fully booked out apparently. Two hundred tickets sold! It's the first time there has been such a talk there, though; there is no record of anything else occuring in the past. The Manager there, he is very excited. He's never had such interest! The draw is to hear the famous Howard Carter, of course. All of Paris is going crazy with the Egyptian fascination.'

'Thank you.'

The blonde man disappeared.

Fox was standing, opening the window, lighting another cigarette. He spoke softly, thoughtfully: 'That all seems a bit funny to me, Miss. Howard Carter delivered a series of lucrative lectures in 1924 and announced publicly he had had enough. Would never do it again. And he's famous for *not* talking to anyone, anymore. Why would he come out here and speak to two hundred people in a club? Nah! It's decidedly "off". A "mare's nest".'

She was about to comment further when Sergeant de Caunes was back, but this time asking for Posie to attend the telephone.

There was other news.

* * * *

Chapter Twenty

After a series of phone calls, Posie sat in the waiting room of the police station, on a grey wooden bench with a very hard back, piecing it all together.

The first caller had been Inspector Oats, sounding pleased as punch.

He'd had some success with Mr Brookman, the Director of the Night Ferry company, who had wobbled like a jelly on hearing he was up against an enquiry into financial irregularity, but denied everything.

Based on the Director's suspicious behaviour, Oats had arranged for Mr Brookman's telephone to be bugged, and after their meeting, Brookman was taped immediately instructing his own bank to send a recently-received payment of almost fifteen thousand pounds abroad, rightaway, into dollars.

A watch was being made for Brookman at all the ports now, especially at Southampton, where three boats were sailing tonight for America. Also by tonight Scotland Yard would have control of Brookman's bank account and would be able to tell *exactly* who had paid fifteen thousand pounds for the train to run almost empty.

It was a colossal sum.

Oats would ring again later with any news.

The Waiter and the Driver were proving more elusive. As was the Guard, here in Paris. There was no news yet.

The telephone had rung again and the police receptionist had announced that it was Sidney, the office boy. He was calling from the offices of the *Associated Press*.

Excited.

Posie stood at the receptionist's desk in the front hall with her notebook out, writing fast. And at points the hair on the back of her neck seemed to stand on end. She was writing down dates, names, histories.

'Greenlow House? *Who* acted like that? Oh, how fascinating. Yes, that explains a good deal.'

Whole chunks of people's lives, and personality traits, and weaknesses, could be explained by the past.

Always the past, which could never be escaped from.

'No marriage certificate for Lady Caroline? No matter, Sid. I don't think I expected it.'

Posie scratched away at the notepad as Sidney reported his findings.

'And did you come across anything which would be important for Lady Caroline when she turned thirty? Because that was going to be next week. And she was proud of it. No? No matter.'

Posie jabbed her pencil at a name on her page, almost violently.

'And David Greeze, what of *him*? Oh, really? A marriage? Well, what's her name? *Sorry?* He's definitely dead. Can you go to Somerset House again and order his Will. Tell them he died last year. Yes, you can reach me here. And while you're there, think outside the box. Were any babies born? Any divorces entered into? Anything *odd*. Because something is off here. Any information about this man is useful to me. Because something does not hang together properly. Yes, soon as you can.'

Nothing hung together properly.

A game had been played, and not with a straight bat.

Posie sat on the wooden bench, nibbling at the end of her pencil when her call with Sidney was finished.

It had all been very interesting, but bitty, and not satisfactory.

She almost chanted to herself: 'David Greeze. GREEZE. Why and where have I come across you, and only recently? But it was unrelated to any of this.'

Suddenly the telephone had rung, and the receptionist had yelled for Posie again, almost with annoyance this time.

This third call had been from Sam Stubbs. On the scent of a story, almost yelping to get the words out.

'Posie? Look, you know you told me to let you know if there was anything odd, after the news of Dadie Spence and Lady Caroline's engagement broke? A week back?'

'Yes. Go on.'

She tamped down her excitement.

'I didn't think of this. And it's not directly related, but, you know, I was down chatting to Sidney for a bit in our archive room, and I looked over his shoulder and I saw a name which I hadn't come across in a good long while…'

Posie cut in: 'Was it "David Greeze"?'

'Yep. You're very good. Maybe you should become a detective.'

'Ha, ha. Funny.'

'Greeze was an interesting chap, you know. Dashingly handsome. Rich as hell, but tied to the family company, brewing, and he couldn't just do what he liked.'

'And what did he like?'

'Fast women, fast cars, and ancient Egypt. Some said he liked fast boys, too. You know he was there when they opened the tomb of Tutankhamun? Along with Lex Lennart, who we spoke of earlier?'

Posie gasped. 'No. I didn't know that.'

At last: some connections.

Sam carried on, enjoying the fruits of his success: 'Well,

David Greeze never pushed himself into photographs, or spoke publicly about his interests. Not once. He was the "face" of his brewing business, and I suppose he didn't want his two "worlds" to collide. He was greatly respected; had a first-class war record, too. Out of this respect, no-one, not even us newshounds, linked his name to the "mummy's curse" when he died last year, although he was young, and it was very tragic. Cancer, I believe.'

'What's his link with Lady Caroline?'

'It's tenuous, Posie, tenuous as hell. But seeing that name again made me think. It rang a bell. They were cousins, I believe. Cousins by marriage? But you'll not believe what I saw, must have been just over one week ago.'

'Go on.'

'It was a notice. It was placed in our paper, the *Associated Press*, but I've checked, and it was actually placed in every single British paper on the same day. And that was the very day after the *Picture Post* came out.'

'Go on. What did this notice say?'

And Sam Stubbs had read it out.

And then the outline of everything had come together.

How it had happened.

Posie thanked Sam Stubbs and placed the receiver down, wandering through the entrance hall to stand by the one, barred window to gather her thoughts.

She understood more now, that was true.

But Posie still didn't understand *why* the murder had happened.

And why *now*?

And she still had no idea who exactly the murderer was.

Posie checked her watch.

It was past five now, and she could see the darkening clouds of the sky scurrying across the Seine.

Fox was suddenly bounding out in the corridor, looking tense, excited. 'Miss Parker, while you were out here, on the telephone, I made a telephone call myself. Something about that talk at the Blue Garret struck me as "off". So, I telephoned to Howard Carter's London flat and spoke to his Housekeeper. He's not in France at all, he's in Egypt, receiving the Order of the Nile from the King there! He's out there for two weeks. And she confirmed he has decided never to lecture again.'

'What? So, this talk is a set-up, a fake to which two hundred people are going. Two hundred *men*, sorry! Paying an exorbitant fee for. I expect it is a money-making thing, don't you?'

Sergeant Fox nodded. 'Yep, Miss. All too easy to take payment and then announce that Mr Carter is actually sick, or detained.'

'I think we should get Sergeant de Caunes to inform the Blue Garret that the talk is off,' said Posie. 'All monies should be returned, and no more tickets sold. But the booking in Lex Lennart's name should be maintained. And Lex Lennart should *not* know it has been cancelled.'

'Oh? How so?'

Posie grinned. 'Because *we* will go instead. All of us who were on that train last night. The rules of the Blue Garret will have to be bent tonight: let's stuff their stupid "men only" rules. I don't think Caroline Greenlow would have stood for any less. But we'll need Dadie Spence and Charles Loxley out of custody and in attendance, too. Every single person on that train needs to be there. We need Daphne de Bengy, too, from the Moulin Rouge. *If* she's managed to get her job back. And Mrs Shepherd. Can you tell Sergeant de Caunes to organise it all? He should be there, with Inspector Lucille.'

'Of course. I'll do that now. Let's hope Inspector Lucille listens, and complies. I know they're as keen for an answer to all of this as we are. They have other problems here…'

He was about to speak again, but then shook his head, tore off down a corridor.

Back in the small, empty, interview room, Posie sat down again, exhaled, got out her red 'Dolly' file.

'Sorry, old friend,' she whispered. 'I'm here for you, but I've neglected you. I haven't even called Rufus. Not once.'

Posie took out the note from the train, with the word 'LISTEN' on it, and she also took out the small picture of the drowned woman's face, *L'Inconnue de la Seine.*

Posie heard the door open, and saw Suzannah come in, holding a tray with cups of coffee which she must have just prepared.

'I have a confession to make,' said Suzannah, suddenly, collapsing down into the chair next to Posie, twirling her coffee cup nervily, spilling coffee.

'Oh? This sounds ominous.' Posie did her best to grin. 'Is it something about Sergeant Fox? Because I think he likes you, and you could do worse, you know, as you obviously have a thing for policemen.'

Suzannah flushed darkest beetroot under the apricot blush. 'No, nothing like that. It's about that note you're reading.'

Posie let the silence fall about them.

'*I* was the person who gave you that note.'

'Sorry?' Posie whispered, feeling strangled.

'I mean, it's not *from* me. I had no idea what was inside it: *non, pas du tout*. I didn't have the guts to tell you before. But you've been so kind…'

Suzannah swallowed. 'When I was at the station yesterday, one of the Night Ferry staff passed me the note: said could I pass it to you? Well, I had no idea who you were then, did I? Didn't even know your name. So I slipped it to the Guard as I went past him on the platform. *C'est tout*.'

'I see. And that's really all?'

A nod.

'Okay.'

Posie buried her head in her hands, wondering what to make of it all.

The note troubled her. Was it from Caspian della Rosa?

Or from someone who had wanted to scare her before the train started up?

And it had passed through Suzannah's hands. *Was that just coincidental?*

Had the same author of the note also been involved in the vast and cruel deception to get Suzannah out to Paris?

But for what reason?

And tiny link between Posie and Suzannah though it was, the note was still a link.

Posie suddenly remembered the clerk at the station, when she'd picked up her own travel docket yesterday morning. After Suzannah had left.

The clerk had almost given something away; something confidential which linked her and Suzannah. She recalled his abrupt words: '*…it seems the passenger before you, the foreign lady in black, has actually been set up on the same…*'

He had tailed off, realised he shouldn't have spoken.

What had he been about to say? The two women had been set up on the same *what*? *On the same account?*

Were Suzannah and Posie out here, like puppets, dancing on strings for an invisible master?

But why?

Because if this was Caspian della Rosa's work, what on earth did he want with Suzannah?

Posie suddenly had an unaccountable desire for Richard. For his strong arms, his cool head.

But she knew she must make a call or send a telegram to Rufus, check he had really wanted her out here to search for Dolly. *What a fool she would look if not.*

She hastily stuffed the note and the picture of the death mask back in her bag, and she put on her green coat.

'I need to send a telegram, Suzannah. But I also need to go somewhere I should have gone in the first place: when I stepped off the train today. Perhaps you would care to join me? It's nearby. And I think we will take Sergeant Fox along, too. I still have the weird feeling that I am being watched. Followed.'

'I have felt it, too, Posie. *Oui.* All along. And it seems others were frightened for you.'

Posie nodded, uncomfortable at the reminder of Jegouzo's telegram insisting Durrant was recalled.

Durrant.

And what on earth was he up to?

So far she had not yet discussed his reappearance with Suzannah; he'd acted so weirdly when she'd mentioned Suzannah's name, and then sworn Posie to secrecy. What kind of man was he, really?

Perhaps it was easiest to let her think he was dead?

Posie quickly wrote two lines of a telegram, and scrawled the London address at the top of it. Meanwhile, Suzannah was buttoning up her smart new coat. 'Where are we off to then, Posie?'

'Well, I'm waiting for some crucial bits of information on the Caroline Greenlow case, so I'm going to turn my attention to my friend Dolly for a bit. It should be a safe outing; let's hope we all come out unscathed.'

Unlike poor Inspector Jegouzo.

For whom Posie's safety had come at a hard price.

And what about Dolly herself? Did it seem even remotely conceivable that they would ever find her out here in this dreadful mess of darkness?

Vanishing cats, vanishing friends, and a trail as dead and cold as ice did not promise very much.

But, after all, this was the City of Light, and sometimes light managed to seep through the darkness, giving clarity and answers, even if it was very, very faint.

* * * *

Chapter Twenty-One

Having instructed the receptionist to send her telegram to Rufus immediately, Posie set off into the biting cold, Suzannah and Sergeant Fox following on, close behind.

The Paris City Morgue was only ten minutes walk away, on the Île de la Cité, the same island as the Police Headquarters, but the cold as they walked was fearsome.

The Morgue sat at the back of the Notre Dame Cathedral and in a scrubby little park all of its own, hard up against the river, and the place was cheerless and grim. Especially now that darkness had fallen properly.

A couple of boats with 'POLICE' marked on them were moored at the bottom of some steps leading down to the river, lit up with green lights, and they clanged and clattered like unholy bells as the choppy waves rollicked over them.

'You certainly bring us to all the best spots, Miss Parker,' said Sergeant Fox, smiling tightly, and he and Suzannah filed in behind Posie to the well-lit entrance-hall, past a few black-canvas-shrouded vans parked up outside the main door.

It was rather towards the end of the day, half-past five, and there was no-one on reception. Posie pushed through some big baize curtains into a huge, cavernous room.

In truth, she wasn't counting on finding out much, but she did have the form signed by Inspector Lucille, allowing her access here, and so she thought she'd better use it.

And then there was the matter of the note on the train, too, with its picture of the death mask from here. The credit for the photograph had been attributed here, to the Paris City Morgue. That detail alone needed some investigation, albeit cursory.

As soon as they entered the huge room Posie nearly regretted her decision to come. Suzannah, who hadn't been that enthusiastic, hung back, looking immediately sick. Even Fox looked as if his eyes were watering with the formaldehyde, and the other, worse, stinks.

The stone-cold room was floodlit with stark green overhead lights and over on the left-hand side twelve marble slabs on tables ran in a row, all occupied with dead bodies, all with thick cloths over them.

Three black marble slabs were placed in the centre of the room. One was occupied but a cloth was over it.

'Hullo?' Posie shouted, rather cheerfully actually, egging herself on. 'Anyone here?'

A tall, reedy man in his late thirties in casual flannels and a striped shirt beneath an open white doctor's coat emerged from a small room on the side: '*NON!* No tourists! GO AWAY!'

Posie stepped forward anyway. 'I have a permission from Inspector Lucille,' she said, brandishing the note as if it were a talisman.

The tall man, who had a long dark face which wasn't unattractive, came forward, put on some round glasses, read it, snatched them off.

'Sorry. I thought you were tourists; we've had so many after that wretched book was published a week or so back, with the famous "*L'Inconnue de la Seine*" on its front cover. People asking who she was! Well, how should I know? It was forty years ago that she was in here, and I wasn't yet born. And now she's mouldering among a heap of paupers somewhere in Montparnasse Cemetery.'

Posie was slightly taken aback. 'Oh! Well, yes: that must be inconvenient for you…'

'Don't mind me! I'm very pleased to meet you.'

The man stuck out his hand, and laughed at Posie's reticence. 'I've cleaned up for the day, so don't worry! I'm all scrubbed down. I'm Doctor Rousse, by the way. I run the Morgue here, for my sins. I'll be pleased to help you. If I can. And you lot are?'

Posie introduced them all, and Sergeant Fox even showed his English Police Identification fob. She was relieved when Suzannah peeled off to go and sit at the back of the Morgue on a bench, where she picked up a newspaper and idly turned the pages. Fox stood resolutely at Posie's side.

'This is a long shot, Doctor, but it's worth a go…'

Posie explained about Dolly coming to Paris in June last year, and disappearing.

About how Posie had vowed to look for her. About how the police had basically closed the file down.

Posie described Dolly carefully. She brought out Dolly's photograph.

'This was her. See the dyed blonde hair? She was pretty and striking. I'm wondering whether you recognise her? She was last seen at the Gare du Nord.'

Posie threw caution to the wind, described everything. 'Oh, and she had a cat, a bald cat, with her. In a cat basket.'

Because even though Isadora Duncan had mentioned a bald cat at Violette's, and it seemed it probably was Dolly's, you could never be a hundred per cent sure.

Doctor Rousse looked slightly caught off guard for a moment, but then studied the photograph and frowned. He handed it back to Posie without comment.

'A special *cat*?' He exhaled noisily. '*Non*, I do not think I have ever dealt with a corpse with a bald cat in tow before.

And the girl, well, sheer numbers make it difficult to try and remember them all, especially given the time that has elapsed.'

He ran his hands through his short brown hair, but he seemed jittery, on edge. 'We have more than a hundred corpses a week come through here,' he explained.

He motioned towards Sergeant Fox, raised a sympathetic eyebrow. 'We have a good many policemen who die, too, unfortunately, like today, all lined up over there. But most civilians are dragged up from the Seine itself. And at least twenty corpses remain unclaimed, every week. Poor souls. Like that famous *L'Inconnue*.'

He gave a theatrical sigh. 'But give me the date your friend disappeared. I'll go and check in my reports from last year. I take photographs of all the corpses' faces. For moments like this, I suppose. I may have to seek permission from the Governor of the Morgue, excuse me for a few minutes?'

Posie checked her silver notebook. 'Sure, it was Tuesday 16th June, at the Gare du Nord. She was never seen again.'

'Wait here.'

Doctor Rousse disappeared into a tiny room with a big glass window looking out onto the big room itself. He had his back turned to them and was pulling down huge ledgers from a shelf high on a wall. He flicked through pages, and then picked up the receiver of a black telephone on the desk and spoke in rapid French.

Posie strained to hear him, but she thought she caught the words '*Oui, aujourd'hui. Une fille, avec un chat sans fourrure. C'est très bizarre.*'

What was that? He was talking about Dolly, and the bald cat?

Fox had floated over to the row of twelve black slabs with their grisly cargo. Bare feet stuck out from each table, with a blue 'POLICE' tag affixed to the toes of some of the bodies. He moved along the row, reading them all inquisitively. As he went, he flicked the sheets back on the faces quickly, irreverently.

Posie stayed put, feeling apprehensive and slightly sick.

'Here's old Jegouzo, poor old sap. Date is today. He's been shot. And here's a stabbing. It's…no, never mind.'

Fox seemed to be willing himself on. 'And here is Caroline Greenlow. By Gad, she was a looker, eh? And here is…oh! Oh, my! That is *weird*.'

'*What?*' hissed Posie, uncomfortable.

'Come here, Miss. You have to see this.'

Posie was over at Fox's side in a second.

He hissed: 'This is horrible, but you need to see it. It's not Dolly, don't worry. But you might get a shock, so don't scream.'

He flipped back the sheet, and on the slab was a girl.

Petite, she had been pretty in life. She was probably about five years younger than Posie, dressed in a good plain maroon suit of nice jersey wool. She seemed familiar to Posie, somehow.

She had been shot in the head, and the dark tarry blood marred her smart haircut. Around her neck was a small silver necklace, not expensive, and it had a 'V' on it. It looked familiar.

'*Look!*' directed Fox urgently. 'In her hands!'

He pulled the sheet back more. There, in the dead girl's hands was a cat lead with sparkling crystals set in it. And below, curled up, was a dead bald cat.

Posie was almost sick where she stood.

'*Move!*'

'That's Violette,' whispered Posie, her heart drumming like a caged beast against her rib-cage. 'Oh, no! I almost didn't recognise her, her hair's different since I saw her in London. But it's definitely her; because the Cardigeon twins "chose" the necklace for her one Christmas; I remember now. Oh, golly! She's been murdered, and the cat, too… It's awful. Hideous.'

'Our doctor is a liar, Miss Parker. He said he had never dealt with a bald dead cat before. I think you should bear that in mind.'

And, stomach heaving, Posie turned as Doctor Rousse stepped back into the main room.

Posie smiled.

Doctor Rousse was holding a huge leather ledger for 1925. He placed it on one of the unoccupied black slabs in the centre of the room and beckoned Posie over.

'I looked at the dates you told me about. Nothing came in on that day, but we *did* have a body the next day, which seems a good match.'

He put a hand softly on Posie's arm.

'Brace yourself, please, Madame. It does seem likely this was your friend.'

He read aloud from the big ledger. 'This corpse was a woman with peroxided hair, short, only five feet tall. She was well-dressed, with brown eyes. She was a long-term smoker from the state of her lungs and fingertips. She had no personal belongings with her, and no identification documents. It looked as if she had had a very bad accident under a coach or a motor-bus, perhaps even under a train. And what seems the important thing is that she was brought in from around the Gare du Nord area.'

Posie stood frozen.

She'd come here more as a courtesy, as a way of eliminating a possibility, and here she was being told all her worst nightmares had already come true.

Doctor Rousse closed the ledger, leaving a scrap of paper where he had been reading from.

Doctor Rousse spoke slowly: 'I am not going to show you the accompanying photograph on the next page, as her face was unrecognisable. It would give you nightmares. There was, however, no cat, no basket. But perhaps, like her belongings, it got taken away. Stolen by vagrants? *Son probable.* Or perhaps she was meeting someone, and then had an accident, and they didn't know what to do, and they panicked? Perhaps they kept all her things? Including the cat?'

Perhaps this was how Violette had ended up with the cat?

After an accident?

Isadora Duncan had said Violette had the cat from last summer onwards, didn't she? And there had never been any sign of Dolly staying or visiting Violette's flat.

Posie felt like she had been hit in the stomach, all the air gone, as if she was about to fall to the floor.

So, the writer of the note *had* known, then.

That Dolly was forever silent.

Posie had been led here. To obtain this knowledge specially.

Breathe, Posie told herself.

A deadening lull in her stomach was like an ache. But Posie willed herself not to cry, not here.

You were my best friend.

'Thank you, sir. And she is buried…where?'

'Montparnasse, I'm afraid. The paupers' hill, in an unmarked grave. I'm so very sorry.'

Well, it seemed appropriate somehow. Dolly, who had come from nothing, and been everything – Suffragette, Wardrobe Mistress, Countess – had gone back to being nothing right at the end.

An accident, though. Really?

Posie had been holding onto her snap of Dolly throughout. And now she tried to stuff it back inside her bag roughly, through tears, and she accidentally dropped the bag.

Everything tumbled out all over the hard flagstones: the red file; a tube of lipstick; the key Inspector Jegouzo had given her to the office on the Champs-Élysées; her jewellery roll; her red money-purse; the recent letter with its cutting from Mrs Walter, still gone unanswered, with the purple words of her address 'ETON COLLEGE,

WINDSOR' prominent, and one of her usual photographs of two little boys, both in fancy dress, also covered in her purple scrawl, with names this time, FRIEDRICH, DAVID.

Posie's bottle of Parma Violet perfume was smashed, shards of glass everywhere, and the liquid itself was seeping out into Mrs Walter's purple writing and over the faces of the boys and obliterating everything.

The perfume also seeped out over the black and white postcards of Jeannette de Montparnasse, which began to curl up damply.

The doctor laughed, easily.

'*Ne t'inquiète pas*. Don't worry, Miss Parker, I'll sort this glass out later, and at least there's something here with a nice smell for once!'

He was squatting down, picking everything up and handing it to Posie, who was dabbing at her eyes, hoping the mascara didn't run.

She took everything gratefully. But the doctor straightened up suddenly, holding one of the postcards of Jeannette.

He whistled softly. 'Oh! There is another one buried at Montparnasse...'

Posie sniffed, threw herself into professional mode. 'You had *her*, here?'

'Oh yes. In 1920. I remember it clearly as I'd just started working here. She was another English girl; another one with the specially-dyed hair.'

He flicked his head backwards to the long row of slabs. 'I have another one right now, actually, although this one here, today, she was truly a red-head, and she dyed her hair bottle-blonde. But Jeannette was brown, and dyed her hair red. A strong flame-red. It somehow always burnishes on death. The dye goes almost green.'

'What happened to Jeannette, Doctor?'

Doctor Rousse tailed off, thinking.

'It was a tragedy. *Ma foi!* Amedeo Modigliani had died the week before, and Jeanette was found drowned in her bath, having taken pills. It was awful. They were friends; probably much, much more. She was his muse, although she was a talented artist in her own right, with half of Montparnasse in love with her. Half of Montparnasse celebrated at her funeral, from what I heard, too. Which was just as well, as her family, her English family, had disowned her. Well, apart from one. He came here specially, but he was a cold fish, you say? He didn't give his name, simply stood there, drinking from a gold hip-flask. He wanted to see the photograph of Jeannette, dead. Said he wouldn't believe it, otherwise. It was luck we had her full name – her real name – it was on some insurance papers.'

'Could I…?'

'You want to see her file? I suppose so. So much time has passed.'

The doctor left again, back to his ledgers.

Posie felt numb, but she noticed that Fox was looking genuinely worried.

'Miss,' he hissed. 'Look at this. Do you remember old Lucille speaking earlier about Jegouzo and the dead green parrot?'

'Budgerigar.'

'Whatever. Now, on the count of three, while that doctor isn't looking, have a ganders at this lad on the slab here.'

'No! Not again! This is turning into a horror show, Sergeant.'

'You need to.'

He pushed Posie slightly, and, with his eyes on the rigid back of Doctor Rousse, he pulled the cloth quickly from the place where the head of the corpse was, and replaced it again quickly.

Posie almost dropped her carpet bag to the floor all over again.

'Miss, did you *see*?'

'*Of course I did*,' she hissed. 'He's been shot at point-blank range, but his mouth was stuffed full of green feathers!'

'What does it mean?' asked Fox, who was tapping his packet of cigarettes nervously from one hand to the other, desperate for a smoke. 'The tag says he was brought in only one hour ago, from the Rue de Berri, something about being found on top of a fruit cart in the street, as if he'd landed there from a great height. Are you okay, Miss? You look green about the gills.'

Posie felt absolutely sick. 'I know him...I *knew* him.'

He had unruly red hair, and he was young, and his eyes which were still open – glazed and milky-covered – were very blue.

Posie had seen the boy earlier, several times, at the Hotel Maigret.

It was the punctilious receptionist.

But Doctor Rousse was back, and he had the fat ledger from 1920 with him.

Doctor Rousse propped it on an empty slab and flicked through some pages, found the right place. He cast a half-angry look over at Fox.

'You peeked under the cloth, didn't you, Sergeant? I can't tell you how often this happens! Even with mighty police inspectors, or judges, or top officials. People just have to have a look... But the one you just looked at, over there: that is an odd one. The boy was shot, then the feathers added afterwards. You don't happen to know him, do you? Because at the moment I have matched him to a description which accords with the identity of a country lad who ran away to the theatre here in Paris, but that was over a year ago. So, it's probably not correct. Well, if anything comes to you, let me know. But here, here is Jeannette.'

And Posie looked at the closed, dead face of Jeannette de Montparnasse and she recognised that face also.

****

Chapter Twenty-Two

They sped along by the Seine, the three of them cramped in a motor-taxi, with the Paris night drawn tight around them, and the twinkling lights along the Embankment looking cheerful.

They swept onto the Rue de Rivoli, and on, on past the Louvre, and around the dark Jardin des Tuileries.

Sergeant Fox was smoking, muttering in low whispers to Suzannah Scotland in the darkness.

Posie was lost in her own world, thinking of hip-flasks.

Of best friends.

Of loss.

Perhaps all three.

'How stupid I've been,' she muttered to herself, noting that she needed to make a call on their return to the police station. To a woman she had misunderstood, shelved. Not taken seriously enough.

Fox had misunderstood. 'You're not being stupid, Miss. If you think that dead lad with the red hair and the feathers in his mouth was your receptionist at the hotel, we'd better check, hadn't we? But if he *was* an actor, like Doctor Rousse at the Morgue said, well, that's maybe more understandable. Mrs Scotland here was telling me that the paper today is all about actors at the moment: it seems that many theatres in Paris went bust this winter, and they're not doing well. Theatres are being turned into nightclubs, and the actors are hiring themselves out as touring troupes, heading off to the Provinces in search of work. The front pages are covering a story about one group in particular, the *Perle de Pigalle*. Mrs Scotland says they haven't been seen for days. They were last heard of going to Nice, in the south. Maybe this lad was one of theirs? The uncertainty of life and the job all got too much?'

'And what about the green feathers?'

Posie bit at her lip, not meaning to have snapped.

She waited but Fox didn't answer immediately.

When he spoke, she heard resignation in his voice:

'Look, I need to tell you something, Miss. I was going to save it for later, when we were alone, or with your husband? But I'll tell you now: we can trust Mrs Scotland here to be discreet, I'm sure.'

'Oh? What?' Posie was only half-listening.

'When you were looking at the photo of that dead artist girl, Jeannette, I decided I'd just check something out.'

'Another corpse, Sergeant?'

'No, Miss. But information *about* one. You know Doctor Rousse read you out a bunch of facts about your pal Dolly, supposedly being dead. And he said he wouldn't show you the photograph? Because you might be upset?'

Posie spun her head fast in Fox's direction: 'Yes?'

'He was lying, Miss. There was nothing on those pages where the bookmark was. They were blank. No words, no photos.'

Posie froze, a half-hopeful gasp in her throat: 'Maybe you slipped, Sergeant? You got the wrong page?'

'No, Doctor Rousse was bluffing. I'm certain of it. There were no photos in that book at all, and he was telling you a load of old rubbish. Making it up. So please, don't be upset because of that. Dolly's whereabouts are still very much a puzzle. I have no idea what that man was up to, or why, but we'll try and find out, eh? What's more, I reckon he was following instructions: do you remember he had to make a call before he brought out that book?'

'Yes. He was saying something about a girl and a cat on the telephone. But that could have been about Violette...'

'Mnnn. Or about your pal, Dolly? We'll try and trace the call. Your husband will insist on it, I know it.'

Posie nodded in the darkness, wiped away a tear.

'Thank you.'

And now it seemed Posie would have to block the whole issue of Dolly from her mind.

She knew she needed to concentrate on the Lady Caroline Greenlow case and the night at the Blue Garret, which was fast approaching, and which she seemed to be in charge of. At the moment that whole case seemed to be like a rudderless leaky ship, desperately needed more work, but which couldn't be advanced until further information had come in.

And anyhow, bigger worries were gripping her.

The worries felt familiar, too.

All this recent talk of theatres, and of pretence, and of charade.

Once, in 1921, when Posie had only just met Dolly, Posie had worked on a case centred on a theatre in London. There had been actors and actresses in abundance, but the theatre had turned out to be a fake, a front for a huge drug-smuggling cartel. Caspian della Rosa had organised and run the whole thing.

What if here, Posie had become involved in, or a victim of, something similar, but the other way around?

What if she had been dealing with things which were meant to look everyday, but were, at their very core, constructs? Theatrical stage-sets with actors acting in them?

They'd taken the Place de la Concorde at speed, whisking around the Obelisk, and now they were about to hit the Champs-Élysées. They were near to Jegouzo's Police Station, and the toyshop.

A horrible thought struck Posie. She could check it out right away.

'Oh! Can the driver stop at the police station here on the Rond-Point?' Posie asked Suzannah, suddenly.

'Miss Parker?' asked Fox, worried, as Suzannah leant forward to issue the instructions in French.

'I need to check something. Something I had just assumed was all right…'

And they were approaching the huge circular roundabout, well-lit despite the now-complete darkness.

The taxi driver braked: '*Nous sommes ici!*'

They all got out, bidding the taxi to wait. Posie spoke brightly, falsely cheerful: 'Here we are, Number 8.'

Posie started to dip her head, to go underneath the wooden door-jamb into the still-snow-dusted courtyard.

But they heard banging on the glass window of the taxi. Suzannah looped back to the taxi driver who was pointing in a jerky manner.

'He says that's not the police station! It's here, just this small office, right at the front.'

Posie shook her head. 'He's wrong.'

She dipped under the door-jamb and crossed the courtyard, but it was all in darkness. Something like a lick of fear pulled at her heart, made her chest suddenly very tight.

Had this big office closed because Jegouzo had died?

Fox was behind her, and he pulled out a large yellow pocket-torch from his coat pocket, swung it about.

The large glass windows where Posie had seen men on telephones earlier were dark, the offices unlit. The door to the right which had had a bronze sign saying 'ENTRÉE – VISITEURS' swung open on its hinges. There was no sign up now.

'Miss Parker, are you *sure* you were here earlier?' Fox

whispered. 'I don't like this. Not at all. And I'm completely unarmed.'

He pushed open the door anyway, stood in the hallway. It was empty. There were no benches, no reception desk. There was no budgerigar.

Fox flooded the corridor with the torchlight, and Posie, heart scudding, ran on ahead, ran like an idiot. She ran through the empty rooms where the policemen had been on telephones, and at desks, and on to Inspector Jegouzo's office at the back.

But here there was no desk, no telephone. No carpets, no tatty watercolours up, no picture of a wife, and no ash over everything.

Instead, the room which had been Inspector Jegouzo's was painted white and was very neat and clean, and two small beds, as if for children, were lined up there. A child's mobile was hung from the ceiling, and nursery-rhyme pictures ran around the room in a frieze.

The other rooms also had beds in them, small desks, and bookcases. It felt as if a boarding school was about to move in, or had recently vacated.

Silently, they left.

They walked across the courtyard, and saw the taxi driver was standing on the street, smoking, motioning to a building right in front of where he had parked.

It was the toyshop.

Only, it wasn't a toyshop anymore. The candy-striped awning and the gleaming black wood and golden signs were gone, and a small sign marked 'POLICE JUDICIAIRE' stood to the side of the door Posie had walked through, only hours before.

'This cannot be real,' she whispered.

The door to the place was ajar but it was dark inside.

Within the small space of the toyshop were two desks, and two chairs. Two official certificates were up on the wall, and one said 'JEGOUZO' and the other 'DURRANT'.

Green feathers covered the floor, and the same cage which Posie had seen earlier was on its side on the floor.

At the back, where earlier a smart girl had wrapped gifts, was a large cupboard which had been sealed off with police tape, the words 'INCIDENT' large and awful in the torchlight. There was a dark patch of what was probably blood on the floor.

The three of them stood there in the silence, not understanding and not knowing what to do. Not knowing how to feel.

'So this was the real Police Station,' muttered Sergeant Fox. 'He must have died here, poor old fella.'

Posie nodded, miserable. 'I feel a fool. But it was so convincing as a toyshop. However, something did strike me as bizarre here today, but only slightly.'

She rushed on. 'It was a discrepancy. When I bought presents from here, the toyshop sent them around to me without any problem, even though I had forgotten to give them my exact hotel details. I wondered how it was possible, when the parcels arrived, but I was too busy to connect the dots. The pretend police station and the pretend hotel must be connected… Didn't you say, Sergeant, that Richard was having trouble reaching me? That the Hotel Maigret was not listed anywhere?'

Everything connects, everything comes full circle.

'I think we'd better go to your hotel, Miss. Check it out, then get back to the main police station, and report on all of this.'

Posie nodded.

All along the Champs-Élysées, and onto the Rue de Berri, Posie sat frozen.

It had all been a show. For her benefit?

But why?

Perhaps unsurprisingly, The 'Maigret' sign at the bottom of the building had disappeared, and they took the staircase, rather than the lift, in case something was wrong with it. In case it had been rigged.

'What will have happened to your toys? And what about my suitcase?' Suzannah kept saying, between puffs of breath, all the way to the top floor.

'Does it really matter?' puffed Posie, equally out of breath.

'We can buy you a new one,' murmured Fox, delicately.

'*Non*. It's not the same. My life was inside that bag...'

They reached the top floor and the darkness hit them at once. The open swinging door, the lack of any reception desk.

Fox got out his torch once more.

The lights of Paris sparkled in the attic windows here, this high up, and the Eiffel Tower, illuminated with the word 'RENAULT' was like a beacon you had to keep looking at.

But there was nothing else anywhere.

No breakfast room with a coffee table and newspapers, no bedrooms. No American tourists and no vicars. No telephone. No electricity. An empty room where formerly a bath had sat.

The doors of the breakfast room were open very wide and the place was even colder than before.

A slight smell of gunshot lingered in the air here, and something else.

Bath salts. The smell of 4711.

Posie stood at the space where she had called to the Adelphi in Liverpool, by telephone.

'By Gad, they thought of everything. I really thought my call was genuine.'

No wonder Richard hadn't received any news from her.

The telephone had been a mere prop, it hadn't been connected to a real network; it must have been rigged with an actress at the other end of the line. A convincing actress, able to pretend to be an Operator, and then to fake a Liverpudlian accent, pretending to be a receptionist.

'I'm pretty sure that red-haired lad at the Morgue was

the receptionist here,' said Posie quietly. 'But why was he shot?'

'Don't let's jump to any conclusions,' Fox murmured. 'I think we should go.'

'What about my suitcase?' whimpered Suzannah. 'All my lovely shoes?'

And Posie had been about to get really quite cross, when suddenly all three of them heard a banging.

A panicked, insistent beat. Metal on metal.

'There's someone else here,' hissed Fox in alarm.

But Posie had already taken off.

She was running, holding aloft the torch and thankful for its bright light.

There was only one place where the noise could be coming from. And it was enclosed, and had contained a boiler. A boiler which had needed stoking in an elaborate show earlier which had been very convincing.

She flung open the boiler-room door, and there, as well as the boiler, was Richard.

* * * *

Twenty-Three

Richard had been tied up and gagged, and the noise they had heard had been his wedding ring striking against the pipework.

She was down on her knees and ripping at the gag and tearing at the ropes with her house-keys, until Fox bounded up, with his efficient pen-knife, cutting through everything.

'Posie, oh my darling!'

Richard was on his feet, rubbing at his wrists, rubbing at his fingers, bringing back the circulation. He was wearing his Chief Commissioner's uniform, and even in the semi-darkness his buttons and braids twinkled like gold stars.

'What are you doing here, Richard?'

'What the blazes do you think, my love? I was looking for *you*. I was told by several sources this place didn't exist, so naturally I thought the worst, almost panicked. I arranged a flight out here, and just before I boarded the plane I got given a telegram which you had sent me, with this same address on it, and it gave me a little hope that you were fine. When I arrived at four o'clock, I made it my first priority to come here. Only trouble was, there were others up here, and I disturbed them. There were gunshots and I ended up being bundled off into that cupboard. It wasn't my finest hour.' He laughed bitterly. 'None of today has been my finest hour.'

He ignored Fox, and the dark shape of Suzannah looming behind, and he reached for Posie, holding her tightly, murmuring into her ear. 'By Gad, I'm glad you arrived, darling. Just wait until I get you home…'

Fox coughed awkwardly. 'Did you see the fella who fired the gun, sir? Only we've got some very odd happenings going on here. In addition to Lady Caroline Greenlow, I mean. We've got missing police stations, and this weird place, and one Inspector who was shot, and –'

'Yes, I heard about the death of Alphonse Durrant, Sergeant Fox. How can we forget that? I only heard about it on the plane over. A very sad business.'

Posie frowned, and beside her Suzannah's strangled sob caught in her throat.

Richard carried on. 'We'll need to help the French police find out who did that. Terrible business. I feel half-guilty myself, as I believe he was coming to assist Posie over here.'

Posie stood silent, holding onto Durrant's secret, as she had promised him she would.

'You asked about the man who was shooting up here, Fox? Well, it was hard to see, lad. When I arrived, the door was wide open and there were people ahead of me, certainly. In that room with the windows wide open. Some sort of scuffle going on between a boy with red hair and a bottle-blonde. She had a gun. I was going to intervene when I was grabbed from behind by another man. I didn't see his face. Just the turquoise of his suit. He was small, felt quite puny, but obviously he also had a gun, so I didn't argue. I think he may have been American, because he said something about the Blue Garret and I think there was an accent there.'

'*Lex Lennart!*' chimed Posie and Sergeant Fox, together.

And then they all ran down the staircase, into the

waiting taxi, and hurried back to the Police Judiciaire on the Quai des Orfèvres.

It was almost seven o'clock.

And despite the very odd trip out, and the dreadfulness of the Morgue, and finding Violette there, dead, and finding yet more confusion over Dolly, Posie found herself busier than ever.

She was burning with a purpose now.

Posie stood by the reception desk, on the telephone, waiting for the International Operator to make a connection, while Lovelace and Fox and Inspector Lucille sat ensconced in the same small incident-room, gesticulating and arguing.

They were also waiting for dinner, which was being organised by Sergeant de Caunes, and Suzannah Scotland had gone to help him.

Inspector Lucille was out of sorts. Irate.

As she waited, Posie listened in on them.

The trouble was that no-one could decide exactly what had occurred today, at the police station on the Rond-Point, or *why*, and what had also occurred on the Rue de Berri, at the fake hotel, despite Fox's protests that a young man with red hair was lying dead in the Morgue and he had earlier been sighted at the fake hotel. The mention of green feathers in the red-headed man's mouth did not help matters.

Inspector Lucille shouted for a police dispatch rider to go to the Morgue immediately and bring a photo of the young man at once.

Then the policemen started to argue about Lex Lennart and his involvement in Richard's imprisonment at the fake Maigret Hotel, and whether to bring him in for questioning. They decided against this, as he would be crucial to the evening's gathering at the Blue Garret, and it all needed to go smoothly.

'Is your wife really up to running this?' Posie heard

Lucille snapping at Lovelace. 'I hope things don't get out of hand.'

'Posie knows perfectly well what she's doing,' she heard Richard reply defensively. 'She even knows who the murderer is.'

Well, that was going too far, actually. And it wasn't quite true.

But, still...

Her thoughts were interrupted by the English Operator. 'Putting you through now. Eton College, you said, Miss?'

It took a while to reach the right person, and Posie stood, gathering her thoughts.

In her mind's eye she saw purple ink; names disappearing into her spilt perfume.

A name she had probably seen over and over again in the last months, but she'd thought nothing of it.

It had been scribbled on photographs and cuttings, by a mother desperately looking for her son.

DAVID GREEZE.

Posie thought about Alphonse Durrant, too. He'd told her he'd come from seeing his very sick father, who was nearing the end.

He teaches mathematics at a famous boys' school.

But until Posie had seen the telegram from Inspector Jegouzo requesting Durrant should return, she had not connected Durrant's father with Eton, Windsor.

Mrs Walter, her cold case of a client, was a Matron at Eton. And she was used to caring for the sick. She was also, without her son, very lonely.

Inspector Durrant had told Posie there was someone looking after his father. *There is a woman there who has taken good care of him, so it is all fine. He's in good hands.*

Didn't it seem likely that the woman was Mrs Walter?

Everything connects... Everything here must come full circle.

A voice was suddenly on the line. A hesitant, kind voice, with the vestiges of a German accent still.

'Oh, hullo! Mrs Walter? It's Posie Parker. Yes, I'm calling from Paris. No, sadly, I don't have any news about your son, Freidrich. But I need to ask you, are you there with Mr Durrant? The maths teacher? Yes? You are? Oh, he's had a dreadful shock? The son? His wonderful boy? A Police Inspector? Gosh: yes. What terrible news. But listen: I'm so sorry to intrude at this awful time, but I also need to ask you about someone else you wrote to me about. You called him "David"?'

Posie listened intently, captivated. 'Really? You don't say. *Gold*, did you say?'

And then, after this intriguing conversation, Posie called the City Morgue, which she had visited so recently.

She hoped against hope that Doctor Rousse, who had acted so weirdly with the truth, was still there.

Fortunately, he was , and he gave Posie his full attention while she heard the noises of the police dispatch rider arriving in the background.

'Doctor Rousse? That dispatch rider will ask you for a photograph for Inspector Lucille. Could you also add a snap of Inspector Jegouzo, please? Just so I can be sure of things. Actually, add a snap of everyone brought in today, please. And oh, could you tell me: you spoke of a cold fish, sir. Coming to call on you, after the death of Jeannette de Montparnasse, in 1920. Was he a blonde, or dark cold fish?'

She noted down the reply and then she called through to her own office in London where she knew Sidney was sitting waiting. He had left messages for her to call him back.

'Sidney? You got sight of David Greeze's Will? Tell me.'

'Yes, Miss. He died last year, 1925. June…I told you he was married? So I checked *her* Will too.'

'Sidney, I could kiss you. You are definitely due a raise.'

'I won't deny that wouldn't be welcome, Miss. Now, are you ready?'

Posie listened, scribbling everything down. She asked him to repeat the details again.

'Ah! I *see*.' Things were fitting in place now. Puzzle piece by puzzle piece.

Posie counted something on her fingers, nodded: 'Mnnn. Next Friday. Yes. That makes sense.'

Sidney was bubbling over with excitement. 'You asked me to check if there was anything else, didn't you? Anything odd. Well, two things cropped up, Miss, and both are weird.'

'Weird is often good. Go on.'

'Well, next to the cabinets of deaths at Somerset House, are the cabinets of all British names, changed by deed poll. And you'll never guess what?'

'What?'

But Posie had not guessed it.

'And there is also a cabinet there, which is about challenges made to Wills, Miss. And listen to this: there was a challenge made last year to David Greeze's Will. After he'd died, last June. It was horrible, Miss. Really nasty. You want to hear about it?'

'Please.'

Posie sat quietly with her notes now.

Reading and re-reading them.

And then she paced around the waiting room, waiting for the police dispatch rider to come back.

As he entered the hallway she stood with her hands out convincingly, and he placed the slim file into her custody, barely questioning her authority.

She quickly rifled through the photographs the man had picked up until she reached the one with the typed heading 'INSPECTOR JEGOUZO'.

This showed a large, older man with a walrus moustache, but with a very different face to the man Posie had met earlier on.

Posie stormed into the small incident room, where the policemen still squabbled angrily, and threw the photographs on the table.

'Was *this* man Inspector Jegouzo?' she asked, pointing, silencing them all.

Inspector Lucille frowned. 'Yes. Why?'

'Then I did *not* meet him today at all. The man I met was an imposter, probably an actor. Perhaps from the *Perle de Pigalle* theatre group, of whom there are maybe one hundred actors, and whom perhaps you need to look for? Haven't they all gone missing? Perhaps they are in danger. Because I now think this other man…' she pointed at another of Doctor Rousse's photographs, the one of the young red-head, from the fake hotel, '…he was also from the *Perle de Pigalle*. Poor boy.'

She cleared her throat. 'He was actually a pretty good actor, for his sins.'

Plates of beef and potatoes and green beans and a big tureen of soup were being carried into the small room, but Posie felt sick at the sight of it all and turned away. For once she wasn't hungry.

She paced up and down again, desperate to get her story straight.

She looked over to the photographs of dead people on the table, the waste of life there: Caroline Greenlow, poisoned; Inspector Jegouzo, shot; the red-headed boy, shot; Violette and the bald cat, shot.

And then she saw another. She saw the typed words at the bottom.

ALPHONSE DURRANT.

She walked over casually, pulled at it. She recognised the texture of the blazer, the small stripes of the shirt collar, the long dark hair. But the face was bloodied and unrecognizable, the features obliterated by a madness, an intensity of hate like no other.

The man in the photograph could have been anyone.

****

PART THREE
The Blue Garret

Chapter Twenty-Four

The Blue Garret was above a casino with a golden door, which was closed.

Outside, the whole of the Rue Lepic was picked out in twinkling jewel-like colours, and restaurants and tiny theatres advertised their wares with much yelling in the street.

The new craze for *Le Jazz Hot* had really taken root here, and saxophone music and the rhythmic 'THUMP-THUMP' of the double bass could be heard pretty much everywhere, like a heartbeat.

There was a rumour that Josephine Baker had fled Berlin, and was about to start up her own show at the Moulin Rouge, and this rumour alone was proving a big draw for the area.

Crowds of men, mainly students, were swarming around the steps to the closed Blue Garret by ten to eight, which was when the police cars pulled up.

A sign which was the very same as the advert Posie had seen on the noticeboard at the Sorbonne was pinned to the golden door, but with a big 'FERMÉ' scrawled through it now.

Students had started to bang on the golden door, yelling out. Angry.

Inside the Blue Garret, above, lights were flickering on, and the whole situation looked like it might get ugly.

But, in the event, Inspector Lucille came up trumps.

He'd foreseen the problems and quickly placed uniformed policemen around in a tight cordon, promising that those who had paid for the Egypt talk would receive their money back, and also, as a sweetener, offering free tickets to the Moulin Rouge, for tonight's show, to anyone who fancied going.

This offer was well received and the studenty crowd dispersed in a couple of minutes, moving off down the street towards the big red sails of the windmill of the Moulin Rouge, where a huge crowd was amassing.

Once the crowd had dispersed, Sergeant de Caunes opened the golden door to the casino, and before them all was a blue-glass staircase, the glass inlaid with small glittering golden nuggets.

He motioned for Posie and Lovelace to lead the way, and Inspector Lucille hovered down by the golden door, watching everyone else go up, checking them off a list.

Here was Mrs Shepherd, in black, like before, with the lace mantilla still fixed in place, and here was Doctor Dance, in a dark tan suit and matching tan Panama hat.

Dadie Spence, in the same much-crumpled mauve suit he had worn on the train yesterday, arrived in handcuffs between two policemen, looking surly and in need of freshening up.

Charles Loxley, obviously allowed a better sort of custody, arrived between two policemen, but without handcuffs, and he had been permitted a shave and a fresh suit.

Suzannah Scotland was dressed in her new set of clothes, and Daphne de Bengy arrived outrageously attired in a gold lamé split-thigh ball-dress, with a fake fur bolero over the top. Her fake eyelashes were also gold, and she had small gold sparkles attached to all her nails.

Posie had been all geared up to wear her pink woollen dress, which would have been fine, but just before they had all climbed into the waiting police cars, a package had arrived for her.

Opening it, she had found a royal-blue velvet column dress, plain at the front but draped with a low cowl at the back. A huge blue diamanté hair slide matched the dress. There was a note, too, in very bad handwriting but meant with a lot of heart:

POSIE,

I HEAR WE ARE MEETING AT THE BLUE GARRET. WHAT LARKS, EH?

I'VE MANAGED TO KEEP HOLD OF MY JOB! I CONVINCED THEM MY RUN-IN WITH THE POLICE EARLIER TODAY WAS ALL A MISUNDERSTANDING. THANK THE GOOD LORD!

I THOUGHT THIS DRESS MIGHT SUIT YOU, AND THE OCCASION.

I SAW IT IN THE DRESSING ROOM HERE THIS EVENING AND THOUGHT I'D BORROW IT FOR YOU, EH?

ONLY A LOAN, MIND, BUT PERFECT, HEY? IT'S THE COLOUR OF YOUR LOVELY EYES.

YOURS EVER,

DAPHNE.

Posie had raced back into the empty incident-room and hurriedly changed, in about two seconds flat.

The dress could have been made for her by Paul Poiret, it was so wonderful, and it stupidly, strangely, gave her a lot of confidence.

Around her neck she fastened Caroline Greenlow's precious scarab necklace, feeling its weight, knowing its history.

And now they stood grouped together at the top of the blue staircase in the Blue Garret, almost silently, most people gathered here not knowing *why* on earth they had been summoned.

And then, all in a rush, Inspector Lucille sent in his constables, a fast stream of about twenty men in uniform, all armed with guns, running up the stairs in hob-nailed boots.

The sound was like shots going off.

BANG, BANG, BANG.

The lapis-lazuli blue doors to the club were thrown open and a cosy small auditorium displayed, with blue crystal-glass walls, and one entire wall which was a fish tank, with only silvery-blue fish swimming within it.

A blue-glass chandelier threw out a strange light.

A small blue table had been set up under this light, in front of rows of pale-blue chairs.

Another bigger table to one side was groaning under the weight of golden amulets and face masks, and pots and packages that twinkled and sparkled beneath the eerie blue light.

Posie recognised Jakes, Lennart's Valet, who was standing next to the treasures like a sentry, his eyes darting about warily. Lex Lennart had been pacing up and down, checking his fob watch, but he now stood open-mouthed in shock.

The constables ran inside the room, a swarm of black angry bees, buzzing. They surrounded the walls, hung back.

Lennart, in his familiar turquoise blue, froze.

He called out. 'Say, why are the police here? And all of *you* lot? What in hell is happening here?'

Richard Lovelace shrugged. 'I might ask you the very same question, sir, and it is my job to ask questions: I am the Chief Commissioner of New Scotland Yard.'

'But I have a talk happening here!'

Lovelace laughed. 'Not any more, you don't, sir. And I would request your manservant to pack all that stuff away. The Antiquities team at Scotland Yard will be happy to assist in going through it, working out which items have been rightfully paid for by you, and which have been appropriated, and therefore needing to be returned to the Egyptian government. I think we will also engage Mr Howard Carter to help, because he might have returned by then, from Egypt. Or, forgive me, is he meant to be dropping in on you, here, this evening? As you have so cleverly advertised?'

Lex Lennart seemed to crumble. He stood back from the table with its gleaming riches, his eyes downcast.

Lovelace was at his most imperious, and Posie thought he was making up for his bad day.

'Fox, go and watch the manservant pack up, please. Everyone else, please take a seat around that central table. Sit in the front row. Now, I suggest everyone is given a drink, no, nothing blue, and then we can begin. Oh, and turn that ruddy blue light off, will you, Sergeant de Caunes? We all look sick as dogs. We may not be learning about Tutankhamun tonight but we *are* in for a real treat.'

Posie swallowed. *If only that were true.*

There were still holes in the story.

She watched the group sitting down, close to the blue table but at a distance from each other, as if they didn't trust each other one bit.

A bright light was suddenly switched on, bathing them all in a clean white beam.

Sergeant de Caunes rushed up to Posie suddenly, brandishing a telegram. 'This is for you, Miss Parker. From your Inspector Oats?'

'Sorry? What? Oh, yes. And you've got the scarab beetle, have you? The one Dadie Spence had in his pocket?'

'*Oui.*'

Posie read the telegram in a rush, but not too fast to marvel at how clever it all was.

Fantastic, in fact.

Smiling incredulously, she hurried to the table at the front.

Stood at it like a lecturn. She had a few notes and papers, but she put them down there, tried to speak without holding anything.

'Welcome, everyone. I had the joy, and the pain, of travelling with you all last night on the Night Ferry train. And it is my job to make sure the truth is told. A woman died in the early hours of this morning in horrific circumstances, and we need to make sure her murderer is properly punished.'

There were a few 'hear-hears' and all eyes had swivelled to Dadie Spence, who stared down at the floor and looked like he might cry.

'Inspector Lucille asked me this morning what linked us all, on that train. I said it was probably wealth. But now I know differently. You see, the train we were on was not a normal Night Ferry train. The Night Ferry is currently very busy, and can't cope with passenger numbers, but last night's train was different. Instead of up to eight sleeper carriages, it only had two sleeper carriages, which is the very minimum it can run with. So this train was unusual to begin with. And even more unusual was that one of the sleeper cars was virtually empty.'

She paused.

'Now, why would the train be running like this, during a time of intense busyness?'

She picked up Oats' telegram. 'I have concluded that it ran like this because the train was needed as a mobile stage-set.'

She looked out, her gaze running on past the constables who looked so threatening, lingering on the people right in front of her.

'The train *needed* to be understaffed, devoid of servants, with as few passengers on it as possible, so that it could function as a place primed for a murder to take place; a murder with as few witnesses as possible, and with many opportunities for confusion. And someone paid the colossal sum of fifteen thousand pounds for this to happen. The level of the money involved and the planning of the murder goes some way to showing us how much Caroline Greenlow was hated. Because this murder was all about revenge.'

A gasp ran around the room.

Lovelace whistled and looked impressed. 'Go on.'

'The money was paid one week ago. The inimitable Inspector Oats has since picked up Mr Brookman, the Director of the Night Ferry company, tonight at Southampton Docks, where he was caught trying to leave the country to start a new life in America. Mr Brookman had sent on almost fifteen thousand pounds there, as dollar bonds. He had reserved a small fraction of the money, however. And why? So that he could pay it out to a very small skeleton staff who could oversee last night's journey, and make it go exactly as was desired. I have heard from Sergeant Fox tonight that the Guard of the train has now been picked up at Le Touquet Airport, carrying more money than he would receive in ten years of work, and we expect to have similar news of the Waiter and the Driver very soon.'

Inspector Lucille had now entered the room. He stood at the back, by the blue-glass doors. He lit up a cigarette and looked about testily.

'So, who was it who paid the money, Miss Parker?' he asked irritably. 'If you have the proof. They say money always talks, *n'est-ce pas*?'

Lovelace looked at his colleague angrily, crossed his arms in silence. Nodded. 'Go on, Posie. As you were.'

'Unfortunately, it is not as simple as you would like,

Inspector Lucille. Because there is *much* behind this carefully-planned murder that is not straightforward.'

She shrugged. 'The plan was also open to pitfalls. For example, the train *should* have been even emptier. It was carrying four extra passengers who were not in the grand, planned design. At the very last minute, the day before the train left, another big sum of money, five thousand pounds, was paid over to Mr Brookman so that *I* could travel on the train, and also so that Suzannah Scotland could do so. I now believe we were both lured onto the train under false pretences: but that is for another story, not this one. And Daphne de Bengy also managed to get onto the train, mainly due to her own personal charms, of which there are many. And Inspector Alphonse Durrant, he also got on, citing police necessity.'

Posie looked over at Dadie Spence, who was watching her carefully. He looked a mess, but not addled, and not as dreadful as the night before. His wide-set purple eyes were very alert, very watchful.

Posie picked up the now slightly battered copy of the *Picture Post.*

She waved it all around.

'This was Caroline Greenlow and Dadie Spence telling the world about their blissful, surprise engagement. It was released just over a week ago. It was unexpected news, and, indeed, no other newspaper had got a clue, despite the fact Lady Caroline had prepared other interviews. Apparently not even their closest friends knew. But this story caused huge problems, started up deep shock-waves. You see, it spoke of an "imminent" wedding but it gave no date. It seemed to hint there was nothing yet planned. But the person this angered could take no chances. So, *this,*' she waved the magazine again, 'proved to be a death sentence. It was straight after this was published that the Night Ferry train was specially booked, and also when Caroline Greenlow got her invitation from Paul Poiret, here in Paris, and the deadly plan was put into action. But before I tell you why she was murdered, I first need to tell you a little story, all about Caroline Greenlow.'

Posie picked up her notes.

It was everything she had pieced together over the telephone, mainly from Sidney.

Hoping it held together, she read aloud:

'This story starts with a house full of women. An ancient, aristocratic, grand house in Surrey, lived in by a woman whose husband had suddenly died, leaving only a girl-child, who could not inherit the title. There was not much money anyhow, despite the grandness. The woman had three sisters, and along with two of these, this woman went to parties, spent all her money in London: on clothes, alcohol. Fast living. The child, I am afraid to say, was left on her own a good deal, while they partied in town. She should have been educated, nurtured, but she ran free in the grounds of the house, where her one joy was a huge, tall treehouse. She fell from it once, smashing her nose, and it wasn't set properly, but fortunately it didn't detract from her beauty. She was from a family of beauties, you see. Her mother and two of her aunts were well-known society beauties; all of them red-headed: the scandal of their day. The house was Greenlow House, and the little child was Caroline Greenlow.'

Posie explained that a tragedy had occurred when Caroline was about eleven.

A fire had enveloped the house, destroying it, killing Caroline's mother and her two aunts. The child had miraculously survived, and had been discovered up in her treehouse.

Afterwards, the girl had been sent away to school. There had been another aunt, married, and rich, but she had not wanted Caroline.

Posie looked about grimly.

'The third aunt did not want Caroline for a number

of reasons. The child reminded her of her sisters and their loose ways. Caroline was also red-headed, although lately she has dyed her hair very blonde. But mainly the aunt didn't want Caroline because she was trouble. Even though she was extraordinarily clever, Caroline got into bad ways. There had even been rumours that Caroline had set Greenlow House on fire herself, as an act of spite and revenge at her own mother. Police reports from the time certainly detail the child's condition on that night up in the treehouse: her clothes soaked in petrol; unable to account for how she had got there or why she was out of bed. But nothing ever came of the reports, and any sort of investigation was dropped. These reports were probably enough to convince the third aunt to leave Caroline well alone. After all, this aunt had her own life, and her own child, too. She didn't want Caroline spoiling any of that. Oh, I forgot to mention: Caroline's surname was *not* Greenlow. She should never have been that; only if she had been born a boy. Then she would have been Earl Greenlow. But her real name was Lady Caroline Duff-Shepherd.'

'How did she manage that?' boomed out Charles Loxley obnoxiously. 'She misappropriated the name? Doesn't surprise me!'

Posie replied calmly. 'No, Sir Charles. She changed her name, by deed poll when she was twenty-one. That was when, if she had been a boy, she would have come into the Earldom of Greenlow.'

'Pah!' shouted Loxley, shaking his head. 'Lot of nonsense. I always knew she was a fraud. A fake!'

Posie rustled her papers. Looked about at the people in front of her.

'I've already told you that the murder motive here was revenge. Pure and simple. But, as I find in so many, many cases, this one too, right behind everything is *money*.'

'Money, eh?' Lovelace nodded. 'Yep. Sounds about right.'

Posie looked at every face turned up to her, letting her eyes linger on Dadie Spence, then Suzannah Scotland.

'But I need to bring someone else into the story now. I need to introduce you to someone who was *not* on the train last night, but whose personality and power over this story was such that he might as well have been...'

Everyone stared.

Daphne de Bengy looked over at the closed blue door as if expecting a surprise guest to burst through it dramatically, and everyone followed suit, craning their necks.

But the door remained firmly closed, Lucille guarding it.

'There is no point hoping for a last-minute arrival. Which is a shame, as by all accounts this man was quite wonderful. He was a man of beauty, of wealth, with a war record to boot. But a man who was, underneath it all, a coward.'

Posie cleared her throat, looking at Charles Loxley first. 'The man I need to tell you about was a man for whom money, too, was the most important thing. To really understand what happened last night, there are four stories I need to tell you about this man. Because they are all equally important. And his name, by the way, was David Greeze.'

Dadie Spence yelled out: 'Who are you talking about, Miss Parker? Caroline has never mentioned his name to me, not once. Not ever!'

'No? Well, I am not surprised, Mr Spence. I have never met this man, but, once in a lifetime, there comes along someone for everyone who causes the heart to burn like crazy, who is unforgettable, someone for whom one realises what "love" is for.'

Posie didn't look at Lovelace.

She wasn't actually sure she was describing her husband. *Perhaps once, for her, there had been such a man, but he had been swept away by a sea of change and the tides of life, ebbing, flowing.*

And there was nothing left of that love.

Avoiding Richard's gaze, she spoke to everyone: 'David Greeze was that love for Caroline Greenlow. I think he must have been utterly magnetic. I suppose Caroline did not mention him to you, Mr Spence, because there was nothing to say: yours was a new relationship, Mr Spence, and any talk of old, unimaginable passion was probably not the best way to navigate it.'

Doctor Dance called out: 'Where was he, then, last night? This Mr Greeze?'

'Dead,' said Posie, simply. 'He died last year.'

Doctor Dance stared, and Lex Lennart bowed his head. Dadie Spence looked like he might cry.

Posie read from her notes: 'Caroline met David when she was about twenty. But she never married him. He was promised to another, and, although there was a minor wobble at his own engagement party, he stuck to his promise to marry his intended, even though he did not love her. What I have *not* told you about David Greeze was that apart from being absolutely magnetic, he was frighteningly rich. And his arranged marriage made him richer still. It seems he could not give these riches up, and that is why I have called him out as being a coward.'

Daphne de Bengy called out: 'Plenty of men like that, Miss! Doesn't surprise me at all. The blighter!'

Posie nodded. 'Well, David Greeze went one step further. He hoped to have his cake and to eat it: right after he met Caroline, he put in place a scheme very quickly whereby he "kept" her, in secret. He paid her a monthly amount and she lived in a flat he rented for her in London. But their story was tragic: a look through the newspapers reveals a history of ill-health for Lady Caroline which was probably synonymous with pregnancies, and perhaps lost babies. Whether it was the alcoholism which caused it, or something else, I do not know. It must have been dreadful.

But I know they loved each other through all of this. In 1916 he had a priceless jewel made for her. A scarab beetle. Which she wore until this morning, when she died.'

Posie unclasped the necklace and showed the jewel all around. In the bright white light, it sparkled like a cursed thing.

'Where does *this* get us, Miss Parker?' called out Inspector Lucille.

'It tells us the first story. You should also know that Lady Caroline was with David Greeze right up until the end, when he died, last year, very young. He had leukaemia. It is stated on his death certificate. She loved him, nursed him. Adored him.'

I would have loved him forever.

Posie now told the second story. 'Something else you should know about David Greeze was his fascination for ancient Egypt, an interest he'd had since a boy. When others were dressing up as sailors and pirates, he was dressing up as an archaeologist. He was actually there when the Tomb of Tutankhamun was opened, and I even believe he put a good deal of money into the quest. But perhaps Mr Lennart here can tell us more? Because you knew him, did you not, sir?'

Lex Lennart had been sitting nursing a glass of untouched whisky. He stood suddenly, looked about himself, shame-faced.

'Gee, I can't tell you any more. David was a private, reserved kinda guy, and we all knew he had deep pockets. While I sunk nearly everything I had into Howard Carter's discovery, Greeze paid over even more. But he made it a rule not to be photographed, and never came along to any of Howard's lectures, either. I don't know what he was scared of, perhaps the mummy's curse?'

Lennart wiped his hands quickly across his eyes. 'Say, I'm beginning to think the curse is real. David died young, didn't he? Out of the blue, almost. All I know is that when we were all goin' crazy, grabbing at the treasures down there in the tomb, he didn't go wild at all. David looked kinda sick at it. He told me he had only ever taken two scarab beetles from a dig, before the Great War, and he had paid for them properly. He said he'd given them to people he loved.'

Posie nodded at Sergeant de Caunes, who passed the plain scarab beetle up. Posie held it aloft, together with its much more richly-adorned 'twin'.

'These two are that very pair of scarabs. But this one,' and she waved the plain one, 'was intended as a murder weapon last night.'

'But not by me!' stammered Lennart, quickly.

Posie shrugged. 'Perhaps, and perhaps not.'

Lennart shook his head mournfully. He indicated his two boxes of treasures, now packed up. 'David would have hated all this, *here*. This circus of curiosities, with lies attached. But we can't all be saints, can we? A man's gotta make his money some way, hasn't he? Especially when you find you've been suddenly declared bankrupt. Not all of us are loaded with a steady stream of money which never ceases…'

He shook his head and sat down.

Posie looked over at Lovelace and he gave her a small, encouraging smile.

But Posie continued to address the American:

'I don't think, actually, Mr Lennart, that David Greeze was a saint. Not at all. And this is the worst thing about the third story connected to him, which I must now tell. He *was* startlingly rich, from a brewing family, and his wife came from an even richer brewing family. Their marriage was, on paper, perfect. But I am rather afraid he was a complete rotter to his wife. In fact, he virtually killed her.'

Posie took a deep breath.

'Is that not so, Suzannah Scotland?'

****

Chapter Twenty-Five

Everyone swivelled to look at Suzannah, who was placed rather near the back at the door. She looked about herself, wild-eyed.

She made a '*Who? Me?*' gesture.

Sergeant Fox, sitting next to her, hissed something in her ear, and she gasped audibly.

'Oh! THE POSTCARDS! *Oui!* Jeannette de Montparnasse! She was David's wife!'

Suzannah stood up, and pointed over at Mrs Shepherd, who was sitting in the front row. 'You, Madame! You can talk about Jeanette better than me, can you not? You were with her picture a good deal of today. *Non*?'

Posie turned quickly to Mrs Shepherd. 'Would you like to tell us how Jeannette de Montparnasse fits into all of this?'

There was a deep silence.

Mrs Shepherd stared at Posie with her small brown eyes narrowed, her mouth a hard, angry line.

'I'll explain then, shall I?' Posie asked.

At the silence she shrugged and continued. 'Jane Morrell was your daughter, Mrs Shepherd, wasn't she? She became Jane Greeze. And you are really Lady Ottoline Morrell, but you reverted to your maiden name of Shepherd when you lost everything. You are also the aunt of Caroline Greenlow; the aunt who refused to take her in after the fire.'

The silence continued.

Posie picked up her notebook, read the few lines she's scribbled about Jane.

'Your daughter had dark-brown hair. She looked exactly like you; I've seen a photograph. She was not a beauty. But she was madly in love with her husband, both before and after their wedding, which happened in late summer, 1916. She forgave him for ruining their engagement party, for embarrassing her in spectacular style. But soon after the wedding she realised that, to her horror, her cousin Caroline was still very much on the scene. Jane knew David loved Caroline above all things, and so, she started to act like her cousin.'

Posie watched Mrs Shepherd's impassive face, the way her arms were tightening around her now-shrunk body, which had previously been huge and bosomy and magnificent.

Posie continued: 'Jane Greeze dyed her hair red, and she started to paint more, a hobby she had always enjoyed. But then she pushed it even further. She started to drink heavily. I suppose this must have driven you crazy, because she was acting just like your own sisters, and just like your own niece, Caroline. The bad blood in the family was now coursing through your own child's veins…'

People gasped. Dadie Spence tried to stand up to get a better look at Mrs Shepherd but he wobbled in his handcuffs and was restrained.

Posie carried on: 'I can only piece together what happened, but I suppose Jane decided to try and get David's attention with a sudden "shock tactic". A year into their loveless marriage, she upped and moved to Montparnasse. In 1917 this was the "place to be" in Paris, if you were an artist, as Jane fancied she could be, and she quickly met Amedeo Modigliani.'

Posie held up one of the postcards from the cemetery. 'Jane became Modigliani's muse and the subject of some of the most brilliant and shocking works of art Paris had ever seen. But the rest is all a sad history. Jane drank herself silly, and forgot all about her previous life.'

Posie put the postcard down, face down on the table.

'Mrs Shepherd, I think you disowned Jane, or *Jeannette*, as she had become known, for there is no record of your attending her burial three years later when she most probably committed suicide. And David Greeze did not attend, either. Although he did come to Paris, to the Morgue, to check Jane Greeze was really dead.'

Doctor Dance took off his tan hat and dabbed at his watery eye and Posie smelt the iodine across the room.

'Why on earth did he do *that*, Miss Parker? Seems a pretty odd thing to do. If he had lived without his wife, happily, for more than three years?'

'I suppose because of the Will, Doctor Dance,' Posie answered. 'Which I have had recourse to. Jane Greeze, or Jeannette de Montparnasse, left everything to her husband David on her death. It was all the shares in her family company – the controlling interest – provided that he did not marry again. I suppose the wealth was worth several million pounds.'

Charles Loxley whistled. 'Can of worms, this, eh? Little Jean got her revenge in death, eh? So David couldn't marry his beloved mistress if he wanted to keep his riches! What a clever little Will, though. Clever mousey little Jean…'

Mrs Shepherd stood up suddenly, the lace mantilla falling from her head. She snapped her head towards Loxley.

'Her name was *Jane*.'

Her anger was below the surface, flat, calm, but it was terrible, like a lion about to spring. She stayed standing, facing Posie.

'What you hint at is indeed correct, Miss Parker. David

Greeze destroyed my family. When Jane left for Paris, and when we found out how she was living, in 1917, after that disgusting exhibition, my husband had a stroke. It basically killed him. He'd made the mistake of handing over the company shares to Jane before she went off the rails. He never recovered. I'm glad he never lived to see or hear about the day she died, unhappy and in agony. In a dump in Paris, in 1920. I too got very ill after Jane died. I felt like dying myself. I've not really recovered. And while I'm vastly unhappy that her Will left *anything* to him at all, I was always happy that David Greeze never married my dreadful niece.'

The woman's anger was terrible to behold. 'Caroline was the cause of all the unhappiness, and for my daughter's unhappy marriage. Caroline was a terrible child, and a terrible woman.'

Lovelace was darting anxious looks at Lucille, who tapped at his watch meaningfully.

'So is Mrs Shepherd the killer, Posie?' Her husband called out hurriedly.

'Bear with me.' Posie moved on hastily. She picked up another piece of paper.

'There was a notice placed in the advertisement section of every newspaper in London last week, the day after the *Picture Post* was published. I'll read it aloud for everyone to hear.'

GREEZE

Bad Debts need to be immediately dealt with and investments paid out. Interested? Speak tomorrow, latest.

Contact THIS PAPER: PO BOX 129

'By Gad! And was this answered?' asked Lovelace, quietly.

'Oh, yes,' replied Posie. 'We have proof from at least one newspaper that the PO BOX was set up for Mrs Shepherd, and she collected the replies in person. Of which there were two.'

Inspector Lucille cut in: 'You mean, Miss Parker, Mrs Shepherd advertised for murder? She advertised to see if anyone else would want to join her in killing Caroline Greenlow? Caroline Greenlow was the 'bad debt' to be dealt with?'

Posie nodded.

'But why now, Posie?' yelled out Daphne, who was smoking, lazily curled up in her chair.

'It sounds to me like Mrs Shepherd had every right to want David Greeze dead, and Lady Caroline dead too. They'd taken her daughter for a fool, spent the family money, and basically had a good old time. But this situation had been going on for years and years. Since Jane's death? When did you say that was? In 1920? So why *now*? Why the urgency?'

Posie picked up the *Picture Post* again.

'We know Lady Caroline and Dadie Spence were going to marry, don't we? Incidentally, we also know Caroline was pregnant, and that they had to hurry before it became a scandal.'

Posie saw Dadie look away, hurt, exposed, and she felt awful. But she was trying to be thorough here.

'And again, this comes down to *money*. Caroline used everything up after David's death, she struggled. His monthly payments to her stopped, of course, last year, on his death. But Caroline knew he had provided for her. It was a question of not being too destructive, and just waiting. You see, David's Will had made provision for Caroline to inherit everything he had, which, importantly, included all of Jane's shares, but only if Caroline was still unmarried at thirty.'

‘By Gad,’ whispered Lovelace, lighting up a Turkish cigarette.

‘So even if Caroline Greenlow married at one day *over* thirty, she’d inherit the lot?’

‘Exactly, darling,’ whispered Posie.

And louder: ‘And that was what she was going to do. She had pre-prepared interviews in some of the newspapers, all about turning thirty, and being unattached. But we know she was going to get married in Westminster next Saturday, the day *after* she turned thirty.’

‘Blimey!’ muttered Fox. ‘And what if, like is the case, Caroline didn’t make it? Where does David, and Jane’s, money go now?’

Posie explained that if Caroline did not inherit David’s money, the Will of David Greeze enabled the money of Jane to go back to her family, and for the original money of David to be used for any causes to do with Egypt, to be freely administered by Lex Lennart.

Lovelace inhaled, exhaled. ‘By Gad! This is a strong motive. One of the strongest I’ve ever come across.’

He looked straight across at Lex Lennart. ‘And you knew about this Will, did you, sir? About your potential to get your hands on a fortune, to use it for something you love?’

Lex Lennart nodded. ‘David told me, when he was sick, last year. He wrote to me. I was delighted. I’ve run my own resources completely down. Well, look at me here, faking things for money. David’s money seemed a great chance to do some good work.’

Or rob some more graves, thought Posie to herself archly.

‘You were one of the people who answered the PO BOX, weren’t you, Mr Lennart?’ said Posie, sweetly. ‘You listened to the plan, which I suppose was Mrs Shepherd’s, about the train, and travelling with no servants and a reduced staff. You heard about the proposed invite to Fashion Week, and you thought it a good one. It was, after all, easy for Mrs Shepherd to concoct the invitation; she'd been sent some of Paul Poiret's writing paper only the year before and it would have appeared convincing enough. You probably couldn't help her by putting up money to pay for the train, but you were prepared to travel on that train and give the whole thing credence: help muddle things, if necessary, throw evidence around.'

'By Gad!' Lovelace shook his head. 'But what about the poisoning itself? How was that done? Was that you, Lennart?'

Posie shook her head. 'No. There were two replies to this advertisement, remember? And there were four stories attaching to David Greeze. I have not yet told you the last...'

Mrs Shepherd looked away, a surly expression on her face.

Posie held a photo in her hands.

'Somebody else in this room tonight had loved David Greeze more than life itself, ever since they were small. It was probably reciprocated. This person hadn't minded when David married Jane Morrell, as it was clear that Jane meant nothing to David. But when David met Caroline, this person despaired. It was like a promise of their own true love being broken; a vow being ripped apart.'

It had been staring Posie in the face all along.

Those pictures of boys in pairs. One dark and one blonde.

The two flasks.

The two scarab beetles.

Charles Loxley and Dadie Spence were turning to Daphne with a sudden gruesome interest, and gradually the whole room did so too.

'*What?*' Daphne shrieked. 'I never met this David chap! I swear on my life!'

Posie smiled.

'You're all wrong.'

People turned then and stared at Suzannah Scotland

instead, who flushed bright red under the harsh lights.

Posie held up her perfume-ruined photograph of two small boys.

'You are all wrong again. Wrong sex, even. Because David Greeze had a special friend at school, at Eton. A boy. A boy who loved him so much he would have followed him to the ends of the earth. A boy who followed him into battle, and, apparently, when he realised he had lost David to Caroline, a boy who threw himself into the war obsessively. Destructively.'

'Good Lord! You mean Doctor Dance?'

Lovelace was standing now, as was Fox, coming towards the front of the room where Doctor Dance was sitting, dabbing at his eye, playing with his decorative *pince-nez*.

Posie shrugged.

'I don't have all the photographs with me, but ironically, Doctor Dance, your mother, the Matron at Eton, contacted me to try and find you. She sent me pictures of you with David, when you were tiny, and she'd tried to follow you through the years, although it was hard, as you disappeared after a battle in 1917. You never returned. Not to *her*, anyway. Which was cruel, as she only had you in the whole world. She never stopped believing you might be alive. She told me recently that you and David had had matching hip-flasks. Very expensive. Gold. David bought them for you both when you entered the army together.'

Posie stared at Doctor Dance, who stared right back with his one eye.

'You changed your name so you couldn't be found, didn't you? You stopped being Friedrich Walter – David called you "Waltzer", apparently, or sometimes when he was feeling affectionate, he called you "Matilda", as in "Waltzing Matilda" – and you later changed your name to Derick Dance out of fondness for his old nickname for you. David gave you one of his scarab beetles during the Great War, didn't he? A plain one, to remind you of him.

Although it was as nothing compared to the one he gave to Caroline. After he met Caroline, I think you stayed in touch with David, but only sporadically. Mainly you stayed away. Went to Africa. But you came back when you heard David was dying of cancer.'

Doctor Dance threw his head back and laughed. It was a harsh sound, full of a lifetime of pent-up bitterness.

His hat fell off and the terrible white beam caught his face, and lit up his scragged-together features. And all the pain and all the pity, was mulched there together for everyone to see, in plain sight.

'David wasn't dying of cancer!' Doctor Dance said jovially, as if discussing the weather.

'I knew that David was being poisoned. It was Caroline, angry at never being married, never being provided for with the riches which she thought were her due! She got her revenge on him, in the most awful way.'

Dance shrugged. 'Rat poison, I thought. Or pure arsenic. Over a long period of time, certainly. But what could I do? I was too late; it is my eternal regret. I visited him in hospital, in June, near the end, and made sure it was at a time *she* wasn't there. I hadn't seen Caroline Greenlow for years, by then. Not since 1916, in fact, at that wretch of a party, when she took him away from me. I was away a lot last year: India, Africa, the Middle East. But it was a shock when David died. He didn't leave me anything. Even the "match" to my gold flask went to Caroline. Although he'd had the presence of mind not to give her his fortune outright. Made her wait. Clever lad.'

Posie consulted her notes, jabbed at a line angrily: 'You contested David's Will, though, didn't you? You declared he wasn't in his right mind when he made it, as he was being poisoned and in agony. You named Lady Caroline, too, as being the suspected poisoner. Which must have been awful for her, as there was an official enquiry. It could have ruined her if they had found against her. Is that what you really wanted? As it was, the evidence was inconclusive. Paltry. Perhaps you even placed it, yourself? I wouldn't put it past you…'

Doctor Dance shrugged. 'I hope she suffered during that enquiry, like David suffered at her hands.'

Lovelace shook his head. 'You, sir, are supposed to cure, not to kill. And so you replied to Lady Shepherd's notice, too, did you? Signed up for this joint venture? Got yourself added to a list of speakers at the Sorbonne, probably last minute, eh? To give yourself a nice bit of credibility. I'll check it out, and I'll nail you down, you piece of filth. And you helpfully provided the murder weapon, I suppose. You got the antimony in Africa, did you? A nice touch. To poison someone who you believed to be a poisoner…'

Posie felt tired now. Staggered by the sheer dreadfulness of it all, but the story was almost done. 'And on the train ride you managed to use everything David Greeze had ever given you, didn't you? You choked Lady Caroline on his plain scarab beetle, which you'd had the chance to dip into arsenic. And you used the flask David had given you, filled with poisoned drink, to "double swap" it with hers, at dinner, by pre-arranging with the Driver for the train to stop at Canterbury, and for the lights to go out so you could get rid of the original hip-flask. Very clever.'

Doctor Dance was shaking his head. 'This is all circumstantial. There is no proof of any of this, anywhere.'

Lovelace was grabbing at Doctor Dance; Fox was pulling out handcuffs.

'I'll find proof, sir, if it kills me,' raged Lovelace. 'And whose decision was it to get Charles Loxley on board? Yours, too? I'll make it my business to find out: I swear it. Clever, to get someone on board who had a long-running feud with the intended victim. And I suppose it was you, Doctor Dance, who "placed" the arsenic in Loxley's bag, and then put the poisoned hip-flask in Dadie Spence's duffle bag when you were 'helping' him with a sedative.

My God, what must Lady Caroline have thought when she got onto that train yesterday and it pulled out of the station? She was having dinner with two of her deadliest enemies in the world and she'd walked right into your trap. She must have realised it was tightening all around her.'

'Calm yourself, Commissioner,' said Doctor Dance cheerily. 'Even if what you say is true, which it is not, both Mrs Shepherd and I are both much changed since 1916, and I don't believe Caroline would have recognised either of us for a second. Besides, she was too drunk. She spent her life being drunk.'

But Posie knew this was not the case.

At dinner Caroline Greenlow had looked at Doctor Dance as if she had seen a ghost. Had placed him.

Because voices remain.

And she had obviously known Mrs Shepherd was her aunt from the very start, even if she was a mere shadow of her former self.

Lady Caroline had tried to block her aunt out by closing her eyes, by erecting a screen of rudeness, hiding hurt which went back years.

Posie remembered the taut, trapped nerve in Caroline Greenlow's face when her aunt had spoken of her sisters in their Paul Poiret dresses, of the way they had burnt to death, at the hands of an arsonist...

Yes, the trap had been tightening, even then.

There were glittering handcuffs out now, and Sergeant Fox and Sergeant de Caunes were looping them around the hands of Lex Lennart, and putting them on Mrs Shepherd.

But Inspector Lucille was calling out, stabbing his cigarette into the air angrily:

'What I don't understand is the money. *Non.* All of these people you have just arrested spent a fortune on setting up a train in order to kill a woman they hated, for different reasons. They needed to pay a great deal of money for this murder to happen, and none of them seem to have money. In fact, Lennart and Mrs Shepherd needed the money from David's Will. So how did they pay?'

'It was ingenious,' said Posie.

'Some years ago, Mrs Shepherd bought one of the paintings of Jane by Modigliani. But she couldn't, or wouldn't, have it in her house. Instead, she visited it here, in Paris, on the date of Jane's death every year. And recently, feeling that she would now be avenging Jane properly, she decided she didn't need it anymore. She sold it. For a massive amount. When my friend Suzannah went to visit the picture earlier today, she was told she was only just in time to see it, and I believe it will be packaged up and sent on to its new home, not far from here, tomorrow. Fifteen thousand pounds were paid straight to Mr Brookman's bank account last week. And it came directly from the Louvre Gallery, here, in Paris.'

* * * *

Chapter Twenty-Six

Downstairs, policemen were shouting, and those people who had been arrested were grouped in the hallway to await being led out to waiting police cars.

Upstairs, Dadie Spence was crying and Daphne was comforting him, and Charles Loxley, now freed from his handcuffs, was drinking whisky at the blue-glass bar. His red briefcase was right at his feet and he seemed to be counting down the minutes until he could leave.

Sergeant Fox came over to Posie, who had sat down at last. She saw he looked awkward, uncomfortable.

'What is it, Sergeant?'

'One of the French lads just brought a cable up for you: it's been sitting over at the Police Station this last half-hour. It's from the Earl of Cardigeon. The Earl says he never asked you to leave for Paris yesterday. He never booked you on the Night Ferry. He thought you were talking about collecting your Lagonda when you called him on Monday night and told him you were accepting something from him.'

Posie nodded.

Well, that made sense at least.

For a second, alone, Posie remained sitting at the table. She saw that Sergeant Fox was now talking animatedly to Suzannah in the corner, their heads very close.

Alphonse Durrant had said someone else would be around the corner for Suzannah, hadn't he? Well, he'd been right.

Poor Durrant, who had been attacked and stabbed on the train very early this morning, after an argument in his locked berth.

Most people, except Posie, and perhaps Inspector Lucille, believed he had actually died today.

Well, he *could* have been killed, couldn't he? Others had been falsely imprisoned and implicated for his murder, albeit not for long.

There had even been that guard of honour for him at the station.

Someone had wanted him dead, and now everyone believed him dead, but his almost-murderer was still out there, free.

Posie remembered Suzannah's recollection about what she had heard through the door of the berth as she had waited for Durrant, before she fell asleep.

I heard the word 'school' mentioned by Alphonse, I'm sure.

And the word 'love'.

Posie was so tired.

Hearing these two words made her think again of Doctor Dance, and the dead David Greeze. Theirs had been a love which had flourished at school, and beyond.

'Oh! My days! Of course! They *knew* each other!'

What if Alphonse Durrant, like Doctor Dance, had attended Eton, for free, just because of his father's job?

What if Durrant and Dance had known each other as boys?

And what if, yesterday on the Night Ferry, they had been thrown together once again? A strange, dreadful, and hugely unlikely coincidence.

Because even though Doctor Dance was changed, voices remain.

Characteristics remain.

Posie stood up: *yes, that made sense*. As did the strange glances, the slight frisson of hostility between the two men at the green-glass bar, and then the argument which had occurred later.

It would have been a bad one.

Posie bounded downstairs. Would they already have left?

She was in luck.

Inspector Lucille was still waiting with his prisoners inside the golden door.

'Doctor Dance?'

Posie came right up to him.

'Why did you try and murder Alphonse Durrant this morning? Was it because he recognised you as being little Friedrich Walter, whose mother spends her days searching for his very existence? Did he tell you she was heartbroken? That she was a good woman, and was helping nurse his own father? Did Durrant tell you he had just come from there, from Eton? Where your mother never stops wondering what happened to you? What on earth did Alphonse Durrant *do* which was so dreadful to you?

Doctor Dance stood stock-still in his handcuffs, in the strange blue-golden light of the corridor.

And then he shrugged. 'I was overrun by coincidence. Durrant threatened to tell my mother I was still alive. I couldn't allow that. Not with this face! I can't stand her pity. I won't go back to her, not ever. She chokes the life out of everything. Durrant was always a do-gooder, even at school. Always had to stick his nose in. He said he'd give me until tonight, then he'd ring my mother and tell her he'd seen me. And he'd give her my new name. I couldn't let that happen, could I? He had to die.'

Posie stared, appalled at the complete lack of feeling. 'And others could take the blame?' she hissed angrily. 'You're appalling!'

'I'm practical,' replied Dance, from over his shoulder.

The golden door was now open onto the street. Cars and crowds of policemen were waiting outside. 'And I'll be practical about this situation I find myself in now, Miss Parker. Just you see.'

And then the prisoners were being herded out, Lovelace looking pleased as punch, and sharing some kind of improbable joke with Inspector Lucille.

Suddenly Daphne de Bengy was beside Posie in the hallway, all in a fluster.

'Awwight, lovey? That velvet sure suits you. Look, there's someone outside who's waving, she obviously wants to talk to you. A woman, with very blonde hair, in a motor-taxi…'

And then Posie was snatching up her carpet bag and she was running, because on the cobbles of the Rue Lepic was a taxi, pulled up, parked, and inside it was Dolly.

Outside, on the road beside the motor-taxi, was Anatole de Poilac, still in his black university gown.

He was beckoning, quickly. 'Look who I found, Miss Parker. I tracked her down for you. Quick. Get in, she wants to explain.'

****

Chapter Twenty-Seven

At least, it had looked like Dolly from afar.

But when Posie got in the car, the girl with the short peroxided hair turned properly, and Posie saw it was another girl altogether, much younger, with blue eyes, not brown.

And a hard expression where Dolly's had only ever been soft.

'Oh!'

The car moved off, and Anatole de Poilac was left behind, standing on the cobbles of Montmartre, laughing heartily, glad to have inconvenienced Posie, to have got her back for rejecting his advances.

Revenge.

The girl in the car laughed too and lit a cheap cigarette. She stared out of the window as they went very fast over cobbles and bumps in the road, down dark streets and past shut-up villas.

Posie's mouth was dry, and she sat gripped by fear.

'Who are you?'

But the girl evidently spoke no English, and didn't want to communicate, and Posie tried to stay calm.

This must all be down to him. Caspian della Rosa.

I've stayed alive this long, perhaps he'll let me live a little longer.

She thought of the faces of her babies, Phyllis, Katie, Kit.

Of how much she loved them and wanted to kiss them one last time.

They were pulling up now at the Champs-Élysées. Number 77. The blonde girl got out of the car and took Posie's arm tightly. Posie felt a gun being pressed into her back.

This must have been the girl Richard had seen earlier, at the fake hotel, with the gun. And, come to think of it, hadn't Posie seen this girl earlier, too? Dressed in a paper cap at Jegouzo's office, serving cakes?

And perhaps later on, too, in a wig, wrapping up toys in the toyshop.

Perhaps she did a good Liverpudlian accent too? The queen of the *Perle de Pigalle* Theatre Troupe? Or just one of Caspian della Rosa's crooks?

Posie found herself being marched to the side door by the jewellery shop. The girl was ringing the bell for 'Galerie FF'.

They were buzzed in, but there was no Porter here this time. Posie found herself stepping, like in some dream, into the glittering lift. She had no thoughts as to running away, or breaking free of this blonde girl who was her captor. There was just a dumb acceptance.

And here was 'GALERIE FF' but, of course, there was no firm of lawyers here, no sign saying 'REDON'.

The door to the place was closed.

The girl beside her spoke. In perfect English. 'You have the key, *non*?'

Posie found herself fishing in her carpet bag, bringing out the key.

The big, solid door opened easily and together, she and the blonde girl stepped into a parqueted hallway, with white flowers in vases, and gilt mirrors above occasional tables.

It was an upmarket apartment. A home.

'HULLO?' Posie called.

She walked down the hallway, noting rooms at each side, bedrooms, a room with a white piano, a small ballroom.

She came to the last room, a huge living-room which looked out over the Champs-Élysées, with the Arc de Triomphe to the right, ablaze with golden electrical light. A balcony ran around the living-room, and all the doors leading onto it were open.

Posie walked to the balcony. Gazed out at Paris in all its gorgeous, bewitching glory.

She suddenly realised her blonde companion with the gun had disappeared.

Thank goodness.

She heard a familiar voice behind her. One she had not heard in more than a year and had hoped never to hear again.

'Don't turn around.'

'Caspian della Rosa, we meet again?'

'We do indeed. And tell me: how have you enjoyed your trip to Paris?'

'It's been eventful.'

'I knew it would be. That's why I put you on that train.'

Posie swallowed. Strangely, she felt no fear now. None at all.

'I started to suspect that was the case. But how did you know…?'

'What would happen on board? To Lady Greenlow?'

There was a manic, sinister laugh. 'Well, I listen to everything, you know. Literally everything. All across London. Just for fun. I bug your telephone lines; your husband's telephone lines; your little pal Rufus' telephone, too. And when I got wind of this clever plot, I thought you should be on that train: you should sort the murder out.'

There was a burst of dreadful coughing from behind Posie, a hacking sound which was almost pitiful, but she didn't turn.

'Oh? You knew Caroline Greenlow would die?'

'That's right. It was complicated, darn clever really. I thought you should get justice for that girl, not that she really deserved it. But mainly I thought I would help *you*: give you a bit of a nudge upwards for your professional profile. You've been a bit quiet of late, haven't you?'

'Er...well.'

Posie was trying desperately hard to see Caspian della Rosa in the reflection of the window. Mainly to see if he had a gun on him. Or a knife.

But she couldn't see. It was too dark.

'Don't turn, Miss Parker. You're twitching, like you might turn around. I was telling you, I paid for you to be on that train, and then I gave you a nice little jaunt around Paris, too. A kind of fictional jaunt.'

'Do you mean the police station at Ront-Point and also the hotel which didn't exist?'

There was that crazy, high-pitched laugh again. 'Exactly.'

Here we go, thought Posie. 'But what on earth was the point of it all? It seems excessive, even for *you*.'

'How you flatter me. It was to show you I could still put on a good show. To give myself a kick! It was so much fun: too good an opportunity to pass up.'

'What was? Using the *Perle de Pigalle* Theatre troupe?'

The coughing started up again, but the man rushed on huskily: 'You've got so clever, Posie Parker. Yes, exactly! A whole theatre troupe were acting things out for my benefit, no, sorry, for *your* benefit, across the city! It was wonderful. Like a game. You know how much I love disguises, the theatre. It really perked me up no end. I also had to create something alternative as that idiot Jegouzo wouldn't play ball.'

'No? Why did you kill him?'

'He would have protected you. I called him up personally and tried to explain what I wanted to do, and he wasn't having any of it. He'd already sent a telegram off to that poor sap Durrant by the time I went and had it out with him with my gun. He probably warned Durrant you were in danger! Yes, a shame. But people die. That's what happens, sometimes.'

Posie almost gasped at the callousness of the man but she forced herself to bite at her lip instead.

She had to try and survive this.

'Yes, as I said. A shame: poor ickle wickle birdie, too. The feathers went everywhere.'

'Mnnn. I saw that. They were in the toyshop, and at the hotel. Even at Violette's flat…'

There was a 'pah!' sound of annoyance.

'That lad I put in charge, the red-head, at the hotel, he stuffed everything up with his carelessness. He told me you had seen a green feather at the hotel, and you looked curious about it. It shouldn't ever have been allowed to be there! The whole place should have been swept clean, otherwise you might have made a connection between my various constructs. Sheer carelessness!'

'So, he had to die, too?'

'Yes.'

Posie swallowed, she felt like gagging, tried not to remember the dead lad's face. That roll-call of the dead from today, all at the City Morgue. She felt an intense anger now.

'And what about Violette? You killed her too? For what? You marched her out of her flat with all her possessions and then you killed her? And the cat? That's simply dreadful.'

There was a pause, then what sounded like a sudden, deep sigh. 'No, Posie. On that you are wrong. Very wrong.'

There was another small silence. Outside there was the sound of laughter, an accordion somewhere, a taxi hooting merrily.

'Violette Lagarde did *not* die at my hands. We had an understanding, me and her. Would you believe it, I liked her? True, initially I got her to do some work for me; up here, as it happens. I got her to try and get your little pal Dolly over here, but it failed. In fact, I think clever little Violette may have double-crossed me by meeting Dolly and taking the cat from her, somewhere else in Paris. It was all roughly around the same time, but I couldn't get exact proof. But I forgave Violette, and we sort of became friends. I visited her often, and I paid her rent. I looked out for her, in my way. I almost thought I loved her.'

Posie couldn't believe what she was hearing.

She remembered Isadora Duncan's description of the 'funny little man' in a beret who used to come by.

She let Caspian della Rosa's silence beat on.

He cleared his throat. 'I was listening to you today, in that fake police office, telling the fake Inspector Jegouzo that you had got Violette's address. I had been about to burst in on you when I realised that if *you* now knew Violette's address, others would now know it too, and she would now be in danger. I turned around and phoned the red-headed boy to get over to Montparnasse and tell Violette to clear out, but it seems he dawdled, and by the time he got there, she'd been marched out. To her death, it seems. He was generally very ineffective.'

'Oh! But who would want to kill Violette?'

There was another slight, almost thoughtful pause. 'I am not sure exactly, Posie, but you think *I* am bad news? Think again. And I'll tell you something else: your telephone is bugged by others apart from me.'

'By who?'

'I don't know. The government? Rich people? Your friends? A combination of all these things together?'

'You mean spies?'

'I have no idea. Not even I have been able to find out.'

'And you don't have Dolly here?'

Another sigh. 'I wish I did. I tried my utmost. I even pretended on occasion, like that time when I was at Dieppe, but no: I do not have her.'

'Where do you think she is?'

Posie couldn't believe she was actually asking her sworn mortal enemy for help, advice. But life was strange.

'Where do *you* think she is, Posie?'

Posie looked out into the darkness above the opposite houses.

'I suppose I think she's dead, or else she's hiding, or she's being hidden by someone. Today at the Morgue, I was pretty much convinced she was dead, but it seems I was being tricked.'

'Mnnn. Maybe you should investigate that. But I need to tell you this: she's not coming back.'

Posie nodded.

Yes.

She knew that too.

Posie rubbed at her eyes with the heel of her hand. It had been a long day. She wondered if she had been missed yet.

Had Richard noticed she was gone? Or Fox? Or Suzannah? Wouldn't they have sounded some alert? Be looking for her?

Suzannah.

'Oh!'

Posie watched the dark shadow behind her reflected in the glass. 'And why did you put Suzannah on the same train as me, Mr della Rosa? Suzannah was brought to Paris for *what*? Other than to cause her pain. That wretched letter from Paul Poiret…'

This time the high-pitched unearthly laugh grated on Posie's nerves.

'Yes: I copied that idea, I'm afraid. From Mrs Shepherd, while I tapped her telephone. The pink Poiret notepaper from last year was so easy to get hold of, and the ease of tricking someone is just a joke…'

Posie was angry, but she kept a lid on the rage.

'And was that *you* who gave Suzannah a note to give me? A weird anagram? At the station?'

'No. Not guilty.'

She had to hold on to something firm. 'But *why* is Suzannah Scotland here? Me, I can understand. You want me. Alive or dead, I'm not yet sure which. But poor Suzannah has nothing to do with any of this, nothing to do with you.'

'*Au contraire*, Posie. She has everything. I wanted to give you a present. And that present is Suzannah. To replace the friend who will never come back. I realised she would run into trouble over at Paul Poiret's place, and then knew she would come looking for you. Voila! A new friendship is born. I had not, of course, foreseen all that hoo-ha with the death of poor old Durrant. The way she would be detained for a bit. Although as it turned out, someone on that train saved me a job. If he'd stuck like glue to you as he no doubt would have done, Durrant would have ended up in the Morgue anyway. But *I* would have shot him.'

Posie laughed, as hollowly as she dared. 'You of all people must know Durrant is still alive?'

'Sorry?' The response was quick, unguarded. It sounded genuine. 'Of course he's dead. What are you talking about?'

'Nothing.'

Posie heard a click behind her. She jolted, shuddered, despite herself.

A gun?

She willed herself not to turn around.

Keep talking. Sure as bread is bread someone will come soon.

And as if God had answered her prayers, she heard sirens below, coming from what sounded like every direction, and then a terrible banging starting up at street level below.

The buzzer was jangling.

She could hear dear Richard's voice on the street way, way below. 'I SAY! Bally well open up, would you?'

Caspian della Rosa laughed, but he sounded exhausted. 'Ah, your good husband. He doesn't give up, does he? It was me at the hotel this afternoon, clearing the last bits out. I was forced to tie him up when he appeared out of nowhere.'

It was now, or never.

Posie turned.

She faced him.

She'd never have recognised him. Not really.

He was, like Mrs Shepherd, a shadow of his former self. Shrunk, haggard, crabbed. Posie supposed he must be in his mid or late forties but today he looked like he was a hundred.

It wasn't make-up which made him look so bad. His skin was yellow and his eyes were too. There was, however, something familiar about his face, from today.

Caspian della Rosa laughed. He saw her puzzlement.

He pulled out a pair of buck teeth from his pocket, shoved them in. His face, although without the police cap, had been transformed into that of the Duty Sergeant at the fake police station earlier, the man who had shown her through to Inspector Jegouzo.

But what was utterly bizarre was that he was now dressed in almost the exact same clothes as Lex Lennart.

Same turquoise jacket, black cravat, same scarab beetle. He even appeared to have the same fob-watch.

'I don't look as bad as Doctor Dance, eh? But I still look pretty awful. No, don't lie! I can see it on your face how terrible I look. I'd always hoped I was a survivor, and I even survived a gunshot wound, but it seems my luck has run out, Posie.'

Posie stared. She had no idea what to say.

Was he just lying? It was absolutely possible.

'I've been given weeks to live. It's dreadful. Painful, too. I'd given up on getting you over here to be my wife, or partner, or any of that lark, of course. I'd written to you promising you a hotel, but still you didn't come. So I'm happy I managed to intice you over here now, anyhow.'

Posie cleared her throat. 'And what did you want of me, now? How can I help?'

Caspian della Rosa nodded.

'There are two things, please. You can accept my gift. It's a jolly good one. The key which opens this apartment is also the key to my gift. You, or your clever husband and his friends were searching in the wrong place for it. The Palais della Rosa is not a hotel in France. It is in Arosa, in Switzerland. And it is yours. Look after it for me. I very nearly changed my mind the other day and gave it to Violette, but what good would that have done? Where she has gone she has no need of anything, let alone luxury hotels. So, you know, every cloud…'

Posie swallowed. She could hear banging now, closer, like there were people tearing up the stairs.

Oh, please.

She'd have to humour him along.

'Well, fine. Thank you. I promise I will accept and visit it and look after it well for you.'

Caspian della Rosa had a small revolver in his hand. He started to raise it.

Posie opened her mouth, stammered: 'How else can I help you? You said there were *two* things? Sir?'

The man in front of her laughed, but quietly.

'I decided to dress up as that loony archaeologist for my final act,' he said, calmly. 'I like what they believed, the ancient Egyptians. Like on that little charm you are still wearing around your neck, Posie. Tut! Tut! Don't forget to give it back to Egypt now, will you? But I think you should remember what it says… "*so I may be placed among the imperishable stars and may never die*".'

Posie had a dreadful sense of foreboding, and then suddenly there were knocks at the front door.

Followed by a battering sound. The small blonde girl who had looked a bit like Dolly emerged from one room and then ran off into another.

Caspian della Rosa strode forward. He held out his hand to Posie, and she took it, squeezed it.

He let it go.

He moved towards the balcony.

'The second thing I wanted you to be here for was a little selfish.'

He placed the gun to his temple.

'I wanted you to be here for me at the end.'

* * * *

Epilogue

A week had passed.

Posie had never been more glad to get back to London, even if it was cold and grey, and rather unexciting, as the end of January always was.

She'd been thrilled to see the three children, and had insisted on buying stacks of presents for them at Hamleys before she got home, to replace the presents she had bought, then lost, at the fictional toyshop in Paris.

The Lady Caroline Greenlow murder case was much in the news.

It had been splashed all over the newspapers, and pictures of the dead beauty were to be seen all over town, together with the sordid details of every aspect of her personal life.

Sam Stubbs at the *Associated Press* seemed to have most to say on the subject.

Dadie Spence had never been so much in demand as a society photographer before, and London was gripped by a ghoulish thirst for information about the case, and for information about the suspects in the murder trial, which would be heard in a few weeks.

Posie's name and photograph had been in a pleasing number of newspaper articles, and there had been plenty of references to Richard, and Inspector Oats, who was now due a promotion and a medal from the financial vice squad.

Which he was tickled pink about.

Richard's worries about the mess of the case in Liverpool seemed to have come to nothing, obscured by the Caroline Greenlow case and the need to speak about it fairly often.

More work was trickling in now, for both Posie and for Len.

And Posie had come back to find Grape Street transformed.

Not only tidy, but bright, with new white paintwork throughout, and new sprigged curtains up at the windows and matching cushions on the sofa.

It seemed that Len's parents-in-law had been busy. And it all looked lovely.

What was also lovely was that Suzannah Scotland had agreed to act as their temporary secretary at the Detective Agency, just until they could find a replacement for Prudence, or, it was also agreed, if Suzannah liked the job well enough, she could choose to stay on.

What this meant more practically were more frequent visits from Sergeant Fox.

Today was one of those days.

It was coffee-time and he'd thrown himself down on the couch in the clients' waiting room, in front of the roaring fire.

Posie came in to find him eating cakes with Len and Suzannah. She snatched one, an Eccles cake, off the small paper Lyons Cornerhouse tray he had brought the treats up on.

'Sergeant?'

'Hullo, Miss. Couple of bits of news. Your husband's busy today, Miss. Says he won't be home until late.'

'Oh?'

'Mnnn. Something awful happened up at Pentonville today. You know old Doctor Dance?'

Posie looked up quickly. Stopped chewing her cake. 'Yes?'

'Doctor Dance is dead. He took a cyanide capsule.'

'*What?*'

'Mnnn. We're not sure where he concealed it. But probably in the iodine apparatus he insisted on keeping with him to look after his eye. What a disaster, eh? His mother was coming to visit him for the first time tomorrow. Poor woman.'

Posie got up and walked to the window. Leant her head against the glass.

She remembered the man's words to her. '*I'm practical.*'

Well, yes.

Not a coward, no. No-one could accuse Dance of that. But there was a sense of evading justice here which left a bad taste in the mouth.

Poor Mrs Walter.

Downstairs, the doorbell for the office rang.

Rather than ring the person up, Posie decided to go down personally. She needed the air; to clear her head.

When she opened the door, there was no-one there. She leant out into the street, peered into the shadows of the buildings where bins were stacked, overflowing today, waiting for the rubbish collectors.

She saw a man some way down the street, hunkered into the side of a building, smoking, kicking at some rubbish which had fallen to the floor.

Posie closed the door behind her, some instinct driving her on.

She was sure this man was here for *her*.

'I say! Can I help you?'

The man stayed where he was. He was a poor man, dressed in grey tatty clothes, with a dirty face and a big bushy beard. But his eyes were bright and oddly familiar.

'Oh! It's *you*!'

'I told you to keep me a secret, and you have. So, thank you.'

Alphonse Durrant pulled out something from his pocket. It was his French police fob, the leather and metal all twisted and ripped. Gruesomely so.

'See this?' Alphonse laughed. 'This saved me. When Dance attacked me with a scalpel, this took the brunt of it. He left me for dead and I must have collapsed. When I woke up Lucille was already organising my funeral and sorting out clever details like corpses, and casting me into my next life: which is where I am now.'

Posie must have looked puzzled, because Alphonse shrugged heavily.

'They had some dirt on me, you see. That's how the organisation works. I *was* a ladies' man, and I had certainly got in with one particular lady who was very wrong. Wrong for me, maybe. Not so wrong for the President…'

'Oh! Gracious. So now you're a spy?'

'Don't ask questions, and I can tell you no lies, Miss Parker. But I'm here, today, and I wanted to thank you for your loyalty. I have something for you.'

'Oh?'

He had a white envelope in his hands. He passed it to her.

'I need you to look at this and then burn it on the fire in your own office upstairs. Not the one in the waiting room, see? No-one can ever see this, and no-one must know. Not your husband. Not *her* husband.'

'Fine. You mean…'

'Yes. Your pal. The one you wouldn't give up on. She even tried to tell you to stay away, I think; gave you a nasty note to warn you off. She knew the danger you could get yourself in, and the danger others who had helped her in the past could be placed in.'

'You mean Violette?'

Alphonse Durrant nodded. He was playing with the ruined leather police fob, and then he threw it in a nearby bin, as if it meant nothing to him at all.

'Violette must have helped her once. Perhaps she took the cat, and offered a disguise? A brief sanctuary? She was probably very brave, hiding your friend from various parties. But it was to no avail. Violette's involvement was all known to the people who now employ your friend. But when *you* blundered along, looking like you might interview Violette and find out exactly what had happened, and then make it all public, they couldn't take that chance. The girl was disposed of.'

Posie gasped. This was awful.

She had caused a death, and there was nothing she could do to make things better.

'I want you to move on, Miss Parker. Your pal has been forced to move on. But I need you to know that when she's not studying on librarian's courses, or serving coffee in train stations, or working for the government, she's watching you, and she loves you. She was sorry to leave her life as it was. But now, move on.'

Alphonse Durrant put out his hand to Posie and they shook hands.

'I told you, Miss Parker, it's the way the organisation who employ us work. They always find dirt on people.'

'So Dolly is a spy, too?'

Alphonse Durrant shrugged and started to walk off. But he stopped, almost tripped over some rubbish on the floor.

'Oh, would you look at that!' he muttered. 'How careless some people are.'

Posie looked at his feet and saw an old, muzzed-up pair of theatrical glasses on the floor, and next to them was a pair of buck teeth.

Nearby too was a big, thick, fake black plait.

Posie stared up again but Durrant had gone.

Bounding up the stairs to her office, she burst in to the waiting room.

'Suzannah,' she panted, breathlessly. 'You said a Night

Ferry employee had given you that odd note to deliver to me, on the platform, last week. Do you remember what he looked like at all?'

Suzannah, who was jolly close to Fox on the sofa, looked momentarily taken aback.

'Well, yes. I do remember actually. But it wasn't a man. *Non*. Did I tell you it was? It was a woman. I think she was serving the teas, although not very well, I remember. She had these awful thick glasses on, and terrible teeth. And she was a bit tubby, with long black hair in a plait.'

Posie's heart was racing.

The description fitted the one given by Isadora Duncan, when she had said a cousin of Violette's had come to stay last summer, studying for a librarians' course. Violette had said the cousin was Belgian, but who could really tell the difference between a Belgian and a French accent? And Dolly's French was fluent.

Dolly. You were there all along.

In a terrible, fantastic disguise.

Good enough to stay out of even Caspian della Rosa's clutches, hidden from his network of spies.

Posie started to head towards her own office, but Fox called out.

'Miss? I said I had two bits of news for you. The second bit is almost more interesting than old dead Dance, really.'

'Oh?' She tried to sound casual, like she had all the time in the world.

'Mnnn. You know Sergeant de Caunes, well, he's been busy as a bee organising old Durrant's funeral, which I expect I'll go over for next week. But he did have time to put a trace on a call for us. You know that strange Doctor Rousse at the City Morgue? The one who pretended he had Dolly's details, when he hadn't?'

'How can I forget?'

Fox had got out his notebook. He flicked through until he found his page, excited.

'Doctor Rousse placed a call at five-forty, French time, last Wednesday. And de Caunes has traced it. It was a call to the International Operator, and then on to London. And you won't believe *where* in London?'

Posie could guess, but she'd better act the innocent. 'No idea.'

'Whitehall. The Secret Intelligence Service, the Foreign Section. You know, *spies*. So our good Doctor Rousse was in their pay, doing their dirty business for them; covering up tracks. But *why* remains unclear.'

Posie licked at her lips, which felt very dry. 'I don't really understand, Sergeant. I suppose we'd better pass the information on to Richard.'

Fox looked slightly put out, but shrugged. He put his pad down, picked up another cake.

'I thought it might mean the Countess of Cardigeon had gone over to the dark side.'

'The Secret Intelligence Service?' Posie laughed. 'Dolly sticks out like a sore thumb. How could she ever be a spy?'

Minutes later, she was on her own, in her own tiny office, in front of the small fire there. She prodded at it, added another log and some extra newspaper.

She ripped open the white envelope from Durrant with shaking hands.

There were two things inside. One was a photograph, in grainy black and white, the sort which Len might take, from a distance, as part of a surveillance mission.

But this was of a level of subject which Len could only ever have dreamt of.

In his wildest dreams.

There, outside a London club, in what looked like a back exit, was the Prince of the realm, the Prince of Wales.

His was a familiar figure, blonde and dashing and with those haunted big eyes which seemed to contain all the pain of the world in them.

But in this photo, he was engrossed.

Because in his arms was Dolly Cardigeon.

'Oh, Dolly! Oh, no…'

They always find dirt on people.

Posie's heart almost seemed to stop, and for a moment she felt like she might faint, but she leant down, and she fed the photograph right into the heart of the fire.

As she had been instructed.

How long had Dolly's affair with the Prince been going on for?

Had it been very serious?

And had Dolly really needed to disappear because of it? Couldn't it have been resolved in some other way?

Perhaps not.

Perhaps it had been more serious than all the other affairs the Prince was known to have had?

It was true he had a thing for older women, but Dolly was, even though she was a Countess, exactly the *wrong sort* of older woman.

Perhaps there had been some talk of Dolly divorcing Rufus?

Of things becoming public?

Perhaps the Crown itself had seemed like it would be put in jeopardy?

Posie saw she had almost missed the second thing. It was simply a scrap of white paper, torn from a notebook, in what looked like a rush.

There, at last, was Dolly's handwriting.

Posie,

You should have listened, not gone.

I am no longer me.

Like I told you, I am silent. I was in too deep. We were in too deep.

I fled to Paris, when Violette called. I thought she was someone I could trust, and that she could hide me. She tried, even though she wasn't supposed to. Even though she should have handed me in.

But it wasn't safe there, not at all. And they came for me anyway.

For the safety of the children, I had to disappear. Become someone else.

Thank you for everything.

I will always love you,

D

Posie found that tears were coursing down her face, unbidden, useless tears.

She pulled at the necklace she still wore around her neck, that jewelled scarab which she would have to get back to its rightful place, soon.

She read the back of the scarab's inscription again, as she watched the last of Dolly's words burning on the fire.

She flicked away the last of her tears and stood, throwing the necklace into one of her drawers.

'You will always be a star to me, Dolly,' she whispered to herself.

'But I will move on. I promise.'

And she stood by the window of her office, watching the workers, far, far below, all of them smoking, chatting, gossiping. And she watched the pigeons circling, and the slight bit of blue showing above all the grey office roofs, and she was overwhelmed by how wonderful the city was.

She turned to her desk, where a few new cases were stacked. There was something from the House of Harlow, the fashion house, which looked interesting.

But she pulled the very first one towards her.

It was a thick envelope, covered in foreign-looking red stamps. On closer inspection she saw they were Swiss.

She pulled out the enclosure, and smiled.

It was a brochure for a glossy hotel in the mountains, and there were papers with it, too. From lawyers in Zurich.

Something new to start on. A new adventure.

Now *this* would be fun.

* * * *

Historical Note

All of the characters in this novella are fictional, unless specifically mentioned below.

Weather, timings, general political events, and places (and descriptions of places) are historically accurate to the best of my knowledge, save for any exceptions listed below.

As in the other Posie Parker books, I refer to the First World War of 1914–1918 as the 'Great War' throughout, which is simpler for the modern reader, although it would not have been referred to in this way in 1926.

As ever, Posie's work address in London (Grape Street, Bloomsbury, WC1) and her home address around the corner (Museum Chambers, WC1) are both very real, although you might have to do a bit of imagining to find her there.

1. (Prologue) The Battle of the Somme started on 1 July 1916 on the upper reaches of the Somme river. As described here, the losses suffered were huge, totalling more than 60,000 British men on the first day of battle alone. The Battle of the Somme would later become synonymous with the futility of the Great War, and indicative of the bad military tactics employed at the time by British generals.

2. (Prologue) The archaeological dig which David Greeze speaks about (in which he found two scarab charms) was indeed at Abydos, and was run by the Egypt Exploration Society under Thomas Whittemore, running from 1910 into the 1920s.

3. (Chapter One) As described in this novel, a terrible and bitter cold front did grip England from 14 to 16 January 1926, with plummeting temperatures and deep, frozen snow and ice packing the roads in London, meaning it was difficult to get about. The extent to which this cold weather affected the railways (and travel to and from the Continent by the 'Night Ferry' services from Victoria) is entirely my own fancy.

4. (Trains – throughout) Please note I have played hard and fast with the available facts here. The Golden Arrow train was introduced in 1926 (on the French side from Calais to Paris, with the English 'arm' of the service being added in 1929), but the Night Ferry as described here was not introduced until 1936. It ran as described, from Platform 2 at Victoria Station every night, leaving at 9 pm and arriving into Paris at 9 am for breakfast.

   The actual sleeping cars (of which only one remains) were chained onto the special ferry, which sailed from Dover to Dunkirk, and which had the capacity to carry at least four sleeper carriages, plus some automobiles and post-related freight. As described in this novel, each navy-and-cream sleeper carriage (all of which were first class) had capacity for nine berths, each berth of which could be used by one or two occupants. To have berths left empty would have been unusual. As described here, a Pullman carriage would have started the journey with the main train from Victoria, being used as a dining-car for dinner for the overnight guests.

It would then have been unhooked at Dover and not sent across on the ferry. Another dining-car (a French one) would be attached for breakfast in Dunkirk. Please note that the Director of the company, a Mr Daniel Brookman, and any financial irregularity he may have engaged in, are fictions of my own.

5. (Chapter One) The John Singer Sargent Exhibition which Posie attends at the Royal Academy was real (and took place from 14 January 1926 until 13 March 1926) and was recognised at the time as being the greatest art show of the year in London.

   Likewise, the play, *Juno and the Paycock*, by Sean O'Casey, which originally opened to rave reviews in Dublin in 1924, had just transferred to London in 1926 and was showing at the Royalty Theatre, Soho (now demolished). It is still regularly performed and is regarded as one of Ireland's classic works of theatre, and is often heralded as a masterpiece.

6. (Chapter Two) The *Woman's Penny Post* of which Len speaks (in which Posie appears, to his wife's chagrin) is fictional.

7. (Chapter Four) '*L'Inconnue de la Seine*' was real, and, in all likelihood, she was a poor girl who died (whether suicide or accident is unknown) in Paris, in the 1880s, and whose unfortunate death had the bizarre ripple effect of achieving for her a kind of post-mortem notoriety. Her beauty was such that a plaster cast of her face was taken (in the Paris Morgue, behind the Notre Dame), and the tragic fate of the forever-unknown girl morbidly captured the hearts and minds of many artists, poets and writers, who concocted stories about the girl. In 1926 the girl was in the news again as a new book (*The Eternal Face,* by Ernst Benkard, as mentioned in this novel) collected reports of the most

notorious death masks of all time. And the mask of '*L'Inconnue*' features heavily.

8. (Chapter Five) My government minister, Charles Loxley, is fictional, although the controversial cuts to workers' pay which the government of Stanley Baldwin was hoping to introduce (as mentioned here) were real and culminated in the miner's lock-out of 1 May (in protest at the planned cuts) and then led to a catastrophic General Strike from 3 May onwards across the country, as whole industries came out in support of the miners and their position.

9. (Chapter Five) Charles Loxley carries a red briefcase as Chancellor on this trip abroad. I have stretched a point here. Historically, since William Gladstone was Chancellor of the Exchequer in 1860, the iconic red box of a briefcase (still in use) has only been used to carry the budget papers to and from the House of Commons. In my story, I have the Chancellor using the bag for all of his government business.

10. (Chapter Five) Likewise, although Loxley is fictional, the case with regards women voting in the United Kingdom is as described and would not be altered until 1928 and the *Representation of the People (Equal Franchise) Act*. Caroline Greenlow, and her support for the Act, is, of course, fictional.

11. (Chapter Five) Dover Marine Station, spoken about by Sir Charles Loxley, no longer exists. It is now Dover Western Docks.

12. (Chapter Six) The fruit punch served in the Night Ferry Pullman car is a fiction all of my own.

13. (Chapter Seven) I am afraid I am guilty of letting

Posie have a Bendicks mint four years early (they were not on sale until 1930) but they seemed so very right here in the green Pullman car.

14. (Chapter Seven) As Mrs Shepherd describes, Paul Poiret was indeed a wildly successful Parisian fashion designer whose empire took in fashion, perfume, home furnishings, furniture and accessories, which he and his teams created in his 'Atelier Marine' workshops. His 'Perfumes Rosines' perfume line was legendary, and the bottles are still among the most collectable in the world today.

    Paul Poiret was the designer who 'took on' Man Ray, the legendary photographer, whose own later fame scaled dizzy heights but who started by photographing Poiret's designs and dresses. Overreaching himself in the Paris Art Deco Exhibition (the 'International Exhibition of Modern Decorative and Industrial Arts') of 1925, Paul Poiret's gradual selling off of art, houses and assets and eventual relocation to No 6, Rond-Point did nothing to turn his fortunes around, and by 1929 he was finished.

15. (Chapter Nine) Dorothy L. Sayers' second detective book featuring Lord Peter Wimsey, *Clouds of Witness* (which Mrs Shepherd is reading in the French dining-car), was indeed published in 1926, although it was actually later in the year.

16. (Chapter Twelve) The hotels Maigret (where Posie stays on the Rue de Berri) and the Raspail (where Suzannah has a room booked, on the Avenue Kléber) are both fictional. The streets are real.

17. (Throughout) The idea of 'Paris Fashion Week' happening during this novel is a plot concept and conceit all of my own. New York Fashion Week did

not begin until 1943, and Paris Fashion Week – as it is now known – not until the 1970s.

18. (Chapter Fourteen) The Carrefour Vavin is now called 'Place Pablo-Picasso'. But the legendary 'roaring twenties' café hotspots, the Dôme and the Rotonde, as described here, are still there. The Rue Delambre was the location of the famous American Photographer Man Ray's studio, and was also home to a number of small hotels and studios which were the homes of artists such as Modigliani. The (real) Dingo Bar on Rue Delambre was the original initial meeting place for Ernest Hemingway and F. Scott Fitzgerald.

19. (Chapter Fourteen) I have placed Isadora Duncan (1877–1927), the legendary expressive dancer, here on the Rue Delambre, where she did live in the last years of her tragic life, but my interpretation of her is simply that, and I do not have an exact address for her.

20. (Chapter Fifteen) The 1922 discovery of the tomb of Tutankhamun, which Sam Stubbs speaks to Posie about on the telephone, was led by the controversial archaeologist Howard Carter, but financed by Lord Carnarvon. Lex Lennart and his financial contribution (in this story) is fictitious, a fancy all of my own. But the legend of the curse of Tutankhamun is real: Carnarvon famously died of an infected mosquito bite only weeks after the tomb was opened, and others who were associated with the discovery (but not Howard Carter) also died in unusual, premature ways.

21. (Chapter Nineteen and again Chapter Twenty-One) Amedeo Modigliani was a famous resident of Montparnasse until his untimely death in 1920, aged just thirty-five. As detailed in this story, he had his first and only show in 1917 at the Galerie B. Weill. It was

a set of nudes and was closed down by the police. The story of my 'Jeannette de Montparnasse' is fictional, although there was a real-life 'Kiki de Montparnasse', among the same crowd, and, in real life, Modigliani had a partner, Jeanne Hébuterne, who committed suicide just after his death.

22. (Chapter Twenty-Four) Josephine Baker did not have a show at the Moulin Rouge in 1926, but she did dance at the Folies Bergère at this time. In 1928 she would return to Paris and set up her own club in Montmartre.

****

Thank you for joining Posie Parker and her friends.

Enjoyed *Murder on the Night Train to Paris* (A Posie Parker Mystery #15)? Here's what you can do next.

If you loved this book and have a tiny moment to spare, I would really appreciate a review or rating on the page where you bought the book. Your help in spreading the word about the series is invaluable and really appreciated, and reviews make a big difference to helping new readers find the series.

Posie's other cases are available in e-book and paperback formats from Amazon, as well as in selected bookstores and at Audible and other main audiobook retailers.

You can find all of the other books, available for purchase, listed here in chronological order:

http://www.amazon.com/L.B.-Hathaway/e/B00LDXGKE8

and

http://www.amazon.co.uk/L.B.-Hathaway/e/B00LDXGKE8

You can sign up to be notified of new releases, pre-release specials, free short stories, and the chance to win Amazon gift-vouchers here:

http://www.lbhathaway.com/newsletter/

About the Author

Cambridge-educated, British-born L.B. Hathaway writes historical fiction. She worked as a lawyer at Lincoln's Inn in London for almost a decade before becoming a full-time writer. She is a lifelong fan of detective novels set in the Golden Age of Crime, and is an ardent Agatha Christie devotee.

Her other interests, in no particular order, are: very fast downhill skiing, theatre-going, drinking strong tea, Tudor history, exploring castles and generally trying to cram as much into life as possible.

The Posie Parker series of cosy crime novels span the 1920s. They each combine a core central mystery, an exploration of the reckless glamour of the age and a feisty protagonist who you would love to have as your best friend.

To find out more and for news of new releases and giveaways, go to:

http://www.lbhathaway.com

Connect with L.B. Hathaway online:

(e) author@lbhathaway.com

(t) @LbHathaway

(f) https://www.facebook.com/pages/L-B-Hathaway-books/1423516601228019

(Goodreads) http://www.goodreads.com/author/show/8339051.L_B_Hathaway

Printed in Great Britain
by Amazon

20186419R00212